Circles of the Moon

Circles of the Moon

Carole Ann Camp

White River Press
Amherst, Massachusetts

Circles of the Moon

Cover photograph by Barbara Brady Conn

First published 2014

White River Press
PO Box 3561
Amherst, MA 014004

whiteriverpress.com

ISBN: 978-1-935052-67-8

Library of Congress Cataloging-in-Publication Data

Camp, Carole Ann.
Circles of the Moon / Carole Ann Camp.
        pages cm
Includes bibliographical references and index.
ISBN 978-1-935052-67-8 (pbk.: alk. paper)
1. Women priests--Fiction. 2. Goddesses--Fiction. I. Title.
PS3603.A4558C57 2013
813'.6--dc23
                    2013042935

Circles of the Moon

PART 1:
Preparation

Chapter 1

"Blessed be!" Henith murmured after the final prayer. Seconds later the silent night erupted into the chattering voices of the thirty women of Living Water Circle. Slipping away from the others, the young initiate moved quietly between the shadows of the stones. Closing her eyes and blocking out the sounds of the voices around her, she willed herself back into the feelings of the last few hours.

"Henith, wasn't that spectacular? What a night! I never imagined it would be like this!" Carog's loud voice jolted Henith back. Groaning inwardly, Henith felt the heat of anger burn her cheeks. The full moon reflected in Henith's disenchanted eyes as she turned to face Carog, the floating sensations destroyed.

"Tonight's ritual was more than I expected," Henith responded without enthusiasm, walking slowly, hoping Carog would go quickly down the path to join the other women.

"Aren't you excited that we have finally become initiates of the Goddess? I thought I'd never get through the last few years of boring classes," Carog continued, oblivious to Henith's reluctance to engage in any further conversation.

"I liked the classes," replied Henith defensively, a feeling that occurred too frequently when she was with Carog.

"Just imagine, next spring, we will become priestesses at the spring festival. I can't wait."

Henith tried to imagine the four initiates from the other villages that she had never met but who were also preparing for initiation, and wondered if they were as annoying as Carog. Trying to get rid of Carog was like trying to remove a burr from one's tunic.

"How did you do with your class on Spirit Flying last moon with Nancillia? I have that next. Did you ever do it? Is it hard?" continued Carog as she slid her hand into Henith's. Henith pulled away pretending to adjust the rope belt around her waist.

Henith didn't want to share what had just happened, but the words came out of her mouth before she could control them.

"Well, during the lessons with Nancillia, I was never able to spirit fly. Nancillia said I was too impatient." Henith smiled remembering the day that her last moon's teacher had scolded her about her impatience. Henith had wanted to spirit fly right away, but she couldn't seem to relax her wandering mind—until tonight.

"That's too bad. I wonder if I'll be able to spirit fly. My mother said that it takes some women years to master that mystery. My mother also thinks that spirit flying is the most difficult of all the lessons," said Carog.

"Well, I flew tonight," Henith said, trying to sound casual, but enjoying the effect her words had on Carog.

"What! You spirit flew tonight? What was it like?" Carog turned to look at Henith with new respect.

Henith couldn't help enjoying the moment. She liked being able to brag to Carog.

"Yes, I flew. At first, I was afraid of what was happening to me. I couldn't figure out how I could be in the circle with all the women and be above the circle at the same time; but I was. It didn't last very long, though—only a few minutes—but I know I was spirit flying. I could see all the women and all the stones below me. I couldn't believe what a perfect circle the stones were in. I wonder how they got to be that way."

"Nobody really knows," Carog interrupted, "even though the storytellers say that the Great Goddess herself put five stone circles on our island thousands of years ago; one at each of the four directions and one in the center."

"I know that," said Henith curtly, "but until you've seen our circle from above, you don't really realize what an incredible feat that must have been."

Henith saw the picture in her head—a perfect circle of bluish-gray stones situated in a clearing on top of the knoll just to the south of her village. She knew that there were no other stones on the island like these, except for the ones in the other four circles. She had also heard that the stones in the center of the island were twice the size of the ones here. She couldn't imagine it. The smallest stone in her circle was almost twice as tall as she was.

"Tell me what else you saw. How far away did you go? Did you go to the center?"

"No, I stayed just above our circle." Henith wondered why it hadn't occurred to her to go somewhere. "I was so struck by what I was seeing that I just stayed there," Henith replied, pointing toward the moon suspended above them. "The women looked like petals of an iridescent flower," Henith continued, "reflecting the moonlight. And as we moved and swayed to the rhythm of the chanting, it appeared as if the flower opened and closed." Henith closed her eyes, hugging herself, remembering the beauty of the flower below her as if it blossomed in some indistinguishable breeze.

"Did you see anything else?" Carog asked again.

"No, as soon as I started to analyze how I had managed to spirit fly after I hadn't been able to do it once last moon, I found myself back in the circle," disappointment crept into Henith's voice.

"I didn't see your mother tonight. Was she here?" Carog asked as they neared the edge of the cottages.

"No, she's still recovering from her wound." Henith remembered the day last week when she found Zendar leaning over her mother, and more blood than she had ever seen before.

"That's too bad, for her to miss your first ritual as an initiate. Do you know what really happened? I mean in Trenig. No one seems to talk about it. I only hear little pieces of the story," Carog paused, "I'd love to go to Trenig. Sometimes I find our life here very tedious. I need some excitement."

5

"Carog, how can you say such a thing? Our work here is holy! Why would you want to go to Trenig, where all the violence and fighting are? I'm not sure I ever want to leave Mona."

"What happens if you are selected to be one of the priestesses to serve in a circle in Trenig? What will you do then?" Henith disliked the taunt she detected in Carog's voice.

"I will do what I am told to do. If I have to go to Trenig, I will go. Maybe Morgan won't choose me. Not everyone has to go there, you know. Especially now, when not many people worship the ways of the Goddess." A feeling of foreboding passed through Henith. People from a far-off country were plundering village after village in the great land to the east, disrupting her world of peace and calm. She didn't want to have to be in a battle and risk being wounded like her mother had been.

"Well, if I'm chosen, I'll gladly go," Carog replied.

"Don't you like it here, learning all the mysteries, being a priestess of the Goddess?" Henith looked at Carog and an uncomfortable feeling passed over her. She noticed it, but couldn't identify its cause. Carog was the same age as she was, but Carog didn't seem serious enough to be a priestess, Henith thought.

"But doesn't all the quiet bore you sometimes? And some of these lessons! Ugh!" They reached the cottage that Henith shared with her mother.

"There's Zendar. She must have been checking on my mother," Henith turned toward the old woman coming from the cottage.

"How is my mother, Zendar?" Henith barely waved as Carog started toward her own home.

"She is much better. The herbs I put on her leg have drawn all of the poison out of the wound. She should be well in a few days' time," the healing priestess responded.

"Thank you, Zendar. I will see you tomorrow."

Henith looked forward to the lessons that would start tomorrow. She had heard some of the others say that the time with Zendar was intense, but having the opportunity to learn the sacred mysteries of the herbs was truly a gift.

Zendar's house intrigued Henith; there were so many smells and aromas about it and so many subtle colors: lavenders and blues, greens and grays. Henith liked watching the seasons change the colors in the garden, especially the purples. She remembered being surprised by the number of subtle shades of color and the vast array of different petal shapes and sizes there were. As a child she would just sit at the edge of the garden trying to count the different variations of color.

"Mother, Zendar says you will be up and dancing by the next moon." Henith, her face still flushed from the excitement of the evening, greeted her mother with enthusiasm.

"I feel better—much better. Zendar truly is a master. Tell me everything about tonight. I heard the chanting and remembered my own first moon ritual so many years ago. How I wish I could have been there with you." There was a longing in Canth's voice that caused sadness deep inside Henith.

Canth rearranged her leg into a more comfortable position.

Henith pulled a pillow close to her mother's bed and sat down. Letting her mind wander slowly back through the feelings and experiences of the evening, Henith told her mother about the ritual: about how thrilled she had been when the circle of energy had been drawn and how elated she was to finally be included in the group of priestesses. She told her about the feeling of floating, how she wished she could have stayed there forever, and how, when she started to analyze how she had gotten there, she had come crashing back to earth.

Canth laughed, "Henith, it is unusual for anyone to have flown so high for so long with so little experience. You shouldn't be so hard on yourself. Very few women are able to master spirit flying without many years of patience and practice. We should tell Nancillia, even though your moon-time with her has finished and you start your herbal craft with Zendar tomorrow. She will be excited to know, that in spite of your frustrating experience last month you may have been chosen for this special gift."

"Mother, will you tell me about what happened to you in Trenig? How you got hurt? Why you were there?" Henith had been reluctant to talk about her mother's injury before, because watching Canth, who was always such a jolly woman, lying still in and out of consciousness had scared Henith.

"These are hard times, Henith," Canth looked at her daughter, tall and slender as a young birch sapling with those piercing blue eyes, even bluer than her own, and sighed.

"I know—but yet I don't know," Henith said, "there seems to be a strange unrest. I feel different than when I was little, and days and moons passed without event. Yet I still don't know why Morgan took you to Trenig, and I don't know how you were wounded." Henith's voice was shaking—something had shifted in her life, something imperceptible—somehow she was different. She felt as if she had crossed a bridge without knowing it. Could it have been the moon magic of the evening? Or was it Carog and her restlessness?

"I don't even know what our island is like. Carog asked me if I had flown to the center to see it. I was embarrassed because it never even occurred to me to do that, to try to fly anywhere else except up above the circle." Henith looked down into her lap.

Canth laughed again. "Oh, Henith, so many questions for so late at night? The moon has worked its way with you. Can they last until morning? I promise I will try to answer some of your questions then."

Henith looked disappointed. "But I have to go to Zendar early. I'm sorry, Mother, I know you are tired." Henith kissed her mother. "I can wait until tomorrow. It feels like I've waited a long time; I guess that I can wait until tomorrow. It's just that I haven't had so many questions before. Life was so simple and orderly. Maybe spirit flying has given me a new perspective." She smiled at her own cleverness.

Canth held Henith's hand. "There are many things to learn, and there are many questions that need answers. You will have this year of your initiation to ask your questions and learn the craft from all the wise women of our village. Now let us get some sleep."

❧❦

Henith watched the light of the moon slide across the wall as she drifted off to sleep. Memories of the last fifteen years, and thoughts and questions about the future vied for consciousness. She reflected on her life which had been spent right here in this village. Tonight she found it strange that she had never even been to other parts of her own island. She marveled at herself for not even thinking about what the other women on the island were like, and who the other young initiates were that she would meet for the first time in eleven moons. She tried to imagine the other three villages, each with its own circle of stones. She tried to imagine what the priestesses of the four directions in the center circle looked like. Why hadn't she flown to the center? Next time, she thought, that's what I'll do.

Fragments of recent conversations swirled around the stones.

"Men advancing north in Trenig!"

"Another village captured."

"Mother, you are hurt."

The gash in her mother's leg terrified her; she had never seen anything like it before. She'd witenessed minor scrapes and scratches. Never anything like this. Henith knew that Morgan never left the center of the island; yet Morgan had been here, had taken her mother to Trenig, and had brought her mother back, almost dead.

What could be happening in Trenig that would cause Morgan to make such a dangerous journey? She tried to imagine how Canth had been wounded, but couldn't. Images of blood and screaming women shattered the peaceful harmony of tonight's moon ritual. Henith tried to open her eyes and focus on the moonlight, but her lids were heavy, and the images wouldn't leave her alone.

Canth watched the same moonlight, remembering her surprise when Morgan came to her village that day. Canth smiled, recalling how regal Morgan looked striding with great purpose toward her. She and Morgan had been friends since that night of their initiation, neither one suspecting then that Morgan would be High Priestess of all of Mona. In the bliss of that festival, thoughts of violence, blood, and men were as far away from them as the moon herself.

Then there she was, Morgan in the western village. Canth remembered the shock and dismay on the other women's faces. For Morgan to leave the center was unheard of. Fear swept through the village like a wind before a thunderstorm. Morgan came directly to her and Canth held her breath.

Morgan was always direct, never a wasted word. Some of the women on the island were surprised when she had been selected as High Priestess of Mona. Some of the older women knew her fiery temper, knew her tendency to action rather than meditation and reflection. The High Priestess should stay centered at all times. And here she was in Canth's village, coming directly toward her.

Canth remembered being shocked that Morgan was dressed for traveling in loosely fitted trousers and tunic. She radiated a different kind of strength than the quiet strength of the High Priestess in long flowing robes.

"Canth, I need you to travel with me to Trenig," Morgan said without preamble, looking directly into Canth's blue eyes.

Canth put her hands on the table to steady herself. "Trenig?" she remembered mumbling.

"I need you. You are the most skilled woman in all of Mona at drawing the protective power. Another stone circle is under attack. Word has come that, if we hurry, we may be able to surround the circle before the invaders try to destroy the stones. There is talk that they plan to build fires around each stone and pour cold water on the hot stones, causing them to crack. Then they will be able to carry the stones away in pieces." Canth could hear the rage in Morgan's voice. A power that made Canth both energized and terrified at the same time.

"Did you call Cait from the south village?" Canth asked, wondering why Morgan had traveled an extra day to the west village for her.

"Yes, she will meet us at the east village, along with Jone and Paet, but we need to hurry. And yes, I wanted to come for you myself, so we will have time alone before we join the others." Morgan's blue eyes smiled imperceptibly.

Canth laughed, remembering how skilled Morgan was at mind-speaking and mind-listening.

"Just let me change into my traveling clothes. I will hurry."

They left Living Water Circle within minutes of Morgan's arrival. Canth didn't even have time to say good-bye to Henith, who was with Nancillia that day walking on the beach.

For the last week Canth had put these memories out of her mind, because she had needed all her strength to bring healing back into her body; but tonight it was time to begin the slow process of healing the memories. She brought back the images of that night. Men everywhere, preparing fires around the stones. Fear gripping at her stomach, realizing they might be too late. At least twenty men and only five women Morgan—strong resolute Morgan—telling them to stay in the trees at the edge of the circle, out of sight, hoping that they might have a chance of surrounding the stones with a wall of protective power before being detected. Trying to surround the circle with the cone of power. One of the men lighting a fire.

Seeing those men in that circle, laughing, was more than Jone could tolerate. She went screaming from the trees like a wild woman, hoping to surprise and frighten the men before any more damage could be done.

Unfortunately, she hadn't anticipated their response. The men turned their destruction of the stones onto the five women. Canth had to shift her attention from the stones to surrounding the women with protection. In the confusion that followed, the details still locked in her memory, Canth remembered a pain in her leg that was like nothing she had ever experienced before. As she lost consciousness she remembered seeing Morgan dancing in the fire around the northern stone.

Her next memory was of Zendar. She could not remember what had happened to Jone, Cait, or Paet. She could not remember if they had saved the circle, she could not remember how she had gotten home to her bed, which included several days walk and a dangerous channel crossing back to the island.

Zendar had told her that the other women had returned to Mona and that Morgan was back at the center. She closed her eyes, and there was Morgan dancing in the fire. In the fire, of the fire, but not consumed by the fire. The fire calmed her and she slid into sleep.

11

Chapter 2

In the morning Henith rose early and quietly slipped out of the cottage, knowing she would have to wait until evening before she would get some of her questions answered. Under a barely blue sky, Henith walked to her favorite spot at the top of a hill, where a cliff overlooked the great sea. The trees and shrubs looked as if the fairies had had a busy night dusting everything in sight with a filmy haze. A perfect morning to begin her new moon's lessons. The gentle breeze blew her long blond hair into a dance about her head. Several small gulls, diving off shore, fed on tiny fish that flourished in the cool waters off the coast. She wondered if there were people far beyond the water to the west, and if they worshipped the Goddess. She thought about Trenig to the east and imagined what it must be like there. She could not see the vast land of Trenig from here because the rolling hills of Mona blocked her view. In spite of what she told Carog last night, she was curious about Trenig—a land more vast than her own island, a land with many people, a land with men. Henith realized she had never seen a man, and realized that she did not know much about them, except that they almost caused her mother to die and they wanted to destroy the circles of stones.

She loved her life here, the calm and the peace, the order of every day, and now the excitement in learning the sacred mysteries, but she had to admit to a slight curiosity about Trenig.

Her thoughts were a collage of her mother's stories, last night's events, and the coming year's lessons. Many questions struggled within her. There was so much to learn. She watched the sea and tried to clear her mind. She did not want to begin her instruction with Zendar in a state of confusing thoughts.

A gull screeched overhead, calling her back. Saying good-bye to the sea and gulls, Henith sighed as she walked down the path to Zendar's cottage and her first herbal lesson. She passed the central cooking fire where others ate and chatted, selected some warm bread and honey, and broke her fast.

The fragrances of Zendar's garden reached out to her and pulled her in to the space that surrounded the house on all sides. While all the women of the village grew the food they needed and special herbs that they traded in Trenig for items the women could not produce themselves, like tools for working in the garden, Zendar's herbs and plants were especially prized.

Henith waited quietly in the doorway, not wanting to interrupt Zendar. How strong she looked, even for one so old. Her hair was still dark brown although streaks of gray were visible in the long braid that hung like a rope to Zendar's waist. Henith thought she detected a worried look on the old women's face. She seemed far away while she was grinding some light gray green leaves in a small bowl.

"Come in, Henith. We are in troubled times. I fear for our island and our mysteries. Come, let me teach you what I can while there is still time."

Henith entered the room with more awe and respect than ever before. She had waited for this moment for many years—a chance to learn from this great healer. Henith looked around the room. Herbs and plants of every design, hue, and variety hung from pegs along the ceiling rafters. Bundles of tied branches decorated the walls. On the shelves stood bowls and vessels of various shapes and sizes. Tears came to her eyes as she realized that finally she would learn about these great and exotic plants.

"Henith, first you must understand that each herb is unique. Used in certain ways, these plants have tremendous powers, but used in the wrong ways, they can be dangerous. Each woman learns the secrets of the plants during her year of initiation, and only a few are chosen to learn the most sacred of the plant mysteries. Each woman has a special gift, and after this year you will know yours. Now is your time of waiting and patience. You must be open to hear the call of the mysteries, listening carefully, watching for signs. You must not choose before you are ready. There will come a day when you will know which of the sacred mysteries will be your special one. Until then, you will learn what the plants have to teach you."

Henith looked at Zendar and felt very humble. Zendar's skill was revered by all the women in the village. Henith watched her teacher move with grace around the small room and tried to determine how long Zendar had been on the earth. She must have lived through eighty or more summers, though one might guess forty from her appearance. She was one of the wisest and oldest women on the island.

"We will begin your first lesson. When entering my house, you will take the blindfold from that hook and wear it during our time together. You will learn about these mysteries with your nose and with your fingers. Each day you will smell and feel and learn from the herb itself what it is and how to use it. I will be your guide, but the herbs will be your teachers. Now, put the scarf over your eyes and explore the room, touch and smell all of the plants that I have here. Take all the time you need. I will not talk with you until you are ready—until you call me. If you have a vision or a strong feeling from a certain herb, remember its smell and tomorrow we will start your lessons with that plant. Try to remember what you see in your mind's eye as you touch and smell each plant."

Henith spent the next several hours exploring the smells of the room, amazed at how many different aromas she could identify. It was like the game she used to play trying to differentiate the subtleties of color, only this time it was trying to identify the slight nuances of smell. There were as many smells as there were colors. Henith wondered why she had not thought about trying to sort out the smells before. Some were sharp, and some bitter, some sweet, and some mellow. Some she liked immediately and some frightened her. Occasionally she became confused and thought that she was smelling the same herb again but in a different place or container.

Her eyelids grew heavy, she wanted to lie down and rest. She felt a burning irritation in her nose, everything was beginning to smell the same. Her head felt very strange, and her stomach was starting to feel sick. Then she smelled something different, very different than the others. It was to her right. How had she missed it? She was certain that she had been in this part of the room before. Henith put her hand out and felt for the plant with the distinctive fragrance, and put it to her nose. It was as if this plant had called out to her. She smelled it again and slipped into a dream-state. She saw herself grinding this herb in a small broken gray bowl, while women on the ground called her name. Around her was a stone circle, but not the one she had worshipped in last night. The tall stones cast eerie shadows in the moonlight. She could not recognize any of the screaming women. An old woman, who looked older even than Zander, helped her minister to these strange and wounded women. She saw herself giving something to one of the women who was bleeding badly from a wound similar to her mother's. Henith tried to find someone she recognized but could not. She was alone and frightened. The vision cleared.

"Zendar!" she heard herself calling. Her voice sounded odd, as if it were coming from outside of herself, echoing strangely around the room.

Zendar responded by leading her into the yard. "Take your blindfold off and tell me what you saw."

Henith related the vision to her teacher, who listened intently without comment, her eyes never leaving the young girl's face.

৯৽৵৹

Henith had been with Zendar for almost three weeks when a great commotion erupted in her village. Henith usually spent the early hours of each day at her favorite place overlooking the sea before she went to her teacher. As she was passing through the village on her way to Zendar's house, she noticed several women talking together very excitedly. Usually, the women spent the early morning time alone in prayerful reflection before they did their chores. The frenzy that greeted Henith on the return from her hilltop cliff was far from the typical early morning serenity. She reached the edge of the group that was gathering around a young woman not much older than herself, and heard the young woman tell the group that the women of East Wind Circle had seen great bonfires across the channel on the shore of the mainland.

The inhabitants of the mainland knew that Mona was sacred to the Goddess, and that only the women who had been born there lived on the holy island. The people who had lived in Trenig for centuries would never cross the dangerous channel to come to Mona. The fires could mean that the people in Trenig were in trouble and were appealing to the Goddess and to the priestesses for protection. One of the women from the east village thought the fires may be part of a raiding party of the foreign invaders that were taking over Trenig. Some of the women in the eastern village were afraid that the foreigners would not respect the laws of the Goddess, as the people of Trenig had, and might attempt a channel crossing. Fear of a pending invasion had overtaken the women in East Wind Circle. The High Priestess summoned the best mind speakers and listeners to the east village to try and discern who had set the fires and for what reason.

Lycin and two other women prepared for the trip to the eastern village, while others gathered food for the travelers. Henith did not know Lycin very well, but she knew that Lycin frightened her. She was a huge woman with intense green eyes that saw right into your soul. Henith feared that, when her moon came to learn with Lycin, she would not have any secrets. Fortunately, that moon's work would not arrive for some time yet.

Henith arrived at Zendar's later than usual troubled by the story she had just heard, hoping that the talk of invasion was only idle speculation. She remembered her vision from earlier in the month and shivered. She was not a healer yet; she had barely begun to differentiate one herb from the other. She remembered that the women she had seen in her vision were unfamiliar and so were the stones. She knew somehow that the events in her vision had not taken place in her village. When she had asked Zendar what it had meant, Zendar had said that they both needed to sit with it for some time before the meaning would become clear. It had not become clear to Henith, and it still frightened her to think about it. Zendar had not mentioned it again.

Chapter 3

Henith was about to remind Zendar of her promise that today was the day that she could work without her blindfold, when Zendar began speaking very softly.

"I see two young women in a place far from here. One has long light hair, the other short curly brown hair. They are far away. I see a man who is chasing them through the trees. They are running toward a house. The one with long hair is trying to follow, but she cannot seem to run fast enough."

Henith came closer, trying to hear what was more like a breath taking on a vague shape than actual words being spoken. Zendar continued whispering, rubbing an herb between her hands.

"She is fading into a great darkness. She is struggling through a deep blue darkness. I hear her calling, but I cannot help her. I can see the blue, but I cannot find her even though I know she is in it."

As the words floated around the room, Henith could feel minute shivers running up and down her spine, a hand was grabbing at her stomach.

Zendar came back with a start. "Oh, Henith, these visions are constantly upon me. I find myself spending more and more time in that place and the pain of these seeings is exhausting me. We are heading into a destructive time. I cannot even force a dream that does not end in darkness."

Zendar's revelation astonished Henith, causing an unsettled feeling in the pit of Henith's stomach. She had never heard her teacher speak so before. Henith worried why this strong, solid, wise woman, who always appeared so calm, was shaken by the dreams and visions that several of the women in the village had shared last night.

Zendar seemed far away today, as if she were speaking from some distant place. Henith had found this old woman, whom she was now watching with some concern, to be a very patient and marvelous teacher. She was much more serious in her craft than her last teacher had been. It was not that Nancillia was not careful, but she was so much more light-hearted, often joking and playing with Henith. Zendar, on the other hand, rarely joked or smiled. It was as though she always carried a very heavy burden. Once Henith realized that this serious countenance was part of who Zendar was, and not the result of some behavior or lack of skill on her own part, she relaxed and set her whole being to the task of learning about each herb.

Henith decided not to remind Zendar of her promise and put on the blindfold. She had grown fond of this temporary blindness and felt a comfort, like coming home, when she put it on. She also had looked forward, however, to working with the colors of the plants along with their textures and scents. She and Zendar quietly spent the remainder of the day meditating on the herbs and waiting for the news from the eastern village.

๛

The meal that evening was different than most. Usually the supper meal was joyful, and one of the storytellers would tell a story about women from their village who had passed, but tonight everyone was on edge. Eyes kept darting to the path from the eastern village expecting to see Lycin and the others. Henith heard the sound first. It was a call not unlike an owl—they were close. The women left their tables and ran down the path to greet their friends. As the group gathered back at the tables, the servers set out more food for the travelers. Everyone asked questions at once. Lycin quieted the group.

"Let us first have some time to center and re-gather ourselves. Our energy is spilling everywhere. Let us have a few minutes to rest. Then we will tell you everything we have heard."

The travelers ate the soup of vegetables and warm dark brown crusty bread. When they had finished, the women of Living Water Circle gathered around Lycin and the others. A hush fell as Lycin began the story. "When we arrived in East Wind Circle, Morgan was already there. The women there thought they detected some boats setting off from Brithdir, the little harbor on Trenig, closest to the safe channel to our island. We were fairly certain that the people from Brithdir wouldn't try to cross to Mona. We knew it must be a raiding party of foreigners. I contacted the priestess there who had gathered some people together to light fires to alert us of the pending attack. We decided to set up a wall of energy between us and Trenig. When the boats, about four in all, reached the stones that mark the safe crossing, the tide was running very strong. The men in the boats were unable to navigate the channel against the force of the running tide and the boats crashed against the rocks. As far as we could determine all the men in those boats drowned," Lycin paused mid story.

A shiver passed over the group. Henith pulled her cape over her shoulders, even though the evening was warm.

"I think we should go to Trenig now and kill the rest of those monsters who are threatening our peace and our ways!" Oalii shouted angrily above the general chattering.

A nervous silence fell on the group. Several of the older women dropped their eyes in shame, saddened that one of their sisters would suggest using violence in any way against any human being.

Oalii continued, taking advantage of the silence caused by her remark to speak of that which had been troubling her for weeks.

"We can no longer sit and wait to be attacked. We can no longer resist only by surrounding ourselves and those we are protecting with the energy field. These intruders will keep at us until this whole island is destroyed and we, our mothers and our daughters, will be made slaves to those warring creatures!"

"Silence, Oalii! Can't you see that your words cause pain for your sisters? No one has ever spoken these words before. The times are difficult, but it is no reason for us to neglect the teachings of the

Goddess. We must be careful of ourselves and of others," an older mother of the village spoke these words calmly and with strength.

Oalii glared at her and screamed, "The words may never have been spoken, but we have had them in our minds and our hearts. You know that it is true. I am only putting into words those thoughts that we have all been afraid to speak of for months now. What do we fear? We are strong; we know all of the mysteries. Certainly, with all of this power we can put an end to the violence that is sweeping through Trenig—that which may soon jump into our own beds."

A loud gasp traveled around the gathering. Another woman responded, "Oalii, Oalii, quiet yourself. What has happened to you? You know that aggression for the purpose of destruction, especially destruction of other creatures, is against all that we hold holy. You know that the Goddess has entrusted the sacred mysteries to us for the purpose of teaching the people the ways of love and peace."

Oalii would not be quieted and spoke out again, "But what good is the power if we sit here and allow ourselves to be destroyed, and all the mysteries with us? Is that what you think the Goddess would want?"

Myle, one of the oldest mothers in the village, stood up. "I agree with Oalii." Another gasp. Several women shifted positions. Another low murmur swirled aound the group.

Henith, watching and listening from the edge of the group, remembered many other lively discussions among the women, but nothing like this had ever happened before, at least not in her memory. Another shiver crept over her body, she pulled her cloak tighter.

Myle was speaking again. "I am one of the ancient ones in our village. I have practiced the ways of the Goddess and have protected her mysteries for many moons and many suns. The times we are in are strange, stranger than maybe we can even imagine now. I certainly do not want to break my sacred vows, but I believe that we must be prepared for that possibility. Our very survival depends upon our actions." Myle sat down.

Not a voice was heard. Nobody moved.

Finally, Lycin spoke.

"We have all been taken to places in our hearts that we have never dared go before. Further words at this point would be useless. The Goddess blesses each one of us with a special gift. I suggest that we declare a three day vigil of silence—each woman to her special mystery, and all to our dreaming. In three days' time we must come together to share our inner journeys. Then we may have a clearer vision of what is expected of us at this time."

Many of the women nodded agreement. It was a time that called for special insights. Even Oalii agreed to the suggestion; three days of silence and inner journeys.

Chapter 4

The sun would soon be setting. Five priestesses arrived at the very center of the island as they did every sunset to gather the energy of the island. It was their daily task to gather the power of Mona and then redirect it, spreading it out over all the inhabitants like a protective blanket. The five priestesses, Morgan, Beorin, Fratez, Esli, and Deese, began their preparations for the evening ritual.

Morgan, the High Priestess, watched the four other women as they got ready. She tried to remember the first night she had stood in this room as High Priestess of Mona. She remembered her surprise when the council had selected her after Janu passed from this life. That was nearly ten years ago when life in the community was an orderly pattern of rituals. We have practiced our celebrations in the same way for centuries, she thought. None of the tales that the storytellers told had prepared her for what was happening. The order and regularity that had governed their existence for centuries seemed to be in jeopardy. She longed for the days when decisions were uncomplicated. Now the very fabric of their lives tore apart before their very eyes.

Thoughts of her initiation flooded her mind. That was the first time she had seen Canth. Canth, whom she had taken to Trenig. Canth, who had nearly been killed because she, the High Priestess, had left Mona against the advice of the other women. She felt her eyes fill with tears and tried to refocus them on the room. She looked at the large windows that opened in all directions. Here she could see the tall stones that encircled them. From the roof of this room, one could see the whole of the island and the land to the east—the land of Trenig, where all the disruption in her life was coming from. I have to stay focused, she kept telling herself. She made herself look at the floor that was green like the earth and the ceiling, that was blue like the sky. She looked at each of the candles marking the four directions. She recalled the first time she had entered this room as High Priestess, coming up the staircase from below as High Priestesses before her had done for centuries. No one except the High Priestess and the Priestesses of the Four Directions ever came into this room. During the full moon rituals, Morgan and the others would spiral up from within the earth to greet the full moon in the temple of the sky on the roof. Morgan jumped when Beorin spoke.

"Morgan, are you planning to send more of our women to Trenig?" Beorin watched the High Priestess pace back and forth between the center of the room and the windows facing east.

Fratez didn't wait for Morgan to answer.

"I don't think we should. We need to try to protect ourselves here. The invaders wouldn't dare cross the channel again after what happened the last time they tried. And besides, if they did try, we could surround Mona with an energy wall that no one could penetrate," Fratez tried to hold her voice steady, hoping the others wouldn't detect the feelings of fear inside her that she couldn't seem to control.

"Fear is not a feeling that is familiar to us. Ours has been a gentle life of love and peace."

Fratez smiled in spite of herself as Morgan turned and looked directly into her eyes.

"When we allow ourselves to be threatened by external forces, we run the risk of losing our sense of who we are and what we are on earth to do. Our only role is to practice the sacred ways of the Goddess and to live in peace and harmony with each other, all the other creatures of the earth, and the earth itself. When we try to make decisions from fear, we may not be thinking as clearly as we should be."

Morgan looked at each of the other four women; the natural sparkle was gone from her eyes.

"Last moon I went to Trenig with a few of our most skilled women in power drawing. The damage to our bodies as well as our minds was heavy. The energy expended to surround the stones required such a sustained outpouring of power, I feared none of us would make it back to our home. I'm not sure that was the wisest decision I have ever made. Maybe the older women are right. Maybe it is the role of the High Priestess to stay centered, to stay totally in tune with all the mysteries, to stay in tune with the Goddess. The part of me that wanted to solve this problem, to make it go away, was so strong. I fear that it overpowered my good sense. I should not have put myself or any of the women in danger like that."

Esli tugged at her shawl, trying to keep the minute hairs on the back of her neck from responding to the chilled wind that had come from nowhere and was causing the candles to flicker in an uncontrollable way. The light from the south candle danced as if gasping for air, sending a series of rapid reflections across the ceiling of the holy room. Esli saw the look of recognition cross Morgan's eyes and pulled the shawl tighter.

Morgan steadied herself and continued.

"I still find it hard to understand why the men of this new religion are actually willing to use death producing weapons to destroy us. We have no weapons like the ones they wield, nor do we want any. We need to discover ways to protect the sacred ways of the Goddess and our way of life without succumbing to their means of violence. Once we retaliate in violent ways, we will have lost everything we hold holy. Responding out of fear leads to violence."

"But do we not need to protect the Goddess's circles and the people that are still faithful?" Deese questioned. "Our history teaches us not to take what is not ours, and yet they try to take the Goddess's circles. We are not to strike out against another human being in violence, and yet they strike out against us. Surely the Goddess does not want us to give our bodies and her mysteries over to this brutality that comes increasingly closer with every day."

"But, Deese," Fratez responded, "we are creators not destroyers. I believe that She will not let us be destroyed. She will give us the strength necessary to withstand this momentary disruption of our way of life."

"Fratez, how can you say momentary? This thing has been creeping towards us for years. We have known about the slow but steady spread of this other religion. Always towards our island. At the beginning it was thought to be temporary, that surely the force of the Goddess would protect all of Trenig and the lands beyond it that remain faithful to Her, but this new energy keeps flowing. Circle after circle falls into ruin, and the people, once faithful to the Goddess, turn towards other ways and other laws. Fratez, this is not temporary, this is permanent," Deese's voice rose sharply.

"Listen to what is happening here. We must constantly be aware of how we are treating each other. We must not let ourselves emulate the very force which threatens our existence. The sun is nearing the horizon. Let us not allow this foreign energy to keep us from our daily ritual, for surely that will weaken our power faster than any sword."

The women watched as Morgan took her place in the center of the room. Beorin then slowly walked to her place in the north, Fratez and Deese to the east and west, and Esli to the south. Morgan lowered her voice to a soft reassuring level, "We will do our ritual with extra special care tonight because our hearts are heavy. The women of our land are troubled and gripped by fear that may be new to them. Some of the women have never experienced fear before, not like this at least, and many do not know what to do with these new feelings. We will do as we have always done, but now we will ask for a special blessing from the Goddess. And with Her help, we will send as much energy to each village as we can."

Morgan faced the west, raised her arms, her azure blue robe turning violet in the last rays of this day's sun as it shone through the western portal.

"Great Mother of the universe, send down your power, fill us with your wisdom. Guide us tonight. Send dreams to fill our sleeping and visions to fill our waking. Help us now as we focus your energy on the four villages of your island."

"Great Spirits of the west, guard our western shore, keep evil at bay, far across the great waters," Deese chanted as she turned from the center and faced the west, focusing her attention on the village in her protection. Soon she would have spiritual contact with these women, for they, too, would have gathered for the evening ritual of renewal.

The great spirits of the other three corners of the earth were invoked, each in turn by Beorin in the north, Fratez in the east, and Esli in the south.

Each priestess closed her eyes, cleared her mind of all temporal thoughts, and allowed herself to become the channel. The four who performed this task each had the gift of mind-speaking and mind-listening. The dual aspect of this mystery was difficult; some women found using the mind in one-way communication much easier. Particular skill was involved in being able to totally clear one's mind, and at the same time open it to the thoughts of others.

During evening renewal, each of the temple priestesses was in mental touch with the woman in each of the villages responsible for mind-speaking. Fratez focused the energy of the center toward East Wind Circle, the village most in danger from what was happening in Trenig.

Deese's village, Living Water Circle, had already begun their three-day vigil of quiet and inner journeying. Consequently, she was receiving strong comforting energy from them. She learned from Lycin of the group's agitation and of their decision to spend three days strengthening themselves from within and waiting for visions and dreams. Deese immediately channeled the suggestion to the others. Peace began to spread around the island. All of the women would spend three days in silence.

Morgan developed the plan further. After the three days of inner reflection, the women's experiences would be shared within their village. The moon would be full in seven days, at which time an all-gathering would take place. In this way, all of the stories could be shared with everyone. This all-gathering was truly a bold plan. Usually the women of Mona only gathered together once a year for the Spring Initiation Rite. The women appeared to find comfort in this plan, and a calm continued to settle over the island. At the end of the prayers for this evening, Morgan and the others went down the spiral staircase into the earth to begin their own three-day vigil of reflection. The holy island of Mona was silent.

Chapter 5

How am I going to spend the next days? Henith thought to herself, remembering the many times in the past when the women in her village took a day of quiet, and she and the younger girls had been exempt from having to stop talking for a day. Now I'm almost a priestess of the Goddess, she mused and hugged herself. I know I can keep quiet for three days.

This would be a good time to practice spirit flying, she thought. Maybe I will fly to the center of the island or to one of the other three villages. A thrill passed through her body and she hugged herself again.

As Henith reached her special rock, she noticed that something about the place seemed odd to her. That's strange, she thought. Throughout the year she enjoyed watching the seasons cast their multi-colored spell over the trees. She couldn't remember anything like this before. The soft shades of golden greens and silver blues were the same, but somehow the colors were more subdued than usual. It was as if a silky cloak of fog were tempering her senses. She could see all the rocks and trees and birds, yet they looked more dream-like than usual.

She decided to test her eyesight by searching out objects farther and farther away. While she was playing at this game, she thought she saw something move in the trees down the hill. At first she thought it might be a bird or a small animal. She stared into the darkness between the trunks. Maybe one of the others has come this way to be alone too; I'll pretend not to notice, she thought to the trees.

She wished whoever it was would go in a different direction. In spite of her resolve to try not to notice, she found herself peering into the dark underbrush. She could not see anyone now, but she felt that someone was very close. An unwanted shiver caressed her body.

"Henith, Henith." Someone was calling her name in a whisper from the patch of woods below her on the hillside.

"Henith, Henith." The unfamiliar voice called again. A soft whisper. Straining her eyes, she still could not see anyone in the woods. Surely her mind was just playing tricks with her. She would forget about it, try to think about something else. She turned her eyes away from the trees and looked out over the sea.

"Henith, Henith!" There it was again. This time much clearer. Anger began to creep across her thoughts. She was trying to practice being quiet for the three days. This was difficult enough without having someone calling her. The temptation to answer was great.

It must be Carog. Anger welled up inside of her. Henith did not like Carog, but there were so few other young girls Henith's age that the two of them had been together for much of the last few years. Carog was always playing pranks and tricks on the women. Henith wondered why none of the others seemed to mind.

Canth had told Henith that Carog was a gift. Some gift!

"Every village needs a trickster. She gives us an opportunity to see ourselves." Henith remembered her mother's exact words, but still didn't know what her mother had meant. Certainly Carog's behavior seemed to be exactly opposite to everything taught about the Goddess. Canth suggested that Henith watch Carog, and someday she would understand. Henith found that it was easier to avoid her than to watch her. Her face burned with rage. She could not face Carog now. She turned her back on the dark woods, and looked instead over the treetops at the sky watching the clouds and the birds. Her eyelids slid closed as she lowered herself to the ground and leaned against her rock. Darkness took her away.

Chapter 6

C anth gathered a loaf of bread and some cheese, filled her bowl with grape wine, and left her house. She was able to walk now with only a slight limp. She knew that Henith had gone earlier that morning to the top of the hill just outside the village. Henith had told her about her favorite rock and how she went there to think. Canth wondered how each woman selected her special place. Some women's space was high on top of the island, or on top of a ledge, almost as if they were reaching for the sky. She had noticed that other women chose to be near the water's edge on the shore or by the pools in the stream. The place that had called Canth many years ago was a cave on the other side of the hill that Henith had chosen.

As she left the village, she noticed that most of the women had already retreated to their quiet places. Some would be away for the entire three days, and others would wander back and forth. She smiled at the woman who was preparing food for the village women.

Canth chose to walk around the hill to avoid passing Henith. It was better to let Henith struggle in her space with little distraction. Canth smiled to herself thinking how her daughter, such an outgoing, sparkling child, was now a young woman. Henith was like the small brook just outside of the village, running, bubbling, gurgling, happily skipping over the rocks in her path. Canth wondered if Henith had reached her first deep pool yet, as the brook did at the foot of the hill just before it turned to run quietly into the sea. Maybe Henith would find that place in this quiet time. This was the first time in her life that she had to remain quiet for so long.

Canth remembered walking this path for the first time many years ago, when she was about Henith's age. She had been looking for a place to be alone. Her friend had told her about a terrible dark place on the other side of the hill. According to her friend's description, that dark place was the last place on the island to go. Her friend was several years older and very brave. It struck Canth as odd that such a brave person could be so frightened of any place on the island.

Her friend admitted that she would not even go near that side of the mountain. On that day many years ago, Canth decided to see for herself. She was a bit apprehensive as she started out and could not decide whether to tell anyone where she was going or not. If she told where she was going but could not enter the dark place, everyone would know of her fear; but if she did not tell and went into the dark hole and was captured by a monster, or fell into a deeper hole beyond the entrance, no one would know where she was and she would probably die.

Her feelings today were so different than when she had first tried this route! On that awesome day, so many years ago, her body tingled from a mixture of absolute fear and absolute excitement. She wondered if the excitement had driven her on, or if there had been some other force compelling her forward. She remembered thinking that at every turning in the path she had expected to trip and fall into a black bottomless pit.

From her friend's description, the cave was not in the path but in the side of the mountain, almost exactly half way around the hill from the village. She was getting close and then, almost without warning, she came to a clearing in the woods. The grass was soft and greener than any she had ever remembered seeing on the island. It was as if the trees had deliberately refrained from dropping their seeds in this space. She marveled at how well-kept and tidy this little patch of green was. She did not think many of the women came here, at least from her friend's description. As she moved slowly into the middle of the greenness, the thought of choosing it as her place flitted through her mind. She really did not have to find that old cave anyway.

Canth laughed at herself now as she recalled how close she had come to abandoning her resolve to explore the cave. Thank the Goddess for youthful curiosity. Canth remembered dancing on that plush carpet, swirling around with sheer delight, when her eye caught sight of the cave. The cave—neatly tucked into the side of the hill— hid behind some small poplar trees, which acted as guards protecting the opening. She stopped in her dance and stared at the opening. The weight of the decision now facing her was tremendous. What she had already found was so delightful, so cheery; it certainly was a gift from the Goddess. No one would deny that she had chosen wisely, and yet there it was, so close. It could not hurt to take just a peek into the opening. She would not be like her friend, afraid even to take a look.

But her friend had told her stories. Maybe she had been trying to frighten Canth, maybe she was playing a joke on her, or maybe she was testing her. She remembered how frightened she'd been of monsters, of a deep hole. She was very young then, but still she had wondered if the Goddess would allow monsters to live on the island and eat her chosen priestesses.

Maybe it was a trap. Maybe she had done something to irritate the Goddess, who might have chosen to have a monster devour her. Her fears had choked her. Back and forth the battle raged inside her. Finally, Canth fought off the urge to run away from this place. She had pleaded with the Goddess for protection, and now slowly, ever so slowly, she approached the cave, calling with each step the spirits of the north, south, east, and west to protect her.

When she reached the opening, she could smell the coolness of the walls mixing with the sunlight at the very edge. She took a deep breath and stepped inside. It was very dark, and wonderfully cool. She had not been able to see anything, as her eyes had not yet adjusted to the lack of light.

She had managed to step inside the cave, wondering how much further she would have to go to prove to herself that she had actually ventured into this darkness. She remembered reaching out with her hands and feeling along the floor with her foot, expecting to reach the back of the cave or a big hole into which she would drop forever. She was unable to see anything at all. As she poked along she was amazed at the size of this room.

Canth remembered the trembling of pride and exhilaration in her body. As she started to leave, her foot had touched something that moved on the floor. Immediately, fear consumed her whole body. The monster's foot! Fear took hold, she could not move. She waited for the great roaring monster to attack her. Nothing happened; no sound, no attack. How quickly her feelings changed! Her mouth had become very dry, her throat constricted so that she could not swallow; her legs lost their rigidity and had turned into liquid. She must either move or fall down. As her body forces reassembled themselves, she found herself bending over to search for the object she had kicked with her foot.

Her hand touched something, momentary panic engulfed her again. Moving very slowly, she started to feel for the object, bumpy smooth, and about the size of a small rock; she picked it up. It was much lighter than a rock and, while it had a very uneven surface, it was also very soft. She left the cave with it in her hand.

When her eyes had readjusted to the brightness of the day outside, she stared at the object in utter amazement. Then a slow crawling giggle coming right from her middle engulfed her. She remembered rolling on the grass in uncontrollable glee. She kept looking at the object and laughing. All of the fear and anxiety, the sheer terror, had all been over a half melted candle!

As Canth approached the green space now, she could see herself holding the candle. The event still made her laugh at herself when she recalled it.

After the incident with the candle, Canth had an enlightening idea. Obviously she had not been the first one in the cave. Why not bring a candle when she returned? It was so simple an idea she wondered why she had not thought to bring a light with her the first time.

On her next visit to the cave, she was still fearful, even though she had brought several candles. She had not had an opportunity to find out much about the cave before her second visit and, while armed with light, she still did not trust what might live beyond the edge of darkness.

Her plan that day had been to explore the size of the cave, to determine whether anything might be hiding in its crevices or corners. She would never forget her surprise when she lit her first candle inside the cave.

She discovered an old stool and sat down, forgetting her plan to explore the whole cave. She just could not believe what her eyes were seeing. Maybe she was dreaming? As she looked straight ahead from where she was sitting, something on the wall caught her attention, something covered in part by mildew. She went up to the wall and tried to brush aside the dampness, but she was afraid of damaging the painting underneath. Whoever had used this space before had filled the walls with pictures. The colors of the dye were still quite vivid in spite of the moss and mold that had begun to grow on the walls and ceiling. She would have to bring some herbs to clean the walls. She tried to make out the other pictures on the wall. She lit more candles, and was so overwhelmed that she had to sit down again, losing all sense of time. The room was small, but very beautiful. She wondered why any place so beautiful was not visited regularly by all the women here.

During the months following her discovery, Canth learned a great deal about the cave. It had belonged to Dena, who had left this earth many, many summers ago, long before Canth was born, long before many of the women in her village had been born. At first Canth had thought to keep her discovery to herself but changed her mind, deciding it was too beautiful not to share. In the time that followed, all of the women came to help clean the cave of the years of disuse. They also discovered another small cave adjoining the first. It was an awesome place. While the first room was brightly colored, with many jubilant drawings, the second room was darkly painted with hideous and frightening figures. Canth did not like that room, and wished it had not been discovered.

After each woman experienced Dena's cave pictures, the women of the village decided that because Canth had been brave enough to traverse the cave's darkness, she would have it for her private space until she chose to leave it.

The storytellers now included Canth's discovery in the Dena stories, but no one ever came to Canth's place. The women had accepted Dena's gift to Canth, and let it be.

And so it was. For the last twenty or more summers and winters, Canth had her special home. During that time she had developed her own private ritual. In the center of the green carpet she placed two vessels that she had stored in a small rock closet just off the path, near the edge of the ring of trees. In one vessel she kept water, and in the other a coarse granular salt. She sat down in the center of the circle. She had learned that if she started her ritual immediately upon arriving at the green, her meditations were shallow and constantly interrupted by thoughts of her present, daily experience.

Sometimes, like today, the present was so busy she thought her mind would never settle. She was afraid that the chaos surrounding the island and the feelings that ran rampant in her village would interfere with her silent inner wanderings, and she was ready for a long preparation time. She often wished that she could just stay in her cave and not bother with the life of the village, especially now with the threat of destruction.

Canth sat in her circle of green, thoughts of the past and present flying though her mind. She knew she would need a long time to quiet herself. She longed for her cave, the dark hole she could see from where she was sitting. She was always struggling with patience. One would think that after all these years she would be doing better than she was at that moment.

Hours passed, and still she waited. The rush in her heart quieted; gradually she found herself releasing all the tensions in her body. The pain from her recent wound was beginning to subside. When her body was completely relaxed, she knew she was ready, ready for the descent into the comforting, frightening, wonderful darkness. Her ritual could now begin.

She took the vessel containing the salt. Moving just to the west of the cave opening, she began to sprinkle the salt in a circle where the trees met the grass. When she reached the western edge of the green she said, "Goddess of the west, guard this circle; keep evil far away.

Take the thoughts and cares of my life and hold them until I return again to the present."

She continued sprinkling the salt in a circle until she reached the southernmost point, repeating the prayer to the Goddess of the south, she continued her circle, invoking the Goddess of the east in turn.

When she reached the cave, she put the vase of salt on a little rock shelf just above the opening to the cave.

"Goddess of the north, protector of the earth's inner space, protector of my inner journeys, guard my openings, protect them from evil penetrations, protect me for the next three days of earth time, and eternity in your time. So be it."

Slowly she returned to the center of the green. She became calmer with each step. She repeated the process with the water vase. When she reached the cave opening for the second time, she stood for a very long time facing the dark hole and waiting until she was called.

She heard the beckoning from within, and entered.

Chapter 7

Darkness hung like moss. Henith rubbed her eyes, trying to clear a space in the blackness. Trees encircled her like a giant tomb. The path that led to her village must be in front of her. Even the stars had disappeared. She sensed a storm approaching from the west. Her mother's cave was not too far away, she knew, but she could not intrude on her mother's vigil, and it probably would be as difficult to find the cave as to find the path back to the village. She had no idea what the hour was either. As she gazed at the darkness down the hill, the intense blackness she would have to go through to get home, she thought she detected a glow coming from the tops of the trees, almost as if they were being illuminated by some invisible fire. She knew it wasn't fire because the glow was soft and white, not flickering and red. She rubbed her eyes again, the blackness returned for a moment, and then slowly the trees started to glow again. She was surprised that she had never thought before now about whether the trees had auras or not. That must be it. Her moon time with the mother of the aura mystery was not for some time yet. She had always seen auras around people, but had not developed any skill in differentiating colors and changes. She would have to remember to ask Zendar or her mother if trees and plants also had auras.

She was trying to decide whether to risk the coming storm and stay here or try to return home in the dark. She slowly realized that she actually had some fear of the dark and the unknown. She tried to remember if she had ever been alone in the night before. She couldn't remember one time. Even when her mother had gone to Trenig, she had stayed with others in her village. Up until now she had lived a totally safe existence.

"Henith." The voice called her again.

"Henith." It was coming from the cluster of trees down the hill.

"Carog, are you here, too?" she called into the darkness, breaking the vigil of silence; hoping it would help her struggle through the long darkness.

"Carog, are you there?"

"Henith, Henith."

Oh that Carog! She's just trying to frighten me. Henith jumped up feeling herself getting very angry as she started quickly down the slope towards the trees and into the thicket.

"Carog, where are you? Stop hiding from me. Carog!" Her voice echoed in the stillness as she stumbled down the slope, traveling deeper and deeper into the dense wood.

She stopped where she felt sure Carog must be, but saw no sign of her, or anyone. She shivered realizing that she could actually be alone in the woods, and that her mind could be playing tricks on her.

"Carog, stop hiding. I know you are here somewhere."

She thought she heard a twig snap and walked slowly toward the sound. Deeper and deeper she ventured in the darkness. This is foolishness, she thought, I will not be able to find my way back; but I know someone is teasing me and I am going to find whoever it is and put an end to this game.

She noticed as she walked on that she was able to see more and more. Were the trees' auras lighting her way or was it the early dawning light? She must have slept far longer than she had thought at first.

Wisps of fog played beyond the trees ahead and she walked toward it, discovering that the mist was coming from a small lake. She could not recall the storytellers mentioning a pond on this part of the island.

She sat down heavily on a log at the edge of the lake, watching the mist, wondering where she was. Tears started to form in the corners of her eyes. She shook her head to chase away the fear and panic, and brushed the tears away with the edge of her sleeve. How had she gotten here and how was she going to get to her village? Anger started to grow deep in her stomach. She wanted to find Carog, to shake her, and to ask her why she enticed Henith to this lake. The image of Carog loomed large in Henith's vision. Henith was embarrassed by the feelings of rage she was experiencing toward one of her sisters, toward an initiate of the Goddess, toward a priestess of Mona. The feelings were all too familiar to her. She was frightened by the intense anger she felt and the loss of control over her own feelings, as if another creature had suddenly inhabited her body, taking her away from her calm center.

She looked around the edge of the lake where she was sitting. If she could find a stone to hold she would feel better. Stones always gave her strength. As she looked around she became aware of the plants and trees that were growing next to the edge of the lake. They were totally undisturbed. No one, not even an animal had been here for some time, maybe even many suns. The only disturbance in the vegetation she had made by herself. She felt another stab of panic. It was not possible! She distinctly heard someone calling her from this part of the woods. She continued to search for a stone. Where was Carog and why had she enticed her to this lake? The tears formed again. No way home, lost, and she was hearing people that didn't exist. No one would come after her here, no one knew where she was. She tried to stand, but found her body too heavy to move. Fear was holding her prisoner. More tears. The harder she tried to hold them back, the stronger they flowed.

"Henith, Henith," a voice whispered through the swirling mist.

"Oh no!" Her despair was replaced with the fear of being caught weeping. She could not let Carog see her in this condition. She wiped her eyes on her tunic again, and peered into the mist. The voice came from the middle of the lake. She squinted, trying to see into the swirling fog. Yet how could someone be walking in the lake? It was impossible.

She focused into the hazy cloud, searching perhaps for a bird whose call impersonated the saying of her name in the echoes of the woods. Instead the outline of a young woman appeared draped in the heavy fog. She imagined it was Carog. She opened her mouth to call to her, but choked on her words and drew in a quick breath as another figure appeared. She widened her eyes to see more clearly, but the misty vapors obscured her vision. The two figures seemed to be floating above the surface of the water, although Henith could not determine for sure where the surface was because of the mist. The more Henith tried to determine who these women were the more confused she became. At moments the shorter one looked as if it might be Carog. She was about the right height, a few inches shorter than Henith. Trying to focus through the mist was difficult, but the one Henith thought might be Carog wore the simple tunic of the island women, cinched at the waist with a cord. The length and material of the tunic varied with the seasons. In the cooler moons, the tunics, made from wool, were long—almost touching the ground. The wool came from sheep tended by the women in the east village. In the warmer moons, the tunics were shorter and made from flax. Occasionally the women dyed the cloth but usually they left the colors as they were. The woman in the lake that Henith thought was Carog was wearing a long robe the color of spring grass. That must be Carog, who else would wear such a fine robe to run through the woods in the middle of the night? Usually the women saved robes this fine for celebrations and moon rituals.

She still could not see the faces of the two clearly. She noticed that the other woman was very tall and much broader than most of the women Henith had seen. It had to be a woman from one of the other villages; Henith knew the women in her village, and this other person was not one of them—too tall and too broad. She struggled to discern just why this other woman appeared so different. The women in her village were all shapes and sizes but this woman was different, bigger somehow. As she continued to watch the pair she noticed that the other woman was dressed differently than the island woman. A sudden panic stabbed at Henith. Was this woman from Trenig? Henith doubted if anyone from Trenig would come to Mona, and besides, how would Carog have met her? As far as she could remember neither she nor Carog had ever left their village. An uncomfortable thought started to form in the back of her mind. She tried to dismiss it as she continued to watch the figures float above the lake.

The mist cleared for a moment. The woman and the other person seemed to be talking intimately to each other.

Stories about the men and women of Trenig began to come to her mind, but never having been to Trenig, she never had the opportunity to see people from there. She had always imagined that they looked like the island women. But the person she was watching was definitely different than any woman she had ever seen. The uncomfortable thought screeched through her mind again. She closed her eyes trying to make the thought go away, trying to make the person with Carog go away. She opened her eyes, and it was still there. She began to shake as the unwelcome thought became a knowing. This other person must be a man. It was true. The figure she was watching must be a man. A man on Mona! Morgan and the other priestesses would be in a rage if they knew what was happening. How could Carog do this to her sisters? Henith continued to watch the couple, thinking that maybe she should hide because they hadn't noticed her yet. She still had time to slide back into the trees. But why had Carog called her if she did not want to be seen?

The couple was looking intently at each other; they were holding hands. Henith was intrigued by their behavior and somewhat embarrassed that a future priestess of the Goddess would be intimately involved with a man from Trenig, and would break all the taboos by bringing one to Mona.

Now another woman approached the couple. They let go of each other, as if reluctant to be seen touching in such a way. Henith stared at the visitor. This woman was Carog. How could that be? Certainly not two Carogs. Who was the first woman? The man greeted the second woman with an embrace.

Henith watched as the man and the second woman faded into the mist. Henith watched the one that remained, trying to see who she was. Sensing that the woman was in great pain, Henith felt a deep desire to reach out to her and took a step toward her, but felt her sandals getting wet. Henith looked at herself standing in the lake. How could she have forgotten about the pond? But the figures in the mist had been standing and walking on the surface. How could that be, she puzzled.

Henith stepped back to the shore. Maybe if she walked around the edge, she would find them on the land on the other side of the water, but the walking was very difficult. At first there was marsh and mud, and each step required tremendous effort to keep from falling into the mire or having her feet swallowed by the lakeside muck. Maybe she had better go back to where she had first seen them and try the other direction, but she was not sure whether the other way would be any easier. As she stumbled through the dense undergrowth, she was motivated by the hope that this woman would show her a path to the western village. The shore began to get firmer. Walking was much easier. Henith noticed that the sun was beginning to shine through the trees. She must have been watching the figures in the fog longer than she thought. The mist, too, was lifting from the lake. She continued on. Walking was becoming difficult again. Surely she must be nearing the people. She stopped and watched the lake as the last morning mist disappeared in the warmth of the sun.

Oh how beautiful this place is! Carefully she searched the shore for any signs of the three people. She thought she saw something move where the trees seemed to change color around the edge of the lake. Henith searched the shore between where she stood and the hollow in the trees. She would have a difficult time passing that way because a high rock outcropping dropped straight down to the water's edge.

She would have to abandon the shore route and move to a more inland path to navigate this high prominence. Henith turned towards the brambles and thick underbrush. Surely no one had been this way today. It looked to Henith that this path had gone untraveled for many years. The briars ripped at her skin and entangled her clothes. Pulling and tugging her way through the coppice, Henith began to despair, the tears flowing down her burning cheeks. She was more lost than ever, her body was stinging with pain from many cuts and scratches, her bones and muscles ached and she was very hungry, but she could not stop because there was no place to sit down and rest. This entanglement seemed endless. On and on she struggled, winding her way through the thick underbrush.

With each painful step, her heart cried out for someone, anyone, to guide her from this web of briars and thorns. Coming into a small clearing, Henith collapsed onto the soft emerald moss that grew there.

Great sobs rattled upward from her insides, racking her already bruised and weary body. She was too tired to try to hold back the tears that kept coming from what, to Henith, seemed like a bottomless well. Henith couldn't remember ever feeling this way before. She closed her eyes, the heaving sobs quieting in the gentle warmth of the early sun. She drifted into a troubled half sleep. People flew through the air and into the water, swirling around her catching her up, carrying her into the lake, carrying her high above the water, dropping her, falling, falling. Henith tried to quiet herself, but each time she thought she had gained control another wave of desperate sobbing overpowered her. As the pain of loneliness and abandonment ebbed from her body, another attacker waited its turn. She wanted to get up from this place. She wanted to go home, but her arms and legs refused to move. Every muscle that controlled her movement had ceased to function. She floated above her green mossy bed; she could see her head sitting on her limp and inert body. Fear rushed at her from every side. Maybe she was dead. The more she tried to move her body, the more her body refused to move. Would she ever get free from this place?

Screams lurched from her lungs, frightened, terrified sounds, running through the forest, echoing across the lake. On and on she wailed, on and on she ran until she collapsed against a rock and everything became nothing.

She woke with a start, beads of perspiration running down her neck. She looked around, the hunger causing her to feel light-headed and dizzy.

Chapter 8

At first Henith did not recognize her surroundings, thinking she should be home with Canth. She tried to move her body but found it stiff from sleeping on the ground. She stretched trying to bring back feeling in her arms and legs. Looking around, she saw her favorite thinking rock. What was she doing here?

Gradually memory started to return. The three day silence. Memories of a lake and someone calling her flashed through her mind. She remembered trying to walk around a lake, but she could not see any lake from where she was.

The dream became clearer. Had she actually seen a lake and three people? Carog and those other people. But who were they?

She caught her breath as the image of what she thought must have been a man returned. Was there a man on Mona or had it been a dream? How could she have had a dream about a man when she had never seen a man in her life?

Henith struggled to reconstruct all of the dream fragments that she could remember. Peering into the trees she still expected to see a lake, even though she knew there wasn't one close by. She began to question if the trees she could see were real. The lake she had seen and the man in the dream didn't seem any less real than the trees she was looking at right now. She shook her head trying to rid it of the ambiguities of her perceptions.

A disturbing thought floated into her consciousness. She had no idea how long she had been here. It was unlikely that she had slept for three days. She knew it was early morning, she could tell from the location of the sun. She had to decide whether to stay here for the rest of the day or go back to the village. Originally she had intended to spend her evenings in the village and her days at her thinking stone, but she was hungry and her body ached. She decided to go back to the village even if it were early morning. Feelings of failure forced their way into her mind. Would she be perceived as a failure if she spent the rest of the time, however long that was, in the safety of her village? A part of her knew that wasn't true. Many women spent most or all of their time in the village. Some women spent silent time walking or doing heavy labor like chopping wood. Some disappeared and some sat in the village and worked with their hands. No one would find her strange for returning at this hour, if anyone even noticed. She should record her dream somehow, and soon, so as not to lose any of the details. She doubted if her story would be of any interest to the other women of the island, but she knew that all dreams and visions were valuable to the dreamer. She concentrated trying to remember all the details of what she had seen; every color, every image, every feeling, every detail was important.

When she reached her village it was very quiet. Only a few women were visible. Henith went to the room where the food had been carefully prepared for this time. She selected some fruit and some bread. When she looked up from the table, she saw Carog looking at her. The feelings from her vision-dream crashed over her. She had to hold the table to keep herself steady. She tried to avoid Carog's translucent gray eyes. She did not want to be tempted to break the silence. She tried to smile and looked away. Taking her fruit and bread, she left the room, feeling Carog's eyes following her. She found herself shaking as she entered her cottage.

She realized that she didn't believe totally that her dream was a dream. As she had been walking home she had noticed that the stinging on her legs had come from scratches. The only way they could have gotten there was in the dream. Getting scratches on one's legs from a dream would be very difficult to explain. But there was no other explanation. How else could she explain the lake and the man? She thought about the man. She had never actually seen a man before, so how did she know this person she had seen was one? She didn't know how she knew, she just knew.

She wondered what her mother was doing in her cave. She remembered the time about six summers ago, when Canth had taken her to the cave. It was truly a wonderfully frightening place. It had been very warm that summer, but it was deliciously cool in the cave. There had been two separate rooms, the first covered with bright and cheerful paintings. Henith had liked that room, but the other room had scared her. It was dark and the pictures were terrifying. Her mother had told her that the two rooms were like the two aspects of every person. Some parts were bright and cheerful and some were dark and scary. She thought about last night. If she were going to paint her experience she would have had to paint it in the dark and scary room.

Henith knew she needed to record her dream somehow. And even if she didn't share her dream with the women in her village at the end of the three day vigil, she should discuss it during her moon of learning with the priestess of dreams and visions.

Henith selected a newly prepared animal skin and some colored dyes from the cottage where supplies were kept. She would draw her dream on the skin which had been prepared for drawing. Henith liked to draw, that was one of the reasons she had been so intrigued by the drawings in her mother's cave. The skin she selected was larger than she usually used. Usually she drew on little scraps of skin left over from other projects. She had never before felt as if she could cover a whole skin. The dream haunted her, and the feelings generated by the dream were persistent. She had to record it all. Before her drawings were of people and objects she could actually see. She had never tried drawing a dream before, and she certainly had never tried to draw a feeling before. She filled a basket with dyes of different colors, the skin, and her lunch. She would go to the trees behind her house; there was an oak tree there that she liked to lean against because of the strength she received from it. She would stay close to the village today because she still wasn't sure whether she had lost a whole day in sleep or not, and she didn't want to miss the sharing at the closing of the three day silent vigil.

She spread the skin out on the grass beside the tree and carefully arranged the dyes around it. She leaned against the oak tree, feeling its warmth and protection. She looked at the whiteness of the skin wondering how she would fill all that space with drawings representing her dream.

She thought about Carog in the spring green robe, the other Carog, and the man. There was some part of Carog that she disliked, that she mistrusted. That was a terrible thing to think. How could she be a priestess of the Goddess and have such feelings of mistrust for one of her sister priestesses?

The women in her village were her family and her community; the women of the entire island were her extended family and community. Even though she had never met them, she knew they were there. The women held each other sacred. Feelings of mistrust, jealousy, and envy were rare because the women knew the ways of the Goddess and knew feelings of jealousy and mistrust were unworthy for priestesses of the Goddess. From the storytellers, she knew that once in a great while a woman would choose not to be initiated if for some reason she found herself unable to live according to the way, and would leave Mona and go to live in Trenig. Henith wouldn't allow herself to think of not being a priestess, of not living and dying on Mona.

She thought about Carog again. Her mother had told her that Carog was a gift. How could she be a gift if all she caused in Henith were disturbing feelings? She wanted to paint Carog as dark and ugly with grotesque features, not the lithesome young woman in a celebration robe of spring green floating above a sky-blue lake in the mist. She wanted to draw dark trees disguised with faces that had many eyes of bright yellows and blood reds, the branches like hundreds of arms and tentacles, long eerie fingers ready to trap the unsuspecting woman. When she thought of the trees as an enemy army waiting to attack, she thought she felt the bark of the tree on her back turn cold. She looked up at the tree she was leaning against. This tree could never be the enemy, it was her friend. She sent a small apology to the tree and felt the warmth return.

As she started to form the images in her mind that she would draw, she wondered if she shouldn't be stitching the design onto her initiation blanket instead. Each initiate had a blanket on which she stitched events and symbols of what she had learned during her initiation year. The fabric could be decorative or functional. The basic cloth was woven by the birth mother and given to her daughter at the time of her first flow of blood. The young woman then recorded in any way she chose the story of her year of initiation into the mysteries of the Goddess. At her initiation, her blanket was blessed by all the women of the island and it became her special protection. Some women chose to hang their blankets in their rooms as house protections. Some chose to use the blanket for sleep protection. Canth had worn hers like a cloak when she had gone to Trenig.

While working on her blanket was meditative, she feared her interest in sewing was slim. She much preferred drawing and painting with dyes. She knew that it was important for her to have her own special blanket of initiation and protection and that it was important for her to record her story into her blanket, but she participated in its creation more as an act of discipline than an act of joy. Some of the protection blankets she had seen were elaborate with many hours of intricate details. She doubted if she would ever be able to create such tapestries. She wanted hers to be simple.

The fabric her mother had woven for her was of flax. Her mother had left the color natural without any other dyes, and it was soft, even though the weave had been fairly coarse. Henith liked the coarseness of the weave because it allowed her to be less fine in her stitching. At first the size of the fabric her mother had given her had overwhelmed her, it had seemed so large. She was afraid that the task of filling it would take a lifetime, not one year.

Some of the blankets she had seen were very orderly. It was like reading a story. They were done in either rows or columns with each event following the one preceding it. Other women had blanket

47

collages. They were in no particular order, but each important event of her life in its own space.

Henith had planned out the whole design ahead of time. She had decided to have seven concentric circles, each circle a different color of the rainbow. In the center would be a silver and gold spiral. Surrounding the gold and silver spiral would be a circle of purple. Surrounding the purple ring, a ring of blue and so on until the outside ring, which would be red. Each circle would be filled with symbols done in the color of that circle. She had started the spiral when she was training for spirit flying. When she imagined spirit flying she saw her spirit tethered to her physical body by a silver light. Her spirit body would spiral out from her physical body on a silver light and be guided back by a golden one.

In the purple circle she was embroidering the herbs with purple flowers that she was learning to use with Zendar. She didn't know yet what symbols would go in each of the other circles. She thought that something would emerge from her moon-time with each of the different mysteries.

Now here clearly was an experience that didn't fit into her neatly ordered blanket. She wished she could ask someone if she should draw her experience or somehow incorporate it into her protective blanket. Selfishly she decided that she didn't want Carog on her blanket. She didn't feel safe with her. Having her on the blanket that was supposed to be for protection felt like a contradiction. And besides, which circle would she put her dream in? She had not planned for a dark and scary circle. She certainly couldn't put the events of the dream in the purple circle that she had set aside for the purple flowers and herbs. That was the circle she was working on this moon. It would spoil the overall design to put this dream anywhere else on the blanket. She selected the darkest brown dye and started to draw trees on one corner of the skin. She constantly murmured apologies to the oak as the trees of her fears took on a sinister appearance.

Henith looked up from her painting occasionally and noticed that women were gradually returning. At first when she had taken up her painting, she had been alone; gradually the women appeared, one by one, all day long. It was like magic. She had continued to watch and paint the whole day. As time progressed, the painting changed from sinister to calm. The trees on one side of the skin were dark and ominous and the trees on the other side were the trees of springtime, light and airy, with golden leaves. In the center of the painting were three figures, one woman dressed in a long black robe almost a deep purple looking out over the mist. Her face was hidden by the hood of her robe. The second woman was dressed in the spring green that Henith had seen on the woman in the lake. She also had her back to the viewer, but her hair was golden and long. Henith had been reluctant to actually draw Carog on her painting. The third person was more difficult to describe, caught up in the mist, not really defined, but present, more dream-like. At first the viewer would think it was a woman, but if the viewer really studied the person, they would not be able to tell for sure if the figure were a man or a woman. Henith realized that at first she had feared the silence that had stretched endlessly before her, and now she felt as if it might not have been long enough.

Chapter 9

"Do you think I'll be able to make up the time I've missed studying with Zendar? I feel as if I only have just begun to learn about the herbs and plants and with three days of silence and now the gathering in the center, I'm sure that there is a great deal I will miss."

Canth looked at Henith while cinching her protective blanket around herself.

"I'm sorry life is so chaotic for you. We will discuss the situation with the other mothers. All the initiates have the same problem. We are living through different times. I can't remember when all the women of the island were gathered at the center when it was not the Spring Initiation Rite."

Henith thought about what was happening. She had never been to the center before. Usually a woman's first experience at the temple at the center of Mona was when she was initiated as a priestess, but today all the women and even all the young children would be gathering there.

Henith was excited about meeting the other women. She knew that during the great Spring Rite there were several days of fun and dancing. Henith doubted if there would be much dancing this time though. In some ways she was sad to have her initial experience at the center be clouded by such heavy feeling, but at the same time she couldn't wait to see the great circle of Mona. Even though the women were gathering this time to hear the stories of the last three days and to make decisions that might affect the future of Mona, she was hoping that she might meet some of the women from the other villages. She rarely saw anyone from outside her own village. The women's lives, at least up until now, were fairly simple. Daily life had a pattern, and calmness and order usually prevailed. Women would practice their special crafts, listen to the storytellers, and share their journeys. The women spent many hours in meditation. There was no need to do anything else.

Henith helped Canth put the last items into her pack. The women prepared for three days. Each woman shared the burden of carrying the food that would be needed.

Henith and Canth gathered with the rest of the women in the center of the village. When all were ready and the final items distributed for carrying, the women set out. Henith remembered watching the women over the past years leaving for the Spring Rite. Before there was gaiety and singing and high energy. She always felt left out before, but she knew her time would come. The initiates each year were decorated with flowers and were treated with kindness and affection. Henith had been looking forward to that special event in her life.

But here she was just like the rest of the women going to the temple, and everyone was so somber. No laughing and joking, no flowers, no one more special than anyone else. After they had been walking in silence for about half an hour, Henith heard the chanting start from somewhere in the line in front of her. Soon the whole village had joined in. Henith imagined that she was an eagle looking down seeing four long lines of women slowly weaving toward the center of the island. The image sent a thrill through her body.

Henith noticed that the chanting had softened to a whisper. They must be nearing the center. Henith tried to see around the women in front of her, but she was too far back to see anything except the trees. The procession slowed as the chanting became a murmur like the rustle of the wind in new spring leaves.

When Henith looked again, she had to blink several times, because she could not believe what she saw ahead of her. The storytellers had not exaggerated, if anything they had understated the magnificence of the stone circle in front of her. She had been impressed with the size of the stones in her own village, but they were dwarfs compared to the

51

immense stones in this circle. Henith couldn't take her eyes from the stones. She noticed that the other women of her village immediately went about setting up an encampment on the west side of the stone circle. She helped Canth set up their tent and then went to help set up the common eating space. She kept looking at the stones in awe and wonderment. She noticed a small building in the center of the circle. It was like a large house, except it looked as if most of it were constructed underground with a platform where the roof should have been. Henith imagined that would be a wonderful place to spend quiet time. She wondered if one could see the water surrounding Mona from there. She assumed that was where Morgan and the other High Priestesses lived.

Henith had been so entranced by the stone circle that she hardly noticed that the women from the other villages had arrived and also had begun to set up their encampments. Henith was anxious to explore the area surrounding the stone circle. She knew she was not permitted to enter the circle until after her initiation, but she couldn't wait to wander to the other camps, and was surprised to notice that the women were staying close to their own circle.

She found Canth. "Why do the women not visit with the women from the other villages?"

Canth smiled,."There will be plenty of time for visiting, but now it is important for each woman to settle into her own new space, especially after the journey. You are young and have never traveled. It is always disturbing to one's sense of self when there is any disruption in the daily routine and especially when one's home has been moved. You need to familiarize yourself with this new space. Make it yours before you go visiting. If you look around you will notice how each woman is tending her own place."

"Our village will eat together to firmly establish our collective energy in this space. Then we will be called to evening renewal, still each in our own village space, and then we will sleep. Tomorrow we will be told how our time together will be spent. It is an unusual circumstance, because as far as I can remember, we have only gathered together once a year for the Spring Rite, and then we all know what we are to do and what is expected and how the time is planned. We are all wondering about tomorrow. We do know that at some time we will all gather and share some of the stories from our three day silence. We will also have the full moon ritual tomorrow night."

Henith was disappointed. She wanted to go exploring now. Henith looked at Canth who seemed to be thinking of something far away.

"Do you think we will meet any of the other women?"

"I imagine so. We usually spend some time with the women in the other villages who are the keepers of the same mysteries."

"What will I do? I haven't even learned about what mystery I will choose or which one will choose me. I've only learned about spirit flying and I wasn't very good at it; and the herbs, but those lessons were cut short because of our situation." Henith started to look dejected.

"I think you need to calm your center and make this space yours. I expect that some of the ambiguity you are experiencing is because you are in a place foreign to you. Nothing is familiar. Did you bring your initiation blanket with you?"

"Yes."

"I suggest you work on it for a while. Calm yourself. Trust the Goddess."

Henith was more agitated than she had first realized. She knew her mother was right. She knew she needed some time to quiet the feelings in her and she would be happier tomorrow for the time taken today. Henith unrolled her blanket and found the purple threads she was using to create pictures of the purple flowers she had learned about. Henith noticed that the initial busyness of the village women was quieting. There was a feeling of settling in. Very few women were visible. She looked out to where the women from the other villages were. She noticed that they too seemed to be settling in. She could not see the east village women. The huge stones blocked them from view, but she knew they must be settling in also.

Henith turned her attention to her sewing. Henith had asked Zendar if she could learn the plants with purple flowers first. Zendar found those with healing qualities because of Henith's first vision. Henith was stitching the purple flowers onto her blanket. She had already finished the purple coneflower and angelica, and was working on meadow rue. As she was stitching she tried to recall the properties of each of the plants and what each was used for. It helped her to remember by visualizing the stitches on her blanket.

She probably should have stitched some of the other plants and not worried so much about sticking to her color scheme. There were so many plants that she had learned about. She was saving the iris until the end. This was the plant that had chosen her. The roots are dried and pulverized and then ground to be applied to wounds. Zendar said that her first vision was about grinding blueflag roots to be used on wounds. What troubled Zendar and Henith was that very few women suffered from wounds on the island. The vision must have been about the future and the thought of so many women being wounded was unnatural and very frightening.

Henith had many flowers to go before she would do the iris. She had saved it until the end because it was her favorite flower and helped her stitching by giving her something to look forward to. Her time with Zendar was over even though she had not finished, because of all the external events affecting her village and the island. When she returned to her village she would begin her lessons with Penrith. Penrith was the mother of the mysteries of numbers. Henith had always been attracted to the symbol for seven. She wondered if that had any significance. All the young girls had basic lessons in mathematics, learning the arithmetic operations of numbers, but she expected that Penrith guarded more than basic mathematical operations. She expected that there was a vast set of knowledge associated with numbers that she was unaware of. One of the initiates from last year told her that there was too much to remember and that her head ached all the time from trying to keep the secret meanings for each number and combinations of numbers straight.

"Henith, are you coming to supper?" her mother called.

Henith joined her mother as she walked toward the other women that were gathering. She was amazed at how different the group looked gathered here in the shadow of those huge stones. She tried to count how many women including young children there were. She wondered why she had never thought to do that before. She guessed it was not important before, but here away from the village, it seemed different. She thought she had counted about thirty-six women. She wondered if all the other villages were the same. She couldn't see well enough to count the others, plus there was too much movement to be sure you had not counted someone more than once or missed someone.

The evening meal was quiet. Henith decided to really look at the women in her village. She had taken them for granted before now. But today she needed to feel more connected to each one. Over the years she had talked with each woman here, but it wasn't until right now that she decided that she did not know them very well. Typically each woman spent much of her day in silence and alone. Of course there were gatherings and sharings and celebrations, but except for her mother, Nancillia, Carog, and most recently, Zendar, she really did not know these women at all. She found the thought somewhat disquieting. All these years living with these thirty-six women and she really did not know them. She was comfortable with most of them, although Lycin scared her some, and Carog drove her crazy. She looked from woman to woman, trying to identify something about each one, trying to determine who these women were, these priestesses of the Goddess, so close and yet so remote.

"Tonight, we have been asked," Henith pulled herself from her reverie and listened to what Lycin was saying, "to be in silence following our evening meal until tomorrow when we will meet in our sacred mystery circles. The locations are the same as in past years. We will gather together the stories that emerged from the women in our groups, identifying similarities and uniqueness. Tomorrow afternoon one woman from each group will tell the stories from her circle to all of us. We will gather in the large field north of where the northern village is camped, the one usually set aside for dancing and games. Initiates can choose to be with their present teacher or their mothers. The young children will gather together for games and storytelling with the older children in the field south of the south village encampment. We will have the moon ritual surrounding the great stone circle. This is very unusual, but we will form a circle around the outside of the stones this time and be very careful to shield it from the destructive powers that seem to be surrounding us. We will bring down a cone of power that will protect it and us in the coming times."

Henith listened to the rest of the discussion, trying to decide whether to go with her mother or Zendar.

Chapter 10

Henith opened her eyes, trying to figure out where she was. Nothing looked very familiar to her. What was she doing in a tent? Her mother was nowhere to be seen. She opened the tent flap and couldn't believe her eyes. Was she having a dream? The magnificent stones glistened in the sun. The stones were distinctly bluish in color, with flecks of pink. They were at least three times as tall as she was and about one and a half her length in width. She could see that the surfaces facing the inside of the circle were very smooth. Why would anyone want to destroy such a sight? She could see that women were already preparing for the day. She joined the others at the communal tent.

Soon she would have to decide whether to go with Zendar or Canth. Canth would go with the women who were the protectors. Canth had described this mystery to Henith some, but Henith did not know much about it. She knew that it was an ancient power that had been given to selected women. Somehow they were able to send a shield of energy around objects or people that needed protecting. Canth's powers had been over taxed in recent years trying to protect the stone circles on the mainland. Henith decided to go with Zendar. At least she knew something about the healing plants, and she might be more able to participate in the discussion. She was curious, though, about what her mother's group was doing.

She saw Zendar across the camp, preparing to go. Henith went over to her, "I've decided to go with you, Zendar, if you feel that it is all right. Where is the meeting?"

"We will meet at the camp of the east village. I'm glad you decided to come with me. I think you need to share the first vision you had when the iris roots chose you."

Henith was surprised and humbled to think that she had anything to contribute to the group.

Henith and Zendar walked around the huge stones. Women were beginning to gather in small groups around the stones.

"It is good you made the decision to come with me. Your mother will be meeting with Morgan at the center. In the discussion yesterday we forgot that you were not initiated yet. We have never had to deal with whether the uninitiated can go inside the stone circle or not. It just was never anything we had to think about before. We eventually decided to have the women all gather outside the circle for the moon ritual. It made some sense, so we avoided having to struggle with what to do with the uninitiated women. We have lived our ways for so long; sometimes we never question our rituals. Now with this new religion and way of life pushing at our boundaries, it seems as if we have to re-evaluate."

Henith listened as they walked along. There were so many questions she wanted to ask, she didn't know where to begin. It was true what Zendar was saying. Up until now Henith had never thought to question anything either. Now all she had were questions. Henith noticed that groups of women were assembling near the stones. She counted the stones, twelve, of course. Why hadn't she thought to count before, twelve mysteries, twelve stones, twelve groups of women. Somehow the order described in this discovery brought comfort to Henith. She had twelve moons of training before she would be initiated. Each of the megaliths must be a symbol for each of the mysteries. When they arrived in the eastern encampment, they went to the group gathered near one of the stones.

"Welcome, Zendar!" an old woman called and gave Zendar a hug. Henith tried to guess how old the woman was. She must be older than Zendar, and Zendar was ageless, but this woman was even more ancient, and incredibly beautiful. Henith couldn't help staring at the features on this woman's face.

More women were greeting Zendar. Henith noticed that two of the women from her own village were already there and was surprised. Henith was amazed again at how very little she really understood about what was happening in her life. Until this year of her initiation, she had been free to play and go about as she pleased. She ate with the women, listened to the storytellers, and helped with the chores, but she never questioned what this life of being a priestess of the Goddess meant.

She looked around the circle as they began to sit down. There were fourteen women all together. She noticed the two other women from her village. Zendar was the oldest and she the youngest. Across the circle she noticed a young woman about her age. Maybe she was an initiate with her teacher or mother, too. Henith caught her eye, and the young woman smiled at her. Henith noticed a feeling in her stomach that was familiar and unfamiliar. Where had she felt like that before? She tried to remember, but the memory would not come. She looked at the young woman again. She started to fidget and feel nervous. She wished the meeting would begin, so she could take her mind off the unfamiliar sensations happening in her body.

When the ancient woman began to speak, a hush fell over the group almost instantly, "We will begin with centering time. Then we will share parts of our journeys with each other. We have two young women here who have never been to one of our mystery circles before." Henith felt the blood flowing in her cheeks. She tried to smile, but was very uncomfortable. She looked for support in the eyes of the young woman across the circle who must be the other initiate. Their eyes locked for a minute, a jolt of energy surged through her body. "And we need to include them in our most unusual of circumstances. Henith and Braen welcome. Now let us settle into our centers."

Quiet continued to surround the group. Henith closed her eyes and settled into it. She tried to clear her mind of all the new experiences she was having. She found herself thinking of the young woman she had seen for only an instant across the circle and who must be Braen. Thinking of Braen definitely caused a stirring in her that was pleasant and caused a shiver to surround her body. She found quiet time difficult. At times her mind refused to settle down. She opened her eyes a crack and could see Braen, her eyes closed, the sunlight making her hair glow gold. Even though Henith had not had her moon with the mysteries of auras to learn the secrets of that particular craft, talking about auras was part of everyday conversation. The golden color of Braen's hair was highlighted by the golden aura that was surrounding Braen. Henith continued to watch the golden energy dance around the young woman and was so captured by it, she forgot that she was supposed to be centering.

"Let us begin by sharing parts of our stories so Henith and Braen will begin to know us. Then we will share any stories that anyone thinks should be brought to the whole. In sharing our dreamings and visions, it is important for us to notice any patterns that emerge," Zendar said to the women.

Henith listened to the stories as the women went around the circle. Braen was next. The sensations overcame Henith again as Braen began to tell her story. She was from the east village. This was her moon with the ancient woman who Zendar had greeted earlier, the one who seemed to be leading this group. Braen had already done her moon with the aura mysteries. No wonder her aura was so pure, Henith thought. She wondered if Braen's special mystery would be auras. She listened intently to the young woman. When the next woman spoke she found herself wondering about what her own special mystery was to be. It seemed impossible to think that she had ten more moons of learning before she would be ready to be a priestess. She hoped that nothing would prevent her initiation. The events of the past months were so unusual it was hard to predict what would happen in the next ten moons.

During the break for food, Henith went to talk with Braen. She found herself being shy and not knowing quite what to say. Henith couldn't remember ever having to talk with a woman she did not know before and was somewhat surprised by her own shyness. She had never thought of herself as shy before. This was truly a different experience. She had known all of the women in her village since she was born. Once in a while a woman from another village would come as a messenger, but she never had to start a conversation with a total stranger. She didn't know what to say. She began to feel uncomfortable again. She looked around for Zendar, but she had gone off with the ancient woman and they were deep in conversation. The others had formed groups of twos and threes. Henith would have to eat alone or risk talking to Braen.

"When you were talking your aura was intensely gold."

Braen looked at Henith and smiled, and then giggled, "Yours was violet."

Henith looked down embarrassed. No one had talked to her about her aura before, except once when she had not been feeling well, and her mother had told her that there were some cold spots in her aura. Several women had come to her house. They said they were going to heal her aura. They must have healed her because she was quite well the next day. That was years ago, she had not been ill since then.

"Can you tell me what that means? I haven't had my moon with the aura mystery yet."

Henith and Braen sat down near the large stone. Talking to a stranger was a new experience for both young women.

Henith found herself enjoying the conversation with Braen and discovered that their experiences were very similar. Life in the east village was not much different than life in the west village, except now with all the trouble in Trenig, the calm and serenity of village life had been altered somewhat.

"I even saw some men in a boat looking at our village. As far as we know they did not come ashore, but the feelings of being watched were frightening. We didn't even feel safe walking around in our own village. Many of the women stayed inside or went into the woods so as not to be seen. It felt as if these giant eyes had surrounded our village. The storytellers said that no one could ever remember anything like that happening before," Braen recalled.

"What does a man look like?" Henith was curious to confirm whether the human she had seen or thought she had seen during the three day silence was a man. She had not told anyone about that part of her vigil. She had been embarrassed because she was not sure if it were a vision or whether it was real. She also had not been sure if the person she had seen was a man.

Braen started to tell Henith what she had observed in the boat, when they noticed that the women were gathering back in the circle. "Do you think we will have a chance to talk again? I've really enjoyed being able to share with you. I've never really talked with anyone like this before. I feel like a door has been opened into a world I never knew existed." Henith interrupted.

"If we have any free time and are allowed to leave our village encampments, let's meet by the primary stone of the south village."

They took their places in the circle and the women started sharing the stories that they thought might have some bearing on the events at hand. Henith found her mind wandering. She glanced at Braen periodically. Braen appeared to be totally engrossed in the stories. Henith wanted to know more about the island. How had she been chosen to be a priestess of the Goddess? What was it like to live off the island in Trenig for example? What would it be like to talk to people who were not born on the island, who weren't born to be priestesses? What would it be like to talk to a man? A slight shudder passed through her body! She looked around the circle. Had any of them ever talked to men? She was struck again by how little she actually knew about the world around her. How little she knew about these women. She knew that they were priestesses of the Goddess and keepers of the sacred mysteries. They spent their days and lives in meditation and in developing their skill and knowledge about each mystery and about one mystery in particular. They participated in the moon rituals every time the moon was full. And once every thirteen moons when the sun rose above the eastern stone of their circle they traveled to the center of Mona for the initiation rites. All in all, Henith decided she did not know very much. She knew her mother had been to Trenig several times with Morgan, the High Priestess. She decided that she would have to ask her mother more questions.

Zendar was speaking. "I believe that Henith should tell you her first vision with the herbs. It was a very disturbing vision to me, and I believe we all need to hear it."

Henith brought herself back to the circle and told her vision. Some women shook their heads, some groaned.

After several minutes of silence, the ancient woman said, "I do not like what I am hearing. I see too many of our women leaving Mona, I see too many of our women having their bodies violated. We are not seeing a future that is as calm and undisturbed as our past. I am not sure we can protect ourselves and the sacred mysteries against this incredibly violent force that is persistently moving closer."

Zendar spoke, "I have been in constant pain with my dreamings and visions, dream after dream of destruction. I thought for a while that my dreams were about my own personal struggles, but when I heard Henith's vision, a vision from an innocent, I knew that some negative power was making itself present in our spiritual mind space. The weight of that knowledge caused me to go deep inside. Then, not many days later we were called to a three day silence, and then to this gathering. There is something going on that is far beyond my limited understanding. I try not to image the future in negative ways, but when I hear our stories, I know that Mona will never be the same again, and my heart weeps at this knowledge."

The women were silent for a long time. Each fearing that to break the silence would surely mean that the new and terrible time would begin.

Henith looked at Braen in her golden light. Even in this heaviest of times, Henith recognized a surge of joy pass through her, and she thanked the Goddess that she had been given the opportunity to meet and be with Braen even if it had only been for a short time. She knew that when they left to go back to their villages, they probably would not see each other again until their initiation and then probably only for a few moments. Henith decided that it was sad not to have more chances to visit with the women from the other villages.

The meeting ended. Everyone seemed locked in her own space. This was not the time to continue her conversation with Braen, even though she wanted to very much. The women rose and walked in meditative silence to the northern village, to the gathering of all the women. She wondered if Morgan would be there. Morgan rarely left the center of the large stones, except in those rare events lately when she had gone to Trenig. Henith was anxious to see Morgan. She couldn't help but wonder what it was like to be High Priestess of Mona and she was already anticipating the thrill of seeing all the women together. She would like to meet the other initiates, whose year of instruction was being interrupted by these unusual events.

Chapter 11

Henith looked around the large crowd of women. Again she was stunned with the sight of so many women she did not know. How had all these women lived on so small an island without her seeing them before? She found the idea astonishing. It occurred to her that she lived with thirty-six women and had taken them all for granted. The days in the life of the village were so ordinary, so calming. A secret thought crept into her mind. She detected a slight thankfulness in her for the disturbances caused by the outsiders. There was an excitement in her, too. Because of the unrest, whole new ideas and thoughts and questions had opened up for her. She never would have had this experience if it had not been for the outsiders threatening them.

She saw her mother talking to a woman near the edge of the circle that was beginning to form. The woman seemed to radiate an energy field around her that was visible even to Henith's untrained eyes. The woman was taller than her mother, with light brown hair. She was the most beautiful woman Henith had even seen. Her long flowing purple gown gave her the appearance of great importance.

Henith walked over to her mother, hoping that she could ask her some questions before the meeting began. Canth saw Henith approaching, and said to the woman next to her, "Morgan, this is my daughter Henith."

Morgan smiled at Henith. Henith's body felt a jolt of energy as Morgan reached out her hand to her. Henith was surprised by the informality of the introduction. She had thought that Morgan was unapproachable, that as High Priestess she could never be seen except during the Spring Rite and then only as the High Priestess—the personification of the Goddess, untouchable, removed, beyond. Henith stood looking into the blue eyes of this woman scarcely able to speak. The color of those eyes was the blue Henith loved in the sky on a clear fall morning.

"These are strange times, Henith, times that call for exploration of new behaviors. I can't stay hidden and beyond reach in such times as these."

Henith felt embarrassed. Of course, Morgan would sense what she was feeling and thinking.

Morgan laughed. "Henith, you were right. I have been remote. Our uninterrupted ways had gone on for hundreds of suns. There was no need for the High Priestess of Mona to do anything different than what the High Priestess had done for centuries.

"I'm afraid that the fates have something different in store for me, for us, and even for you. You must find all of this activity different and possibly even exciting. Your mother tells me that this is your initiation year and you are doing well in your studies."

Henith responded, "It does surprise me that I didn't realize how many women lived on the island. I can't believe I hadn't ever had an opportunity to meet them before now. It would seem impossible for the outsiders to penetrate the island with all this energy collected in one place."

"The problem is that we have to protect the ways of the Goddess in Trenig also. This new force is like nothing we have ever experienced before. On the one hand, some of the teachings of this new religion are similar to the teachings of the Goddess, although the words used to describe them are different. Yet at the same time, there is a kind of violence that is growing in the people. I am still amazed that after so many centuries of living the ways of peace and love this violent energy can so easily take over the hearts of the people in Trenig."

"We had better gather. The women are waiting for you, Morgan," Canth suggested, as she looked around at all the women watching them.

Canth and Henith sat near the women in their village. There were so many women here, Henith tried to find Braen on the other side of the circle. She secretly hoped that Braen was looking for her, also.

Carog caught Henith's eye and waved. Henith felt a lump in her stomach. She found herself wanting to keep Braen away from Carog. Tears came into her eyes when she thought that Carog and Braen would become friends and leave her out. She brushed the tear away and tried to focus on Morgan who had walked to the center of the circle. She moved like a breath and, as she reached the center, waves of quiet rushed over the assembled women. Morgan turned to the east. Raising her arms to the sky, she began to invoke the powers of the four directions. As she began, another woman standing on the outside of the circle began to walk slowly around the circle. Henith knew the woman was drawing a circle of power to keep the evil forces out and the Spirit of the Goddess—in her many forms—within. Henith recalled some of the feelings she had at the last moon ritual.

Henith found herself holding her breath as the circle of power fell on the women. Morgan, surrounded by an intense light of white and gold rays, shimmered in the center. The purple of her gown was almost obliterated by the light surrounding her. Henith watched, amazed. As the circle closed, the light from Morgan spread over the women. It was as if a cloud of iridescent light had descended upon the group. At that moment Henith noticed the four other priestesses, each taking a position on the cast circle, one in each direction. Morgan stood in the center. All eyes were riveted on her. Just as Henith began to wonder what was going to happen next, a feeling of calm came over her unlike anything she had ever experienced before. She felt calmer than when she was a small girl and used to nestle in her mother's arms. She felt as if she were about to lose consciousness. She couldn't keep her eyes open any longer. She was falling and couldn't stop herself, but she did not want to stop herself, and allowed herself to tumble gently into the blue light that seemed to be waiting for her. Out into the blue light she went, into a hole in the wall of the universe. She was being pulled into the blue, an intense cobalt blue, not unlike the blue of Morgan's eyes. She heard laughing and singing women's voices.

Further into the blue she went as the singing grew stronger. The words were sounds she was not familiar with, words she had never heard before. Into the blue she went and the music became deeper, the voices lower. She could not remember hearing women's voices that low before, almost like the rumbling of the waves crashing on the western shore during a storm. As she traveled further into the blue, the music became crying and weeping. Still all she could see was the blue light, pulling her through the darkness. The weeping turned to wailing and screaming. Henith tried to open her eyes to stop the screaming in her ears, but her eyes closed tighter. She tried to go back to the earlier sounds, the sounds of women singing and dancing, playing, and happy, but the screams became louder in her ears. Tears started to flow down her face. She was caught between two universes, between two times. She did not like the one of the screams, but she could not bring herself back. When she voiced the word "help" in her mind, a rush came upon her. Morgan was calling her name, and she thought she heard Braen calling her also. She began to come back. She opened her eyes. She was here with the women of her island. They were not screaming. In her mind she voiced a "thank you" to Morgan. Her mother, who was sitting next to her, reached over and touched her hand. She looked around. Where had she gone? How did Morgan hear her cry for help? More and more questions flooded her mind. It was nice to hold her mother's hand. At least her mother felt real. Henith couldn't stop the trembling in her body.

Canth whispered in her ear, "It's alright, you just have to learn how to bring yourself back." Canth smiled. Henith looked at her mother. Did everyone here hear her calling for help? She felt embarrassed.

Morgan stood and moved to the edge of the circle near Canth and Henith. "We will hear from each group in turn and then have an open discussion. We need to plan our time carefully in order to have time to prepare ourselves for our moon ritual tonight. This time is a sharing, a collecting of the stories and the events. We will not try to formulate any plans today. We are only here to gather and share information. We will all take the information and stories home and work with them until we meet again at the great Spring Rite in ten moons. At that time we will stay together until the plan for the future is determined. In three moon's time, each village is to send two women to the center for a meeting exchanging stories and ideas that have occurred in the three moons' time. It is absolutely imperative that we disrupt our way of life as little as possible. We must continue our rituals, because it is through our rituals that we maintain our strength. We must continue to learn what we can from each other, and we must maintain as much silent centering time as possible. The outsiders will surely be able to take us over if we scatter our energy, if we lose our centers. So now more than ever we have to stay disciplined." Morgan sat down next to Canth.

An old woman from the north village stood.

"Today we heard the stories from our sisters who keep the ancient wisdom of the runes. After a long meditation time, when we passed the sacred stones to each one in the circle, each holding and feeling the energy of the stones, we laid out a spread for the island. We decided to share the reading with all of you so you may meditate on the collective wisdom during the coming moons. We feel strongly that even though we are the keepers of this sacred mystery, this reading belongs to all of us and we all need to meditate on its meaning.

"This is the reading. In the position of the present, comes this rune." Henith watched as the woman showed the group the first stone that had markings that resembled an arrow pointing to the ground. Henith did not know the meaning of this rune, but she could sense that the other women were not pleased.

"What does that one mean?" Henith whispered to her mother.

"It is the sign of danger," Canth responded.

The woman speaking continued, "The rune that fell in the position of challenge is this one."

Henith couldn't quite make out the markings from where she was sitting, and started to ask her mother what it meant, when Canth whispered,

"Separation."

"The outcome rune is termination and new beginnings."

Henith saw what looked like two straight lines with a line across the top on the rune. The group was very still, it was if no one dared to breathe.

Gradually, one woman from each of the other sacred mysteries rose to share the stories from their groups.

Henith was exhausted after listening to all the stories. There was so much information, so much that she didn't understand, and the meeting was coming to an end. The sun was lowering in the sky. The women needed time to return to their encampments to prepare for the moon ritual. Henith hoped she would stay awake for it. She was so tired. Her head was swimming with ideas and questions. She felt like she knew nothing compared to these other women. She doubted if she would ever be able to master all of the knowledge that these women embraced. She was totally overwhelmed.

As the women started to leave, Morgan came to Canth and said, "I would like to see you after the ritual. Can you come to my room?"

Henith looked at her mother and was surprised that she was so familiar with Morgan.

Canth smiled at Morgan and nodded assent.

Henith and Canth walked back to their tent. Henith noticed that her path had taken her completely around the stone circle today. She was even more impressed with their grandeur, the more she was near them.

"There are so many questions I want to ask you. I'm not even sure where to begin."

"I'm sure that the day has been very confusing to you. How was your meeting with Zendar and the other healers?"

"I met another initiate, named Braen, from the east village. Her aura was spectacular," Henith smiled to herself remembering the morning. "This afternoon's meeting was very confusing to me, because there is so much I haven't learned yet. I didn't understand much of the discussion."

"This is a difficult way to be initiated into the mysteries. Tonight's ritual will be very powerful. Morgan will be calling the energy. When she does, one can almost feel the ground move. It will be much more intense and powerful than this afternoon. If you find yourself disappearing, open your eyes and ground yourself by moving. I will be next to you, and I will be there for you if you need me. I will call you back as Morgan did this afternoon, if I sense you are in trouble."

Henith nodded, wondering what kind of trouble she might encounter.

"You look tired, Henith," Canth put her arm around her daughter. "Why don't you sleep? I will call you in time for the ritual. You need to re-gather some of your strength."

To the Goddess Canth silently asked, "What kind of a life do you have in Henith's future? What are you calling her to do? What are you asking of all of us?" Canth sighed and went to find a quiet place to wait for the moon.

Chapter 12

"I'm having difficulty staying grounded, even though the ritual ended hours ago. The new initiates must have been overwhelmed by the power of that circle. I had to practically carry Henith back to our tent and put her to bed." Canth looked at Morgan silhouetted against the window. The full moon's light made her look unreal in the semi-darkness of the room.

"Ummm," Morgan looked from the southern window out over the large stones. The moon was so bright and the sky so clear that the stones cast shadows into the circle. She could see the tents of the southern village, but not many women were visible. Usually there was singing and dancing after the Spring Rite moon ritual, but tonight everyone was lost in the power of the circle.

"Morgan?" Canth looked at the High Priestess, "Morgan?"

"Oh, Canth, I'm sorry. I also seem to be floating away. I had the most eerie feeling when I called the power tonight. It was different than I've ever felt before. In some ways it was easier, possibly because we are so in tune with each other after all the discussions and sharings we've had today, but there was something working on the far reaches of my mind, like this may be one of the last times I will call the power. It may have something to do with the dream I had the other night. I saw you far away from here, in one of the villages in Trenig. There were men all around you, threatening you with swords and knives. I was outside the group hidden behind some trees. I tried calling the power to protect you. I guess it was working, because the men seemed suspended in time, but I didn't know how long I could hold it. I knew if I let go for even an instant that the energy field would drop, and they would capture you or kill you. I heard a rustle in the leaves behind me and then I screamed and woke up. I was so glad when I saw you yesterday, that you were all right, and that the wound from the last encounter with the men had healed. I kept telling myself that the dream was my inner self working through the terror of that last event. But I couldn't help wonder if it wasn't preparing me for a future event."

"There's a sadness in your voice that I've never noticed before." Morgan put her arm around her friend.

"For the very first time in my life, I understand fear. In my routinely ordered life, I bask in the love and knowledge of the Goddess. I so want to protect our simple holy life, but these disruptions are causing feelings and sensations in me, around which I have no previous memories and experiences. Violence is not a way of life we know about. We have lived for hundreds of years in peaceful joy and harmony, developing our skills and gifts, spending time in meditation and communication with the Goddess, and even on rare occasions having some special time with a friend," Morgan pulled Canth closer to her.

Canth smiled in the moonlight. She enjoyed these times when she and Morgan could be alone together, even if the events surrounding their meeting were causing unusual feelings to surface.

"What did you hear in the stories today?" Canth asked, moving to sit down.

"Too many women are having dreams and visions of violence. Even if we remake the dreaming to try to change the future, I'm not sure we can withstand the new forces that appear inevitable. I don't want to project any negative energy into the future, but I do believe that life as we know it is going to change. I keep thinking about what the new beginnings might be that came up in the runes. I want to make a special effort to keep our lives as ordered in the present as they were in the past, and at the same time I believe that we have to begin to prepare for an uncertain future. Our strength is in maintaining our rituals, in grounding ourselves in our mysteries, but we cannot be naive enough to think that this new religion is going to go away, that somehow we are going to be ignored."

Canth took Morgan by the hand.

"Come and sit by me, let us forget the future for a while. Just let us be together. I need to go back to my village in the morning."

Morgan sat down next to Canth; she closed her eyes, and let the tensions of the day flow into the ground as she allowed herself to be comforted by her friend.

Chapter 13

Several moons' lessons had passed as Henith prepared to begin aura reading. Life in her village was back to normal. There had been no more threats from the mainland. The tensions and fears of a few months ago were waning. She was progressing with her lessons. She found that even though the new mysteries she was learning were fascinating, she still was most interested in the healing mysteries with the herbs. She remembered fondly the meeting she had attended with Zendar, the one where she had met Braen. She wondered what lessons Braen would be doing this moon.

Braen had already had her moon's time with the aura mysteries; the one Henith was beginning today. By the next moon ritual Henith would be half way through her training. In six moons she would see Braen again. Maybe there would be some time to talk with her again.

"Henith." Henith turned to see Zendar waving to her and went toward where the old woman was standing.

"Within the next day or two, Oalii will be giving birth and it is important for the initiates to be present and assist me. I would like you especially to be by my side. I sense that maybe you will be a chosen healer."

Henith's eyes lighted at Zendar's compliment.

"I'd be honored, Zendar. I have only studied half of the mysteries, but so far the craft of healing is the one I am most drawn by. I start aura reading today."

"A good healer uses the skills learned in the craft of herbs and the knowledge gained from aura reading. The skills from both are vital to a healer. Learn your lessons well, Henith. Please come to see me after today's lesson, and I will share with you what is needed for the birthing."

"Thank you, Zendar."

Henith walked toward her new teacher's home thinking about the event that was to take place.

Birthing was not a frequent occurrence in her village, happening once every two or three years. Again she realized how very little she knew about the process, because she had never attended a birthing before.

She greeted her new teacher.

"Zendar told me that you are to assist in the birthing that will take place."

Henith was surprised that Dala already knew.

"Yes, she spoke to me just now. I am very honored, but I know nothing about it. I only vaguely remember the last birthing."

"Your other teachers have told me that you are a very good student of all the mysteries, but Zendar thinks you may be a chosen healer. If that is true, then learning the craft of aura reading will be very important to you. Tell me what you have already learned about this mystery and what you have seen."

Henith described her experience at the gathering a few moons ago. She described Braen's aura, and what Braen had said about hers. She told Dala that she had seen glows around women when she was younger, but didn't notice them any more unless she looked a certain way. On a rare occasion when she really concentrated she could see color, but usually only a glow. The goldness of Braen's aura was spectacular.

"Who is Braen?"

"She is an initiate from the east village."

"Oh?"

"I met her at the circle I went to with Zendar. She was there with her teacher also."

"Did anything else happen between you and Braen?"

Henith was surprised by the question.

"No, we only talked that once. I think about her some, and I look forward to seeing her again."

Dala smiled at her.

"Oh," Henith said, "there was one other thing. When we were centering during the afternoon meeting, I allowed myself to float too far away. Braen and Morgan called me back."

Dala smiled again.

Henith was starting to feel uncomfortable and gave Dala a questioning look.

"Don't worry. It is all right. I was just curious. Now we need to begin our lessons."

❧

Henith had spent most of the day in quiet meditation. This was developing into a pattern. With all of her lessons so far, each teacher had started with hours of meditation. Henith enjoyed the silence to be alone with her thoughts. At times Henith thought she spent more time meditating than in actual learning. However, Henith found that the more she spent in silence the more she learned. Somehow the knowledge came from deep within her. Each teacher acted as a guide. She surprised herself sometimes wondering how she had discerned the knowledge. She couldn't remember actually having been taught certain skills and yet there they were. Her experience meditating explained to her why the island women spent so much time in silence; they were learning more about their crafts.

"Welcome, Henith," Zendar embraced the young woman warmly. "How was your first day?"

"Fine, we mostly spent the time meditating."

"Good, then we can begin immediately. I expect the birthing will be in the morning. So I will teach you as we go."

"Zendar, do you mind if I ask you a few questions?"

"No, ask whatever you like."

"I have not actually witnessed a birthing before. Why do so few women give birth? It has been a while since the last one. How is it that there are no males born? Women in Trenig must give birth to both males and females. Are the island women different than women in the other parts of the earth?"

Zendar started laughing before she could ask any more.

"You have asked some good questions. I will do my best to answer them. One of the reasons that all the women do not give birth is because all the women do not want to. The second reason is that the total number of women has to be maintained at about one hundred and fifty women, about thirty-six in each village to study the twelve mysteries and a few from each village to serve in Trenig. When we had more women serving the Goddess as priestesses of the stones in Trenig, we had more births. It is important not to overtax the food supply of our island. When a woman passes from this life to the next, then another woman is chosen to give birth. You remember last year when Tanil passed from us to join our mothers with the Goddess, Oalii was chosen to be the next mother."

"How is it that Carog and I are almost the same age then?"

"Because two women passed within a few weeks of each other the year before you were born. That was quite unusual for our village. They had been serving in Trenig for several years and had developed a sickness. They were near death when they were brought home. It was too late for the herbs to save them."

"You said that the women are chosen from those that desire to give birth. What allows some women to give birth and not others?"

"As you know there are no men on our island, but in order for a woman to give birth it is necessary to fertilize the egg that the woman has in her body with fluid produced by men."

"I don't think I understand."

"When we need to have the fluid of a man, a priestess from the east village goes to Brithdir, the village in Trenig nearest the shore across the channel from our island, selects a man from the village that she decides would make a good donor. She holds a Purification Rite, to remove all evil intentions from him. He donates his fluid into a special pouch made of deerskin that has also been purified and blessed. In the meantime, the woman receiving the fluid goes to the east village and is prepared to receive the fluid. If the Goddess chooses to merge the fluid with the egg in the woman's body, she gives birth ten moons later. Sometimes the Goddess does not allow the fusion and nothing happens. That also is a rare event."

Henith was fascinated by what Zendar was saying, and wondered if she would ever decide to become a mother.

"But what about the birthing of male babies?"

"Once in a very great while a male child is born to an island woman. In that case, the child is taken back to Brithdir and given to the man who was the father."

"Does that mean I have a father, too?" Henith was having trouble trying to understand this new information.

"In a technical sense, yes, but the island women do not relate to fathers or brothers in the way women in Trenig do. The reason the women rarely give birth to sons is because the part of the fluid that creates male children dies in the journey from Trenig to Mona."

Henith couldn't help but be amazed by the plan the Goddess designed to provide the women of her island with women. For some reason Henith was gladdened by this thought.

"It sounds as if the women are preparing," Zendar said.

Henith looked up from her task, at the sound of the women's voices outside.

"Is it time? How does a woman know when the baby is about to be born?"

"Her body knows when the baby is ready to start living on its own, and pushes it out into the world. Let us gather our herbs and join the others."

The women were heading to the stone circle of their village. Henith could see Oalii, she and several of the other women were up ahead. Some of the women were singing. As the procession entered the stones the joyous song turned into a chant with a pulsating rhythm. A place in the center of the circle was being prepared with flowers and candles. The chanting became hypnotic. The women were swaying and chanting as if they were all part of one being. Oalii went to the place created for her. Zendar followed with Henith and Carog. Henith was annoyed to see Carog there with her. She had tried to ignore Carog for the last few months. This had been easy to do because the life of an initiate did not allow much time for anything except studying, meditation, and working on the initiation blanket. Most of her time she spent alone or with her teacher. Whenever she was feeling too smug about herself, Carog appeared and an uneasiness nibbled at her insides.

The two young initiates smiled uneasily at each other, and positioned themselves next to Zendar.

The intensity of the chanting increased. Pulsating sounds floated up to the heavens. Oalii's breathing was in tune with the chanting.

The pulsating rhythm of the sounds coming from the women was causing Henith to slip into a trance. She had to keep re-focusing in order to stay present to the events taking place. The chanting was intensifying in volume and was taking on a groaning quality. Still Oalii's breathing matched the sounds of the women. On and on the groaning continued. Throughout the night Zendar would take Henith's hands and place them on Oalii so Henith could feel the baby's movement. She could also feel Oalii's body pushing the baby out. Zendar took up the rhythm of the women, telling Oalii to push; sweat glistened on Oalli's naked body as a slight glow began to appear in the eastern sky. The women's groaning and chanting turned into a loud wail, and just as the sound of the women reached a feverish pitch, Oalii screamed and Zendar received the baby into her hands and held it up for all to see.

Pandemonium broke loose. Zendar was busy wiping the baby with special herbs. Henith helped the best she could. Carog and a few other women were massaging Oalii's stomach. Zendar placed the baby on Oalii's breast while Henith tied and cut the cord. Canth and Lycin were blessing the baby and Oalii with water, earth, fire, and air, and everyone else was singing and dancing. Zendar had been right. The baby was a girl. Prayers of thanksgiving were offered up to the Goddess.

The afterbirth was blessed and put in the earth near the center of the circle.

Oalii was laughing and crying. All the women were laughing and crying and hugging each other. Henith found herself missing out on all the gaiety that this birth had created, but she also felt privileged that she had been able to assist Zendar. The wonder of the birthing started to overwhelm Henith and tears started flowing down her cheeks. Exhaustion started to overtake her body.

Oalii was ready to go home with the baby asleep in her arms. The procession started again. The women sang very soothing songs. Almost as if everyone was trying to put everyone else to sleep. Dala came up to Henith as they approached Henith's home.

"Sleep as long as you need to. Come to me when you are well rested. I plan to sleep at least until the sun is high in the sky."

Henith could only smile her thanks. She was already asleep as she climbed into bed.

Chapter 14

Eyes wide open, the room still in darkness, Henith woke startled from a dream. Ever since she had spent her moon time learning about dreams, three months ago with Lile--the keeper of the dreaming mysteries—recurring dreams troubled Henith's sleeping.

In the dream fragments that remained in her memory, she could see Braen. Braen, with hair the color of deep autumn, was standing in a field of lavender iris that matched the gown she was wearing. This dream piece caused warm pleasant sensations in Henith. Wishing that this was the only part she remembered, she tried to hold this feeling of peace and calm as long as she could. But wishing didn't work, and gradually the other images persisted until she felt cold and frightened. Braen's auburn hair had turned to gray like a misty morning in winter, her soft smooth skin had wrinkled, and her tall straight graceful body had become smaller as she stooped over a few remaining iris in a garden gone to seed and back to the earth mother.

The tears running down Braen's face were no less real than the ones running down Henith's, while her words echoed around the room, "No, no, it is impossible, we will never see Mona again. You can't go back, ever."

And from nowhere Carog's voice sounding like a flock of seagulls fighting over some coveted sea creature, screeched at Braen, "You think you're so clever, with all your mysteries, what good are they doing now?"

The first few times that Henith had the dream she thought that she and Braen were on Mona, possibly in one of the other villages, because it wasn't her village, but lately she knew that they were somewhere in Trenig.

During the last few weeks, the dream came to her again and again. Thinking that it was a warning dream, Henith had decided never to leave Mona. But how could she prevent Braen from leaving?

Trying to forget Carog's voice screaming in her ears, she wouldn't allow herself to imagine that she might not always be on Mona, that she might not always be a priestess. She forced herself to think of the next few weeks, the last days as an initiate, finishing her protective blanket. She was dismayed that some of the dream fragments had appeared on the red circle as flames of fire, and no matter how many times she had taken out the stitches to make them less menacing, there they were.

She imagined herself in the blanket that Canth had woven for her from flax, the color of lilies of the valley, and as soft as the petals of the iris. She tried to have the butterflies, that she had designed onto the sash for her initiation gown, chase away the last remnants of her nightmare. She was proud of her own handiwork, which had gradually improved during the past year, and now her sash was alive with butterflies of every color of the rainbow. Someday, she thought, I will go back and redo the flowers of the purple circle so they will be as neatly done as the butterflies.

Henith focused her attention on the room, her room for so many years, her room for only three more weeks, after which she would leave her mother's house and live with her teacher, Zendar of the healing mysteries. The walls were changing from deep purple shadows to rose and pink, as the sun gradually warmed the earth for another day.

The stirrings of the women merged with the sounds of the birds. One more day closer to becoming a priestess. The dream slipped away as thoughts of the coming days came with the coming light. The procession. The magnificent stones at the center. Braen.

Henith slipped into a tunic and joined the women at the morning dream table. She chose again not to share her dream, instead she took some bread and some jam made from last year's raspberries and started toward her thinking rock.

She had noticed as spring began to make itself felt that the women were getting excited about the spring festival. Extra food was being prepared. Some of the women were even making new robes, or re-decorating their old ones. Henith could feel the anticipation throughout the village.

This spring festival was to be different than those of the past. In addition to the traditional initiation rite and the festivities that usually accompanied that event, the women were planning an extended time in the center of the island. Canth told Henith that Morgan wanted the women to stay together in the center for as long as it took to develop a future plan, in case there was any possibility that the men of the new religion would try to cross the channel again. There had been agreement at the last all-gathering that drowning men was not the best plan, but alternate plans that were consistent with the teachings of the Goddess needed more discussion.

Canth had been one of the women to meet with the others selected from each village and with Morgan throughout the last year. The messages from Trenig implied that the women were in no immediate danger right now. Lately, the men of the new religion had only visited the villages in western Trenig, and Rento, a priestess serving in northwestern Trenig, had sent word that during the last year most the foreigners had gone further east. She had not seen many of them for several moons. An uneasy calm had settled over the area near the village of Brithdir and the island of Mona.

The horizon was far away this morning. Henith couldn't remember a day this clear for a while, no fog mists or rains, unusual for so early in the spring. As she climbed to the top of the cliff, she gave thanks to the Goddess for this beautiful day, which would be a good day to accompany Zendar into the woods to see what the earth mother was providing for them. Zendar, whom she had become very fond of, had told Henith that if she ever were selected to serve the Goddess in Trenig that she would have to know how to find what she needed on the lands where she would be. Because of last night's dream, she secretly prayed that she wouldn't have to leave Mona.

Henith was staring out over the water for a long time, trying to remember everything she had learned yesterday when she thought she saw a stick move on the water near the western horizon. It must be a bird she thought. More sticks appeared on the horizon. Maybe as many as twenty. She squinted her eyes to see better, but they were too far away for her to determine what they were. She remembered hearing about the boat that the women in the east village used to take the women back and forth to Trenig.

Straining her eyes to count the sticks, she decided they must be boats and large boats for her to be able to see them at this distance. If that's what they were, that were moving very rapidly from west to east. Sighing with relief, she realized there weren't any coming in the direction of the island, and that they must be headed for some southern port of Trenig. Henith didn't know why that thought sent a chill down her back, because as she thought about it she realized that surely boats must come and go to Trenig all the time. She just hadn't noticed them before because she had been so intent on her studying. She continued to watch them as they appeared from nowhere and continued to sail off the edge of the earth.

PART 2:
Initiation

Chapter 1

Laughter and singing woke Henith early. Today was the day she had yearned for, the day of initiation. She thanked the Goddess that nothing had happened to interfere with this day. She had not told anyone about the boats she had seen. What would have happened if the ships had surrounded Mona and the women had been unprepared?

She had kept watching. Every free moment she had, she went to her lookout point. Her mother asked her about why she seemed so agitated and suggested she meditate more. Henith used it as an excuse to go to her rock more often in order to scan the horizon for those same sticks.

Several days had been very foggy and seeing even as far as the beach had been difficult. How very easy it would have been for those boats to get close to Mona without detection. Every day Henith put a protecting wall around Mona, she knew she was expending her energy and should have asked for help, especially from her mother, but the Goddess had been good and no more sticks appeared.

The women were singing, and today they would escort her to the center. Some of the women had already gone ahead to prepare the encampment, while the rest along with the teachers and the mothers joined the initiates in the procession. The rite itself took several days beginning today with the procession and presentation. Henith's mother had told her that on the second night at the moon ritual each new priestess would be given the symbols of her ministry, and the third day was spent in celebration, games, story telling, singing, dancing, and feasting.

Canth came into her room as Henith was dressing, and looked at her daughter.

"I have given you your earthly birth," Canth said, "but today you truly begin your life. Being a priestess of the Goddess is a sacred calling. You were born to this role. I will always be your earthly mother, but the Goddess is truly your mother. After today you will no longer live in my house. I will miss you, but I know that you are walking your own path." Tears were running down Canth's cheeks as she continued, trying to keep her voice steady. "This is a joyous day even if it is the beginning of an uncertain future. I do not know what the Goddess has in store for you or for me or for any of us." Canth held Henith in her arms, her tears shining like crystals in Henith's hair.

She hugged her mother and didn't want to let go. For the first time she really saw Canth, not just as her mother, but also as a priestess of the Goddess. Only yesterday she thought she was totally prepared for her initiation, but now, clinging to Canth, she felt inadequate. The future loomed like an incredible dark shadow into which she would have to walk. Where would she find the strength for the task set before her?

She remembered her lessons, the time she had spent with each teacher, the skills she had mastered. She wondered if all initiates felt this way, totally humbled by the sacredness of the events in her life, or was the foreboding due to the outlying fear that the peace of the last few centuries was about to change and that Henith as well as the others would not be able to live their lives as women in the past had—as priestess on this beautiful island, practicing and studying their crafts, worshipping the Goddess in her many forms, living a routinely calm and peaceful life.

"Are you ready?" Canth held Henith at arm's length and looked at her gently. She pulled her daughter to her again and kissed her.

"We must prepare for the procession. Do you have your initiation blanket? You will need it tonight for your sleep. I have the robe you will wear tomorrow and Zendar has everything else. May the Goddess's love be made manifest in you. Let us go."

Carog was already waiting with the rest. Henith hadn't noticed before but Carog had grown taller, and was now taller than most of the women in the group. She had her hair entwined with flowers, and she had a serene calm about her. *Maybe I've been misjudging her. After all she also is about to be initiated into the ways of the Goddess.* She wondered if she also appeared as calm and serene to Carog. Feelings of jealousy poked at her. Henith dismissed them as best she could, deeming them unworthy feelings for a priestess to have and joined the women who were now assembled waiting to begin the procession.

Another first was happening at this Spring Festival. All the young girls were also coming because no one knew how long the meeting following the rite was going to be. Next year's initiates would tend the younger children during the sacred rites as they had during the last all-gathering.

The procession would take most of the day, arriving at the east village encampment by midafternoon. Henith felt happier than the last time she went down this path, women singing and talking to each other, the younger women running ahead, spreading flower petals in the path.

Carog and her mother were up ahead in the procession. Wishing she were with own mother, Henith searched for Canth and saw her further back in the procession laughing with Zendar and Lycin.

Her moon with Lycin had been the most difficult. She did not like mind reading and mind-speaking because she did not want to know what others were thinking, and she didn't want others to know what she was thinking. During the month with Lycin, she had learned how to block others from reading her mind and how to focus her thoughts to one specific person, but Lycin's power was so intense that Henith always had difficulty holding her thoughts from her. By the end of the lessons, Henith had been able to sustain a block for several minutes, but it was exhausting work.

The women were beginning to sing a lively song, and Henith found herself skipping down the trail with the others, becoming engrossed in the activities of the procession. Up ahead some of the women were putting a flower crown on Carog, and, as the group came towards her to place a crown on her head, she couldn't identify all of the feelings that were overflowing her; she was ecstatically happy and yet sad at the same time. She found herself both proud to be in this procession and

91

humbled by the awesome responsibility she was about to assume; she wanted to leap for joy and sing and dance, and she wanted to quiet and center herself.

The procession flowed as the women gathered by a spring up ahead. Zendar dipped a chalice into the spring and held it high in her hands, addressing Carog and Henith, she said,

"This spring is the half-way point on your journey from our village to the center. Drinking from this spring is the turning in your life. From this point on, we will progress in silent meditation, preparing ourselves for the presentation. Let us all drink from this precious gift of the Mother, reminding ourselves that what is past is past, and we open ourselves once again to that which is to begin. The seasons remind us that our lives are a continual process of dying to the old and being born to the new."

The cup of water slowly passed around the circle. Everyone sipped form the cup except Henith and Carog.

"Henith and Carog, you are to stay here for a while in silence looking back down the path from which we have just come. We will go ahead. When you are ready, turn around, take some water and start toward your new life. We will wait for you at the entrance to the east village." The women became silent. Even the children, sensing the mood, became quiet, and the procession of women left Henith and Carog alone.

Henith went to the path to look back sensing Carog behind her also looking back. The last fourteen years of her life streamed passed her consciousness. She stood looking back for a long time. When she turned, Carog was not there. She dipped water from the spring, took a deep refreshing drink, and began to walk down the path set before her.

Chapter 2

The sight of the magnificent stones defiantly holding up the late afternoon sun was even grander than she remembered. Reaching out to her as a mother, they took her breath away again, as they had late last spring. Approaching the women with her feet barely touching the ground, she quickly searched the group for Braen, noticing Canth and Zendar standing near one of the tall stones. Two other young women, wearing flower crowns and carrying protecting blankets were standing beside Carog as Henith continued her search for Braen. As Henith joined her mother and Zendar, the women from the east village were forming a semi-circle facing the stones. The young women, their mothers, and their teachers formed the other half of the circle facing these women. Except for Canth and Zander, the other women that had been part of Henith's procession had joined the women from their village who had arrived earlier to set up camp. With a look of relief, Henith noticed that all the young women were not present yet, counting twelve presenters, six mothers, six teachers and only four initiates. Fearing she had been the last to arrive, Henith approached her place between Canth and Zendar as a young woman entered the circle from the south and went to stand between two of the older women.

Henith began to be anxious. Where was Braen? Henith looked around the circle. No one else seemed worried except her. One of the two older women left must be Braen's mother and the other her teacher. One was the ancient woman that had been Braen's teacher when she and Henith had first met. Henith wondered what mystery had chosen Braen; she had secretly hoped that it had been the mysteries of the healing plants, so that at least once a year they would be able to see each other during future spring celebrations.

From where she was standing she could see down the path that led to the east village, and hoped Braen hadn't changed her mind about becoming a priestess. What a ridiculous thought, she scolded herself. Where do those ugly thoughts come from? Thoughts like that were losses of her power. She closed her eyes, calling on the Goddess for peace and serenity because she wanted to be in a state of perfect harmony when she was presented to the women who were the guardians of the east. Henith sensed a shuffling next to her, and opening her eyes she saw Braen coming slowly into the circle. Again Henith was struck by the intense glow of her aura that was dazzling in the late afternoon light. Managing a slight smile when she was able to breathe again, Henith found herself sending messages to Braen who didn't appear to see her. She was walking as if in a trance. Henith had imagined this meeting with Braen for months, their eyes would meet, they would smile, they would nod, they would mind speak, but Braen had not even looked for her. She didn't even know Henith was there. Henith was sad and then embarrassed knowing that she had let her thoughts stray to Braen instead of focusing on thoughts of the Goddess. She was glad Lycin wasn't here because she would have known exactly what Henith was thinking. Center yourself, center yourself, center yourself, she keep repeating to herself as a tear escaped. Hoping no one would notice, she tried to flick it away with her hand.

The ancient woman from the east village stepped into the center of the circle and faced east. Lifting her arms to the heavens, she intoned, "Hail to thee, O Great Goddess of the east and of the sky. Goddess of all beginnings! Come and be present at our rite as we perform according to your sacred ways. Send your Holy wind to purify these women that they may walk forever in perfect love and perfect trust."

The ancient woman returned to her place in the circle.

The woman next to Braen spoke as Braen moved forward slowly to the center of the circle.

"Great Goddess of the sky, I present to you Braen, who has chosen to follow your ways of love and whom you have chosen to be a guardian of the power drawing mysteries."

Braen remained in the center as another young woman walked forward.

"Great Goddess of the sky, I present to you, Jana, who has chosen to follow your ways of love and whom you have chosen to be a guardian of the dreaming mysteries."

Carog's mother spoke as Carog slowly walked to the center of the circle to join Braen and Jana.

"Great Goddess of the sky, I present to you Carog, who has chosen to follow your ways of love, and whom you have chosen to be a guardian of the sacred runes."

Henith moved to the center with the others who were forming a small circle within the larger one and stood facing Braen whose eyes were closed.

"Great Goddess of the sky, I present to you Henith, who has chosen to follow your ways of love and whom you have chosen to be the guardian of the healing mysteries."

Henith choked back the tears as she heard her mother's voice raised to the Goddess. The last two initiates from the north village were presented. The six young women in a small inner circle were surrounded by the older women in the outer circle who were now chanting and moving in a circle around them. The ancient woman of the east village was holding a small earth colored jar containing burning sage, a scent very familiar to Henith's trained nose. The holder of the sacred sage started to spiral inward, until all the women were in a tight spiral surrounding the inner circle, their bodies flowing with the chanting. The women, holding hands, began to unravel the spiral. As the last woman in the spiral took hold of Braen's hand, the six initiates were unraveled into the larger circle.

After the circle dance had lasted for some time, the presenters and the initiates left the east village for the south village encampment where the women had already formed a semicircle facing the stones and the arriving women took their places completing the circle facing south.

The Goddess of the powers of the south, fire and passion were invoked, and each of the young women was presented to the Goddess of the south and the women of the south village. The chanting and spiral dance began again with a candle being carried into the inner circle as a blessing from the fire.

In the west village, Lycin invoked the Goddess of the powers of the west and of the waters of the sea. During the spiral dance, the initiates were sprinkled with water from the jar that Lycin carried.

In the last village, the Goddess of the powers of the north and the earth were asked to be present. Several hours had elapsed since Braen's presentation in the east village, and the sun was beginning to set as the last spiral dance was beginning, but something different was happening here. Henith noticed that Morgan was standing just inside the stone circle, and now it was time for her to enter the great stones, a moment she had dreamed about since the all-gathering. A shiver fluttered over her body. "Please let me be worthy of this great honor," she whispered to the Goddess.

The women had formed an archway leading to the place where Morgan was standing, the women in two facing lines, each pair holding flowering branches. Morgan was at the end of the tunnel in a white robe, tied with a turquoise sash. Attached at her shoulders rested a cape— deep purple on the outside, and cobalt blue on the inside, reminding Henith of a waterfall. Henith thought that surely if the Goddess were personified on earth, she was present right now in Morgan. Henith smiled to herself, when she remembered that the Goddess was also present in Braen, and Jana, and even Carog. That must mean that the Goddess was also present in her; her knees weakened at the thought.

Braen was preparing to enter the flower tunnel created by the north village women. Deese greeted Braen at the opening of the tunnel.

"What is your desire?"

"My only desire is to serve the Goddess in perfect love and trust."

Braen slowly walked through the channel of women into the sacred circle of stones. Jana was next, followed by Carog.

Deese then addressed Henith, "What is your desire?"

"My only desire is to serve the Goddess in perfect love and trust," Henith responded, entering the canal.

When she reached Morgan, Morgan held her and said, "Welcome, Henith, chosen healer." A surge of power engulfed Henith from Morgan's touch. The energy field within the circle of stones almost knocked Henith over and she struggled to maintain her balance. Henith felt as if she were walking through an invisible wall; she could feel it, but she couldn't see it. Henith was escorted to the stone at the eastern point of the circle where she and Braen had first met. She noticed that each of the others had been escorted to sit by a certain stone. Braen was at the western stone, Jana was at the stone to the west of the southern stone and Carog was near the stone to the east of the southern stone. The other two women were at stones flanking the northern stone.

As Morgan walked to the center of the circle, the women from the villages filled in the spaces between the stones. The initiates were completely surrounded by a circle of women and stones. Henith removed her protecting blanket from her shoulder and placed it on the ground in front of the stone and sat down upon it. Just being able to sit now was such a relief; she hadn't realized how tired she felt from all the walking and dancing until this moment.

The women in the circle began a chant that flowed in waves around the circle, causing Henith to feel as if she were leaving her body, as if she were spirit flying. So easily without thought or intent, she floated above her blanket and around the circle. She found herself visiting each stone, lingering with some, looking into the eyes of each woman, floating around the circle many times, sometimes quickly, sometimes slowly. With each pass, she noticed something she hadn't seen before. When she passed the western stone, she saw Braen asleep on her blanket. Even in her sleep, Braen was golden. Henith let the love she felt for Braen flow forth, she couldn't have held it back if she had tried. As she floated around the circle, Henith sent a wave of love to Canth and to Zendar, and the chanting continued to ebb and flow, rise and fall.

Henith felt herself being drawn into the center of the circle where she met the essence of Braen and of Morgan, who was taking them into the center of the earth, into the very womb of the Mother. Then they flew with Morgan into the blue of the heaven, deeper and farther they went. As the chanting continued, the sounds pulsating stronger and stronger, Henith felt totally safe flying into the center of the universe with Morgan and Braen, who had taken her by the hand, and was sending a surge of love into Henith's body. Henith was reaching ecstasy, pure unmarred joy, being one with Morgan, Braen, and the universe. They were out in the stars, and yet Henith could see the stones far below, could see her body lying on its blanket, could see Braen and the others on theirs. She could see Morgan standing in the very center of the circle with her arms held high and her robes flowing around her. And she floated on and on into the blue.

Chapter 3

The new initiates stayed within the protection of the stone circle, meditating and sleeping, while the older priestesses had gone back to their tents for their own dreaming and meditation. Feeling lightheaded, because she had not had anything to eat since yesterday noon, Henith wished that this part of the purification process would soon end, and that she could have a piece of bread or at least some water. The sun was half way between noon and sunset, and she had been sitting here since last night, but soon she knew she would be called into Morgan's rooms to talk with her about her last year. Her turn would be next; Carog had gone in not too long ago. She was frustrated that she couldn't see Braen from where she was seated by the eastern stone, because the Temple of the Sky, where Morgan and the other four priestesses lived, blocked her view.

As Deese came toward her, she stood smoothing her gown with her hands, her legs weak from sitting for such a long time. Following Deese into the lower level of the Temple of the Sky, trying to calm herself, she had a strange sensation that she wasn't entirely sure where her own body was. Calm yourself, she repeated over and over. Surely Morgan would be able to detect any type of anxiety. Morgan was looking directly into Henith's eyes. Henith tried to look away, but couldn't release herself from Morgan. Morgan greeted her.

"Welcome again, Henith."

"Thank you," Henith murmured, trying to maintain her balance in the presence of this powerful woman.

"Your teacher has already prepared you for tonight's ritual, what you will do, where you will stand, all the details, so I won't go into that with you now." Morgan moved closer to Henith.

Henith nodded, not wanting to move, fearing her legs would not support her.

"Some of your teachers have told me that you have learned your lessons well. I am pleased. As you may have observed at the all-gathering, I am very fond of your mother. You have been especially blessed. I understand that the Goddess has been working through you in your dreams and visions as She has with the other women. I would like you to tell me about your last year. What were your special learnings? Where do you still feel inadequate? What unusual dreams and visions have you had?"

Henith was worried that she wouldn't be able to tell Morgan everything in the time left. Henith stood near the entrance of the room, a room lit by so many candles, that the room itself glowed.

"Come Henith, sit here with me. You needn't fear this interview. I just like to know each woman personally. And during these times it is important for me to hear all of the visions and dreamings of the women, in case I am called upon again to make decisions that may affect the future of Mona and the ways of our beloved Goddess." Morgan held Henith's hand as she led Henith to the cushions near the center of the room.

"It is hard to know where to begin, so much has happened. I have learned more than I thought possible and now I realize I have only mastered a very small amount of what is possible to learn. I marvel at how much Zendar knows. I have had many seeings about a land far from here that is not Mona. I assumed it to be Trenig. I have also seen many women who have been wounded and hurt, like my mother was." Henith watched the High Priestess close her eyes as if trying to shut out some pain that would not go away. The smile on Morgan's lips disappeared as Henith caught a fleeting glimpse of the woman, Morgan.

"As a result of these visions, I have specialized in the healing mysteries, especially the herbal medicines. Zendar suggested that possibly I was being called to be a healer." Henith tried not to think about the implications of this calling. She was not happy thinking about having to travel to Trenig. She wanted to remain on Mona and learn as much as she could from Zendar.

"Tell me about you and Carog and Braen," Morgan demanded abruptly.

Stunned by Morgan's statement, the words choked in Henith's throat. Henith sat staring at Morgan, wondering how she knew about Carog and Braen.

"It's all right, Henith, don't be so frightened. All our feelings for one another are real. We just have to understand them so that they do not take us over inappropriately. We should not hide our feelings from ourselves. I listen to all the stories. Your mother has told me about some of your feelings about Carog. Dala mentioned your experience at the all-gathering with Braen. I also know that at the all-gathering, Braen responded to your call for help almost as quickly as I did. And last night, you and Braen and I were obviously spirit flying together."

"I'm just startled that feelings I try to keep buried you already know so much about. Somehow I experienced Braen and I being with you last night, but I didn't realize you also would experience it in a similar way."

Morgan laughed. "That is one of the difficult aspects of being the High Priestess. I want you to know that I have had last night's experience seven times plus the time of my own initiation, but last night was different. The intensity of it cannot be matched in my experience. Usually, there is some spiritual bonding, but nothing that comes close to the depth of last night. On occasion one or two new priestesses connect with me or with each other for a moment or two, but usually these encounters are very brief and of no lasting significance. I have heard Braen's story about last night and now I want to hear yours."

"I'm embarrassed about my feelings for Carog." Henith thought that between the two, it was easier to share her feelings for Carog than for Braen. "Ever since we were little, I have disliked her. I know we are called to love all of the Goddess's creation, but Carog unsettles me. I just can't find it in my heart to trust her." Henith looked down wondering whether to continue, knowing that what she was thinking could be turned back on her. Morgan waited. Finally Henith continued. "I don't think she is serious enough to be a priestess. I have tried to avoid her this past year because I didn't want to be distracted from my studies." Hearing her words in the air, Henith began to feel uncomfortable again. Her feelings seemed so small and petty.

Henith could feel Morgan looking deep into her soul. Being with Morgan was even more intense than being with Lycin.

"And Braen?" Morgan continued probing.

"I don't know what to tell you about Braen. I've talked to her only once in my life. I'm not sure if she even remembers me. I was surprised last night when we were spirit flying that she reached for my hand. I have thought about her many times since the all-gathering, and she does appear in one terrifying dream that I have. I haven't known what to do with the feelings I have for her, so mostly I try to ignore them."

Morgan's eyebrows rose, and then her face became blank. After several minutes she said,

"Thank you for sharing with me. In a few minutes the others will gather with Deese in preparation for tonight's ceremony. The moon Goddess is about to shine on us in her fullness. Go now and during the next days, let us talk again."

Henith left Morgan with an unsettled feeling. There was no resolution. She had wanted more from Morgan. Henith felt naked and vulnerable. Henith had told Morgan feelings she had never voiced before and Morgan had just listened, except for raising an eyebrow when she had told the High Priestess about Braen. Henith wondered if she had said too much, but then really what did it matter, Morgan probably already knew anyway.

By the time Henith reached the room designated by Deese, the others were already there preparing for the next part of the ritual. Feeling shy because of the conversation about Braen made her feel shy with the others, and she remained silent as she began to change her clothes. She noticed that Braen was already robed, her gown flowing about her gently from her shoulders, with a cape of soft white linen lined with gold into which intricate patterns had been woven with golden thread. The golden strands in her auburn hair which was loose and falling on her cape matched the golden threads. Instead of a sash she wore a woven braid of golden rope around her waist. Henith found herself staring at the intense beauty reflected in Braen's face and had to force herself to look away. She was faint from her fast and wished she could sit down, but there were no chairs in the small room or any other furniture to hold onto. The room was intensely quiet, the awe of the up-coming ceremony outweighing any excitement that the young women might be feeling. Henith changed into her new white gown that her mother had woven for her, and was thankful for the softness of the cloth that was now caressing her skin. She cinched her waist with the sash of butterflies, fearing that they were too playful for such an occasion as this, especially compared to the dignity of Braen's golden rope. Henith's cape was made of soft white wool with a blue lining very similar to the color of Braen's eyes.

Henith felt as if the butterflies on her sash had escaped and were flying around in her stomach. She closed her eyes to calm herself, as parts of her conversation with Morgan kept coming into her mind. As the young women prepared to leave the room, Deese paired them, the two novices from the north village followed by Carog and Jana, and then Braen and Henith. The warmth from Braen's body flowed into Henith, and, to Henith's surprise, was very calming. Henith smiled a thank you to Braen, who smiled back, a gentle calming smile.

The young women were unprepared for the sight that greeted them as they emerged from the underground rooms of the Temple of the Sky. All the women of the island were present inside the stone circle, dressed in white gowns, but each with a cloak of a different color. Henith felt like she had been dropped into a flowing rainbow.

The six young priestesses were followed into the center of the circle by the four priestesses of the temple and then by Morgan, who was dressed in a silver gown, made from a material that Henith had never seen before. The shimmering cloth picked up rays of light and reflected them in a myriad of directions, and it was as if Morgan and light were one.

The procession around the circle began in the east. As the procession continued, the mothers and teachers of the novices joined in between the young women and the four priestesses of the temple. After the women from the north joined in the procession, they turned to the center, climbing the small set of stairs that led to the flat roof of the house in which Morgan lived. The elevation was high enough to see practically the whole island. For the first time Henith saw the dark outline of Trenig far to the east, and in the other directions the darkness of the sea. Henith noticed that as they were climbing to the top of the temple roof, the four priestesses had dispersed to the four directions.

As the priestess who had been chosen to cast the circle walked around the circle of stones, the women joined hands, and then when she had finished, she joined the circle. As the circle closed, Henith felt a surge of energy course through her body. Morgan raised her arms, facing east just as the brilliant white moon, highlighted in orange gold, appeared to rise out of Trenig. Another surge of energy cascaded through Henith's body. Henith had never felt anything like it before, not even at the all-gathering where she had nearly collapsed from the intensity of the power. The invoking of the four directions commenced. As the powers of the east were being addressed by Morgan, the priestess of the east carried purifying incense around the circle. Braen's mother purified those on the platform. Next, the purification with the fire, then water, which Zendar did, and then the earth. When all had been cleansed and purified, the final act of initiation began.

Morgan said, "Creator of the Universe, Your daughters have come once again, to pay homage to Your Way, and to present to You our sisters, whom You have called and blessed, and who have chosen to answer your calling. I am honored to give back to You, Mother of the Earth, Jana." As her name was called, Jana knelt down at Morgan's feet with her forehead touching the ground. Morgan turned slowly and called each by name, until all were kneeling in a circle surrounding Morgan as one by one each young woman was presented to the Goddess.

After the presentation, and while the young women were kneeling, the mothers and teachers left the roof of the Temple and joined the women in the outer circle. When Henith stood, she could no longer see her mother or Zander. She realized that she was no longer a novice,

104

an initiate; she was a priestess like all the other women here. She could feel a smile growing inside of her. Looking around at her sisters, who were also glowing, Henith thanked the Goddess for this moment and for her life, and asked for guidance in the days and months and years ahead.

Morgan continued to stand in the center with the young women in a small circle around her and a sound started, a deep, low, barely audible hum that surrounded the center. Ever so slowly Morgan and the six lifted their arms to the moon while the hum became a sound increasing in pitch and intensity, becoming multiple tones, groans from the depths of the women's souls echoed from the stones. Soon the stones themselves joined in the chorus, vibrating their own sounds. Henith could feel her body dissolving into her pure spirit self, totally alive in the vibration, totally in tune with Mother Earth, pulsing to the rhythm of the stars. Thoughts ceased as she became red light like the fire, she was on fire, she was fire. The flames of her burned without burning. She roared in the raging flames and danced in the flickering embers. She was yellow light, light as the wind. She was the wind. Howling wind and gentle breeze. She was green light, the green of Mother Earth. She was the earth, the tall trees, the tiny blades of green grass. She was herbs and plants that had been her teachers, she was the teacher. She was blue light, the blue of the water, the crashing waves, the ocean depths, the bubbling brook, the small still pond. She was sound and she was light. She was part of a beautiful golden ribbon of love that flowed forever in the universe. With every breath the golden love surged through her body. She became the gold light and was sustained by it.

The vibrations were slowing; the sounds of the women became a low earthy hum, and Henith's body began to re-assemble. Slowly and gently she lowered her spirit self into her body self. The sound became a whisper, just audible above the sounds of the rustle in the trees.

Henith knew that she had been gone a long time because the moon was almost at its zenith. Morgan was holding a chalice high and pouring new spring wine into it. She filled six other chalices, holding each to the moon, and then poured some wine into the earth for the

Goddess. The new priestesses drank from the first chalice, and then Henith and the others each took one of the other chalices to the circle of women below, while the priestesses of the four directions brought baskets of bread and fruit. When all had been fed and nourished, Morgan raised her arms to the moon, now directly above the southern stone, and thanked the Goddess for being present. The priestess who had cast the circle earlier walked around the circle in the other direction. When the circle had been opened the priestesses of the four directions followed Morgan into the rooms below the ground. As the last priestess disappeared, Henith and the others were surrounded and overwhelmed with hugs and kisses.

The mood and intensity of the circle spontaneously turned into gaiety and more food appeared. Some women had flutes and stringed instruments. Music erupted again, and small groups of women began to dance, while others talked and ate. Henith laughed at the change of mood. It was as if all the intensity of the last several hours burst forth in one explosion of joy.

In spite of all the excitement surrounding her, Henith discovered that she was very hungry. She gradually pulled herself away from the women from her village who were surrounding her with embraces and went to the baskets of food. Several others had already gathered there.

"Henith." She turned to see Braen approaching the food baskets.

"Hello, Braen, are you as hungry as I am? I can't remember when I ate last, and the wine has made me very giddy."

Henith looked at Braen, tall, majestic, ethereal. Giddy would not have been a word Henith would have chosen to describe Braen.

"Would you like to sit down and rest before we join in the dancing?"

Henith and Braen selected apples and oat cakes from the baskets of food, and walked to sit near the eastern stone, as if they had been friends their whole lives.

"It has been a long time since we had lunch on the other side of this stone. I have learned so much since then. I was truly saddened that we were unable to talk again after the last time," Henith said shyly.

"I thought about you often during the last months. Did Morgan ask you about me? I was stunned and somewhat embarrassed that she asked me about you. It is shocking to realize the powers that she has. She mustn't read everyone's minds all the time or she'd go crazy." Henith was surprised by Braen's casual confession.

"She asked me about you also, Braen. There must be secrets about being High Priestess that we haven't learned yet."

Braen laughed, "There must be, but there were times this past year when I thought I couldn't possibly learn any more. Have you had enough to eat? The dancing is beginning. Do you like to dance? I love to. Come on; let's join that circle over there."

Braen pulled Henith to her feet. Henith had rather enjoyed the quiet rest. She was amazed that Braen still had so much energy left.

Morgan had also joined the circle. She had changed into a white gown like the rest of the women. Canth and several others she recognized were also there. Once Henith started to dance, she was able to float in the spirit of the music. At times she danced with Canth, and with Morgan and a few others, but she found herself always coming back to Braen.

As the moon began to set in the west, the dancers faded also. Some women went to their tents; some were asleep near the stones.

"Would you like to come to my tent? I'd like to talk to you about the last few months. I'd like to hear your journey, too."

Braen and Henith walked to the eastern village encampment. The camp was very quiet as many of the women were already asleep. Soft voices could be heard coming from a few tents.

"Come," Braen said, holding the tent flap open for Henith to enter.

PART 3:
The Journey

Chapter 1

The morning was half gone when Lycin entered Zendar's cottage where Henith had been sorting through some freshly picked plants, tying them in small bouquets, hanging them to dry. Henith looked up, surprised to see the older woman, who did not make a frequent habit of visiting.

"Lycin, are you feeling well?" Henith asked somewhat alarmed.

"Yes, Henith. Morgan asked me to send you to her."

An astonished look came over Henith.

"I don't know what she wants," Lycin replied in answer to Henith's unspoken question.

After the days of discussion following the spring festival many moons ago, the women returned to their villages, their mysteries, and their rituals. Henith had moved into Zendar's house, where Henith would spend at least another year, learning from Zendar, and continuing her studies with the plants. During the spring festival celebration discussions, the decision to continue life as usual had been agreed upon, because the immediate threat to Mona had lessened, and it was now almost two years since the time of the campfire scare in Brithdir.

The fears that had gripped the island and Henith during her initiation year seemed far away, as far away as Trenig seemed from the plants Henith was holding in her hands. She had given up all thoughts of ever traveling to Trenig, but in spite of her disinterest at the possibility, a slight thrill entered Henith's mind thinking that Morgan was calling her. She hadn't seen Morgan since her initiation, and couldn't imagine why the High Priestess would send for her unless she were being sent to Trenig to minister at one of the circles there. But that was impossible, because she was far too young for such an honor, and she had to continue studying with Zendar before she would be asked to leave Mona.

"When am I to go?"

"You are to leave after the moon ritual in two days' time."

"So soon, I will barely have time to finish preparing all these plants." Henith looked at the work that still remained, at least a week's worth of sorting and tying replacing the already dried herbs. They would require at least three more weeks to grind and prepare for use. "Thank you, Lycin. I will be ready to leave at that time," Henith said reluctantly, knowing that one did not refuse the High Priestess's summons. "Has anyone else been called?"

"No, you are the only one she asked for. Last night during evening renewal, when I was mind-speaking with Deese, she said that Morgan wanted to communicate with me this morning at sunrise. I was surprised myself, Henith. Usually my only contact is with Deese at evening renewal, but this morning Morgan specifically sent for you."

A chill, as if a cold breeze had swept through Zendar's cottage, passed over Henith.

"Has there been any more trouble in Trenig?" she asked, closing her eyes as if not wanting to see the answer. She had been unaware of any new happenings in Trenig lately, and she did not want any interference in her life, which was as calm and regular as it had ever been.

Lycin didn't answer the question. Either she knew and wasn't going to tell Henith, or she didn't know. Henith watched as Lycin and Zendar went out into the yard. She couldn't hear the conversation, and was soon busy with her own thoughts and work.

Three days later, early in the morning following the moon ritual, Henith rolled her protecting blanket, filling it with several herbs, and prepared herself for the journey to the center of Mona. There had been no more messages from Morgan for her, and curiosity about the High Priestess' request caused her to almost run. She had to keep telling herself to slow down, but she found herself walking quickly, sometimes breaking into a slow run. As she approached the temple, she could feel her anxiety as well as her curiosity mounting.

The sun, causing sweat to glisten on Henith's skin, was nearly overhead when the gigantic megaliths appeared before her. Pausing to catch her breath and to absorb the beauty and power of these standing stones, memories of her initiation flooded her mind and body. Scanning her memory for the few times that she and Morgan had talked did not suggest anything that helped her predict this upcoming meeting. She remembered with fondness the precious times she had had with Braen, the warmth from inside her body, now competing with the warmth of the sun causing her cheeks to glow red like the poppy petals she had packed in her blanket. She allowed herself to remember her initiation. Even though many moons had passed since then, the images were still vivid in her mind. I wonder what Braen is doing, she thought, wishing to see her again but knowing that would not occur until the next initiation celebration. For several weeks after last year's celebration, Henith had found it difficult to focus on her studies. Memories of the ritual, of spirit flying so easily with Morgan, and talking for hours with Braen had filled her mind, but gradually as the days became weeks, she became absorbed in her studies, and in her desire to become as skilled a healer as Zendar was.

Henith slowed her walk as she entered the stone circle, and as she was approaching the center, Deese appeared as if she had just materialized out of the ground.

"Welcome, Henith. Morgan is waiting for you in the temple room. We saw you coming. Have you eaten?" Deese guided Henith through a corridor to a spiral staircase that led to Morgan's room. "Follow me up here."

Following Deese up the spiral stairs, she emerged into a round room, flooded with golden light, the windows opened to all the directions. Henith caught her breath taking in the view from here that was almost as breathtaking as from the temple of the sky on the roof of this room.

Morgan, in a gown the color of blue hickory flowers, her long chestnut colored hair hanging loose down her back, said, "Come, Henith, sit here while we wait." The High Priestess pointed to one of the cushions near the eastern windows where she was standing. "You must have run the whole way, to arrive so early. I wasn't expecting you for some time yet."

Henith wanted to ask, "Wait for what?" but decided that would be inappropriate. The High Priestess would tell Henith what she needed to know when she was ready.

Henith sat near Morgan and welcomed the rest, not realizing until now how anxious she had been to get here. Deese offered her some barley cakes and some new Spring wine. The warmth of the liquid caused the earlier glow to reappear in her cheeks. Savoring the cakes, she remembered that she had not stopped along the way, and hadn't eaten anything since early this morning.

The room was very still and calming. Deese had left the room after serving Henith, and none of the others were there except Morgan. The wine on her empty stomach and her fatigued body were pulling Henith into sleep, and she was working with some difficulty trying to keep her eyes from closing.

"Why don't you sleep while we wait?"

Henith smiled, remembering Morgan's skill at mind reading.

"Thank you." The permission to sleep was a gift from the Goddess. Henith realized that if someone had asked her to move right now she would have been unable to do so, her body as heavy as one of the standing stones. Soon she was in a deep total sleep.

When she opened her eyes again, the room now in dark purple light didn't look familiar. Slowly, as her eyes adjusted to the light, she could see Morgan across the room talking to someone Henith couldn't see.

"Henith, good, you are awake, just in time to join us for evening renewal. Braen will join Fratez in the east and you may join Deese in the west. After the ritual, we will have supper and I will explain to you why I have called you both here."

Henith was standing, looking at Braen, trying to listen to Morgan's voice, but caught in the beauty of the woman who was looking directly into her eyes. Unable to speak, Henith obediently followed Deese to the western windows, nodding a greeting to Braen who was changing places with her as she moved to the eastern window. Never having anticipated the possibility of seeing Braen before next spring festival, she was unprepared for the feelings that were flooding her now. She wondered why the possibility of seeing Braen here today had never crossed her mind. Henith managed a smile, as feelings tumbled about inside her that she had not anticipated, and tried to center herself for evening renewal.

"We are thankful and honored that our sisters are joining us tonight. Braen and Henith, you may lead us in the invoking prayers." Henith watched Braen turn to face the east, and in a clear voice that danced like music through the room and to heaven, Braen invoked the powers of the east. Henith could feel the energy flow into her as Braen raised her arms to the Goddess, her golden aura brightening the semi-darkness.

The ritual continued as it had every sunset for centuries.

⇛⇚

"It occurred to me a few weeks ago that we do not have a very clear idea about what is happening in Trenig in terms of the foreign invaders. We only hear stories when one of our women returns from there. For a few years prior to this last one, we had sent a few women to certain villages that needed assistance. Your mother was one, remember Henith? During the past year, we have heard very little from Trenig. We do not know if the men of this new religion have given up or are just moving more slowly. We have heard some stories from the Brithdir, but I don't know whether to rejoice at the calm or not. I'm still very uneasy when I think of Mona's future and our lives. I've asked you both here to discuss a plan I have. It is a very unusual request. After hearing the plan you may choose not to do it. That is your right. You are free to make your own decision. You each have to follow your own inner voice and what you think the Goddess wants you to do."

Henith watched Morgan as she talked, wondering what this plan could be.

"You are both highly skilled priestesses in your own craft and in all the crafts. The experience we had together at your initiation was unique and powerful, which is why I believe that more is being asked of both of you."

Henith lowered her eyes, humbled by the compliment.

"I would like the two of you to go to Trenig, to travel extensively throughout that country. I want you to visit as many villages as possible. I want you to learn about this new religion, and to talk to the people of this new religion to find out what they are really like, what they believe, how they feel about the Goddess. I want you to visit all of the priestesses that we still have in Trenig. I'm embarrassed to say that I do not even know where they all are. Each woman serving in Trenig serves for seven years. When she returns she explains to the woman taking her place the location of the stone circle that she was protecting. This has been happening for centuries. I doubt if any woman on Mona knows for sure, where all the sacred stones are. We have some ancient drawings that may be of some help to you in locating all the stones, even the ones that have been abandoned. I'd like to know, especially where the stone circles that have been abandoned were, how the Trenig people live, and whether they still follow the ways of the Goddess.

"This journey will take many years. There is some part of me that does not want to send the two of you so far away for so long, because the women of Mona need to share in your strength, skill and youth, but I find it very difficult trying to make decisions with so little information.

"If you decide to do this task that I ask of you, it is important that you continue to practice our craft. You may have to practice in secret, because you may find yourselves surrounded by people who have chosen different ways and different gods, and may not be friendly and accepting of you. Your strength comes from the Goddess. You will be safe if you continue to remember that. When you return, we will listen to your stories and be able to understand more clearly what is happening in the world outside our world. It will be important for your stories to be added to the tales of our island, so that future generations of priestesses will understand more clearly than we do.

"I have one other request. I suggest that you do not talk to each other until I have met with each of you tomorrow morning. I realize that you have much to share with each other, but I want each of you to listen to your own inner selves. I want each of you to struggle with your own anxieties and fears alone, in the darkness of the night.

"Esli and Deese will take you to your rooms. Pay special attention to your dreams tonight, as they will guide you in your decisions."

Without speaking, as they had been requested, Henith and Braen followed the priestesses to their rooms.

"Why is it we always have silence when I have so many unanswered questions?" Henith thought to herself as she prepared to sit in the darkness before actually going to sleep. She knew that when the candles were extinguished she would be in a darkness she had never known before, because these rooms were totally underground. After Deese left her, she sat in the candlelight, slowly lowering herself into the calmness of herself. Slowly she moved to extinguish the four candles, guardians of the four directions. She returned to the center candle. When she was ready to enter the darkness at the center of the earth, she extinguished the last candle.

Chapter 2

Rain had been pouring steadily for hours. Braen's hair lay in strings on her cloak.

"Maybe we should find a place to get out of this weather," Braen's voice hinted at frustration.

Henith regarded her friend, smiling at the remembrance of their initiation, now three years ago, and how much had happened since then. That day, with Morgan in the Temple of the Sky, Braen had shone in pure golden light. Now, soaked through, she looked like one of the too many beggars they had seen in village after village this past year.

"Are you sure we are on the right road? In the last town I thought they said that the circle was only a few hours walk. It must be past noon," Braen wiped the water from her face.

"Maybe the man was mistaken. Maybe he intentionally misled us. I find it difficult to understand what happens to some people when we tell them that we want to find a stone circle. I can't believe that it was less than one hundred years ago when all these people were followers of the Goddess, and now they are afraid to be associated at all with the stones. Maybe we should try to get shelter at that house across the field," Henith pointed to a small cottage down a dirt road to the west, surrounded by carefully maintained fields of barley.

"I think we should at least try it. I'm not sure how much more walking in the rain I can endure today. Maybe if we are close to the stones, the person there will know about them, although, after the last experience, I almost hesitate to bring them up in conversation again. The fear that has been generated about them is difficult to understand."

Standing at the intersection where the road to the house turned off, Henith said with encouragement, "There is smoke coming from the chimney. At least we might be able to dry off, and it would feel good to rest and warm up."

Henith followed Braen as she knocked on the door. Braen turned to smile at Henith, "What story shall we tell this time?"

Before Henith could answer, the door opened slightly, and the warmth of the building and the smell of fresh bread floated out into the rain and surrounded the two women. Trying to reclaim her composure, Braen said to the woman standing in the opening, half hidden by the door, "We have been traveling all day. I fear we may be on the wrong road, and we were wondering if we could warm ourselves in your home."

The door opened more, and the woman motioned for them to come in. Henith noticed immediately the great variety of herbs that were drying around the room. The woman, whose green eyes held caution, watched as Henith surveyed the room.

"I'm Henith and this is Braen."

"I'm Megen. Take your capes off and hang them over there by the fire, and I'll fix you something warm to drink. Sit there by the table."

Henith noticed some of the rarer herbs that Zendar had told her about and was intrigued to find out how this woman had gathered so many. Her supply wasn't as extensive as Zendar's, but it was impressive. She had not seen a display like this since she left Mona.

"You must like plants and herbs." Henith smiled at the woman, pointing to some of the plants hanging near the fireplace, trying to initiate conversation.

"Yes," the woman replied, reluctant to say more.

"Henith and I have been traveling throughout Trenig, learning about the people who live here and have lived here for centuries."

Megen raised her eyebrows at Henith, as if not believing what Braen was saying.

"We spent the last moon in the village north of here. We were told that there was an abandoned stone circle near here, and we were trying to find it when we got lost."

A frightened look came into the woman's eyes.

"Did I say something wrong? You look frightened."

"No one has mentioned the stones since I was a young girl. We have been told that evil spirits live there."

"What kind of evil spirits?" Braen tried to ask in a gentle tone, wanting more information and not wanting to frighten the woman into not saying anything. In the last several moons, Braen had noticed that, as they traveled south in Trenig, more and more people were reluctant to talk about the stones. In the last village no one would talk about them at all.

When they had first entered the village, the people had been friendly, offering the women lodging and meals, and were more than happy to talk about their lives. As it became known that Braen and Henith were interested in the stones, the villagers' reception cooled. By the end of their stay, it had been increasingly difficult to find someone to take them in for the night.

"I'm not sure. I've never been to the stones. My father told me to stay away from them before he died," she turned so that Henith could not see her face, although her voice had a slight quiver.

"We've seen many stones and many circles and none of them had evil spirits," Henith said.

Watching the woman flinch, Henith wished she hadn't been so bold, but she was frustrated that this woman was so fearful. Henith wished that Megen could experience the joy and love that being a priestess of the Goddess brought to her.

"Aren't you afraid you will die if they catch you near the stones?"

"Who will catch us, the evil spirits?"

"No, the authorities."

"What authorities?" Braen was confused.

"The authorities that live in the city to the south and east of here."

The two priestesses had heard about this city before and were traveling in that direction, but it always seemed to be further south and further east from where they were.

"How many days travel is the city from here?"

"About twenty days, I've heard. I've never been there. Once in a while some men come through on their way back and forth to the sea. Sometimes hundreds at a time. They are the ones that tell us not to go to the stones. They say something dreadful will happen to us if we do. We never know when they are coming, so it is easier just to stay away from the stones."

"How far is it to the coast from here?"

"It is less than a morning's walk west and less than a day's walk south."

The two priestesses were surprised that they were so close to the coast. Braen and Henith had been trying to make a map of Trenig and match it to the ancient drawing Morgan had given them. They had discovered that Trenig was much larger than they first imagined. At first they thought that they would visit all the stone sites identified on the old drawing, as well as all the present stone circles, while at the same time traveling along the coast in order to determine the size and shape of Trenig. At their present rate of journey, they would be away from Mona for many more years, which didn't appeal to Henith at all. While this past year of travel had been exciting, and she had learned more than she ever expected to learn, she longed for home and the serenity of Mona.

Trenig was more expansive than anyone had ever implied, especially compared to Mona, and they had been told that there were even more countries to the east. Henith and Braen found this information difficult to comprehend even though they had been traveling for more than a year, and they still hadn't reached the southern coast of Trenig.

"Can you tell us something about the land around here, about the towns and villages?"

Megen looked at the two women, thinking it strange that they be traveling around Trenig alone.

"The coast turns east, south of here. There is a large port on the western coast not far from here, Boscawen. Many travelers from the land across the sea have been coming here in recent years, mostly men. If you had traveled further down this road, you would have come to a major road leading east to west. Several years ago the road you were on was a major road to the north. For some reason, the men decided to go east instead. Lintern is east on that road. Many people were happy when the men came, even though their beliefs had to change. You see, the men were in need of supplies and other necessities, and many of the merchants in town became very prosperous. Our simple ways have changed considerably since these people have come to Trenig. Towns have grown, our way of life changed."

"What kind of changes?"

"My grandmother told me stories before she died. She said that before the men from the foreign lands came, the people lived in peace with each other. Now there is much fighting and violence. Before, women were treated with respect and honored, now they act like slaves. Some of the men have no respect at all for women." A sadness came into Megen's eyes.

"Tell us about your grandmother. Is she the one who taught you about the herbs?"

Megen looked up in surprise. "Yes, how did you know?" Then she fell silent.

After several minutes, Henith asked the question again only very gently, "Tell us about your grandmother."

Megen looked from one woman to the other, trying to decide whether to tell her story or not, whether she could trust these strangers.

"I promised my grandmother I would never tell her story. I don't know you or what you are doing here, but I knew when I saw you coming down the road in the rain that I would have to let you in and that something important was happening. Then when you asked about the stones, I became frightened. It is difficult to trust anyone any more. Not many people come here. They mostly leave me alone. I think most people are afraid to be associated with me. A few women come for herbs once in a while, but mostly I'm alone. I have one friend, but she lives in Boscawen on the coast. She trades my herbs for me and visits once in a while. She's the only one who has been inside my home for years except you two. Usually I meet the others out by the fence. They don't want to come in."

"Tell us about your grandmother," Henith tried again.

Megen was quiet again.

"Have you been traveling in the north?"

Braen and Henith nodded.

"Then you must have heard about Mona."

Henith said, "Yes, we know of Mona."

"Then you may also know that for centuries before this last one, priestesses were sent from Mona to live in the villages near the stone circles."

The two priestesses nodded again.

"My grandmother was the priestess guarding the circle that you are looking for."

In surprise, Henith asked, "Oh, I thought all the priestesses returned to Mona after their service here?"

"They usually did, but my grandmother couldn't."

There was a long silence. Henith and Braen waited patiently for Megen to continue the story. Megen looked away from the women to the window. "It looks like it is clearing. The sky is brighter in the west."

Henith asked, "Are you afraid to tell us the story? We know much about the priestesses of Mona." She was tempted to tell Megen who they were. When they first started their travels a year ago in the north, they were proud to tell the people who they were, but as they wandered further from Mona, they were met with more and more hostility. They had revised their story many times, seeking a reasonable tale to explain the reason why two women were traveling alone together. Until the last few months, as they ventured further south, that had not been a problem, but it was becoming clearer that some of the people in the south, especially the women, thought that they were in danger traveling unprotected by a man. Henith shivered at the thought. It was so unusual for the island priestesses to think this way that Braen and Henith still chose not to heed this advice.

"We would really like to hear your grandmother's story. Since we started our journey, we have become fascinated with these stories. We have become so intrigued with the stone circles that we thought it would be a challenge to see how many we could find and the stories that went with them."

Megen began again.

"My grandmother was a priestess from Mona. While she was here she fell in love with my grandfather. She told me that the priestesses of the Goddess were forbidden to marry and that after they had spent their time in Trenig they would return to Mona and live the rest of their lives in peace and harmony. But my grandmother's love for my grandfather was too strong to ignore. He was a handsome young man from the village down the road. They spent much time together, and I guess she was lonely. I know that I am lonely here at times. The young men from the village now are not the way my grandmother describes them; they are all caught up in the ways of the men from across the sea. I doubt if I'll ever marry. I'm nearly forty now, almost too late for children. I regret not being able to share what my grandmother taught me about the herbs with my daughter or granddaughter. The men are afraid of me, I think, but I'm not sure why.

"My grandmother had a difficult time trying to decide whether to go back to Mona or stay here with my grandfather. Then they had a son, my father, and she knew she could never return, because she could never leave her son behind, and male children weren't allowed on the island. I can't imagine an island with only women, although there are days when I'd like to experience it."

Henith repressed a smile, remembering having exactly the opposite thought, that she couldn't imagine a country with men, but that she'd like to experience it, having no idea at the time that her experience was to last several years. She missed the routine, the study, the meditation, and especially the moon rituals. For the last three moons, she and Braen had not been able to find a stone circle at the time of the full moon, and so they found a field and had performed the sacred rite, but it was different, lacking the power the women created within the holy place of a stone circle. Henith was hoping that they would find the old stones of this village before too long, knowing that even if it were only she and Braen, it would make a difference in how she felt; at least the power of the stones themselves would be present.

"Tell us more about your grandmother."

"When she knew she could never return to Mona, she sent a message to the island that she had died and that the circle had been destroyed by the foreigners. She and my grandfather and their son lived in this house. It was hers when she was a priestess. She continued to celebrate the moon rituals, but gradually over the years the people turned away from her. I don't know if it was because she was living with my grandfather or if it was because the people moving into the area brought their own religion. Some of these people said that she was an instrument of the devil and of evil and that they alone had the one true religion. Eventually she gave up, even though she continued to grow herbs. Some people still came to her for healing and for help with birthings. The men tried to discourage the women from coming to her, blaming her for strange things that happened in town, but the women came anyway. She was well known for her healing skills.

"When I was still very small, my grandmother taught me about the herbs, how to grow them, which ones were used for different ailments. I've tried to keep her plants as she had them. Some I've forgotten about because I haven't had a use for them in years. It is sad that I've forgotten so much, and I have no one to share this knowledge with."

"Did she tell you anything else besides the use of herbs?"

"I have some of her things, but I don't know much about them. She gave me her special blanket. It is covered with pictures I don't understand. She also taught me some of the moon ritual. Once in a while I go to the stones and do the ritual. I feel awkward, though, standing there alone in the rubble of the circle. Many of the stones have been pushed over. Only a few are left standing, and I'm not sure I have it all correct, the ritual I mean. I only dimly remember watching my grandmother, and wish now that I had been more attentive. But, what difference does it make? I have no one to pass on the information to." A deep sadness sounded in her voice as she finished her story.

The three women sat in silence for a long time. Finally Braen said, "I'd like to see the stones. Would you feel comfortable showing them to us?"

Megen replied, "I suppose it would be safe enough. Most of the older people have forgotten about them, and the new people don't know much about them except for a few stories of evil spirits. Since my grandmother died about twenty years ago, the stones have been pretty much ignored, except for when I go there occasionally. Let us wait for the rain to stop, and then you will not have to get all wet again."

⌀⌀⌀

"They are down this road and in the field to the right," Megen said leading the others out into the yard.

The three women fastened their cloaks as the setting sun was breaking through the remaining clouds, creating streams of golden light that danced to the earth. Together they walked quietly down the path Megen indicated. The smell of the moist earth arose as the freshly washed plants greeted them.

"Some of the stones have fallen over or have been pushed over, and some have even been broken," Megen reported with grief as she turned into a field of barley with no apparent marker. They went through the barley for at least five minutes until they came to a clearing.

"I planted the barley to shield the stones from the road. Unless you know where they are, it is difficult to find them. I know it may seem silly, but it was all I could think of doing to protect them from any more destruction." Megen managed a faint smile.

Braen and Henith stood looking at the circle of toppled stones. They were small by comparison to the ones on Mona, but in their own way they commanded awe. Here, hidden in the middle of a field of barley, protected by this lone woman, not even an initiated priestess, they remained. Looking at the stones, remembering Mona and the power of the circles there, remembering how long ago it seemed since they were with a group of women safe within the cast circle, safe from destruction and violence, Henith felt tears streaming down her face. She could feel the warmth of Braen standing beside her and the soft gentle hand that was searching for hers.

Megen was walking closer to the western stone that was still upright and appeared to have been undisturbed for years. She leaned against the stone and waited for the others who were different from the other

126

women she knew. She didn't know what it was, though, and she was taking a risk showing them the stones, but she almost couldn't help herself. It was good to share these secrets with someone after all these years. She had not told anyone what her grandmother had taught her except for her friend, Tana, who wanted to know about the herbs and their healing properties, but was more timid when it came to hearing about the stones. Megen remembered the night years ago when she had brought Tana here, hoping that they could do the old rituals together, but Tana had been too uncomfortable and Megen never suggested it again. Megen didn't know whether she should ask these strangers if they would like to join her. They had not said much about themselves as she related her stories. She may have said too much, but they were so interested in what she had to tell them. Living alone for so many years, she had forgotten how good it felt to talk to other women. She longed for her grandmother.

She watched the two women looking at the stones. Were they afraid to come closer? They were just standing there, staring. She waited, leaning against the stone, allowing the strength of the rock to seep into her body.

Braen gently squeezed Henith's hand. "Should we tell Megen who we are and invite her to join us in the moon ritual even though she is not initiated? She obviously is one of us, struggling here alone practicing and protecting the mysteries as best as she can. Her dedication to the Goddess is apparent, in spite of the lack of support from her friends and neighbors."

"We could stay here a while, if she will have us, and teach her some more of the mysteries. I don't think we will be violating any of our sacred vows by sharing some of the craft with her. She already knows much about the herbs from her grandmother," Henith responded as they started to walk slowly toward Megen, still caught in the power of these stones and the tenacity of them, and this lone woman to survive such abuse.

"I would like to do a ritual now, maybe our evening renewal rite, the sun is setting. We could at least invoke the powers to protect these stones and this woman," Henith continued.

"That's a good idea." Reaching Megen, Braen said, "We are moved by the power of this circle that still remains. Your grandmother protected them well. Would you like to join us for the evening renewal rite?"

Megen looked startled. "What? Who are you?" She was obviously disturbed.

Henith reached for her hands, "We are priestesses from Mona." Megen went limp with the news. "We have been sent to learn as much as we can about the stone circles left in Trenig and about the people who are still faithful to the Goddess."

Megen looked at the ground, feeling very humbled in the presence of two priestesses from Mona. Even though her grandmother had also been a priestess, Megen could only see her as her grandmother, a very wise old woman. The stories her grandmother had told her about the women on Mona had filled her with awe and longing. Never did she imagine that she would meet one face to face and now here were two in her house, her garden, her circle.

"We're sorry we didn't tell you who we were earlier, but we also have learned to be cautious. The further south we go, the more difficult it is to trust people with our true identities. We have found, however, that there are one or two women in each village that are trying to keep the ways of the Goddess."

"I thought I was the only one."

"I am so glad that we found you and that you brought us here."

"Do you know any of the evening renewal ritual?"

"No, I only remember parts of the moon ritual."

"I will cast the circle, and Braen will draw down the power. Did your grandmother teach you about drawing the power?"

"No, but she used to tell me stories about when the High Priestess drew down the power. She said that it was an experience that she missed more than anything else when she chose to stay here with my grandfather. She regretted being unable to go back to her island and be part of the rituals. She truly missed that aspect of her life. I always felt sad when she told me about them. There was always such longing in her voice."

"Well, then, Henith and I will guide tonight, and tomorrow night you can join us." They each recognized that there would be a tomorrow night and wondered how many tomorrow nights there would be.

Henith picked up some dirt she had loosened with her hand.

"I will walk on the outside of the stones tonight to bring them into the protection of the circle." Henith walked to a fallen stone that had marked the east. She ran her hand over it as she passed it, and a deep sadness in her made itself known. She was sad for Megen's grandmother, who was torn between loves, love of a man and love of the Goddess. She was sad for these beautiful sacred stones lying in disarray in a forgotten field. She was sad that she had been away from Mona so long. She missed the holiness of her home.

When Henith was in place, Braen raised her arms toward the sky, the clouds still scattered in the western sky were taking on a deep rose purple hue as the sun was lowering. Henith caught her breath watching the beauty of Braen, her long hair streaming over her cape, her face already transcended to the mystical, silhouetted against the sunset in an obscure field of Trenig. Tears poured from her eyes as she stood transfixed. Willing herself to move, slowly her feet carried her around the circle of stones. As she walked she trickled the dirt she had picked up earlier through her fingers, encircling the stones, Megen, and Braen in the safety and love of the Goddess.

When the circle had been cast, Henith joined the others near the center where she could feel the stones vibrating as if awakening from a long sleep. The three women sat in the center of their world, trancing from the beauty and power and music coming from the stones, the earth, the fields, and the sky.

It was very late when they finally found their way back to Megen's home, each lost in the joy of the last hours. After kissing each other, and without any more words between them, they fell into deep and restful sleep.

Chapter 3

"I wished we could have stayed longer." Henith adjusted her cloak, which was beginning to show signs of wear, as the sun began to warm the earth, and the early morning mist rose from the trees.

Braen, carrying some of the herbs Megen had given to Henith, responded, "It's been over three moons since we arrived at Megen's. At this rate we'll never return to Mona."

"It was such a relief to find a circle so we could practice our rituals. I'm glad that we were able to teach Megen some of the craft," said Henith, taking one last look back. Megen's house was no longer visible.

"I thought her grandmother's blanket was especially beautiful. Did you notice how brilliant the colors were, even after all these years, I hope the protection of the blanket will also protect Megen." Braen pulled the hood of her cloak from her head, allowing the rays of the sun to bring back the golden highlights.

"Maybe we should have stayed to make doubly sure she was pregnant." Henith was concerned that they hadn't stayed long enough. "I don't want her to lose the baby, and I'm not sure we did the ritual correctly." Henith had followed the instructions that she remembered learning from Zendar, but that was some time ago, and the circumstances were very different.

"Maybe we should have stayed for another moon. Then, if Megen had her monthly bleeding, we could have tried again, although I'm not sure Tana would like to get the fluid for us again." Smiling, Braen looked at Henith, remembering the look on Tana's face the day that Henith explained exactly what was needed. But, in spite of her initial reaction of thinking that the request was impossible, she had acquired the fluid. "I keep thinking about Tana trying to find a man that would donate his fluid without telling anyone. I'm not sure I would have been able to do that part." Henith listened to Braen who so rarely showed any insecurity.

"But the priestess in Brithdir does it regularly; maybe one gets accustomed to asking. I wish one of us had been able to do the purification rite for him. We took an enormous risk, an impure male donor that we don't even know, selected by a woman who is not a priestess." Henith recalled the morning when Tana had arrived very early, before the sun rose, carrying the sheepskin bag next to her skin to keep it warm. The hollow reed for insertion had been prepared and blessed. Megen was ready. Henith quickly did the purification rite for Megen and a belated rite for the man's fluid. With Braen's help she had filled the reed with fluid from the sheepskin bag, inserted it into Megen and gently blew the fluid into her.

"But she wanted a child to have someone to share the craft with," Braen barely whispered, also recalling the evening with reverence.

"What if it's a boy?"

"Megen's grandmother had a boy and was still able to share some of the mysteries with her granddaughter," Braen answered reassuringly.

"Do you think it is wise for the secrets of the Goddess to be passed along to the uninitiated?" Henith asked, part of her wanting to honor her sacred vows, to keep the mysteries safe, but feeling that sharing with Megen was also right. Megen had already learned much from her grandmother, especially about the mysteries of the healing herbs. Megen wasn't violating the ways of the Goddess, but was part of their protection, even if she hadn't been initiated at Mona.

"We didn't share all of our knowledge, and besides I'm beginning to think that if more women in Trenig knew about the mysteries, both the women and the mysteries would be safer."

"You're right," Henith agreed thinking about how the priestesses of Mona would respond to this suggestion.

The two women fell silent as they neared the seacoast town of Boscawen, watching the number of travelers increase as they turned onto a major road. Groups of people passed, mostly men on horses, and people traveling in horse drawn wagons.

Braen pushed Henith out of the way as a cart filled with barrels came quickly around a curve in the road. "We must be nearing the town. The air smells different. Look at all the travelers on this road."

Henith readjusted her protection blanket which she had tied across her shoulders. "I hope it was a good idea to come here!" she said, resisting the temptation to turn around and go back to Megen's even though she was tired from the morning's journey and wished she could sit down and have some tea.

"Henith, this place is calling us. There is something we need to learn here."

"I know, but it feels like it is going to be difficult, if not painful."

The excitement Braen was feeling was in opposition to Henith's reluctance.

Braen tried to encourage Henith, "At least we will know one friendly person. Tana will take care of us."

When Tana had learned that Henith and Braen were planning to continue their travel in southern Trenig she offered them her hospitality. She had explained that, since the foreigners had arrived many generations ago, life had changed drastically. She had said that Boscawen once was a quiet village and now it was a bustling town with many people and much activity.

She also told them that Boscawen was important to the foreigners because there were very few places along this coast of Trenig that could accommodate their large ships. Consequently, the town had become their port of entry. The harbor was protected from storms and the waters were deep enough to accommodate their heavily laden ships. Megen said that the comings and goings of these foreigners added a certain excitement to the lives of the villagers. She said that her grandmother had told her stories about what it was like when her grandmother was a child. Tana admitted that she liked the busyness, all the comings and goings, meeting the new people that were constantly passing through. It had been this way ever since she could remember, and she personally liked it the way it was. She now ran the inn that her father had started, a place where the strangers could stay when they needed food and lodging. When her parents died, she continued what they had started. It was hard work, but she enjoyed it.

"She is full of life. Nothing seems to bother her. Even though she was reluctant to join us in the moon rituals, I think she is a fine person. She just doesn't care one way or the other about the ways of the Goddess. She admits that the presence of the foreigners has added a sense of violence and unrest, but she also says that it has been good for her town's prosperity. I wonder how one can measure prosperity when it is at the cost of peace and love." Henith, her eyes watching the ground lest she trip and fall in the ruts left in the road by the carts and wagons, tried to imagine living one's life in all this confusion and noise.

"This town is larger than any we have seen so far, Tana wasn't lying. And to think that the one east of here is even greater than this one!" Braen said, raising her skirt to keep it out of the excrement that the animals had left in the road, wishing she could have dressed in the more comfortable trousers like the men were wearing. But she remembered the severe warning she and Henith had received from the priestess in Brithdir that caused them to leave those clothes behind and dress only in long skirts as the women in Trenig did. More and more people crowded the road. The young women, used to walking silent paths from village to village, found travel difficult having to watch the road for ruts, and to get out of the way of wagons and to keep their boots clear of the slippery leavings of the animals.

By comparison the people in northern Trenig did not travel much, going only as far as the next village or occasionally to the local festival. They were usually content to live where they were.

"Look at all the horses and the way the men are dressed with those strange markings sewn into their shirts. I wish we had our leggings that we left behind in Brithdir." Henith, unsettled by so much motion around her, was picking her way across a deep rut. "Have you ever seen so many people and such confusion?"

"I hope we find Tana's place soon. I think she said it was an inn near where the ships were docked."

The women walked through the bustle of the seaport town asking for directions as they went.

"I'm not sure I'm going to like it here. Where are we going to do our rituals?" Henith looked around in dismay at the buildings crowded next to each other with almost no grass or trees or flowers.

"I think this is not going to be a place where we can be honest about who we are," Braen resolved. "I hope Tana's suggestion about introducing us as friends of her cousin's from northern Trenig, will be good enough. I don't sense that this is a place where priestesses of the Goddess will be welcome."

"Braen, I can't shake the feeling that keeps overcoming me. It sends shivers over my body. My feet want to turn around and go the other way."

"Henith. I think it's because there are so many people here. You're just not used to large crowds." Braen tried to comfort Henith, dismissing her own anxiety about this town.

"Don't you feel it though? I think it's more than lots of people. There's an energy here that I don't like."

"I do feel uncomfortable, but I thought it was my own nervousness at feeling so out of place here. When I get in crowds like this, I wish I were on Mona where it is safe and quiet," Braen admitted.

"That must be Tana's place. Look at all the men going in and out. Do you suppose one of them is the father of the child Megen is carrying?"

Braen looked at Henith in surprise, "Oh, Henith, I hope not. They look so rough, and most of them look like they are not native to Trenig." An awful thought went through Braen's mind. Henith picked it up, and they looked at each other. Why had it not occurred to them before? Could Tana have gotten the fluid from one of the foreigners? "Don't say it out loud," Braen warned, "Maybe it will be best if we don't know."

Henith nodded. The fear she had been trying to dismiss all morning pulled tighter in her stomach.

"Are we going to go in there with all those men? I would be more comfortable staying on the edge of town."

"Come on, Henith, we'll be all right." Braen led the way to the inn.

Henith watched reluctantly as her friend opened the door and went in. She followed slowly, viewing her surroundings with dread.

"Greetings," a voice boomed over the heads of the people seated at tables around the room. Tana's face was flushed, her apron dirty, and her hair looked as if she had been in a wind for hours. Her hearty smile welcomed the travelers as Henith looked around a room filled with people talking and laughing. Their arrival caused some near the door to stare. They must have seemed a strange pair to be arriving at this inn. Tana made her way through the tables, "Come in, come in, don't just stand there."

Henith and Braen slowly moved into the room, Henith using all her will power not to turn around and walk straight back to Mona. She could hear Braen whispering, "Keep breathing, keep breathing."

"I'll show you to your room. A ship arrived today and I did all I could do to hold the space for you," Tana joked good-naturedly.

"Oh, maybe we could find someplace else to stay. We don't want to inconvenience you," Henith replied, half hoping to escape from this alien environment.

"Don't be silly! I told Megen I'd look out for you and that I will. And besides it's probably not safe for you two to be alone without some protection anyway."

Henith bristled. She had all the protection she needed—herself, the Goddess, and Braen.

"Here is your room, overlooking the harbor. It has the nicest view." Walking to the window, Tana pointed to the scene below. Henith followed. Looking out the window, Henith caught her breath, something jammed into the back of her head like a wall, taking her breath away and making her knees weaken, a wave of foreboding washing over her. She reached for the sill to hold herself from falling. Braen noticing the change of color in Henith's face came to her offering her arm for support.

"Henith, whatever is it? You look pale."

"I don't know," lying, so as not to have to say anything in Tana's presence, "maybe I'm just tired from today's journey." Henith left the window, still visibly shaken, and sat down on the edge of the bed. "Maybe a rest would help."

"That's a good idea. I hope you can rest with all this noise, but you'll have to get used to it. Being this close to the docks, people never really settle down, not even in the middle of the night. I don't even notice it anymore myself. Why don't you rest and come down later?" Tana, playing with the edge of her apron, was anxious to return to the many customers that waited in the room below. "I won't be able to show you the town right now, but I'll get my oldest to take you around later, after you've had a rest and have a chance to settle in."

The room was empty when she left. Tana, a large woman full of energy, seemed to occupy all the space she was in, and her absence was noticeable.

"Tell me what you saw." Braen looked out the window toward the ships.

"I can't bring it all back, but when I looked out of the window, a terror ripped through my body, like nothing I have ever experienced before. Something about seeing all those ships, a warning, maybe. We have to be very careful here." Her body shaking, she barely whispered, "This is not a safe place for priestesses of the Goddess."

Sitting beside Henith and taking her hand, Braen said after several minutes when Henith's body had returned to a calmer place, "Did you notice how it felt when we passed through that room with so many men? I can't remember seeing so many in one place before. It feels so different than being with a group of women."

"I don't think it is safe for two women to be alone here either."

"But we are not alone, we are with each other." Braen put her arm around her friend.

Leaning into the warmth of Braen, Henith spoke, a longing in her voice that came more often in the last months, "Sometimes I wish we were still on Mona, practicing our craft, living our lives calmly and peacefully. But then I realize that if we were still there, I'd be living in the west village and you would be in the east village, and we'd only see each other during the great Spring Rite once a year. In spite of all my longings to return home, I am happy that Morgan gave us the gift of being together."

Braen's arm tightened slightly on Henith's shoulder. The two women were quiet in their memories of the last year.

"It has been so long since we left Mona, I wonder how many more years we should travel before we return. I doubt if we will be able to accomplish our task in one lifetime. We haven't located half of the circles on our ancient drawing, and Trenig is far greater than we imagined. We haven't even reached the southern shore yet. The women on Mona will be surprised to hear that Trenig is a gigantic island and that there are more lands to the east and south. How little we know about our Mother earth."

"Ummm." Henith's eyes were heavy with sleep.

"Come lie down and rest. I will wake you when it is time to go with Tana's son."

❧

"Braen! Braen!" Screaming, Henith opened her eyes, looking around a room she didn't recognize. A small room with one window. The window. She remembered. Beyond the window were the ships. Ships full of men. Men who acted so differently than all of the women Henith had known. They were louder, maybe because their voices were lower in pitch. Henith could hear rumbling voices echoing up from the room below. And they were bigger, or at least appeared bigger maybe because of the way they moved through space. And they jostled each other, poking and slapping.

The door opened.

"Oh, Braen, I had a very disturbing dream and when I woke up you weren't here. The Goddess is trying to tell me something."

"Do you want to talk about your dream? Here I brought some tea."

"Thank you. I will share my dream with you later, but I understand why I had the reaction I did when I saw the ships. Several years ago I was sitting on my favorite thinking rock, and I saw hundreds of masts sailing by on the horizon. At that time I had no idea how big a ship was and I couldn't imagine what they were. I never realized that so many men could fit on one ship, and I saw many. The thought of so many strangers coming to Trenig frightens me. No wonder Megen said so much has changed since her grandmother's time here. Their ways and values are so different from ours. If many more come, we will surely be outnumbered, especially in this part of Trenig." Henith sipped from the steaming cup that Braen had offered her. "Thank you for the tea. I do feel more rested in my body, but my spirit feels more unrested. How are we going to keep the rituals in this place?"

"I don't know. We will have to find a way. It is very important to keep ourselves centered, especially now. Morgan was right. More than ever we need to continue our rituals. Maybe we can ask Tana's son to show us some meadow or field when he takes us to see the rest of Brithdir. Certainly there must be some place on the outskirts of town we can go to."

"It won't be safe for us to do that."

"We will have to make this room do." The women looked around the small, uncomplicated room. "It is not a stone circle in a field, open to the sky and the smells of the earth, but we will have to make it holy." Braen watched as Henith held on to her tea, as if trying to absorb all of its heat through her hands. She continued, "We should be going down. I told Tana we would be ready to leave after our tea. You will have to tell me your dream later."

ෙංග

"Tell us about that building," Braen pointed to a building she recognized as a center of worship for the religion that was overtaking Trenig. The invaders had built their worship buildings in most of the towns and villages in southern Trenig, often destroying the circle that had been there for centuries.

The young man headed toward the building. Henith was in no mood to go into the building, already feeling disconnected from herself. She knew that going into this alien place would further accentuate the feeling.

"We needn't go in now," she said almost too strongly. "Why don't you tell us about it as we walk along the wharves? It's too nice an afternoon to go into dark stuffy buildings."

Braen shot a look of caution at Henith.

The boy seemed not to notice Henith's disdain for the building that housed this strange god and his worshippers. It would not be wise to appear hostile to the keepers of the new religion, and might even prove to be dangerous.

"It was built here a few decades ago, one of the first things the newcomers did," the boy offered. "My grandfather said that it was as if the newcomers landed in their ships one day, and the building was there the next. There are several priests that live in that house." He pointed to a small white washed building, with a thatched roof typical of most of the buildings in town.

"Someone told us in other towns that these worship buildings are built over a stone circle. Do you know if that was true here?"

"I don't know, I don't remember that part of the story. Maybe my mother remembers, although it was built before my mother was born."

Braen was trying to count how many ships were coming and going in the harbor. She looked at Henith watching the ships, sharing some of her pain. During the past few years, Braen had come to cherish Henith, and it was true that if these foreigners had not come to Trenig then she and Henith would not have had this time together. There were times when she wanted to grab Henith and run away, run back to Mona, to the women on the island, to escape these people, to see Morgan again. Morgan, who probably hadn't realized the enormity of the task that she had set before Henith and Braen. How could they ever describe what this world was like compared to the life of the priestesses, none of whom had been this far south in Trenig for more than two generations? The calm peaceful existence of life in former times had given way to a time where men fought openly with each other and women were not treated with respect or care. No wonder Megen stayed hidden in her house with her herbs.

❧

"Good, you're back. Did he show you everything?" asked Tana. Braen and Henith smiled and nodded. Henith couldn't decide whether she was happier outside with all the sights and sounds and confusion, or in this room with all the sights and sounds and confusion. She hoped their stay here wouldn't be long. Not three moons, like their visit with Megen, who with the blessing of the Goddess, would give birth to a child. A child Braen and Henith would never see, a child who would probably never know of its beginnings, of how two priestesses from an island far away had found Megen and had initiated its life.

They would never see Megen again, because they had decided to travel east after this town, and then gradually go north again back to Mona. They hoped to return there in two years. The stone circles were getting scarcer, and the influence of the foreigners more secure in this part of Trenig. Feeling at this moment that she really didn't want to learn anymore about this new religion, that she had heard and seen enough, she smiled at Tana and allowed herself to be guided across the room.

"Come, sit. It is time for our evening meal, and more travelers will be coming in soon. Here, sit at this table. It will give you an opportunity to watch the comings and goings." Tana hustled them to a table in the corner, where they would be out of the way and at the same time able to watch the whole room.

"I'll bring you something to eat. You must be hungry."

Henith realized she hadn't had much to eat since early this morning when they left Megen, and she was very hungry.

"Thank you, Tana, I am hungry."

The women sat and watched as the dining room filled with travelers, aware again at how different the atmosphere in the room was compared to a circle of women.

"Can you feel the difference in energy in this room filled with men compared to the gatherings of women at home?" Henith asked.

"Yes, it is very loud."

"Somehow they seem to occupy more space, even though they are not much bigger than we are."

"It doesn't feel calm in here either. The sensation I have is that of tumbling, constant motion, like a persistent waterfall that can never stop, and just keeps roaring forever."

"Would you like some company?" Tana asked as she set the food before them. Henith knew by the smell, that some animal had sacrificed its life for this dinner. Henith would never get used to eating animals. The first time they had been served the flesh of a sheep, Henith couldn't eat it, and Braen had been sick for two days afterward. After a very long discussion that had lasted for days, Henith and Braen had decided that they would have to eat whatever food their hosts served. It had not been an easy decision, but they could not produce their own food, so they decided to thank the animal for its sacrifice, and do the best they could with whatever food was offered to them.

Before Henith could say no, Tana waved to a tall young man, wearing the clothes of the foreigners, strangely embroidered shirts, tight fitting pants, and tall brown leather boots.

"Talendar, I want you to meet Braen and Henith, friends of my cousins in northern Trenig. This is Talendar, one of our frequent visitors. He just arrived today also. He's been away for a few months to his homeland."

Henith looked up and her eyes looked directly into the blue green eyes of Talendar, who was looking directly at her. She managed a slight smile, but couldn't take her eyes away.

Tana noticed the look between them.

"Sit here, Talendar, I'll bring your supper soon."

Henith looked away, relieved that the instant had passed, but nervous that this man was sitting across from her. Henith felt an unknown confusion in her body, similar in some ways to the sensations she had felt when she first met Braen during the all-gathering.

She tried to focus on the food before her, pushing the chunks of meat to the side of the plate. Braen, who was the one who could easily engage strangers in conversation, was asking Talendar about his home.

Henith wished she could disappear into the walls, and was glad Braen was there to do the talking so she could just listen.

"I've been coming to Trenig for ten years. My father is the captain of one of the ships in the harbor," he said, pointing in the direction of the wharves.

"What do you do here?" Braen continued.

"I've been taking supplies to the towns along this road. I go as far as Lintern."

"Isn't that the large town east of here? Is it bigger than this one?"

Talendar laughed. "There is almost no comparison. Lintern is many times the size of this town."

"Oh!" Henith managed. "This town is larger than any village we have visited. I'm not sure I would like Lintern."

Talendar smiled at her, and she felt her cheeks grow hot.

"Where are you from?"

Braen looked at Henith. She hated not to answer truthfully, but somehow she knew that in spite of the fact that Talendar seemed pleasant enough, it would not be wise to tell him the whole truth.

"We're from a small village in northern Trenig."

"Why are you here?"

"We are visiting Tana."

"Yes, I know, but isn't that unusual? I've never met women from northern Trenig before. I didn't know they traveled, especially without their husbands. Women in my country would not be allowed to leave home without their husbands."

The food stuck in Henith's throat, and she could feel her back stiffen. She heard Braen calmly responding, "We do not have husbands."

"What?" the tone in his voice coming almost as a sudden clap of the hand.

"I said, we do not have husbands," Braen said, becoming calmer, as if she were saying nothing unusual.

"Unmarried women would never travel alone! That is worse than a wife traveling without her husband. It could be dangerous for you."

"I don't know what you mean. Why would anyone want to harm us? We've been perfectly safe until now."

Talendar stared from one woman to the other. Henith tried to avoid his eyes, because she could feel herself getting angrier.

"You don't know the ways of our people very well."

"Well, our people would never harm a woman," Braen said, overemphasizing the word 'our.'

Tana arrived with Talenda's dinner.

"I hope everything is going well, and that you are enjoying dinner," Tana interjected.

"Yes, thank you," Braen responded, relieved to break the tone of the present conversation.

When Tana left, Braen tried to redirect the conversation.

"Tell us about Lintern. We thought we might travel there."

Chapter 4

"Do you really want to go to Lintern?" Henith asked. "I was hoping we'd turn north again soon." She placed a candle in each corner of the room.

Braen, who was arranging the candles in the center of the small room, thought trying to simulate a large circle of standing stones in this space was ludicrous.

"I think we should ask for guidance. The Goddess has directed us to this place and She will continue to guide us. If we have to go to Lintern, we will. Do you still have feelings of foreboding, Henith? You were very quiet at dinner," Braen paused, watching the candlelight reflect in Henith's eyes.

"Talendar seems to be a fine young man, even though he has been taught some strange customs about women. Can you imagine only being able to travel with your husband? Why would any woman consent to such a thing?" Braen continued, looking out of the small window at the many masts reflecting back the early evening sun.

"Maybe they have never had any other experience. Shall we begin? Will you please draw the power tonight? I'm not feeling very centered. I will invoke the spirits of the four directions." As the walls made the room seem smaller and smaller, Henith tried to imagine tall standing stones surrounding Braen and herself.

Braen stood in the center for many minutes before she began the chant that always sent a chill through Henith. For an instant, Henith remembered the feelings that she had felt earlier that evening when Talendar had looked into her eyes and tried to dismiss them as she focused on the light of the candle of the east. Henith could tell by the look on Braen's face that she was already in a trance.

How many nights have we shared this ritual together, she wondered. Lighting the third candle she forced herself to focus on the words she was saying, invoking the spirits of the west, trying to raise her own spirit from the low place it had fallen to. Usually she herself would be nearing a trance by the time she reached the fourth candle in the north, but tonight she was detached, just going through the motions. The rituals seemed empty.

Henith sat facing Braen in the center of the room, now filled with rose light from the setting sun. Watching the candle light flicker on Braen's face, Henith hoped that Braen's calmness would also surround her as well. She tried to empty her mind of all thoughts, but images of Megen and babies, Braen and Talendar, danced round and round in her mind's eye. Carog appeared.

She hadn't thought of Carog for months. She imagined Carog at Mona, safe and calm, doing what priestesses on the island had done for centuries. Here she was in a tiny room in a place filled with strangers, afraid to claim her identity as a priestess. Her thoughts assumed a dreamlike quality, with Carog and Talendar and herself dancing around a fire, running in and out of the stones like children playing a game of tag. Carog, Talendar, and Henith pulled at each other. Henith looked around for Braen, who was walking slowly away. Feeling pulled by Talendar, Henith called to Braen again, but Braen continued to walk away. Henith was screaming, "Braen! Braen! Braen!"

Henith felt warm arms take hold of her body, which was shaking with sobs. She was out of her body and in her body at the same time. The room was in motion, the arms continued to hold her.

"Henith, I'm here."

Henith opened her eyes slowly in the semi-darkness, the last rays of the evening were lighting a small square of wall. Braen was holding her. "Oh, Braen," tears flowing down her cheeks, "I thought you had gone and left me with Carog and Talendar. I kept calling you and you kept walking away."

Braen held her friend gently in her arms, "I heard you calling me and I'm here, I didn't walk away. I'm here." Braen rocked her gently back and forth. The gentleness of her voice and the warmth of her body gradually soothed Henith into a calm she hadn't felt for weeks.

"Something is deeply troubling you, Henith. Tell me about Carog. You haven't mentioned her since we left Mona."

"I guess I was feeling sorry for myself, being here so far from home and then remembering that she is home safe, being a priestess."

"We are being priestesses."

"But it's so different. At first during our year of initiation I wanted to leave Mona, explore Trenig, but then I discovered the serenity of living the life of a priestess and had decided that I never wanted to leave Mona. Then when I—we—were asked by Morgan to go on the journey, I was excited again. Now all I want to do is go home."

"We will go home, but I don't think it will be for a while yet. We need to learn more about these people, who they are, what they believe. We can only do that if we live with them for a while."

"Don't you miss Mona?"

"Yes, but I know we have to keep on our mission. It is important that we not fail the women by giving up too soon."

"Oh, Braen, I'm sorry. Ever since I was little Carog has disturbed me in some way. My mother used to tell me that Carog was a gift and if I watched her I would learn valuable lessons I needed to know about myself. At our initiation I thought I had come to some peace with her and that part of me that she represented. I saw her for the first time as a beautiful woman, a priestess of the Goddess. The disturbing dreams and visions I had of her ceased until just now."

Relaxing into the protection of Braen's arms, she continued, "It feels so good to have you hold me. I don't know why I keep forgetting the precious gift I was given, of having this opportunity of being with you on this journey." Henith looked up into Braen's loving eyes. "I doubt if I would have said yes to Morgan if she had suggested that I travel with Carog."

"Morgan is a wise woman. She knew from the dreams we shared with her that we were to be together."

Henith asked, "Did you dream of me before our initiation and did you tell Morgan?"

"Of course, didn't you?" Braen replied, puzzled by Henith's question.

"Yes, but I thought, I mean, it never occurred to me that you, I mean, I wanted you to. Oh Braen! You never told me before," Henith turned and held Braen in the candle light, feeling as if time had stopped.

They were startled back into the room by a timid knock on the door. The women looked at each other in surprise, not expecting anyone to disturb them at their evening renewal ritual. Fearing that the arrangement of the candles in the room might illicit suspicion from anyone familiar at all with the ways of the Goddess, Henith quickly rearranged the candles, while Braen went to the door, "Yes?" she asked, and opened it slightly. One of Tana's children was standing there, and shyly said, "Talendar asked if you and Henith would like to accompany him to see the ships at the wharf."

Henith felt a pull somewhere deep inside her. Wanting to stay here in the protection of their room, and Braen's arms, she said only so Braen could hear, "At this hour? We never do anything after evening renewal except meditate." She wanted to forget about the ships and people, to forget about the mission that Morgan had assigned. She wanted to go back to where she had been a few minutes ago, floating in the glow of the candles within the warmth of Braen's body.

"Henith, I think we should go."

"I suppose we should be polite," Henith responded reluctantly.

"Tell Talendar we thank him for his invitation and we will be down shortly."

Henith wanted to tell Braen about all her thoughts and feelings, but Braen was readying herself for their walk. The spell had been broken. Henith put on her cloak and buried the feelings of sadness that crept into her heart.

❧❧

Henith and Braen let Talendar do most of the talking, telling them about his homeland and the long voyage by water to get to Trenig. He told them about his frequent trips to Lintern, and about his father's ships. He seemed excited and very willing to talk. Occasionally Braen would encourage more talk by asking him a question.

Henith struggled with the feelings inside her, feelings that surprised her again as she walked next to him. Confused and embarrassed by the heat in her face, she tried to tell herself the heat was from walking so briskly. The feelings made her very shy, reluctant to engage in conversation with this stranger, and it definitely made her feel like returning to the safety of Mona as soon as possible.

Talendar was telling them that he was going to Lintern in a few weeks.

"I am taking a supply of goods to Lintern, and from there I am heading north. The priest wants to begin another church further north in Trenig." Henith stumbled on the uneven cobblestones. Talendar reached out to steady her, his arm going around her waist. "It's difficult walking in the dark. We should walk slower." His arm lingered longer than was necessary for her to regain her balance.

Henith wanted to change places so that she was next to Braen and Braen was between her and Talendar. She called out to Braen in her mind, hoping Braen would save her again from the cacophony of feelings invading her body.

She tried to focus on what Talendar had just said. Another church in northern Trenig. That would mean the possible destruction of another stone circle. She could feel her anger turning into rage. How dare this man, who was going to destroy a circle of the moon, touch me! The fact that he was the first man in her life who had ever touched her, and that he was part of this deliberate and willful destruction of the Ways of the Goddess, disturbed her greatly. The blood rushed in her cheeks. The strangeness of this male body next to her caused unfamiliar feelings in her and confused her. The way he walked, the way he talked, was dangerously intriguing. She wanted to listen, but she didn't want to hear the things he was saying.

They reached the ship just as Henith thought she would collapse from the chaos inside of her. She tried to stay behind Braen and let Braen ask the questions. Up close the ship was even more impressive, obviously designed to carry many men and much cargo. It certainly was different from the little boat that had brought her and Braen from Mona to the mainland.

"Many people must be able to be transported on this ship."

"Yes, during the first trips here, we just brought men and a few supplies. We needed to get as many men here as possible in order to establish our ways here. Now we mostly bring supplies."

Braen asked the question that was in Henith's mind, "Why did you want to establish your ways here? The people were very content before you came."

"Don't you know the teachings of God?" Talendar turned and looked at the women, "Oh! you are from the north. You must still practice the old religion."

Henith could feel the tension and the danger mounting.

"Tell us about your god," Braen asked, the tone in her voice soothing the pending anger before it had time to surface.

"We had better leave," Talendar said abruptly. "I will show you back to Tana's." The women looked at each other, questioning this sudden shift in Talendar's mood.

Several minutes passed as the three headed toward the inn.

"You seem quiet. Did I say something to offend you, Talendar?" Braen asked, trying to make sense of the last few minutes.

"It didn't occur to me until just now that you weren't believers. I just made an assumption that you were among the faithful, but you may never have had an opportunity to have heard about the one true way. I should have known this afternoon when you said you were traveling alone that you weren't believers. No women who are believers would do that."

An explosion of feelings, thoughts, and questions burst inside of Henith again. How could this man dare to imply that she and Braen weren't faithful! They were priestesses of the Goddess. She couldn't figure out how to respond without revealing too much of their identity.

"Tell us more about your god," Braen said, in a tone much calmer than Henith was feeling.

"I shouldn't be talking to you at all. It is dangerous for me to be with non-believers. Only our priests are allowed to do that. They are the ones who prepare the way for the rest of us."

"I don't think I understand."

"My soul is in danger."

"From us?" Henith allowed the words to burst forth unchecked.

Talendar began to walk very quickly.

"Please slow down. You are in no danger from us. We really would like to understand your religion and why you have to destroy the religion of the people who have been here for centuries." Henith noticed a slight irritation beginning in Braen's voice.

"I really must talk to the priest before I tell you any more."

Talendar fell silent.

Both Braen and Henith were frustrated and angry.

"You needn't walk us back. We can find our way."

"I'm staying at the inn also. I don't like to sleep on deck when I'm in a port."

The finality of the tone in his voice plunged the three into silence again. Any further questions or discussion was pointless. The silence grated on Henith's sense of self. She had never considered herself dangerous before. A funny paradox drifted before her eyes. She had feelings of being in danger from Talendar and here he was telling them that he was in danger. It didn't make any sense.

She was relieved when she saw the lights of the inn just ahead.

Chapter 5

"Good morning!" Talendar passed by their table nodding recognition.

"Good morning! Would you like to sit with us?" Braen invited, ignoring the fear of a few evenings ago when they had gone for a walk.

Talendar hesitated, trying to decide if it were safe to talk to them in this room.

"Talendar, we would like to talk to you." The young man reminded Henith of a poplar tree, tall and straight.

"We would like very much to learn about your god and your ways. How do you expect us to understand if no one teaches us? We have lived all our lives in the north, and your ways are different from ours."

Talendar looked at the women who seemed so innocent and quiet, and who appeared so eager to learn. He knew that if he brought these two women to the priest for instruction, he would be rewarded. Ignoring his earlier mistrust, he sat down feeling good about the possible reward.

"Will you tell us about your religion?"

"I can't do that now. There are lessons that must be learned in order. Also, each pupil has one teacher."

Henith thought it was not so different from her year of instruction to be a priestess. Braen looked around the room.

"Did all these people have their own teacher? That would be a great number of teachers."

"In our country the father teaches every child. By the time of initiation, the role of the priest is to test the child to see if the father's instruction was adequate. Most of the people here are from my country or are related to people from my country, so they have already been taught. Several decades ago when my people came here, it took several years to convert the people that were already living here. It was necessary to destroy the rituals and symbols of the old religion. With the rituals and symbols gone, it was easy to convert them."

"Why did you want to convert them?" Henith was projecting calm even though her insides were boiling.

Talendar looked at Henith in disbelief. "That's what god told us to do. For every person we bring to god, we are rewarded."

"Rewarded?"

"Yes. The more people we bring to god, the more happiness we will have in heaven. We will be endowed with riches beyond our dreams. That's one of the reasons our families are so large. The man whose wife produces a child a year is a fortunate man."

Henith could feel the bile rising in her. A baby a year!

"Do the women have any choice over how many children they have?" Henith managed, trying to keep her voice even.

Talendar laughed, "Of course not. The wife gladly obeys her husband. She wouldn't even consider asking the question you just asked."

If all the women on Mona had a baby every year, they would have run out of food centuries before, Henith thought to herself.

"Why would women want to obey their husbands and not be able to make their own choices?"

"You have a great deal to learn. In the first place, god says that the wife must obey her husband. Life would be very chaotic if women were allowed to make decisions."

"Do you have a wife?" asked Braen.

"Not yet. I've been one of those selected to find a woman native to Trenig. I plan to go north in a few months, find a woman to be my wife, and then start having children. It is one of the ways to convert the village. Certain men have been selected to take over many of the villages in the north. Some of the work has already started. The first wave, many years ago, tried to destroy as many stone circles as possible.

It is easier to take over when the people are afraid," Talendar explained, apparently committed to the strategy he described.

"But I don't understand why you want to 'take over' as you put it. What is wrong with the religion that the people already have?" Braen continued to probe the young man, who was becoming less appealing as the conversation continued.

"The old religion is evil and it has to be destroyed."

"Evil? What do you mean?" Henith asked, looking deep into the eyes of this man.

"It causes the people to sin. They will never get to heaven unless they renounce their ways."

"I don't understand you. I don't know what evil is. I don't know what sin is." Braen offered Talendar some bread.

"That is why you need to go through the instruction in order," Talendar suggested, looking around the room for someone to bring him some tea.

"You said that we each have to have our own teacher. Can you find teachers for us?" Henith looked at Braen in surprise, not sure she was willing to continue learning anymore about a religion that would deliberately condone destruction of another's beliefs.

"I will discuss it with the priest this afternoon, after I have helped my father with the cargo. Have you seen much of Boscawen?" Talendar inquired, the interview about the new religion obviously over, even though the two women had more questions to ask.

"Yes, it is very crowded. But when will we see you again, in order to receive this instruction as you call it?"

"I will meet you here at the supper hour," he replied. "It is getting late; my father will wonder what happened to me."

The women watched the young man leave. Braen was surprised to see tears in Henith's eyes.

"Do you think that we should go through with this plan? I'm not sure I want to know any more about it," Henith asked, looking around the room, at the men who had come here for their noon meal, wondering where the native men of Trenig were and how they felt about these foreigners who intended to marry the Trenig women.

"How else will we be able to report to Morgan what we have learned? How will we be able to make a plan to survive it if we don't know everything there is to know about it?"

"But going through instruction, we might not be together. Talendar said each person had a teacher."

"We will be able to discuss it together, though," Braen said, trying to reassure Henith.

❧

"Good evening, Henith, Braen," Talendar greeted them just as they were finishing their supper meal. "Let me introduce Cyric. He has agreed to be a teacher for one of you."

Braen and Henith greeted the new arrival, a man of about twenty-five years, shorter and broader in the shoulders than Talendar, with a cautious nod. Something about his eyes made the hair rise on the back of Henith's neck. Realizing how little practice she had with mind-speaking in the last year, she tried to send a message to Braen that they weren't safe.

Talendar was continuing, "The priest said that we could start the instruction immediately, before I go to Lintern. Cyric is studying to be a priest, to go north with us next season, so this will be good practice for him. I convinced the priest that I could instruct Henith until I left, and that he could continue in my absence."

Not sharing Talendar's enthusiasm, Henith asked, "How long does this take?" She was not looking forward to spending a year with Talendar, and didn't want Braen to spend a year with this man, who was looking at Braen in a way that made Henith angry.

"That depends on the student. It takes as long as is necessary for true conversion. We don't want any back-sliding into the old ways." Talendar and Cyric laughed at something that did not seem at all funny to the two women.

"Why don't we begin now by getting more acquainted with each other? Cyric why don't you and Braen find a place to begin instruction, and I'll begin with Henith. We mustn't waste any time, I'm scheduled to leave in a few days, although I may be able to postpone the departure for a week if I'm lucky." Talendar smiled at Henith, and then looked at Cyric with a different kind of smile. Henith felt her knees weaken.

Henith did not want to go with Talendar, and she certainly did not want Braen to be alone with Cyric. She tried again to communicate with Braen.

Braen said, as if not mind-hearing Henith at all, "We are tired from our exploring today, and need to retire to our rooms for a while, but why don't we spend some time tonight getting acquainted. I think that will be all right, don't you, Henith?"

Before Henith could respond, Talendar had taken her by the elbow and was ushering her from the dining room, leaving Cyric and Braen sitting at the table. Feeling trapped, she pulled her arm from Talendar's grasp and preceded him to the door.

Talendar directed her toward the docks. "Let me show you my ship," he said. Henith remained quiet.

As they approached the ship again, Henith was impressed again with its size, with two tall masts, and several cross masts that must hold the sails in some way. Henith was staring up at the height of the mast, when Talendar suggested, "Let us go to my cabin. It will be quiet there, no one will disturb us. We will begin the instruction right away." Talendar led the way to the planks joining the ship to the dock and started aboard. Henith waited on the dock.

"Come, Henith, this will be a good place to begin your studies," he said, putting his hand on her arm to assist her.

Fighting against all the voices inside of her not to go aboard this ship, she slowly joined Talendar, wishing Braen were here, wondering what Braen and Cyric were doing. Again fear gripped her just thinking about him.

"I'm very tired, Talendar, I'm not sure what kind of pupil I will be. Maybe we should begin tomorrow, when I'm more alert." Henith stepped toward the side of the ship, toward the dock.

"You'll be able to be comfortable in my cabin," he insisted, nodding to another man on the deck. "We are not to be disturbed," he commanded with authority, and ushered Henith below the deck on a small ladder-like stairway. The ceiling in the space below came just above Henith's head, and she noticed that Talendar was unable to stand straight in this space. She felt cramped in such small quarters and wanted to be out on deck again.

"Come this way, my cabin is aft." Talendar opened a small door to a room, even smaller than the one she was sharing with Braen at the inn. How could anyone live in such a small space! If all the foreigners traveled in spaces this small it was no wonder why the inn was so busy. The rooms at the inn must seem immense by comparison.

"Sit here, Henith." Talendar indicated a chair next to a very small table. He sat on the other side.

"Before we begin, I want to tell you how happy I am that the priest granted my request. It gives me an excuse to be with you without Braen, and I wanted to tell you how much pleasure that gives me."

Henith looked at Talendar, trying to avoid his eyes. Fear started to grip Henith again. She didn't feel safe. She had never been alone with a man before. Trying to ignore what Talendar was saying, Henith said, "Tell me about your god and this evil that I don't understand."

Talendar smiled in spite of himself. Henith was so perfect sitting here in the dim light of his cabin, so quiet and so beautiful. She was not like the women he had met at home, and certainly not like any he had seen here in Trenig. She reminded him of a goddess which he had heard stories about. She didn't seem real and yet here she was in his cabin. A thought that sent a thrill through his body occurred to him as he searched the face of this woman. I will marry her, he said to himself; she is from the north. I will take her back north with me when I go. Her voice sounded like an angel singing.

"Talendar, will you please tell me about your god?"

Talendar reached across the table and took Henith's hand. Feeling the gentle warmth, he tried to focus his attention on god. "God is the Father Almighty, creator of heaven and earth."

Before he could continue, Henith, her voice no longer calm, asked, "What? Did you say, Father? How can a father be the creator?" She was trying to relinquish her hand from Talendar's without appearing to be rude.

Talendar stood up, dropping Henith's hand. He didn't want to have this discussion about god.

"Henith, listen, there is a catechism. You are to memorize the answers to certain questions. You are not to ask the questions."

"If I don't ask questions, how will I ever understand?"

"Henith, it will go much quicker if you just memorize the answers to the questions, then we can get on with other things." He had walked behind her, and was about to put his hands on her shoulders, when she stood up.

"Talendar, my mind isn't ready to memorize anything tonight. Perhaps tomorrow. I'm sorry I wasn't prepared for this type of instruction. I will be more alert tomorrow, I really must go now." Henith started toward the door.

Realizing that Henith was uncomfortable, Talendar controlled the passion that was burning in the pit of his stomach and led Henith to the dock.

"I'm sorry if I offended you," he said, when they had reached the street back to the inn. "What time should we meet tomorrow?"

"Let me discuss our plans with Braen. We probably should try to meet at the same time that Cyric is meeting with her." She was secretly hoping that would be never.

"Good, I will check with Cyric and see you then." Talendar left Henith at the door to the inn and headed back to the dock.

࿐

"Braen, I don't want to see Talendar anymore, he scares me. He even touched my hand. I was so frightened; I didn't know what to do." Henith looked at Braen as she set the candles in the four directions in their room. "How was Cyric? Did you learn anything about this new religion?"

"Some very strange things! Did Talendar tell you that this god sacrificed his own son? And did he tell you that if you don't believe in this father, god, that you will burn in a fire when you pass from this life?"

"Talendar didn't seem to want me to ask questions, he said all I had to do was memorize some answers to some questions. He said he wanted to do something else other than talk about his god. I was very uncomfortable, so I told him I was tired and couldn't concentrate." Braen noticed that Henith was twisting the edge of her skirt in her hands.

"Would you like to go to the cliff we discovered yesterday? We could go in the morning. Cyric cannot meet again until late afternoon so we will have time. It reminds me of home, maybe it will make you feel calmer. I could sit there for hours," Braen suggested, trying to lessen Henith's apparent distress.

"Maybe we could explore the coast south of here? We could ask Tana for some food to take with us and spend the day. Maybe she could even suggest some roads for us to take." Henith brightened for a moment and then her face became dark again, as if a cloud had passed in front of her.

"I just remembered a dream fragment. There was a field of stones that lay forgotten for years, off the main road."

"Do you think it is around here? These people seem so determined to destroy all the circles! I can't believe they could have missed one so close to one of their major towns."

"I don't know if it was here or not. It was on a grassy bluff overlooking the sea."

"Let's look at the map again and see if there are any markings we can identify. I think we may be able to determine where this town is on the map, although it probably didn't exist when the map was made." Braen unrolled the map that Morgan had given them, and smoothed it on the table in the dim candle light.

"Look, Braen, this could be where we are!" pointing to an indentation on the land near the bottom of the map. "Remember Megen said that the land ended south of here only a few days' walk. So we are probably here."

"But this map suggests that the land goes forever, that Trenig isn't a large island. Maybe where we are is actually off the edge of the map. The stone circle near Megen's isn't marked either, remember?"

"But look right here where the land runs east. There is a marking for a circle. This town could be here, where it looks like a good place for a harbor."

"Maybe we should ask Tana how far it is to the southern shore."

∂∽⑤

Henith and Braen hurried from their room in search of Tana, forgetting for the moment the evening renewal ritual.

"Tana, we would like to go south to see the southern shore. How far is it?"

"That's impossible, there are no roads."

"Are there no people who live south of this town?"

"A few, I guess. Jenli, the young woman that helps me on the busiest days, says her grandmother lives there. I can't believe it though. There are no roads. The ground is very difficult, rocky and rugged, and then it falls into the sea."

"How do you know?"

"Oh, some of the old ones tell stories. You know how they are. The foreigners haven't even bothered to go there as far as I know."

"The more you tell us, the more I want to see it. You said there were no roads, but there must be paths or trails or some kind of markings."

"After you leave town on the road along the coast, after it turns east, you'll notice there is a path to the right. You may not notice it immediately, but there are two big stones. They look something like the ones that used to be in the circles around here, but these two are not in a circle."

Henith felt a thrill go up her back, her excitement soaring. "Why weren't they also destroyed?"

"I don't know. They are not in a circle. Mostly the newcomers only wanted to destroy the circles. I hear that all of the circles along the southern shore of Trenig were destroyed before I was born. Except for Megen's, I've never seen one, only heard about them. I don't know how Megen's escaped destruction. They must have missed these two stones also, when the first purge happened during my grandmother's time. Quite possibly they didn't recognize them. Only the old ones that are still around here know about them. Jenli told me about them when she told me about her grandmother. Since my mother passed, I've been too busy running the inn to do much traveling. The only time I'm not working and mothering, I go to see Megen, which isn't very often. I hope none of these men find out about her. I doubt if she would be safe if they did."

Henith was tempted to ask the question about the donor of the fluid for Megen's baby, but decided she really didn't want to know the answer.

"We would like to see the southern shore. We are trying to visit all of Trenig. Please do not worry about us. We never know how long we will be in any one place because we never know what we will find." Henith wanted to run to their room to pack their few belongings and start now even at this time of night. She couldn't wait until they left this inn and Talendar and Cyric.

"Are you thinking what I'm thinking?" Braen asked as they returned to their room.

"That there may be a circle down that path, and that Jenli's grandmother knows about it?"

"Yes. Doesn't it thrill you to think that in spite of this new religion, which most of the people have converted to, there are these women carrying on our ways?"

"It must be terribly lonely, not being able to share their stories and the rituals with anyone."

"What about our instruction in this new religion?" Braen asked her friend.

"It will have to wait until we get back," Henith replied excitedly.

"We should tell Tana to tell Talendar we will be back, but not to tell him where we are. We don't want to put Jenli's grandmother in any danger."

"Look, Braen, two standing stones, can you feel their energy?" The women recognized the stones and knew instantly that they were guardians of a path. Upon reaching the stones, Henith and Braen touched them as a mother cares for her child. Stroking the gray smoothness, Henith said, "It feels like I've found an old friend, even though I haven't known this particular megalith before. It's a miracle that the strangers didn't see them and destroy them. Anyone who knew the stones would recognize them immediately."

"Henith, someone put a wall of power around these stones that is mighty powerful. Can't you feel it? We just walked through it because we are priestesses and are comfortable with that energy, but someone not familiar with it might not be able to come close enough to destroy them, possibly not even close enough to see them. It doesn't surprise me that the road we were on swings to the east the way it does. The people building the road probably were unaware of what made them turn east there instead of continuing straight south."

"You're right Braen, I can feel it. Someone very skilled in power drawing has cast a wall around these stones."

The young women went between the stones and started to follow a trail that was barely visible. They followed the path for at least an hour as it gradually led to the west. The incline was very gradual, barely noticeable to the climbers. Eventually they had to stop for a rest near a grove of trees.

"I'm surprised that we haven't come to something, the coast, the circle, or Jenli's grandmother by now."

Braen laughed at Henith's impatience. "Henith, we are on the right path, I know. Your impatience may lead you into trouble someday."

"You remind me of my mother when you say that. Do you ever miss your mother?"

"Once in a while I think about her, but she has her mission and I have mine. I am thankful that we are both able to serve the Goddess in our own unique ways."

They walked for at least another hour on a path that was indiscernible at times. "Do you suppose we are going the right way?" Henith looked back, the path disappearing behind them.

"I don't remember seeing any alternatives. Remember, Trenig is an island. We can't walk forever before coming to the sea."

"But we followed the shore from the town to the stones, and I was sure we were going west most of the time. We should have come to the ocean hours ago."

Braen looked ahead. "Do you think the trees are thinning? It's a little brighter over there."

"You're right, maybe we are close." She picked up the pace in her hurry to find a stone circle.

The lightness of the sky showing through the trees encouraged them.

"Braen look. It's like the end of the world." Braen and Henith came into a large clearing that ended with a high cliff overlooking the water in two directions, and fell steeply to the sea. To the south was another peninsula of land jutting out into the sea. Between the cliff where they were and the one they could see stretched a treacherous cove, the surf pounded on the rocky shore far below, certainly not a good place to land a boat. The women explored the field filled with grasses waving in the breeze, and covered with many different flowers. Henith started searching for ones she knew.

"Braen this field is better than Zendar's garden, even though it doesn't look like a garden because it's so wild. Do you suppose someone planted it and let it go?" Henith wandered, bending over occasionally to caress a certain plant and smell different flowers.

"Braen, I've never seen so many plants growing like this. I wonder if I should gather some. We may never find this variety again." Braen was standing so still on the edge of the cliff, Henith wondered if she was meditating. Braen reminded Henith of the Goddess, silhouetted against the sky, so tall with the wind blowing her robes gently about her. Henith couldn't resist the urge to go to her and hold her in her arms. As Henith approached, Braen turned toward her. Braen's face was more serious than Henith ever remembered seeing.

"What is it, Braen? Did you see something?"

"No, but Henith do you know how to get out of here? We can't go west and north into the sea. We can't get down the cliff to the south, and in the east the trees seemed to have joined. I see no way to the trail.

In our excitement to reach the end of the path, we were not careful to notice where we had been."

Henith looked around as Braen spoke. It was true. There seemed to be no easy escape from here.

Trying to smile at Braen, Henith said somewhat wryly, "Well, I can't think of a nicer place to end my days."

"The Goddess led us here, we know that. I am sure we will be safe. We just have to be patient."

"You are a fine one to talk about patience." Braen managed a smile.

"Either we missed a turning, or this is where we are supposed to be. I love it here. It reminds me of Mona, except this field is grander than any garden we have at home."

"It's early for the evening renewal ritual, but we should call the Goddess to this place and ask for guidance. Let us see if we can find the center." The two women explored the field.

"Braen, why don't we walk the circle together and then come here to this mossy place that could be the center, eat some food, and go into silence for a while. Maybe we will get clarity on what we should do next."

The women left their packs on the mossy ground and walked to the edge of the trees, selecting the place that they determined was due east. They faced the darkness of the forest and called the protectors of the east to be with them. Walking slowly to the south, Braen's hand touched Henith's. Holding hands, they approached the southern cliff, with the dangerous rocks below in the pounding surf. They watched the fury of the sea in this inlet before they called the spirit of the south for protection. Still holding hands and walking very slowly as if to make the moment last forever, the women approached the west. It must have been later than they had assumed, because the sun was far lower in the sky than they realized. The sky was fire red by the time they raised their arms to embrace the guardians of the west. Time was disappearing. They seemed to be floating, but still holding hands neither could say later how long it had taken to walk to the northern point on the cliff. However, by the time they reached there, a fog had surrounded them. They called the Guardian Spirits of the north. With the mist curling around them and their arms entwined, they walked to the center. The food was shared, but not remembered. They lay down arms around each other, the soft mossy earth beneath, the dancing swirl of fog above, and with only the flowers as witnesses, they left their bodies as on the night of their initiation, and, drifting in the blueness of the universe, were one with each other and the Goddess.

Chapter 6

Henith opened her eyes. It was very dark and very light at the same time. The not quite full moon overhead was casting a milky luminescence on the field of flowers. The priestess sat up and gently moved her arm from under Braen, thinking that she saw something move in the darkness near the trees in the east. Henith looked at Braen's face, which was calm from the spirit flying. Braen's dark auburn hair with the golden strands spread like a spider's web on the moss.

The fog had cleared totally, and the pounding surf on the rocks far below the cliff sounded out of place in the stillness of the field. Looking across the field to the east, trying not to let her imagination scare her, she saw movement again. It must be an animal, she thought. The circle they had cast had been very powerful. She wondered if Braen knew the skill she had drawing the circle of power. No enemy could get past that wall; the Goddess would protect them. She continued to look in the direction of the movement in the east. She knew something was there, even if she couldn't quite bring it into focus. Now she was more curious than afraid, knowing that whatever or whoever it was must be attuned to the energy that existed here.

Braen opened her eyes. "Is she coming?"

"What?"

"Is she here yet?"

"How did you know?"

"I can feel her, where is she?"

"She's coming from the trees, but I can't make her out yet."

Braen stood, shaking the wrinkles from her gown and straightening her hair with her fingers. "I think we should go to meet her. Where did you see her?"

Henith pointed toward the trees. Staring toward the darkness in the east, they saw her, dark against dark. The old woman appeared, smaller than either of the two priestesses. Her aura, reflecting the moonlight, made her look much taller. She was older than any woman Henith had ever seen before, but she moved with the grace and agility of a young woman.

"Welcome, I've been waiting for you. I knew you would find your way to me."

She embraced Henith and then Braen with a strength that took their breath away. "I've been watching you since you entered between the guardian stones. I understand why the High Priestess sent you on this mission, even two so young. You have been well schooled in the craft. You, my dear," addressing Henith, "must watch your impatience. You are lucky to have your friend here to keep you on the path," the old one chuckled, a twinkle dancing in the corner of her eyes.

"You said you were expecting us. How did you know we were coming, when we only knew ourselves this morning?"

"Come, follow me. I will tell you what you need to know. There is time for questions later, but first let us eat together and then rest. In the morning I will show you what you have come to find."

"Will I have a chance to come back here? There are some plants I would like to take with me."

"Perhaps."

Henith was unsettled by the ambiguity of the old woman's response, and dismissed the possibility that she thought she detected a chuckle coming from deep within the earth.

"Come, let us leave this place."

Braen followed, then Henith, who found herself reluctant to leave. In just a short time she had grown attached to this field of plants, and wanted to stay and learn more from them.

In the darkness it was impossible for Henith to see any opening in the trees that would lead to a path. It was as if they were walking straight into a black wall. The old woman was leading them to the southeast, about halfway between the points where Henith and Braen had invoked the spirits of the east and south, close to where the wall of trees met the edge of the rocky cliff. The night air was silent except for the rhythmic pounding of the surf on the rocks below. Henith was hoping they weren't going to attempt to climb down that treacherous cliff in the dark. That would have been impossible even in the full light of day. The woman was heading for the trees near the edge of the cliff.

Henith focused her attention on following the old woman, who led them into the darkness of the forest protecting the east edge of the field. Henith expected it to be very dark in the woods, but was surprised by the amount of light filtering in from the moon.

The path was sloping downhill, which, Henith suspected, led toward the rocky cove. The sounds of the surf echoing through the trees appeared to come from all directions, but she was certain that the roar originated on her right. They were nearing the point where the cove ended, and the path started ascending again, going around the cove toward the other peninsula the women had seen from the field.

"We are almost there," the woman shouted above the ocean's voice.

Up ahead, Henith could see the outline of a house dark against the glow of the night sky. As they approached, Henith detected the smell of some of the herbs that were in the field, and smiled thinking the old woman must have a garden of herbs here.

Henith was surprised at how similar the house appeared to the one that Morgan lived in on Mona, one room at ground level with windows that faced each of the four directions. Three of the evening ritual candles were lit. As soon as the three were safely inside, the old woman lit the fourth candle.

Henith felt as if a gigantic peg had slid into its home, locking them forever in the power of this room and this woman. Noticing that Braen also detected the forces at work within this room, Henith caught Braen's eye and smiled a sigh of relief. Looking around the room, Henith noted more similarities to Morgan's room in the center of the great stones of Mona, including the spiral staircase going into the earth and to the rooms where this old one lived.

"Welcome to the edge of the earth."

A chill crept over Henith's body. She tried to peer through the windows, but the light of the candles caused just enough inward reflection that she could only detect vague images of the three women being mirrored back into the room.

"We will eat," the old woman said, pointing to a table that had been prepared. "Then we will descend into my chambers and sleep. In the morning we will first tell our stories, and then I will take you to see what you came to see. Let us continue in silence until the morning, enjoying the power that has emerged from our joining." She looked at Braen, whose aura was aglow, brighter than ever. Braen had been intensely quiet since she asked if the old woman had come to them, back in the field.

"You have exceptional skill at power drawing," the old one said to Braen. "Guard your gift well."

ॐ

Morning came so quickly Henith only vaguely remembered the night's sleep. She was calmer than she could remember for a long time. As Henith left her room, she met Braen who also radiated a gentle calm, in the hallway.

Climbing the spiral stairs with renewed curiosity, speculating about the old woman's story, Braen led the way into the room with its view of the land and earth in all directions.

The old one was already waiting for them, again with food prepared for their morning meal—fresh bread, blueberries and strawberries, different cheeses, grains, and milk.

"Good morning." Henith was surprised to see that the woman was even older than she had guessed last night. The bright sunlight streaming in eastern windows highlighted a face carved with the wrinkles of time. She was very small, and there was a frailty about her that had gone undetected in the candles and moonlight of last night. Her eyes were alive, clearly taking in all that passed before them. Pure white hair was carefully braided down the middle of her back. In some ways she was a smaller, older Zendar.

Henith and Braen joined her at the table she indicated.

"You have traveled far to reach me here. I've been waiting for you for several years."

The young women looked at each other. Braen voiced their confusion.

"You seem to know much more about us than we know about ourselves. Will you share your story with us? But first, how did you know we were coming?"

The old woman chuckled. "First things first. I am Shelagh. The healer is?"

"Henith."

"And the one who draws the power?"

"Braen."

"In all my years of drawing the power, I have never experienced the intensity of last night. I thank you and I thank the Goddess that I could share with one so skilled before my life here ends. I have been dreaming for years that two skilled and powerful women would come and take over my work here before I passed. When Jenli told me that two women from north Trenig were visiting in town and were asking questions about the foreigners and about stone circles, I knew that my dreams were about to come true and that it was only a matter of time before you would find me."

"I'm surprised your granddaughter was so observant. I didn't think we were so obvious."

"Jenli isn't my granddaughter. She just says that, because it is easier for her to get away when she says that she is going to see her grandmother. Many of the young women call me grandmother."

"Many of the young women?" Henith asked, surprised that there might be more women than Shelagh here who practiced the Ways of the Goddess.

"Yes, there are twelve at the moment. I will tell you about them later, but first let us share our stories."

169

"When I was ten or eleven, I fell in love with the priestess of the circle north of the town. My mother was a faithful follower of the Ways of the Goddess, and she would take me to all the rituals. I started to notice the priestess. She became more than real to me. I thought about her every waking minute. I dreamed about her in my night dreams. She was so delicate and so strong at the same time. When she led the rituals, drawing the power, my body turned to liquid, my heart left my body and flew to her. All I wanted was to be with her. I was more devoted to her than to my mother. I began bringing her little things, flowers I'd picked, stones I liked. Eventually she allowed me to help her. I spent all of my waking hours as her apprentice. I didn't care what she asked of me, I was so eager to please her. As I grew older, she began teaching me some of her craft. I was a skilled student. Drawing the power was almost natural to me. I remember the first time she allowed me the honor of drawing the power. We were both amazed at the intensity of the circle that night. After that she taught me everything she knew.

"I loved her with a passion that scared me. I don't know if she had the same feelings. We never talked about it. I was her devoted student, she my skilled teacher. I told myself it really didn't matter if she returned my love or not. After all, I was much younger than she was, and I was happy. I was with her every day. When I was fifteen she told my mother that I should have been born a priestess because of my natural skills. She asked my mother if I could live with her so she could instruct me in the ways of the Goddess. My heart was pounding at the thought that she wanted me to live with her. I could hardly breathe waiting for my mother's response.

"My mother said, 'yes' and I went to live with the priestess. That was one of the happiest years of my life. Just the two of us. We spent hours and hours talking and being with each other. She taught me everything she knew. We shared the rituals. That was my greatest joy, to draw the power together, to be one with each other and with the Goddess." Shelagh was quiet for some time. The joy in her face gradually changed. Henith watched the lines that radiated from the corner of her eyes darken as other memories returned.

"We lived together for two years. She was always the priestess, I was always the student. My love for her was deep and intense. I knew that she would have to return to her island someday, but I tried not to think about it. I wished that I might even be allowed to go with her. Even though she had told me that only women born on Mona were true priestesses, I still let myself hope that an exception could be made in my case. She never mentioned her return.

"During our second year together, she began to spend more and more time traveling in the villages. She was a skilled healer and the people called on her more and more. Sometimes I would accompany her, but as time went on I stayed home more as she traveled more.

"I hated the time she was away. I spent the time preparing herbs for her and attending to the other crafts. One day after she had been away for several days, she came home looking very different. She had been putting on weight. Her body had always been so slender and willowy. I had noticed the change in her before, but this time she was so different. I was so happy to see her; I tried to ignore the changes in her appearance and her behavior. As we prepared for the evening ritual, I noticed how her skin had also changed color. I was afraid she might be ill. She told me that after renewal she had something she wanted to tell me. I could not participate fully in the ritual because I kept thinking about her and what could be wrong. I feared she had contacted some dreaded disease from one of the many people she had been visiting. After the ritual that night, we sat down together and she said that she was not going back to Mona.

"I looked at her in disbelief. A priestess not returning to Mona was unheard of. I was relieved and very disappointed at the same time. I discovered that I had rather wanted to go to Mona, and even though that was impossible, I still held onto my dream. The realization of what she said started a smile to grow somewhere inside of me. She was staying here to be with me. Before I could voice my joy at this declaration, she continued, 'I've decided to stay here and marry one of the young men in the village.'

"I couldn't move. I couldn't talk. My whole world collapsed. I refused to believe what she said. I fought to hold back the tears. All of eternity surrounded me.

"A voice far away was trying to talk to me. I heard the word 'baby'; I heard the word 'love.' Love? What did the voice know of love? How could the voice be talking about love when I was sitting right here, when I had been here in love, loving, for several years. How could love be with a man! I refused to hear any more. I wouldn't let this voice destroy the beauty of real love, the love I had for her.

"I managed to stand, although the earth was trembling and the winds were blowing fiercely in my face. I left her sitting there. I never looked back. I started walking and walked for days. I don't remember where I went. I walked and cried and cried and walked.

"Somewhere in those days I decided I couldn't live with the betrayal. Not only had she betrayed her vows as a priestess, but she also had chosen a man instead of me. I was completely devastated. I decided at one point that I should get to the coast and find a cliff so I could throw myself into the ocean. I didn't want to live any more. How could she give up our life like that? I started to head toward what I thought was the west shore. I arrived at the field you found yesterday. The cliff was almost high enough, but the one I could see to the south looked even higher and steeper. I made my way to that field. When I arrived I discovered a stone circle. It was grander than any I had ever seen." Shelagh's eyes became dream-like. "It was magnificent, gleaming in the sun. I leaned against one of the stones, the north one, I think. I don't know how long I was there, but I cried and cried and cried. I must have fallen asleep. It was so long ago, I do not really remember, but I must have slept.

"I don't know if it was the same day or another day or many days, but when I opened my eyes I was at peace. At first I thought I had passed from this life and had arrived at the next. Slowly my memory came back. The feelings of betrayal and abandonment were still intense, but I had a calmness deep within that kept me alive. All of my agony had flowed out of me, and the stone I was leaning on replenished my body with calm. I stayed connected to that stone for hours. I knew the cliff was near, but I didn't even bother to look over the edge. I slept, protected by the north stone. The woods and fields provided me with all the nourishment I needed for my body and the stones provided me with all the nourishment for my spirit. The Goddess had given me what I needed. I was happy again. I eventually realized that I never had my priestess. She was always there, but she had never been mine. She had always been my teacher and I her student. She had never implied anything else in our relationship, but I loved her and I guess she loved me in her own way, but not in the way I had wanted and hoped for.

"That was a long time ago. I'm an old woman now. I have learned much and I have been happy serving the Goddess here."

"Have you lived here alone all these years?" Henith asked thinking how awful it would be not to have Braen to share her life with.

"In a way I live here alone. But the young women come regularly to learn the craft and to participate in the rituals."

"How do they get here without being noticed? The townspeople seem totally converted to the new religion."

"Many, many years ago, when the men with the new religion started coming to Trenig in greater numbers, the women gathered at one of the moon rituals when the stones were still there. It still pains me to remember the day when they knocked the stones over, pulled them away from their circle, and then built their building on the Goddess's sacred ground."

Shivers went down Henith's spine.

"After that the women decided that in order to keep our ways and the ways of the Goddess, we would pretend to have given it up. Some of the women even took instruction. They vowed not even to tell their husbands that they were keeping the old ways. For some reason the village men responded more positively to this new religion with its new ways than the women did. The women kept the rituals as best they could, but as time went on it became more and more difficult.

"After the first few years of total isolation, I began going to town occasionally. On these trips I was able to observe the deterioration of our ways and watch the gradual takeover of the new ways brought by the foreigners. I became friendly with some of the women and learned of their plan to pretend to go along with the new ways. At the time it was a reasonable choice. Our ways of love prevented us from the use of violence to destroy these other human beings that were invading our land.

"At the beginning we couldn't believe how violent these foreign men were. We were naive. They would come into a village and immediately start killing anyone that offered any resistance at all. So we thought we could stop the violence by not resisting. Some of the men would even take the women against their will. They have no reverence for life, and totally disregard the wishes of others. As the situation worsened, I invited a few women to join me here for support and the rituals. Gradually I taught them what I knew about our sacred mysteries. It seemed important to me not to let all the precious knowledge get lost. I had no one else to share it with. Our group was very secret. We knew that if we were found out our lives would be in danger. Many women had been killed for lesser crimes than gathering to continue to participate in a moon ritual."

"Killed! Someone actually killed a woman!" Braen shouted in disbelief.

"Yes. Several women were hung and several were burned."

"That's not possible. No one would destroy anyone that way."

"The men brought some strange customs with them besides their religion."

"Do women still come here?" Henith asked.

"Yes, Jenli is one of them. She told me of your arrival in town. She has the skill of aura reading. She told me that two women from the north had arrived. She said the women had the purest auras she had ever seen. She said one aura was so intensely golden that she was surprised that everyone in town couldn't see it. I told her that I thought I knew who you were, but then she said she saw you engaged in discussion with one of the men and she became uncertain."

"Part of our mission is to learn as much as we can learn about the new ways and the new religion."

"I thought possibly that was what you were doing. I understand the man you were talking to is one of the most powerful men in the new religion."

"Tana introduced us."

"Tana. I don't understand her. Sometimes I think she is one of us, sometimes I'm not sure. We have been very cautious with Tana, but she did send you here. She has also guided other young women to me."

"Do you know Megen?" Henith asked the old woman.

"I've heard of her, but I've never met her. Jenli says that she's the friend of Tana's that grows healing herbs. That's all I know."

"I think she's your priestess's granddaughter. She told us a similar story, except you were not in it. It is possible that there were two priestesses with similar stories, but I don't think so. Her grandmother also taught her some of the craft. I think you might like to meet her. I'm surprised you haven't already, but both of you are so isolated."

"We have to live secret lives. If the men find out what we are doing, they might kill us. We have to be very careful with whom we share our stories."

"One of our learnings is that, in many of the villages that we have visited there is one woman who is guarding the sacred ways. In the northern villages, priestesses from Mona still serve in this way. But as we travel south, it becomes more and more difficult to find a priestess or the woman who is still practicing the old ways, but they are there. Some were taught by a priestess; some just remembered or were taught some of the mysteries by their mothers and grandmothers. The women on Mona thought the ways of the Goddess were disappearing from Trenig. They will be happy to know that the way continues, even if it is in secret." Henith walked to the western window, overlooking the sea.

"Do you want to see the stone circle?" Shelagh finally asked.

"Of course. Here is our map. Do you think it is this one?" Braen showed Shelagh the drawing, pointing to a circle near the bottom of the map. "If it is, it is a very special one."

"It could be. I will have to take some time to study your drawing more. Come; let us go to the circle." Shelagh led them from the house toward the second peninsula. As they were walking, Shelagh said to

Braen, "The moon is full in three days. I would be honored if you would draw the power, Braen."

"It is I who would be honored to share the joy with you."

Chapter 7

"Braen, I really don't want to leave here. It has been so wonderful being with these women, almost as wonderful as home, except the sharing here is different." Henith paused, allowing herself to enjoy the beauty of Shelagh's garden.

Sighing, she continued, "And as much as I want to stay here, I know that we should leave soon, because it will probably be at least a year before we reach Mona, and we need to report what we have discovered to Morgan and the others." Henith stopped in the path to caress an iris. Trying to remember what life was like back at home, she wondered how many young women had been initiated this spring.

She thought about Zendar's garden and this garden, knowing that Zendar would like Shelagh. They both shared a reverence for the sacred plants that Henith was just beginning to appreciate before she left Mona for this mission. During the travels, it had been difficult for her to be with the plants like she was able to be with them here. Even though she always carried a small supply of medicinal herbs with her in case they met someone along the way that needing healing, she hadn't spent time learning from the plants, like she had during her moons with Zendar.

As she reflected, she realized that in many of the villages that she and Braen had visited, there was a healer, a woman skilled in the mysteries of medicine. In some cases Henith had been able to teach the healers about an unfamiliar plant and enjoyed sharing some of her skills with the women. She had been very careful, until they met the women of Shelagh's circle, to keep the most profound healing mysteries secret, but now she wished that she had taught all the women they had met everything she knew.

"It doesn't seem possible that we have been here seven moons. It feels as if it were only yesterday when we passed between the guardian stones," Braen responded, watching her friend select an iris, whose fragrance filled the late afternoon air. A thrill went through her, seeing how happy Henith was with the plants and herbs. Smiling to herself as Henith talked to each plant, gently touching the flowers and thanking the ones she picked for their gift, Braen remembered the first time she had seen Henith in her initiation robe, the same color as the iris in her hands. She had known, in one of those flashes of foreknowing that she frequently had, that she and Henith would be together, but she never imagined that it would be so far from Mona in this beautiful garden overlooking the sea. She also wished that they didn't have to go home, because she liked sharing her life with Henith, and back home it would not be this way.

Picking several flowers and holding them to her nose, Henith slowly continued down the path, idly looking at the wide variety of plants Shelagh managed to assemble here. Shelagh had told her that many varieties had existed before she came here, but the women brought others as gifts. Henith imagined that she would be happy spending the rest of her life in a garden just like this one, especially if Braen could share it with her. Back on Mona she would have to live in her village on the western shore of Mona, and Braen would live in the eastern village. Life on her island as she remembered it would not provide many opportunities for the two of them to be together. She thought of Shelagh's story and how sad it was that Shelagh had lived her life alone without a companion. It was true that there were all the young women that she taught, but it wasn't quite the same. Henith probably would never have known the joy of having a friend like Braen if Morgan hadn't sent them on this mission.

"It must be nearing the time for Megen's birthing. Do you think we should go there to be with her?" Henith asked Braen.

"I'd love to, but maybe some of the others from here should be with her. We can show them what to do. Do you remember the

Birthing Rite? I was present at a few when I was younger, but I never actually had much part in the process. I remember how exhilarating it was when all the women started chanting and breathing together. Megen would truly be surprised if a group of women came to her to celebrate the birthing. It would be good for her to discover that she is not alone." Braen sat on a large stone as Henith continued to wander through the flowers.

"Braen, that's a wonderful idea! Zendar taught me about the ritual. I have even helped her with a birthing. I am sure the women here have developed their own ceremony, but it would be nice to share ours with them. It would be like connecting with them in magical ways. They can also share their Birthing Ritual with us. Let us discuss the possibilities tonight at renewal." Silence floated gently between them. Minutes passed, each lost in the memories of the last few moons, knowing it was time to move on and trying not to think about it.

A dark sadness appeared in Henith's eyes. Moving closer to Braen, Henith asked seriously, "Do you think that we have broken our sacred vows by sharing the secret mysteries with them?"

Braen reassured her. "I don't think so. The only hope of withstanding the invasion is to teach as many women as possible as much about the mysteries as we can. It may be the only way for the craft to survive. From what I have observed, my fear is that it is only a matter of time before the ways of the foreigners become the ways of Trenig. I shudder at the thought, but I don't see any real way to stop it." Braen watched the darkness pass through Henith's eyes again, a sadness so deep that it was too painful to witness. Braen looked out over the ocean.

The intent of the invaders was so strong and so well organized, nothing except a violent resistance would be able to stop it, and even then the outcome could not be predicted. The people in Trenig were not warriors and had not been prepared to fight back. Especially in the early days of the invasion, nothing in their culture and experience had prepared them for what had happened. For the foreigners, violence was a way of life. The women said that even some of the men in Trenig had begun to be more aggressive in their behavior. At first it had been easier to separate the foreigners from the people native to Trenig, but the men from the alien land had married the women here, sometimes against their will. Now several generations later, there were many mixed marriages, and loyalties in families were confusing.

Braen continued, "If we keep all the secrets on Mona, and if the island is taken over by these men who seem intent on moving north, then everything will be lost at once. Shelagh has shown us a perspective we probably never would have discovered if we had stayed on our island, in an illusion of tranquility, spending all of our time trying to find a plan to protect the mysteries. By holding on to them so tightly, we were running the risk of having them lost forever. The more we spread the knowledge, the more difficult it will be for our ways to be completely destroyed. I do think that it is important for us to keep our activity secret, even though that may be increasingly difficult. If the men don't know what is happening, maybe they'll stop worrying about it."

"What about the stone circles? I grieve every time I think that the circles are being destroyed." Henith looked toward the cliff where the stone circle protected by Shelagh was. It was not as large as the one at the center of Mona, but it was more impressive than most of the circles they had seen on their journey. The tallest stone was taller than Braen, but most of the stones were the height of Henith. Henith and Braen were certain that this was the circle on their ancient drawing, which made it the circle farthest south on the map.

"I don't know, but we need to find a way to protect those stones that are still standing."

Even if the ways of Trenig were changing, Braen felt certain that if the women continued to practice the mysteries in secret, and if more and more women learned about the mysteries, then maybe most of the mysteries would be protected, especially the craft of healing. The women here weren't as skilled in all the other mysteries as they were in healing, but they had been very willing students. Braen had learned that many women from Lintern had studied here during the past decades, a very courageous act, considering how treacherous it had become for women to travel unescorted. Many of them could not participate in the moon rituals back in their villages, however, because of the danger of being visible. Braen knew that strength came through celebrating together and worried about the lack of opportunity for most of them to gather in larger groups, given their plan of secret conspiracy.

"Are we coming back?" Henith looked at Braen in wonder, handing her some of the purple flowers she had picked. A shiver passed over Braen as if a cool breeze had unexpectedly blown.

"We have to leave soon, but I don't think it will be forever." Braen wondered if she were having a foretelling or whether she was just saying that to make herself and Henith feel better. In many ways, leaving here was more difficult than leaving Mona. When they had anticipated leaving Mona, it was to go on a great adventure. They had felt proud that Morgan had chosen them particularly for this mission, not realizing until they had been here for several weeks how arduous this type of wandering was.

In their innocence they also had not been aware of how dangerous it had been for two women to travel together without a male escort. The stories these women had told however, had caused Henith and Braen to reconsider their attitude toward these strangers. Braen still thought of them as strangers, foreigners, and newcomers, even though some had been in southern Trenig for at least two generations. Braen had been surprised to learn that Tana's father was one of the foreigners who had married a woman native to Trenig. That explained some of Tana's ease with the strangers and some of her reluctance about participating in the moon rituals at Megen's circle. But she wasn't hostile to Megen, and she even encouraged other women to keep the old ways.

"When I was younger I wanted to spend the rest of my life in the peace of Mona, but now I see that wherever I am doing the work of the Goddess, I will be happy." Henith leaned back against the rock where Braen was sitting, close enough to feel the comfort of Braen's aura surrounding her.

"I'm glad we chose to stay here instead of returning to Boscawen," Braen said, enjoying the closeness of Henith.

"I was not looking forward to the instruction. I feel we know as much now about their religion, as if we had had their lessons, maybe we have even learned more." Henith smiled at the possibility of having learned more about the men's religion from the women here than from the men themselves.

"I wonder what happened to Talendar. Remember he said he was going north to marry a woman and convert the town," Braen said, not seeing the faraway look that had come into Henith's eyes.

Henith's barely audible voice sounded as if she were a hundred years away. "He caused such strange feelings in me. I was attracted and repelled both at the same time. I've never had those feelings before. What was also very strange was that I couldn't bear to listen to what he said without getting really angry." She remembered the night when he held her hand in his cabin.

Braen looked at the back of Henith's hair; her small shoulders seemed to cave in as she spoke just above a whisper. "What kind of feelings?" Braen asked.

Henith was embarrassed, wishing she hadn't said anything, "There was something about the way he looked at me. When I looked into his eyes, my stomach did strange things. It was like some outside force was pulling me to him."

Braen shifted her position on the rock. An edge crept into her voice that Henith could not ever remember hearing, "You never told me about your feelings for him before."

"I had so many different feelings in that town; I was having difficulty sorting them. The feelings I had about him were just among the rest." Henith turned to look at Braen. "What is it? You sound different."

"Nothing, I just do not want you running off to be his wife." She managed a slight laugh trying to lighten the weight sitting on her heart.

"Braen, what a thing to say! I never even thought about that. Marry Talendar! I'm a priestess of the Goddess. How could you even suggest such a thing?" Anger overflowed Henith. Turning from Braen, looking out over the water, she tried to hide the tears forming in the corner of her eyes.

"He's looking for a wife. Remember he said that many men had been selected to do that."

"I don't care what he said. I can't believe you would think it would be me." Several minutes passed as the silence weigh heavy between them. "I would never leave you." Henith could barely speak without choking.

"I'm sorry, Henith, I didn't mean to cause you any pain. I guess I'm just anxious about leaving. I hadn't realized how wearying all the traveling was until we arrived here. I didn't know how much I needed the quiet of a place like this and how necessary it was for me to participate in our rituals with other women."

Turning back to Braen, Henith looked at her friend. She was always startled when Braen shared her feelings of insecurity. Braen always appeared so centered, so calm, so stable. Henith had envied her, especially when her own feelings were out of control, as they had been when she and Braen were in Boscawen, and that night with Talendar on his ship.

"I am anxious, too, about leaving here and traveling back to Mona. We will have to go through many towns full of foreigners. Some of the stories we have heard about the women who have been murdered are especially frightening. It just never occurred to me that men would treat women that way. I guess I'm beginning to understand fear for the first time." The moment of tension slid away, and Henith moved closer to Braen, just barely touching.

"Yet, the women we have been teaching live with it all the time, and still they are able to risk coming here and learning about the ways of the Goddess." The remaining tension floated away on the breeze that had begun to rustle the leaves on the trees east of the garden.

"If what Talendar said is true, we will see many men from the new religion as we travel north." Henith noticed an uncomfortable feeling in her throat at the voicing of his name. "We will have to be more cautious than we were traveling south. Do you still think we should go to Lintern?" Henith was not looking forward to all the confusion of the big town. From the stories she had heard, she knew she would not be happy there.

"I'm not sure there is much sense in going there anymore. We probably will not learn more about it than we have already learned by being here and listening to the stories." Braen smiled at Henith's reluctance to go near the town.

"I'm thankful we found Shelagh. These women were able to teach us much from their experiences. Life for women is so different here compared to life in the north. Sometimes I can't believe how easy it was for the ways of the foreigners to take over. They are so violent, especially towards the women."

"But you heard the stories. The men with their priests would come into a town or village, immediately kill the wise women in the town, and then the other women became fearful. I guess it was easier to acquiesce than to run the risk of being killed themselves."

"I would never acquiesce. I would never give in to their ways," Henith said indignantly.

"Henith, you do not know that for sure. We have never been in a situation where someone was physically threatening us. We don't know what we would do. We have been taught not to harm another human being. So in a violent situation we might decide that the best strategy is not to fight back. Taking the ways of the Goddess into hiding is a good plan. It has some danger attached to it, but just think of how many women are still practicing the craft, when we thought that our ways had been completely eliminated in this part of Trenig. There is something hopeful about the idea." Braen got up from the rock.

"Do you think we should go northeast from here?" Henith asked, following Braen back down the path toward the house. "I guess I would like to reach the eastern shore of Trenig before too many moons have passed, and then go northwest from there"

"Shelagh thought that reaching the east coast would take at least six moons, especially if we were delayed anywhere along the way. Then six more moons back to Mona. We may be able to be back home in a year, maybe even in time for the Great Spring Rite."

Henith stopped on the path. "Home. I had almost come to call this home. Do you think we will see Shelagh again after we leave?" Henith hesitated. "Braen," she almost shouted. Braen turned around, wondering what had happened. "Braen, wouldn't it be wonderful if we could take Shelagh to Mona?"

"What about her work here? She wouldn't want to leave that," Braen said with some concern, not wanting the women to abandon their learning.

"There are many gifted women here. They could carry on without her for a while," Henith replied quickly, the excitement taking hold of her.

The idea was beginning to send a thrill through Braen, too. "Do you think she is strong enough for that long journey?"

"Maybe we could acquire a cart and a horse. The foreigners travel that way." Henith was getting more excited. She started to dance in the path, her hair in a happy state of confusion.

"We don't know the first thing about horses and carts. How would we ever take care of a horse?" Catching Henith's joy and laughing, Braen pretended to gallop ahead.

"I don't know, but wouldn't it be a thrill for Shelagh to go to Mona? After all these years, she could fulfill her life's longing."

Henith allowed the joy of the plan to carry her down the path.

Chapter 8

"It's been many years since I passed through these stones." Henith and Braen watched Shelagh caress the tall stones that had guarded her domain for so long.

Tears formed in Henith's eyes, looking first at Shelagh and then at Braen; leaving the comfort and joy of this place was far more painful than Henith had anticipated. Gradually the two younger women joined Shelagh at the stones. Holding hands and stretching their arms wide they encircled the stone. As they joined hands, a shock of energy rushed through Henith. Looking at Braen, smiling in recognition, all the fear Henith had dissolved in the ecstasy of the moment. Henith closed her eyes as she felt as if she were being pulled out of the top of her head. There ahead of her, flying above the trees, were Shelagh and Braen. She offered no resistance to the sensations splitting her in two. She flew up to Braen and held her hand. Spirit flying with Braen was always so easy. Shelagh was high above. As they floated up to her, they could see the joy that radiated from her face. Her face was an eternal face. In one instant it looked like the face of a newborn, smooth and soft and pink with big round eyes seeing into the universe. In another instant it was the face of a woman older than time itself, mirroring the pain and sorrow of hundreds of lifetimes of women. The past and the future became one in her face. Time ceased and all women's sufferings and joys could be seen in her eyes.

Some noise outside of Henith's consciousness caused her to look away from the face of Shelagh and down toward the earth. As the noise grew louder, Braen and Shelagh heard it also. Letting go of each other jolted them back into their bodies.

Braen said, "We mustn't be seen here. Let us hide in the trees behind the protection of the stones."

Without a word Shelagh and Henith followed Braen back from the road and into a thicket just far enough from the road that no one could see them unless they were specifically looking for them.

Braen gasped as she watched the men and horses and wagons move along the road in the direction of Lintern, coming from Boscawen. There were so many of them. The place where the women were hiding was at the bend in the road and allowed them the opportunity of seeing in both directions.

Henith could feel Braen sending a wall of energy along the edge of the road just outside the two standing stones, and joined her in drawing the protective power. She could feel Shelagh doing the same. At one point she thought that the men must be blind not to see the stones and the path that they protected. She tried to keep her mind focused on protecting the stones and the path to Shelagh's home and circle, while the men continued to walk past seemingly unaware of the wall of energy that the women were sending. On they marched, past the three women in the thicket.

It was long after the last ones were well down the road that Braen released the energy that she had been holding. Feeling her release, Shelagh and Henith also let go. Braen lay on the ground, rolling on her side. She pulled her knees up and was instantly asleep.

"She has a power I have never seen before," Shelagh said as she folded her cloak and put it under the sleeping woman's head.

Henith sat down beside Braen totally drained herself. "Yes, I know two others who may equal her, Morgan and my mother, Canth." Henith looked at Braen with awe, thanksgiving, and love. Braen never boasted of her skill and to look at her sleeping here in the thicket one would never suspect that she was one of the most intensely powerful women in all of Trenig. The skill she had at drawing and holding the energy was incredible.

"We need to let her sleep awhile until she regains her strength." Shelagh advised, looking at the two young priestesses who had come to take her back to Mona.

"What about Jenli? She will be waiting for us. Do you think you can help me contact her by mind-speaking?" Henith inquired, wanting to rest also.

"She is not very skilled as a sender, but she has received messages from me on occasion. Between us maybe we can contact her. We also should rest a while. These old bones aren't used to all of this activity in the outside world. Let us tell her to meet us when the sun is high. That will give us some time to rest. We should also warn her about all the men on this road. She should stay out of sight of them if she can."

Henith focused her attention on Jenli. She was unsure if she had enough strength left to contact someone who had not developed the skill to receive. Henith knew from her moontime with the mind-speaking mysteries that the process demanded far less energy when the persons communicating with each other were both skilled. Henith's body was already tired from the power drawing she had just done with Braen and Shelagh.

"Help me reach her, Shelagh. There is a great interference between us. It could be that group of men that passed; they may be upsetting the channel. I've never tried to find a specific woman in a crowd of men before."

"I will do my best, but this is not one of the mysteries we've developed very well here. It wasn't until you came that we practiced regularly."

"Someone is receiving me. I hope it's Jenli, but it feels different somehow. Can you help me?"

"The person you have is a powerful receiver, but it is not Jenli. Let it go, Henith, quickly."

Henith let go, her body started to shake. "Who was that? Are there any other women around here that are good receivers besides the ones I know? I don't think it was any of them. The ones I practiced with I think I would recognize."

"The only women I know are the ones that have studied with me. I doubt if you picked up one of them. I don't think it was a woman."

Henith stared at Shelagh in disbelief, "What? How can a man be a receiver?" Henith had never considered the possibility that a man might also have some skills in the mysteries of the Goddess. The idea was unthinkable.

"Let us try again to reach Jenli." Henith and Shelagh closed their eyes and focused their minds on Jenli. In a few minutes Henith opened her eyes.

"I think we reached her, but she didn't send back, so I'm not sure. I'm exhausted, we need to rest. The worst that can happen is she'll have to wait for us longer than she thought. I hope she doesn't worry when we're late and try to find us. It would not do well for her to come too near here with the horse and wagon. We would not want to jeopardize this sacred path by running the risk of anyone seeing us here. Let us rest."

In less than a minute Henith and Shelagh joined Braen in a deep sleep.

Chapter 9

"I hope Jenli was able to reach the side road before that troop of men passed," Shelagh said, walking around a tree that was blocking the path. "We will have to be cautious on main roads and stay off them as much as possible."

Henith followed Shelagh around the tree, looking back at Braen some distance behind.

"We should be reaching the cottage in a few minutes. This path comes out on the road just south of the cottage. Jenli should be there if she didn't run into any trouble on the main road," Shelagh continued, leading the women down the path that looked abandoned.

"Braen, are you feeling unwell?" Henith asked as Braen reached the others.

"I'm alright. I'm just not practiced in expending so much energy in such a short time. I was unaware of how long it takes to recover. In training we practiced, but it wasn't the same. We cast protective circles around stones, plants, animals and the women on Mona, but never in a real situation, never against an enemy and never against so much male energy. It was a real learning experience for me." Braen walked in silence for a few minutes before she continued, "If we ever meet a group of men like that again, I will have to be careful. I realized that I could not hold them off forever, and that if I do expend that amount of energy I need a great deal of time to recover. I also realized that, even though that group was not coming directly at us, the collective strength of their undirected energy was overwhelming."

"I see the road ahead. I doubt if anyone besides Jenli will be here. This side road ends just north of here and this cottage has not had people living here since Jenli was a baby. Unfortunately, the road may be too rough for a wagon."

Emerging onto the road, the women cautiously looked in both directions. The cottage, in need of much repair, was to the left, and to the right was an overgrown road showing that a wagon had passed recently.

"Jenli must be here." Henith was surprised at the relief she experienced at hearing those words. Being away from the safe haven of Shelagh's circle, being out in southern Trenig and having seen that troop of men had sent an uneasiness in her.

As they headed toward the cottage, Jenli appeared from the doorway.

"Jenli, have you been waiting long?"

"I was worried when you didn't arrive an hour ago. Earlier I thought I heard you telling me you would be late, but I didn't trust myself, so I have been here for several hours. When you didn't arrive on time, I thought maybe you had sent the message. Then when several more hours had passed, I began to worry again. I knew you would come through on the footpath, and I didn't want to leave the wagon. I also didn't want to miss you by going around on the road. So I waited. I wasn't expecting the first message, so my mind was not clear for receiving. For the last hour I have tried to stay clear in case you sent another one.

Henith laughed, "Why didn't I think of that? It never occurred to send you a second message." Henith hugged Jenli.

Braen embraced Jenli next, and then sat on the edge of a broken step, still weakened by the morning's experience. Looking at Braen, Henith was concerned by how pale her face was. Braen had said something earlier that made Henith reflect on their experience in Trenig. It was true that everything they had learned, every skill they had practiced, every mystery they had mastered, worked perfectly on Mona with women with similar skills and knowledge. At Shelagh's circle, life was relatively simple and uncomplicated, even healing was easy, primarily because the women were healthy and needed very little medicine. Drawing the power at a moon ritual was a joyful experience because other women were present and there was no resistance, but this morning's expenditure of energy was difficult and exhausting.

"Did you see the troop of men on the road?" Shelagh asked, sitting next to Braen on the steps.

"Which one? Five large troops have passed through on their way to Lintern in the last few days."

"Five!" Henith tried to calculate five times what she had seen this morning. "That must be over one thousand men. What is happening, do you know?"

"The stories around the town are that the foreigners are preparing to take all of Trenig under their control. Northern Trenig so far has been left relatively alone with just a few men and their priests scattered throughout the area." Jenli looked at her new friends as she replied.

"Do you think we should continue to the northeast?" Henith wondered.

"I do not see why we should change our plan, except for staying off the major roads. Maybe we can even prepare the people," Braen responded as she started toward the wagon.

"But we don't know for sure when all this will take place and what their plans are," Henith replied, following Braen. "I have that strong feeling of wishing I were back on Mona away from all this." A wistful look came over Henith.

"I think Jenli's right, we might be able to prepare some of the women at least for what might happen." Braen stopped and looked at Henith, knowing that they had to continue as they had planned, even though the task that lay before would be difficult.

"But we can't save all of Trenig." Henith surprised even herself with her own comment, feeling embarrassed as soon as the words were out of her mouth.

"No, but we might be able to save some of the people. I suggest we continue our original plan for now, going northeast as far as we can for five moons, then turning northwest to Mona. Hopefully we will arrive on Mona in time for the Great Spring Rite. We may have to adjust the plan as we travel, but with the wagon it should be easier than walking as Henith and I did." Braen was beginning to regain some color in her cheeks.

"I have the clothes we talked about. I think we will be far less noticeable in these." Jenli held up a skirt.

"We will keep our robes for the moon ritual. Let us pray that we will find a circle by the next full moon and that we will be able to gather women for the rite."

Putting on a headscarf similar to the ones the women in the area wore Shelagh asked, "Were you able to gather any more information about roads and villages in eastern Trenig?"

"Not much more than what we had gathered the other evening when we had the map drawing session. Except for the foreigners, the people don't tend to travel much. I tried to talk to the men at Tana's, but I was afraid of raising too much suspicion. So what I gathered isn't much better than what we already knew."

"I would still like to find this other stone circle that is marked on our ancient map." Henith found a scarf similar to the one Shelagh had tied on her head.

"Trying to put the old map together with the sketchy new information is difficult, but we can at least go in that general direction. There is a town named Merchlyn I've heard about in eastern Trenig. It's near the coast. I've also heard that it is to be one of the first places in the east that the foreigners intend to take completely. I heard two of the men at Tana's say that the plan was to take the biggest towns first and then the villages," Jenli offered.

"I still don't understand why they want to take over Trenig. What good is it going to do them?" Henith had completed dressing and was climbing into the wagon.

Shelagh replied, "They think their god wants them to do it. Remember for each conversion to the new religion they believe that they will be rewarded in the afterlife."

"What kind of god is it that causes men to do violence, to destroy and murder? It doesn't sound like any kind of god I want to have anything to do with," Henith directed her comments to the sky and not to anyone in particular.

"Are we ready? We still have a few hours left to travel today. We do have to go on the main road for about an hour, where you saw the men this morning. Then we can turn north where the main road continues on to Lintern."

"Do you think there will by any more men on the road today?" Henith asked Jenli.

"Probably not. They mostly leave Boscawen in the morning in order to arrive in Lintern by dark the next night. I think we are well behind the group that left this morning. Besides meeting a few travelers, I think we will be safe leaving now."

Braen looked at Jenli. How different she was from the quiet waitress at Tana's, now a strong woman preparing a horse and wagon for an unknown journey.

"You will have to teach us about the horses and how to drive the wagon, Jenli."

Jenli laughed, "Don't worry, I expect we will all be horse masters by the time we get to Mona. You know it's strange, I never knew of Mona before you arrived and now I have the strangest sensation that I'm going home. I am so happy that you asked me to accompany you, after all I'm not a priestess of Mona. I am truly honored." Jenli looked at each of the women and then at the ground.

Braen helped Shelagh into the wagon. The four women were silent for several minutes wondering what lay ahead, thinking of Mona. The sounds of the horse set them in motion again. Braen joined Jenli on the seat for her first lesson.

Chapter 10

The sun was nearing the western horizon as the women approached Merchlyn.

"It must be at least two more hours before we get there. We probably should find a place to camp tonight and wait until mid-morning to arrive in town. It might not be good for us to arrive too late. Four women arriving in the evening might raise too much suspicion," Jenli suggested. "We could stay in those woods I see ahead there. Maybe we can get far enough off the road so we can be safe." She encouraged the horse to trot.

Henith agreed. "Looks like a grove of oak trees. That would be a wonderful strengthening place to stay."

Braen and Shelagh looked at each other in an instant of recognition.

"The road is to the right before the grove. It goes east for a while and then there is a path into the grove on the left," Braen said as if from a different world.

Henith recognized her friend's tone. "Braen do you think there is a circle there?" Excitement in her voice.

Shelagh responded, "We have to go there. Something is pulling at us. I can sense it, too."

Jenli and Henith peered ahead, but the road Braen described was not visible yet. It had been three moons since they had found a stone circle intact enough to be recognizable. The moon would be full tonight and Henith longed to be in a circle. As they approached the grove, Henith sensed what Braen and Shelagh were experiencing.

"Oh, Braen, there must be a circle here somewhere."

The road appeared barely visible unless one knew to look for it. The grass had grown tall from lack of use. One more abandoned circle. The women in this area must have been separated from their center of power, like women all over Trenig.

Shelagh, sensing her outrage, turned and crept up behind her, putting her hands on the young woman's shoulders. She commented, "Henith, the destruction of our ways is difficult for us to watch, but I know they won't be lost forever. Think of a seed that falls to the ground. In some ways the seed dies and is destroyed as a seed, but it is being nourished underground by Mother Earth and may lay in the darkness for sometime before it begins to grow again."

Jenli turned onto the road. "Wait," Braen said and climbed down from the wagon. "Go on slowly, come and help me send strength into these grasses," she said, addressing Henith and Shelagh. "We cannot let anyone know that someone has been using this road."

The three women walked behind the wagon that Jenli was slowly guiding down the hardly recognizable road. The grasses responded to the compassion of the three women and within minutes it was impossible to tell that any wagon had passed that way.

They went on this way for quite some distance, and as the road started to enter the grove, a quiet came over the women as each settled into her own private awe. The intensity of the silence in this place was breathtaking. Jenli stopped the horse as the road turned into a path. She climbed down to join the others.

Shelagh had started down the path, a calmness surrounding her in such a way that she appeared to be floating. The others followed, leaving the horse and wagon at the edge of the trees.

The path had a slight incline and turned gradually to the right. Although it was impossible to see what was at the end of the path, they walked with a sure knowing of what they were going to find.

A gentle breeze caused the leaves to dance on the trees around them. The excitement in Henith was mounting, but so was a calm. She knew there was a circle here. She prayed to the Goddess that it was still intact, that it hadn't been destroyed. Shelagh slowed as they came into the clearing as the others joined her. Ahead of them was a circle similar in size to the one Shelagh had found years ago south of Boscawen. All the stones seemed to be there, and they were standing; none had been knocked over or moved. Henith gave thanks for the gift that she and her companions had just received. Jenli started to walk towards the circle. Braen reached out to gently hold her back.

"Not yet. This is a sacred place. Let us approach it as we were taught. I do have the urge to run up and lean against one of the stones also, but would it not be more powerful to approach the stones at sunset as priestesses? We should spend our time in preparation. It is still early in the day. After we have walked around the circle at the edge of the trees, let us leave and prepare ourselves."

"You are right, Braen, we have been travelling so long in alien lands, our rituals have become haphazard. We do need time to prepare ourselves." Henith took Braen's hand, feeling the joy that it caused in her body as if it were the first time.

"Shall we find a place to set up camp? We won't be able to go into town in the middle of the night." Jenli always asked the practical questions, while the others would have been content to gaze at the stones for the rest of the day.

Henith chuckled, "Yes, you're right. We should spend the next hours setting up our camp and planning the evening's ritual. I would like it to be special."

Shelagh observed, "The four of us have never done the moon ritual alone in an intact circle. That in and of itself will be unique."

A thrill went through the little group, each person feeling the anticipation of the evening. Braen had started to walk to the edge of the trees, noting where the major points were. The others followed slowly, captured by the beauty of this field and its guardian stones and the dense grove of oak trees that sealed it on all sides from the outside world.

"Did you notice anything strange about this circle as we walked around it?" Braen asked the others.

"I was so caught by the beauty, I admit that I wasn't looking for details," Henith replied, trying to see what Braen had seen.

Shelagh responded, "It felt to me as if it wasn't abandoned. Possibly someone or even many people had been there recently."

"That was my sense. It is well hidden and well protected, but I don't think it is abandoned." Braen continued looking for signs of use.

"Does that mean we shouldn't have our ritual here tonight?" A sadness crept into Henith's voice.

"Not necessarily, but we have to approach with some caution. We don't know who has been here recently and for what purpose."

"Suppose it is a group of women like we found at Shelagh's. Wouldn't that be wonderful?" Excitement returning to Henith's voice.

"Yes, but we can't just take over their space and rituals. They won't know who we are and we may frighten them."

Reaching the wagon, Jenli suggested, "I think we should try to find a place that is not so easily accessible by the road, even though it is only visible to those who know that it exists."

"Let us search around. Maybe there is a place we can stay where the wagon and horse will be more hidden."

Jenli found a small clearing well off the path to the south of where they were. It would be difficult getting the wagon to it because of the steep incline, but with care she thought she would be able to do it. By carrying most of their belongings up the trail by hand, Jenli was able to guide the horse and wagon over the worst part of the trail. The clearing was small but far enough from what they determined were paths that might be used, if their suspicions about the recent use of the stone circle were true.

Jenli and Henith made a small dam in the brook that was at the edge of the clearing for a pool for their horse to drink from.

Working quickly, Shelagh and Henith set up two small tents, one for Henith and Braen, the other for Shelagh and Jenli. An efficient routine had developed during their last months of travel; while Braen put the supplies back in the wagon, Jenli set up a cooking fire.

"It is pleasant here. I can't believe we found the circle just in time for our moon ritual." Henith sat next to Braen with her meal. "But I should know by now your incredible skill," she said, smiling intently at Braen.

Braen was looking deep into the woods, a concerned look in her eyes.

"Aren't you eating, Braen?" Henith continued, looking at her friend, detecting her concern. "What is it? Is something wrong? Do you see something?"

Braen looked at Henith, "It's a sense I have that won't let me go. I don't see anything, I just feel a foreboding. I can't get it into focus. I don't want to spoil our ritual, but I do sense that caution is very important."

Shelagh joined them. "I couldn't help overhearing what you said to Henith. I also have a foreboding about this place. It isn't tangible yet, but caution is in order."

"Should we move?" Henith questioned with some concern, reluctant to give up the idea of celebrating the moonrise this evening.

"No, I think we are supposed to be here. And I don't think the foreboding is about tonight. It is more like something in the very near future. Maybe next week or the week after that."

"I agree," said Shelagh. "It feels more in the future than tonight. Let us be alert to any signs that we may be given in warning. These premonitions are for our protection."

"Tonight, after our celebration, let us read the ancient stones. Maybe we will be given a sign through them," Braen suggested.

The four women planned their ceremony and then kept a silent vigil for the remainder of the time before the ritual. They had agreed to wear their ceremonial robes and to meet at the northern point of the tree-edged field just before sunset. Their silence would be broken by the casting of the circle by Braen.

❧☙

Henith had been sitting on her protective blanket leaning against a tree for an hour when she thought she heard something in the woods to her right. A twig snapped and then another. She peered into the woods, straining her eyes, but couldn't see anything or anyone. Picking up her blanket she cautiously went toward the sound that she had heard. She heard another sound further on, but still was unable to find the source of the noise. Aware of the danger that they may be in, she was undecided whether to continue to chase the illusive sound alone or return and find Braen and the others. They had agreed to remain in silence until sunset, and she did not want to interfere with the other's private silence for some fictitious fear of her own. She continued further from the camp and towards the circle.

Approaching the circle, she thought she heard the sound of a woman's voice. Knowing it wasn't one of her three companions, she crept closer to the circle. Standing behind a large oak tree, Henith heard more voices. Her heart began to pound in her chest, and she found that she was clutching the blanket very tightly. She slowly moved to a tree that was closer to the edge of the clearing, going as far as she dared without risking detection. What greeted her took her breath away. Sitting in a small circle, several women had gathered just north of the stones.

As she watched, she noticed that another woman appeared out of the woods and joined their circle. The woman stood and there was much hugging and laughing and they sat down and became intensely involved in their discussion again.

Henith was curious about these woman and their discussion, and wanted to join them, but wasn't sure if she should just appear out of the woods. She continued watching the group and tried to decide what the best way to approach them was. She considered returning to the camp to alert the others and to tell them that they probably would not be celebrating the moon alone.

From where she was hiding, she could only hear snatches of the conversation.

"I'm visiting my aunt."

"Again? I thought you visited her last month."

"I did, she's still sick."

Everyone laughed.

"I don't think Ursula will be here tonight."

"Oh!"

"Her husband became very suspicious last month and accused her of seeing another man and threatened to beat her if he found her running off again."

The group was very quiet for a moment.

The voices continued so softly Henith couldn't detect what they were saying.

Another woman appeared from nowhere. Henith had been so intent on trying to hear the conversation that she hadn't noticed where the woman had come from. She was very tall with long deep auburn hair. Henith's heart skipped a beat. For a moment she thought it was Braen, with the lowering sun casting a golden glow around her head. The women all greeted her as they had greeted the first one.

Henith sensed someone behind her before she heard the sound, and turned just in time to see a very big woman about ready to grab her.

Henith stood quickly and covered herself with her blanket. The woman froze with her hand in mid-air. Neither woman knew quite what to do next.

"Greetings, friend," Henith ventured.

The woman lowered her arm, staring in bewilderment at this strange woman calling her friend.

"What are you doing here? Spying on us? Are you from around here? You don't look very familiar."

Henith was undecided about which story to tell, the one that the four had agreed to and had been using in every place they had been in the last few moons, or the truth. The size of this woman was somewhat intimidating, and she shuddered to think that this woman might have treated her roughly.

"I'm not spying," Henith tried gently.

"Then what were you doing hiding behind this tree trying to listen to the others?" The tone and level of this woman was different than Henith was used to hearing.

Her loud deep voice caused the others to come running.

"Dana, is that you? What is all the noise about?" The group reached the pair and stopped. Some of the women gasped.

"Who is this?"

"I don't know yet, but I bet she's a spy. She hasn't said much," Dana answered, causing more anxiety in the already over-anxious group.

"Don't be afraid," Henith said as calmly as possible, "I'm not a spy."

The tall woman, the one who reminded Henith of Braen, was staring at her and her blanket. Henith recognized the intensity of the message. She was testing her. Henith knew she could trust this woman. She replied, "You are the High Priestess of this circle. I am Henith, priestess of Mona. Greetings in the name of the Goddess."

"I am Zeena. Welcome, Henith."

The other women stared as the two embraced.

"I apologize for appearing to spy, but we have been traveling in secret and we have to be very cautious. I heard voices and had come to see who was here. We had been hoping to celebrate the moon tonight."

"We! Does that mean you are not alone?" Zeena asked, looking around.

"There are four of us. Braen and I are priestesses from Mona. We have been traveling throughout Trenig gathering information about the invasion of these foreigners with their new god. On our way we found two women, Shelagh and Jenli. Shelagh is an old woman whose dream is to see Mona. Braen and I want to help her fulfill that dream. Jenli is one of the women from Shelagh's circle that is helping us with the more practical aspects of getting around in Trenig." Henith smiled when she thought of how useful Jenli's knowledge was.

The women started to ask questions all at once.

Zeena interceded, "Is that any way to treat a priestess from Mona? Come, let us sit awhile and calm ourselves from all this excitement. Then you can go and return with your friends for our celebration."

The women walked from the woods into the field and sat where they had been sitting before.

Zeena asked, "Would you do me the honor of drawing the circle tonight, Henith?"

Henith smiled at this woman. "Thank you for trusting me with so great an honor, but if you would allow me one request, my friend, Braen, truly has the gift of power drawing."

"We would be honored to have Braen draw the power. Would you then invoke the power of the east?"

"We do not want to invade your sacred rites. We are guests only."

"We are honored by your presence. There has not been a priestess of Mona here since before my mother became High Priestess of this circle. I became High Priestess after my mother became too frail to make the journey here from town every month. I am afraid we may have lost some of the old ways. I am not sure we do all of the rituals correctly. We couldn't meet at all for many years when the foreigners were first in our town. It became very dangerous. A few of us met in twos and threes when our husbands were out, but nothing formal. Then the ten of us, nine of whom you see, decided to try our monthly meetings. Getting away once a month has been very difficult. There are only so many sick aunts we can visit."

The women chuckled.

"For example, Ursula can't be here tonight because her husband is very suspicious. There are many other women who come once in a great while, but we are the core group."

Zeena addressed three of the women. "Do you feel all right if we invite our guests to lead us tonight?"

The three nodded agreement.

"Zeena, there are only four of us. If Braen leads us as High Priestess, with your blessing, we would welcome you to invoke the power of the north."

A mist blurred Zeena's eyes. Clearing her throat, she said, "I think we need to begin our preparation, and Henith needs time to return to her companions. Let us go now."

Henith and Zeena embraced as the others dispersed to different places in the trees outside the field surrounding the stones.

Henith was feeling light-headed as she reached where her friends were preparing. In as few words as possible, Henith described what had happened and how they were leading these women in the full moon celebration.

Each nodded agreement without discussion. They waited while Henith changed into her ceremonial robes. Each was dressed in a long white gown. Braen's cape was like an ice blue crystal, her long, dark auburn hair falling down her back. Shelagh, her face ageless, wore a wool cloak of dark forest green. Jenli's cape was the color of the fog that Henith remembered from Mona; it was not blue, not grey, but both. Henith chose her favorite cape, the color of a purple midnight.

When she was ready, Henith led the group around to the north. Zeena was waiting for them. The others had already gathered inside the stone circle. Zeena nodded at Henith as she approached. A shiver passed through Zeena as she looked at the others, so beautiful in their colorful robes and white gowns. Zeena joined the line in front of Braen and behind Jenli. The five women with their robes flowing in the gentle evening breeze approached the northern stones just as the glow of the full moon began to be visible in the eastern sky.

The women in the circle had also dressed in white flowing gowns. Henith heard a slight gasp from the group and knew that Braen must have entered the circle. A thrill went through her body and she sent a quick thank you to the Goddess for the gift she had been given in being Braen's companion.

Henith walked the circle just inside the stones, starting toward the east. Zeena had stayed in the north with Braen. Jenli would stay in the south and Shelagh in the west. When Shelagh reached the west, Braen began to cast the circle, each priestess invoking the power of the four directions as Braen passed. The intensity of the power of the circle Braen cast brought tears to Henith's eyes as she thought about these women risking their lives to come together. A shudder of rage overwhelmed her for an instant. These women were not hurting anyone. Why did they have to be persecuted?

❧❦

"If you arrive mid-morning tomorrow you will be least noticed," Zeena suggested to the newcomers, as the group of women, sitting in a tight circle in the shadow of the northern stone, shared stories.

"But where do you think we should stay?" Jenli questioned.

"Why do we need to go into the town anyway? We already have found what we came to find." Amazed still by their courage, Henith looked around at the women she had just spent the last four hours with.

"Henith may be right. Our mission is to learn about the new religion that is taking over Trenig, to locate as many stone circles as possible, to determine what the needs of the women in each area are, and to try to support them as best as we can. It seems to me that we may be able do that by staying here," Braen looked at Zeena, silhouetted across the circle from her. Their eyes held for a minute.

Shelagh watched Henith as the look between these two beautiful women, almost mirrors of each other, went unnoticed by most except Henith.

"How dangerous is it for each of you to meet with us here? Would you be safer if we went to your town?"

"It is very dangerous for us to be here, even once a month. The new laws have made it all but impossible to travel safely and at will. My husband would become very suspicious if I had to visit my aunt more often. He already is displeased that I do not share his bed this night," the woman sitting to the left of Braen responded.

"Can women gather during the daytime hours?"

"Possibly, but the four of you will be an unusual event in our town. I'm not sure how four strange women unattended by male escorts will be treated. With suspicion, I expect. And that will make it even more difficult for us to be seen with you."

"How long do you plan to stay here?"

"We only stay a few days, because we are trying to reach Mona in time for the Spring Rite," Jenli offered.

"If we can find a way to keep everyone safe, I hope you will stay longer. You have so much to teach us. I know of many more women who would risk coming if they knew who you were. We have tried to keep up our skill in all of the mysteries, but without any guidance many have fallen away." Zeena was staring at Braen. "Never have I been able to draw the power like you did tonight, Braen. I could learn much from you."

Henith shifted in her place. She felt proud that Zeena had recognized Braen's skill and beauty, and she tried to dismiss the uneasiness she felt watching the two of them communicate with looks.

"It is getting late, and we need to determine a plan for the next few days. Should we go to the town or stay here?"

Jenli stood and started to walk around the group. "I have an idea. Maybe we should do both. Two of us stay here and two go to town. Two would raise much less suspicion than four."

A few of the women nodded in agreement.

Jenli continued, "Shelagh and Braen could go to town and visit Zeena. Braen could be Zeena's cousin without anyone asking questions. They look enough alike to be sisters. Shelagh could be Braen's mother and Zeena's aunt, who have come from Lintern for a visit. That was part of our original story anyway. Shelagh's husband could have recently died and she and her daughter needed to leave Lintern because of lack of funds. They're here visiting her only other known relative. Henith and I could stay here. Once a week we could go closer to town and women could visit us in some barn or someone's house on the edge of town."

"Your idea has merit, Jenli," Zeena smiled.

Dana spoke for the first time, "My house is between here and the town, and it is off the main road. We could meet there. It is apparently permissible for women to come to my house to purchase herbs for cooking and other things. Many women still come there. Jenli and Henith can stay with me. Only the women who come to my house would know of their existence. Bringing women here in the next few days would be very difficult."

Henith found herself not liking this plan, but was unable to raise a rational argument against it. "What about the horse and wagon?"

"They could come to my house. I have a large shed where we can keep them out of sight."

"Zeena, you said that you wished we could teach the women some of the mysteries. If we stayed only a few days, we wouldn't be able to do very much. Do you and Dana think you could keep us longer without too much risk to yourselves?"

"I could manage," Dana said. "The authorities don't pay much attention to me for some reason."

"My husband may find it strange that I haven't mentioned my cousin and aunt before and all of a sudden they move in."

A few women laughed. One said, "Tell him Shelagh was your father's oldest sister and left our town with one of the foreigners and was a disgrace in the family."

"That's a good story," another added.

More details followed, each woman playing the game of adding to the story. Shelagh laughed and then was serious.

"Wait, please. If we make the story too complicated, none of us will remember the details. Let us keep it as simple as possible."

"Shelagh's right. Let the story be uncomplicated. The more details, the more chances for being caught in the fabrication."

"Then do we have a plan? Shelagh and Braen will come to my house as relatives and Henith and Jenli will go to Dana's, hopefully undetected except to some selected women." Zeena stood.

No one offered resistance. She waited. "Let us sleep. In the morning we will begin our plan."

Henith tried without success to dismiss the discomfort in her stomach. She watched as each woman found a blanket and went to sleep, each by one of the standing stones.

Zeena explained, "It seems to give us strength to sleep close to the stones. Each woman leaves to go home by a different route at a different time. We do everything we can to avoid suspicion and to try to keep the location of this circle a secret."

Braen looked at her companions. "Maybe we should also keep this custom. In the morning we can gather our things and go into town as planned."

As much as Henith wanted to sleep by a standing stone, she realized that it would be many nights before she would be with Braen again. She found herself not looking forward to the possibility that she might not have the opportunity to see Braen for many days. She and Jenli would have to stay out of sight most of the time. Henith walked to the stone guarding the east, spread her cloak on the ground, and lay down. She put her hand on the stone and could feel its strength flow into her body, but the tears fell anyway, and she let them fall quietly and gently into the ground.

She fell into a troubled sleep. The stone she was against seemed to be moving, shaking back and forth. The whole earth was trembling. She tried rolling away because she feared that the stone was about to fall on her. Stones were falling and crashing everywhere. She called out for Braen, but Braen didn't answer. She called and called. She tried to get up, but the shaking of the earth made it difficult to stand without falling. She needed to find Braen. She knew she had been by the northern stone, but she couldn't see where the stone was. Then when she realized that it had fallen over, she screamed. She tried running to the place where Braen was, but couldn't get there. She ran and ran but didn't get any closer. She screamed again. The earth was shaking her, "Henith! Henith! Wake up!" Still she continued to shake as if propelled by some outside force. Still she continued to scream. "Henith, it's Braen. Wake up, you are dreaming."

Opening her eyes, she saw Braen's face inches away from her own. Surrounding her were other faces. As she became more awake, she recognized Shelagh and Jenli and the women of this place.

Henith fell into Braen's arms, "Oh, Braen, we do not have much time. Disaster is coming to this place. We have to prepare these women as soon as possible, before it is too late."

"I know, Henith, I feel it, too." The two women held each other for a long time. One by one the faces drifted away, leaving the two to comfort each other for the rest of the night.

Chapter 11

"What a day! I can't believe how exhausting it is teaching only one person. I appreciate my teachers in ways I never thought about before." Henith sat in Dana's kitchen drinking tea.

"Dana, you had a brilliant idea, having four different women come here every day, two in the morning and two in the afternoon. But it tires me out. Sometimes I can't remember what I've taught to whom."

"You are doing fine. I'm amazed at how much knowledge you have about the mysteries." Dana laughed out loud.

"What's so funny? Did I say something amusing?" Henith looked at the large woman sitting across the table from her.

"No, I was just remembering finding you in the woods at our circle and accusing you of being a spy."

"Well, in some ways I was spying, hoping to find out if you were still faithful to the Goddess and her ways. Not being able to trust people is very difficult for me."

"The situation has gotten worse in the last few years. According to my mother, there was a period several decades ago when the foreigners made a significant effort to take over this area, and then for some reason they gave up. Some of the foreign men stayed, some married, but much of the original violence lessened. People became less afraid. We thought that the threat to the old ways was gone, so some of the women started meeting again, but it wasn't quite how my mother had described it to me. Most of us are young, we tried to remember our mothers' and grandmothers' stories, but most of the knowledge about the mysteries was lost to us. We only have little pieces. Zeena seems to have the most skill. Her grandmother left her much knowledge. The rest of us do the best we can."

"This is how it is everywhere in Trenig, except for the far north. And I'm not sure what it is like there now. It has been almost four years since Braen and I started out on our mission."

"I hope that you can stay here and teach us for many weeks. There is much we would like to learn, even though it is very difficult for some of the women to leave their homes for any length of time. I noticed that there was more agitation in town this morning. Something is in the air I can't describe."

Henith looked at her new friend. She herself had noticed the charge in the air. Something was going to happen here. Henith thought about Braen and Shelagh, whom she had not seen for almost a week. Henith tried not to think of Zeena, because she knew that the work that they were doing here was important and there was no reason to feel jealous of Zeena.

"Well, our horse is alright in the barn, but I think she would like to get out and run for a while. Do you think that is possible, Dana?" Jenli said as she came into the room and sat next to Henith.

"Maybe there is some way for you to take her for a walk if you stay off the roads. Stay on the paths and don't go very far in that direction," Dana pointed to the northeast. "The town is that way and there are bound to be more people about. Do you think you can find your way around? You really have not had much opportunity to explore this area, being shut up in the house teaching the women all day."

"I think I will wait until it gets darker. I wouldn't want to risk exposing our hiding place. It's strange to be in hiding while at the same time visiting with so many women."

"We will have our evening meal soon. Why don't the two of you rest? It has been a strenuous week. Although, in some ways, it seems as if you have always been here teaching us."

"How long has she been away?" Henith asked looking out the window into the dark night.

"Try not to worry. If she doesn't return soon, I will go in search of her. Can you contact her with mind-speaking? Maybe you can guide her home."

"I have been trying to contact her, but there is much interference tonight. Do you think it would be possible to go to Braen and Shelagh? Braen's skill is much clearer than mine. Maybe she can get through to Jenli."

"That is a great risk. It is not safe for women to be out in the dark these days. There are many wandering men around. Sometimes I do not even feel safe here alone so far from the edge of town, but they have left me alone. Thank the Goddess." A shiver went down Dana's back.

"Do you think it would be possible for us both to go?" The thought of seeing Braen again, if only for a moment, was making her reckless.

"We couldn't see them at Zeena's. Her husband and children would be suspicious if another strange woman appeared on her doorstep."

"Could we get closer, a barn or something, and then Braen and Shelagh could slip out of the house and meet us?"

"I don't know if it's possible to do that. You haven't been in this part of Trenig. Women just don't leave their houses much except for going to market and visiting relatives. They never leave in the dark. It is dangerous and their husbands wouldn't permit it."

"But we have to find Jenli. She may have met with some misfortune. I'm very concerned that I can't get through to her at all."

Dana walked around her small kitchen, poking at things here and there. "I should never have let her take that horse for a walk. It was foolish to let her go alone."

Henith walked over to the woman who was rearranging herbs on the shelf. "Jenli is a strong woman and has a mind of her own. It may have been unwise for her to go exploring in the dark without you to guide her, but you needn't feel responsible for her actions. Maybe the two of us should go and try to find her."

"I just thought of an idea. Joice has a small barn that is far from her house in a field. They used to keep tools in it. It is much closer to Zeena's. I'm fairly sure that you and I could get to it without too much trouble. If we walk through the fields, the tall wheat will protect us. The most difficult part will be to get Shelagh and Braen out of Zeena's house undetected by her family. Can you contact Braen and have her meet us there?"

Henith laughed, "Of course, I have been so focused on trying to contact Jenli. It didn't occur to me to try to contact Braen."

"Let us go then. You can start to contact Braen on the way."

Henith smiled to herself at Dana's confidence at her skill. Henith was not used to having a world of interference to sift through. Stumbling through fields of wheat in the middle of the night needed concentration enough, but to focus on mind-speaking, even to Braen, was a challenge. She had been in contact with Braen every morning during her meditation time. They had agreed on the time. Braen would not be expecting her to try and contact her at this time of night. She may even be asleep.

Henith and Dana set out. The sky was overcast, and Henith thanked the Goddess for the extra protection of the dark. When her eyes adjusted to the night and she and Dana had set up a rhythm in their walking, Henith focused on Braen. She could not remember this type of interference with mind-speaking on Mona. The only other time she had experienced this difficulty was when she and Shelagh were trying to contact Jenli before, the day that troop of men had interrupted their departure. Henith shuddered to think that this much interference might be caused by another troop of men. Henith and Dana continued on, stopping at the end of each field. Crossing between fields was the most dangerous, because they were out in the open for several yards. But the night was still and there didn't seem to be anyone around.

"It's at the edge of the next field. We are almost there," Dana whispered to Henith.

Henith breathed a sigh. She still had not been able to contact Braen. Maybe it would be easier when she wasn't also trying to concentrate on walking.

Dana slowly pushed open the door to the small barn. Only the rustling of night animals could be heard. They carefully entered the room filled with discarded farm tools, leaving very little space to stand. Henith decided that she did not want to spend much time in this cramped space.

"Dana, join me in trying to reach Braen. I have not been able to reach her yet. If we make contact, envision where we are and guide her here."

The two women pushed a few of the tools away to make a space for them to sit down. Henith was grateful that she had remembered to bring her protecting blanket with her. She spread it on the dirt floor and for the first time in her life invited another woman to sit with her on it.

᷍ꙮ᷍

"Shelagh, Shelagh, wake up!" Braen was gently shaking the old woman. "Shelagh, wake up."

Shelagh opened her eyes, "What is it, Braen? I was just having a dream. I saw Henith in a funny little house with all kinds of strange objects surrounding her. She was calling your name, over and over."

Braen almost laughed out loud. "Thank you, Shelagh. We have to go, Henith is calling me. Something has happened. We have to leave immediately."

"Where is she?"

"I'm not sure exactly, but once we get out of this house, I'm going to spirit fly and see if I can recognize the image that keeps coming into my mind."

"How are we going to get out of this house without waking everyone up?"

"We will just have to be very quiet and careful."

They had already started to put on their clothes when they heard a noise in the other room. Both women held their breath, trying not to make a sound. The footsteps were coming closer to their room.

Without hesitating, each woman slowly slipped back under the blankets, half dressed. There was a gentle knock on the door.

Braen whispered, "Enter."

Zeena quietly opened the door and walked over to Braen. "I just had a dream." Before she could go on, both Shelagh and Braen laughed quietly.

"We know, we were on our way." Braen pulled back the blanket. Shelagh got up and continued to dress.

Amazed, Zeena asked, "Where are you going in the middle of the night?"

"I'm not sure exactly, but I know Henith is calling us. We all had the same dream I expect. Did you recognize where she was? We are not familiar enough with the countryside around here to identify where she is. Maybe you could help us."

"How do you know it wasn't just a dream?"

Braen said calmly, "All three of us had the same response to the dream. The same dream. It is more than a dream. Henith is calling me."

"It looked like the barn in a field near Joice's house. It isn't too far from here. Let me guide you."

"What happens if your husband wakes and doesn't find you here? And your children?"

Zeena looked at the floor. "They won't waken."

Braen looked at this woman with new amazement.

"How did you know to give them a sleeping drug?" Braen asked.

Embarrassed Zeena continued to look at the floor. "There are times when I need to be left alone, when I do not want to be bothered. Sometimes I just want to sleep alone. I have been doing this for some time. It's just a simple mixture of hops that I add to their evening tea. They don't even notice. I've been doing it for so long. They wake up refreshed from a peaceful night's sleep. And I have been able to sleep elsewhere or have been able to do other things that I need to do."

Braen put her arm around this woman and gave her a hug. "How insightful of you to have drugged them this night. Hurry and dress. We need to go to Henith as soon as possible. Morning will be coming too soon."

Zeena pulled her nightdress over her head. Underneath she was ready.

Shelagh laughed, "Do you always sleep dressed for a journey?"

Again Zeena looked embarrassed. "I was already planning to leave later. I was just taking a little nap when I received Henith's message."

"Do you go out in the night often."

"Not often enough!"

Braen was surprised by this response and waited for more explanation, but Zeena turned and walked out of the room with Shelagh and Braen following.

Chapter 12

"What was that?" Dana said, getting up to look out of the crack left by the door that wouldn't close after so many years of disuse.

"Maybe it's Braen." Henith rose to join Dana.

"You stay here. I'll go and look. We can't have some local farmer finding you here in this old barn in the middle of the night. I'm easier to explain."

Henith knew that Dana was right, but she wanted to see Braen. The expectations of the meeting interfered with her good sense. She would have run right out into the field, forgetting that she was in hiding.

Dana slipped through the narrow opening and disappeared into the dark. Within a few minutes Henith heard many footsteps, more than enough for just Dana and Braen. She looked for a place to hide. She was afraid that she couldn't get into a safe place without making a great deal of noise. She froze in place as the sounds came closer, trying to will herself into being invisible in the shadows.

The door scraped against the floor. Henith almost laughed out loud as Dana, Braen, Shelagh, and Zeena tried to occupy a space barely big enough for one. "Oh," she exclaimed, "you all came. I was expecting only Braen."

Shelagh laughed, "You need to practice being more focused in your mind sending, Henith, you practically woke up the whole town with your message."

Henith looked embarrassed. "Well, at least you are here."

"Why did you call us, Henith?" Braen asked, sliding past Shelagh to where Henith was standing. Henith wanted to reach out and hold her friend, but that was difficult in this place.

"Jenli went riding earlier this evening after supper, and she didn't return. I tried calling her, but I couldn't reach her. I was experiencing much interference. I thought that you might be able to get through to her. You are much more skilled than I am."

"I think we should move from this place. It is too crowded. We need to be able to focus our energy, and it is almost impossible under these circumstances." Zeena started to move to the outside.

"But where will we go that will be safe for five women in the night?"

"Come with me, I know a place."

The women followed Zeena. Henith and Braen waited until they had all left the barn. "I missed you, Braen," Henith whispered.

"Me, too," said Braen. They held hands as they quietly followed the others through the field of wheat.

Henith didn't know where they were going, but it seemed as if they were headed away from Dana's. Time was passing and soon it would be morning. She was afraid that they would all be caught wandering around in the fields when morning broke.

The little procession slowed as Zeena came to a small house. A candle was shining in the window. "Good," Zeena said. "We will be safe here."

"Here?" asked Dana. "Isn't that Celie's house? What about her husband?" Dana sounded skeptical.

"Don't worry, we will be alright." Zeena quickly darted across the yard between the field and the house. The others followed.

Zeena opened the door. A tall woman, with the darkest hair Henith had ever seen, embraced Zeena. "I thought you weren't coming. I was beginning to get worried." She looked up, startled when she realized that there were four other women staring at her. "Oh, Zeena, who are all these people?" She stepped back into the room, trying to decide what to do next.

"I'm sorry, Celie, I had to bring them with me. Jenli seems to have disappeared. These are the women I was telling you about. You don't have to worry. They are hiding just as much as we are."

Celie looked at the women, recognizing Dana. "Hello, Dana, I didn't expect to see you here." Turning back to Zeena, "I feel very strange. I think we need to sit down."

"Celie, we have to help find Jenli. She may be in danger. We have to find her, so we all can get out of sight before the sun comes up. We may have time to share stories later, but now we have to find Jenli." Zeena held Celie's hands. The tall woman was clearly shaken by the intrusion of all of these people into her life.

"Let us sit in a circle. Those that are able, picture Jenli. The others just ask the Goddess for guidance," Braen directed the women. "We need to take some time to quiet ourselves." She looked at Celie and smiled. Henith knew she was surrounding Celie with light, trying to help her be calm enough to be in the circle without her nervous energy disrupting what they were trying to do. Braen looked at each woman in turn. When Braen's gaze fell on Henith, she felt all of the tension of the last few days flow from her. She felt so light, she thought she would float off the floor. Staring into Braen's eyes, she was connected to the Goddess, connected to all of time. As Braen shifted her gaze to Shelagh, who was sitting next to Henith on the floor, Henith closed her eyes, enjoying the sensations in her body, the flowing, floating feelings.

She couldn't help herself, she was floating away. She tried to stay in the room, but it was so pleasant floating that she allowed herself the pleasure. She found herself floating over the wheat fields she had traveled through tonight. She recognized Dana's house and the path she and Shelagh had taken from the stone circle on the first day they had gone to Dana's. Soon she was over the circle. A cold wind was whipping around the stones. Her body shivered. She needed to escape this biting wind. She tried to float higher and higher. As she looked beneath her, the stone circle seemed to disappear. She wanted to get closer, but she didn't want to get caught in the howling wind that seemed to be blowing dirt in swirls around the circle.

She floated past the circle further south, over places she had never been before. There was smoke coming from a fire. She was compelled to go closer, but something or someone was holding her back. She looked behind her. There was Braen. Braen was pulling her back, but she wanted to go closer to see who was around the fire. Together they floated past the fire. Henith noticed many men, sleeping on the ground around the fire. She looked at Braen, thankful that they were here together. Henith started to feel very uncomfortable. Something was wrong with this place. She reached for Braen's hand, but the pull was intense. Someone or something was pulling her into the fire. Braen was pulling back with equal force. She was going to be split in two. She willed herself to look away from the fire and into Braen's eyes. She pleaded with Braen to get her away from there. She gave over her control to Braen and felt herself lifted out of danger. She risked looking back at the scene, keeping her eyes from focusing on the fire. Some distance from the sleeping men, she thought she detected movement in the trees. She nodded to Braen, who had also noticed it. It was their horse. A jolt of surprise went through Henith's body. She couldn't see Jenli, but she knew Jenli was there somewhere. Braen nodded to her. They focused their thoughts on Jenli. Henith thought she detected a very faint cry for help.

"Henith, come back. Henith." She could hear Braen's voice in her ears. She tried to open her eyes, but they did not want to cooperate. "Henith, come back." She struggled to raise her eyelids. Light and strange faces greeted her attempts. She shut them again quickly. She couldn't remember where she was or who all these people were. She only wanted to see Braen. She tried again to open her eyes. As she did, memories of recognition flooded her mind. There was Braen, looking at her with those intense blue eyes. There was Shelagh, and Dana, and the woman who looked like Braen, with the same intense blue eyes. And there was a new woman, one she couldn't remember seeing before, one with long black hair flowing over her white cotton shift.

"Braen, did you see her?"

"Yes, she has been captured by a group of men. I'm afraid she may have been badly hurt. She was barely able to respond to us, and we were very close."

"Who are the men?" Dana asked.

"I don't know," Braen looked at Shelagh. "Do you think they are the ones we saw when we left your circle? There was something about them that was familiar."

"I'm fairly sure that they are the same men. One of them is dangerous to us, especially to Henith. He is very skilled in mind-speaking and receiving, whether he's aware of it or not. And for some reason he is able to capture Henith when she is focusing her energy outward like that."

Celie looked bewildered. "I'm not sure I know what you all are talking about. I didn't see anything, but I did feel very calm."

Zeena took Celie's hand. "It's alright, Celie, these women are very skilled in mysteries we have only heard about. They have much to teach us.

"What's the matter, Henith?" Zeena asked. "Are you aware that your color just shifted?"

"The men are very close, just south of the circle. We do not have much time to teach you everything we know. We may not have much time to teach you any more."

"Men have come to our town before, and we have survived their arrival." Dana seemed not to have picked up on Henith's concern.

"Yes, but I fear that this time will be different. When we were in Boscawen, we learned that the men had decided to take over all of Trenig, even if they had to take over by force."

"That happened once before, several years ago, and then they more or less left us alone. Except for marrying some of our women," Dana was looking straight at Celie.

Silence fell on the group. Henith waited, hoping Celie would respond, but she said nothing. Henith wondered about these women she was just getting to know. Dana did not have a husband, but Celie and Zeena did. She wondered where their husbands were this night and how they had managed to get free from them.

Zeena responded as if reading Henith's mind.

"My husband is also one of the foreigners. It has been very difficult living this double life, being the High Priestess of the area and being a wife to one of those that seek to destroy our ways. At the time of our marriage, I thought that if I were married to one of them, then I could at least know what they were doing and what their plans were. It has been much more difficult than I thought and somewhat exhausting. The only time I can leave the house undetected is in the night. I have resorted to giving my husband and my two children a sleeping potion regularly, so I can leave. Unfortunately that does not leave me with many hours in which to sleep."

"My husband is also a foreigner. There was a time when I actually thought that it was alright to marry them, that peace might be kept in our town that way, but it also has been very difficult. My husband has gone to Lintern for a few days. That is why he is not here now," Celie said, looking intently at Henith.

Dana looked angry, "How could you marry one of them? How could you give your bodies to the enemy?"

Zeena looked directly at Dana. "We all make choices. At the time my choice seemed like a reasonable thing to do. Years ago, it didn't seem that bad. He and I have had some good times together and we have two fine children."

"But look what you have had to sacrifice for the joy of children. Surely there must be other ways to have children without also having to have a husband." Dana's voice was rising.

Braen interceded, "Friends, there are many things we could teach you, but Henith is right, the time is very short. I also fear that these men are not about to take this town peaceably. We need to think about Jenli. We can't leave her there."

"Where is she?" Celie asked.

"I think she has been captured by that group of men that are camped out south of town."

"We have to get her from them."

"How are we going to do that? It isn't safe for any of us to go there either."

Zeena said, "I will have to be home when my husband wakes in the morning. I couldn't go much further tonight and be back in time. But if we waited until tomorrow evening, we could start off earlier than we did tonight."

Celie looked reluctant. "I'm not sure I can risk going that far away in the daytime either. If my husband came back unexpectedly, my life would be very difficult. He isn't expected until the day after tomorrow, but sometimes he arrives earlier."

"I think we should try to get her now. Risk the light. The longer she stays with those men the more endangered her life will be," Dana started to get up.

"Zeena, what will your husband say if your cousins all of a sudden disappear from your home? He will be expecting to see us in the morning." Shelagh looked at Braen, who was looking at Henith.

"I forgot about that, Shelagh. Braen and I should be home for breakfast. We would raise too much suspicion otherwise," Zeena confirmed.

"But that leaves only Henith and Dana."

Henith's stomach tied into a knot. She envisioned being home on Mona, or at Shelagh's circle, planting in the garden, drying and preparing herbs. She was the only one who wouldn't be missed in the morning, because no one in town knew she was there except for a few women she had tried to teach about the healing mysteries.

Braen was worried. "Henith, you have to be very careful if you do this. Do not let your thoughts go out to Jenli. Keep yourself totally focused internally. I don't understand it, but one of those men can read you as easily as I can. If he senses your presence, you could be in danger. You must not let him know you exist. Do no send any signals at all. I wish we could think of another plan." She came to where Henith was sitting. "Look at me, Henith. You and Dana have to try to rescue Jenli, but you must not say anything or even think anything. Let Dana do all the thinking and follow her blindly. Do not send out any energy at all. You cannot let the fear overcome you and lose your concentration."

"I will do it. But maybe you can send an energy field around us. Do you think you can do it from so great a distance?"

"I will try. Shelagh can help me."

Chapter 13

Dana slowed down. They had been walking quickly through the night toward the place where Braen and Henith suspected Jenli to be.

"We are getting close. I can smell campfires. Maybe they have already decided to break camp." Dana looked at Henith, who seemed to be in another world.

"Yes, I can smell them, too. Do we have a plan? How are we going to get to Jenli, even if we can find her without being noticed?"

"Maybe we can watch the men, just out of sight. See if we can detect what their plan is. See if we can find out what they have done with Jenli."

"I have to keep remembering to keep from thinking outward. I haven't had to control my thoughts so carefully before, but I will try to be just an observer."

Dana stopped in the path. Henith looked around. She could detect the presence of the men. They were very close. Fear gripped her and made her body go rigid. She concentrated on calming herself.

Dana motioned for her to follow. They left the path and started to walk through the trees. The underbrush was so thick that it made walking difficult. Dana seemed to have a plan. Henith followed as quietly as she could. She wanted to call out to Jenli to find out where she was, but with the men so close it would be too risky.

"We may be able to watch them undetected from this rise. They may have camped in the clearing on the other side. Let us hope that they haven't posted a sentry here," Dana smiled.

Dana was very cautious, slowly approaching the top of the hill. Every few steps she would stop, listening intently. As they approached the top of the rise, more and more sounds became audible. Even in these early hours, there were many noises. As they focused on listening, Henith became aware of horses, many horses. As she listened deep into the earth, she could hear footsteps and the soft rumble of men breathing in their sleep. Some of the men had already awakened.

Henith was not prepared for what she saw as they reached the top of the rise. There were many tents, and many men in the field at the bottom of the hill. Henith guessed that besides the men she could see sleeping on the ground, there were many more in the tents. Tethered to one side of the field were many horses. Fires were being built and a meal was being prepared by the men who were not still asleep. How were they ever to get Jenli away from all these men? As Henith and Dana watched, more men emerged from the tents to join those already awake, and morning preparations began in earnest.

Henith noticed how differently these men prepared for the day. Back on Mona, the women were barely visible or audible as they prepared for the day, but these men were blustery, making much noise, pushing and poking at each other. As more and more men rose from their sleep, they grew in size, taking up more and more of the field, until it seemed as if there were no space left and the field had become a wall of men. They couldn't see Jenli anywhere.

Cautiously, Dana led them from the rise around to the south of the camp. They were closer to the horses now. One of the horses started to whinny and act nervous. It was the horse Jenli had been riding. It had detected their presence and now began to snort and paw at the earth. The other horses now too began to shift about, becoming uneasy. Dana, sensing the disruption their presence was causing, nodded to Henith to move back to where they had been. Some of the men had noticed and were coming towards the horses to calm them down. One of the men, taller than the others with blond hair and broad shoulders, stopped in his path, and tilted his head as if listening for something.

"What's the matter?" the other man asked. "Did you hear something?"

"No, I just thought I felt something strange, that's all."

"Not that again. The others are going to think you are crazy if you keep telling them about your strange feelings. Come on, an animal spooked the horses. That's all."

Dana looked at Henith. They had both heard the conversation. All the color had drained out of Henith's face. She tried to focus on being centered. Maybe it had been a bad idea for her to come here, but could Dana rescue Jenli alone? She wasn't even sure that she and Dana could rescue Jenli together. On the other side of the field from the horses were several tents. Getting close to them would be very difficult, because they were far enough away from the edge of the trees to make any approach possible.

Henith and Dana sat down behind a large rock. What they were supposed to do was not clear to them. They knew that Jenli must be here somewhere because her horse was here. Maybe she was in one of the tents. If they waited until the men were on the road, it would be even more difficult to get to her if they had her tied in one of the wagons. Henith knew she couldn't try to contact Jenli, but she was surprised that she wasn't picking up any sense at all that Jenli was here. Then a thought occurred to Henith, and then a knowing. Jenli wasn't here.

Henith jumped up and pulled Dana quickly down the hill, continuing south in the direction that she was sure had been the way the men had come. When they were a safe distance away Dana asked, "What are you doing, Henith? I thought we were going to watch what the men were doing."

"Jenli's not there. I couldn't see her there in the spirit traveling and couldn't sense her there now."

"But the horse is there. Where else would she be?"

"I'm not sure, but I know she's not there. I'm going to call her."

"You can't. The risk is too high. However that man does it, he senses you. I saw it happen, and you were not even sending."

"Yes, that's true, but he does not know what is happening. He randomly picks up on me. And from what it sounded like, no one believes him. He doesn't know what he's doing. If I send another message to Jenli, and he does tune into it, what is he going to do with it? Even if he figures out what is happening, he won't know what to do with it. If he tells the others, they will think he's crazy." Henith smiled to herself. Maybe I could send him some false messages, she thought.

"Braen is not going to be happy if she finds out you are putting yourself in such danger by mind-speaking. I'm not at all convinced that you are right. Maybe he's not the only one picking up on you." That thought hadn't crossed Henith's mind.

"How else can we find Jenli? We can't search all of Trenig. The Goddess gave us these gifts so that we could use them. Now that I know who it is that is picking up on my presence, I think I can focus on Jenli in such a way that he will not be able to draw me into his thoughts. You can help by surrounding me with protective energy so that I can focus on Jenli."

"Shouldn't we get further from the men, then?"

"Yes." Henith was leading the way now. After many minutes, Henith stopped and looked around.

"What is it?" Dana asked, also looking around but not seeing anything except trees. The morning sun was rising above the trees, Dana noticed. The early morning light that was filtering through the rising mist in the trees was making the woods dream-like.

"Is the road to Lintern near here?"

Dana thought a while. "I think so."

"Let us stop here and try to find her, I think she is near."

Henith sat on a rock nearby, and Dana joined her. "I want you to put up a wall of energy between us and the men. I am going to focus on Jenli. I do not think she is between us and them. She is between us and a road that I think is over there." Dana stared in disbelief at her new friend. Dana had lived in this part of Trenig all her life and while she had explored the area regularly looking for herbs and plants, she wasn't sure if the road was where Henith said it was. Henith had been in the region for less than three weeks and had not left Dana's home except for last night. Yet Henith acted as if she knew the area intimately.

Henith closed her eyes and, taking deep breaths, she was soon in a trance. "I have her. She is barely conscious. We must get to her quickly." Dana was startled out of her own trance by the urgency in Henith's voice.

"Where is she?" Dana asked, looking around.

"Follow me, we are very close."

Henith led Dana into a thicket. Dana could see the road not far from where they were standing. "The main road to Lintern must be just over there, we must be very careful, many people travel that road. It would not be good to be found here," Dana cautioned.

Henith looked to where Dana was pointing. "We must keep looking, I know she is not far away." As Henith said this, a color caught her eye just beyond a bush of holly. Quickly she and Dana went to it. Jenli was lying face down in the leaves. Her clothes were torn in many places, and Dana could see bruises on the part of her arms that were exposed from her torn gown. Dana gasped, "Is she alive?"

Henith was bending over Jenli, gently feeling for broken bones. "Yes, she is still breathing. Her heart is beating, but she is very weak."

"Did she fall off her horse, do you think?" Dana asked, trying to explain the incredible bruises on the woman's body.

Henith carefully turned Jenli over so she could see Jenli's face. Henith and Dana both cried out at once. Jenli's face was covered with blood and there were many deep cuts and bruises. Henith took Jenli in her arms like a child and gently rocked her, holding her close to her breasts. Henith tried to hold back the tears that were forming in the corners of her eyes. Henith looked at Jenli. The tears would not be held back.

"We have to get her out of here, Dana. I need to get her to your cottage. I need the herbs that are there. She needs a great deal of care."

Jenli moaned and her eyes flickered.

Henith looked at the woman, surrounding her with healing energy. "Jenli, it's Henith."

Jenli opened her eyes for a second and, seeing Henith, started to cry. She relaxed into Henith's arms.

"She has given her strength over to me. Do you have any idea how we can get her back to your cottage? I'm not sure that the two of us can carry her all the way back through the forest."

"We can't risk the road, Henith, especially not carrying an injured woman."

"Dana, see if you can find two long thin tree branches, relatively straight and not too rotten. We can use my quilt and roll the edges onto the poles. We might be able to carry her by pulling her. I'm going to begin to heal her aura, but I need some time to center myself. Once my mother came back from Trenig with a wound on her leg, but she never looked like this. I have led a very sheltered life," she added almost to herself.

Henith made Jenli more comfortable, moving her from beneath the holly tree and arranging a pillow of leaves for her head. Henith's hands were shaking. She looked down at the woman, blood caked on her face. Henith needed to get her to some water to clean her wounds. She seemed to be in a calm sleep, almost as if her spirit had left this world. Henith's stomach quickened. She leaned her face close to Jenli's. She could barely detect Jenli's breath. Henith took a deep breath, closed her eyes and began to release all of her anxieties and fears. When she felt that she was free from outside noises, she slowly moved her hands over Jenli's body, not touching but just above her skin. When Henith found places in Jenli's outer body that felt wounded, she concentrated her energy into those places. There were so many. This woman's body had been badly abused. When Henith was finished, she opened her eyes. Dana was quietly standing there, waiting.

"I didn't hear you come back."

"You were in a deep trance."

"I guess I was. Were you able to make something for us to carry her?"

Dana showed Henith her creation.

"That is perfect. If we are careful, we should be able to carry-drag her a long way. Do you remember seeing any water near here? I would like to clean her face and her arms."

"I'm not exactly sure where we are along the road. We came here in the most round about way. I'm going to go out on the road and see if I can recognize where we are. You stay here. I won't be long."

"Be careful, Dana."

Dana helped Henith move Jenli onto the carrier and then walked toward the road.

"Henith," Jenli said barely above a whisper.

"Jenli, I'm here. Just rest now. Don't waste any of your energy talking. Dana and I are going to take you home. Just focus your energy on healing."

"Henith," she tried again but slipped into sleep.

Henith had no idea how long Dana had been gone, but she was beginning to get restless. She wanted to get Jenli home, to tend to her wounds. She was beginning to feel unsafe in this thicket so close to the road. She couldn't see which way Dana had gone after she had reached the road. She waited impatiently for her friend's return. There was nothing else she could do. She felt so helpless. Henith was surprised when Dana came back from a totally different direction than she had anticipated.

"Henith, I know where we are. There are three women I know who live not too far from here. A grandmother, a mother, and a daughter. I think we can trust them to take us in. They are much closer than my house. We have traveled a long way this night."

"How will we explain who we are?"

"They probably won't ask any questions. They live by themselves mostly and do not know many people around here. We'll just say Jenli fell off her horse and we came to find her. They won't need to know anything else."

The two women carefully lifted the carrier and started in the direction that Dana indicated.

Chapter 14

"Do you need to rest?" Dana had stopped in the path and had turned to face Jenli who was slowly walking behind.

"No, I want to keep walking," Jenli replied, looking at Dana ahead of her on the trail. Henith, who had been following behind, caught up to them as they paused to give Jenli some rest. Henith was concerned because Jenli had not spoken much in the last three days. Her body seemed to have healed without any trouble or any visible marks, but her spirit had been wounded in some way. Dana and Henith had tried to find out how she had fallen from her horse, but Jenli refused to give any details. The women did not want to pry, but at the same time they were very concerned by the way Jenli was acting. It was as if her body was present but she wasn't. Dana turned and continued toward her home. The day before yesterday, she had returned home alone to tell the women what had happened. She had been able to get a message to Braen and Shelagh. She returned for Henith and Jenli last night. Dana had been surprised to see the almost total recovery of Jenli's body in such a short time, but she could not erase the feeling that something was still very wrong with Jenli. Dana knew that Henith was concerned, too. The three walked on in a troubled silence.

For the most part, the path that went to Dana's from where they had found Jenli was through the forest far from any of the major roads. There was only one place, up ahead where the path crossed a road, where there was any need for concern about being detected.

As they approached the road the three women suddenly stopped in the path. All had heard the sounds at the same time. Henith recognized it as the same rumblings of the earth that they had heard when they left Shelagh's circle. Jenli turned in the path and started running wildly away from the road. Henith started to call after her, but changed her mind when she remembered she might be heard even above the roaring noises coming from the road. Instead she ran after her. Dana heard the two running away and turned just in time to see the two women run behind an outcropping of rock that they had passed a few minutes before. She went after them.

When she reached the rock, she found Jenli in Henith's arms. Jenli rocked against Henith, sobbing, tears pouring down her cheeks.

"What is it, Jenli?" Henith asked softly.

Jenli continued to sob, holding on to Henith. Henith looked up at Dana as she appeared from the other side of the rock.

"What happened?" Dana asked Henith.

"I don't know." Henith was trying to calm Jenli.

"I'm going to go and see what I can learn about who is on the road." Dana turned to go.

Jenli gasped between sobs, "Don't go, don't go."

Henith tried to hold her, but she was struggling to get to Dana. Jenli continued to cry, "Don't go, you can't go, they'll find us. Please don't let them find us." She collapsed against Henith, sobbing deep sobs, unable to catch her breath.

"Jenli, can you tell us what happened to you the other day?"

Jenli just shook her head, crying into Henith's shoulder.

"Dana, please be careful, I will look after Jenli. Go and see if you can find out how many men there are on the road," Henith smiled up at Dana and then down at Jenli. "Be very careful."

Dana was gone several minutes before Jenli calmed down enough to speak. "Henith, it was so horrible. I was riding along. I guess I wasn't very careful. It was such a pleasant night for a ride. We had been cooped up for so long at Dana's. I needed to ride and get some air. Before I realized where I was and what was happening, I came out into the road and there were many men camped in the field. As soon as I saw them, I tried to get away. I didn't think that they had seen me, but I wasn't fast enough. Just as I was turning to leave several of the men noticed me. I headed out of the field away from Dana's. I didn't want them to follow me that way. Several of the men began to chase me. I came to a road. I thought I could travel faster on the road than through the forest. I could hear the horses behind me getting closer. I was terrified. I didn't know what to do. Our horse wasn't used to being ridden so hard. They caught up to me and one of the men pulled me off my horse." Jenli paused and the tears started falling again. Henith held her close. A sick feeling began to form at the bottom of Henith's stomach.

"You don't have to go on, if you don't want to." Henith began to fear the rest of Jenli's story.

"I need to say it, I need to get it out."

Jenli looked up at Henith. "There were five of them. They were laughing and joking, calling me different names. I didn't know what to do, I was so scared. I tried to center myself, but I was so terrified I couldn't shake the fear that was surrounding me. They started to come closer to me. They made a circle with me in the middle, there was no way to escape. One of them grabbed me by the arms from the back. I struggled to get free. The more I struggled, the more they laughed and joked with each other, and the tighter I was held. I can see the face of the one that came at me first. In some ironic way it was a nice face, pleasant features, blue eyes, a nice mouth, and a reddish beard, but the nice face turned into a monster right before my eyes. I had to look away. The others cheered him on. I screamed and screamed, but it didn't make any difference, they kept coming at me. After the second one had raped me, I blacked out. I don't know what happened after that, not until I looked up and saw you holding me. I thought I was dead."

Henith knew she had to control herself to keep from throwing up. She continued to hold onto Jenli. Some women had told stories like this in other villages that they had visited. But here was Jenli, her friend, who had been brutally attacked and raped by these men. She feared for the women in this town. These men had no idea of the sacredness of women. Jenli was softly weeping again. Henith wondered how they going to protect all of the women in this town and all of Trenig from this violence.

Dana appeared. "There are dozens of men. They have stopped on the road for a meal. They seem to be heading toward where we saw the others camped. The others must still be there, or I would have heard about their arrival in town yesterday. We will have to wait here for some time before it is safe to cross the road. They don't look like they are in any hurry to move on."

Dana sat down with the two women. "Is she alright?" Dana asked Henith.

Henith replied softly, "She was assaulted by those men."

The three women slipped into their own private silences. Henith feared for their safety. She wished that Braen were here. She missed her friend. She found herself remembering the first few moons of their journey. Braen had been so quiet. Henith had had to get used to Braen's long periods of silence. At first Henith thought she would go crazy, when Braen wouldn't talk for hours. Eventually Henith came to enjoy the silent times she shared with Braen. They would walk for hours, alone in the silence, but in some ways, very much together in the silence. Henith learned that they didn't need to have many words to share the joy that they had with each other.

They had started their journey in such excitement and joyful anticipation. Henith never imagined that she would be praying for her own safety as well as the well-being of these strange women who so recently had become so important to her. How were they ever going to protect the ways of the Goddess against such violence? She began to cry. There was so much pain in this land. These men had brought so much pain. Couldn't they see what they were doing? The ways of the Goddess were so gentle, so loving, so peaceful.

Jenli had fallen asleep in Henith's arms. After what seemed liked a long time, Henith whispered to Dana, "Do you think it is safe to move yet?"

"I think so. I think I heard them leaving a short while ago. The ground does not seem to be rumbling any more. They have probably moved on. I will go and see."

Dana left and returned a few minutes later. "There is no sign of them. I think we can leave now."

"Jenli, wake up, we are leaving now."

Jenli opened her eyes. "Where are we? I was dreaming I was at Shelagh's circle. It was so lovely there."

"We are on our way back to Dana's. We will have to be very cautious as we approach the road, just in case there are any stragglers. I think Dana should go first. When she is safely across, you will go, and then I will go. We should leave considerable distance between us."

"I'm not sure I can do it alone." Jenli started to shake again.

"I will surround you with energy," Henith said, trying to comfort her friend.

Dana turned and headed toward the road. After several minutes, Jenli left. Henith focused her energy on the two women going before her. Finally she left the protection of the rock and followed the way they had gone. When she reached the road, she listened carefully for any sounds that would indicate travellers. She put her ear to the ground and listened. Way off she could hear the soft rumbling of the earth. It must be the men, she thought. She could not detect any sounds very close, so she quickly crossed the road. She was relieved when she found Dana and Jenli waiting for her on the path.

"It isn't far now. We should be home in a short while." Dana started to walk briskly in the direction of her home. She noticed that the color in Jenli's aura had shifted from ashen gray to lavender. And while Jenli's face still reflected a great deal of pain, she walked with a surer step.

When they reached Dana's, they were surprised to see Zeena waiting for them.

"I have been worried about you. I expected you hours ago."

"We had to wait a long time. Another group of men were in the road. We had to wait until they moved."

"Another troop. That must mean hundreds of men." Zeena looked concerned.

"They may be gathering where we found Jenli." Zeena looked at Jenli, who had fallen into her dark place upon seeing Zeena.

No one said anything for a while. The silence was uncomfortable. Finally Dana said, "Let us have some tea, and discuss what we shall do next. I think that our four visitors should leave as soon as Jenli is able to travel."

"Before the full moon ritual?" Henith asked. "That will be a just a few nights. I was so hoping that we could share that experience again and that we could tell other women to come. It was so important for us last time. I was hoping that Celie would come." Zeena looked slightly embarrassed at the mention of Celie's name.

Dana poured tea into the cups that Zeena had brought out from the small pantry that was overflowing with a wide variety of dried herbs.

"I also was hoping that we could share the moon time with you again. So much has happened in the last few days, I feel like we need that time together," Henith said.

"But it is getting dangerous for you to be here. I don't think we should gather at the stone circle any more either. If we were ever found out, I shudder to think what would happen to us." Dana looked at Jenli.

"Do you know what Braen and Shelagh think?" Henith asked Zeena.

"I think they were assuming that we would invite all the women that you have met in your instruction times, and that we would have a moon celebration, and then when it was convenient, you would continue on your journey. Of course, they do not know that more men are assembling," Zeena responded.

"I'm not sure I can put myself in a dangerous place again." Jenli shifted in her place. "Some men attacked me, Zeena."

Zeena looked at Jenli and a pain of recognition passed over her eyes. "The women of our town are also afraid. Some of them have also been assaulted, some even by their husbands. It would be very dangerous to gather for the moon ritual. But it also would be empowering for them to experience, at least for only a little while and maybe for only one time in their lives, the power of the Goddess," Zeena said somewhat wistfully.

"The risk is very high. With so many men moving into our town, it is hard to predict what will happen."

"Do you think the town's people will fight back?" Jenli asked.

"I don't know. The stories about places where the people fought back are terrifying. Many people are killed, the women raped, property destroyed. And still the foreigners win. In places where the people ignored the foreigners, there was still violence but not to the extent that there was when there is resistance. It is a difficult choice."

"But can you just sit by and watch those men take over your town?" Henith said with much anger in her voice.

"It isn't easy to watch, but what are our choices? Violence seems to beget more violence. Some of the people have moved out of the town, gone further north, to little villages. The foreigners don't seem to bother with the smaller places."

"But what about the women who are married to the foreigners who came earlier? It is so hard for me to imagine being married to any man, especially to one who was a destroyer of our ways."

Zeena responded, a note of irritation in her voice, "Some of us have made choices that right now seem hard to understand, but, at the time, made some sense. For example, both Celie and I chose to marry. We thought that it was safer to know what was going on with the strangers than to live in constant fear. It is true that we still live in fear, fear of being found out, fear of practicing the old religion. But at least we know where two men are all the time, even if we have to drug them to do it." Zeena allowed a slight smile to cross her lips.

"It must be very dangerous for you to be the High Priestess of the circle here and be married to a man at the same time. Life on Mona was so simple by comparison." Henith looked at Zeena apologetically.

"We still do not have a plan." Dana poured more tea.

"We have another problem," Jenli addressed the group. "We do not have a horse. The men must have taken it." The women could detect a bitter edge to Jenli's voice that made them uncomfortable.

"Dana, do you think we will be able to get another horse from somewhere without raising too much suspicion?"

"You can take mine."

"But what will you do?"

"I will manage. I'll say it ran off. Eventually I will get another one."

Tears came into Henith's eyes thinking about the generosity of this woman. It would take her a long time to replace this horse.

"I would like to risk another moon time together," Zeena said.

Silence fell on the group.

After several minutes, Henith said, "I would be willing to stay until the full moon, if it is alright with Braen, Shelagh, and Jenli, but then I think we need to leave."

Zeena looked relieved. "Is it alright with you, Jenli?"

Jenli nodded reluctantly. "I will stay until after the moon time, but I'm not sure I will be able to participate fully in the ritual."

"I will tell Braen and Shelagh of our discussion and ask their opinions. If they agree, I will let you know, and then we can meet at the stone circle. I will try to get as many women there as possible, if Braen and Shelagh agree to the plan." Zeena rose to go. "I hope I will see you at the circle in three days time. We have much to do in the meantime."

"What happens if the men who are gathering on the outskirts of town decide to move in before the full moon?" Dana asked the question that they all wanted to avoid.

"I have a very uncomfortable feeling about this," Dana continued, "I don't think we should go anywhere near those stones until the men have made the first move, until we know what their plan is. We should stay as far out of the way as possible, until they do whatever it is they are going to do. Then it will be easier to have a safe plan. Gathering so many women at the stone circle with so many foreign men wandering about is truly a dangerous and possibly even foolish thing to do." Dana looked at Henith and Jenli.

Zeena nodded and left.

Chapter 15

The early morning mist floated between Henith and Jenli as they prepared the wagon for their departure early the next day. Tonight, Braen, Shelagh, Jenli, and she would be reunited at the full moon ritual, and tomorrow morning they would continue on their journey northwest towards Mona.

The thought sent an instant thrill through Henith, but was quickly replaced by the heaviness Henith had not been able to shake for the last three days. She was looking forward to the moon ritual that evening. Zeena said there would be many women there. Rituals were always very powerful when so many women gathered to focus their energies, even when some were unskilled in the ways of the mysteries. Every time Henith tried to focus on the coming evening event, she was unable to see it clearly. She was troubled by her inability to visualize tonight's moon ritual. She dismissed her anxiety by saying to herself that she was not centered enough because of all of the events in the past week, especially by what had happened to Jenli.

She planned to spend the rest of the day in preparation for tonight after the wagon was packed. She looked forward to the day she would spend in silence. She was concerned about Jenli, however. Jenli had been very restless the last few days and still hadn't decided if she could participate in the ritual tonight. Henith was sure that Jenli's restless energy was affecting her and was contributing to her own foreboding.

Many more men had gathered, according to Zeena, who said that her husband had told her that they probably would enter the town in another week. Zeena did not think that anyone would offer any resistance. The situation in this town was very strange. In some ways the foreigners had already taken it over in the first invasion.

Many of the women were married to these foreigners, and the other men and women were quite co-operative. It wasn't clear to Henith why so many more men were needed to invade the town. All of the visible signs and symbols of life before the strangers first invasion had all but disappeared. The stone circle was still intact, but mostly abandoned except by this handful of women who were trying to re-claim some of the old ways.

One of the reasons Henith was uncomfortable about tonight's ritual was because the stone circle was too close to where the men were camped. They were taking a great risk to go so near the encampment. But Dana had pointed out that the circle was not on the men's route from Lintern to the town and was at least an hour's walk through thick underbrush and forest to get from where they were camped to the circle. Someone would have to know exactly what they were doing to find them.

Henith had reminded Dana that they had found the circle without difficulty.

"But you were coming from a different direction, and besides, the men don't have your skill," Dana had said. Henith had not been relieved.

"Jenli, after we finish here, I would like to be in silence for the rest of the day," Henith addressed the young woman who was loading the wagon with bread and cheeses, and some dried apples and flour that the women of Merchlyn had given for their journey.

"I will also be in silence." A far away look came over Jenli's face.

Henith watched her friend.

"Have you decided whether you are going to join us tonight? You might gain some strength from the ritual."

"I have not been centered enough. If I can find my center in the afternoon's silence, I will come, but not as one of the priestesses. Maybe I could be present as a participant." Henith noticed the pain in Jenli's eyes.

"Jenli, of course that would be fine," Henith said as she put her arm gently on Jenli's shoulder.

Jenli looked away from Henith. She said something Henith could not make out. Jenli sobbed into Henith's shoulder. "I cannot be a priestess."

"But you are a priestess already, what do you mean?"

"Those men took that away from me when they violated my body." Tears ran down Jenli's cheeks. "How can I be a priestess when I continually think about what they did to me? All I want to do is to kill them. Those are unworthy thoughts for a priestess of the Goddess who teaches only the ways of life and love.

"There are times when I plan their brutal and violent deaths. They have infected me with their ways. I have been poisoned, and I cannot seem to rid myself of it. I am consumed by thoughts of revenge and destruction. They not only entered my body with theirs, but somehow in that act they have entered by mind and my soul. They have implanted me with seeds of violence. All I want to do is destroy them. It doesn't seem possible to me that the people in this town are just going to let them come in and take over. How can they yield without offering any resistance?"

"What happened to you should not have happened. It was not your fault. And you are still a priestess of the Goddess. If you choose to come to the ritual, we could do a special healing for you," Henith offered. Somehow her words seemed empty and shallow. Anger started to rise in her also. Henith could not think of an alternative to what these town folks had decided to do. Fighting back did not seem to be a solution. The men were better equipped and qualified as fighting men. The people in the town had no such skill. They would violate the women in both cases. Going away from this place was the only possibility. But could all these people move north? The men would eventually move north also. Was there any other place to go? Henith could not imagine a world beyond Trenig, although she knew that the men had come from a land far away. She was glad that she was going back to Mona. A terrifying thought crossed her mind. Would the men also come to Mona?

"We are living in difficult times, Jenli. I don't know what will become of our ways, or what will become of us. The priestesses on

Mona may also be forced to make difficult decisions as the people here have been. We cannot judge too harshly. We may also be put to the test someday."

"I hope what happened to me will never happen to you. I could not bear to think that any one else would have to go through what I went through. Do you think we are going to be safe tonight?"

"I don't know. I have some uneasy feelings about tonight. I hope Dana is right and that the men are far enough away and in a direction that would not lead them to us. I have been trying to keep my thoughts positive about tonight, but I keep finding myself in darkness, and I have to admit to some fear."

Jenli pulled away from Henith's arms. "I know that I will have to encounter men as we continue our journey, but I am not looking forward to that time."

"Well, we should not see any tonight, and if we are careful, not for some days to come." Henith tried to be reassuring even though her own fears were causing her to doubt their safety. "We should finish our packing so that we will be ready for tonight's ritual," she said, hoping the work would take their minds from the anxiety.

The two women finished packing the wagon in silence, each lost in her own thoughts.

❧❦

Henith was concerned about herself as she dressed for the evening ritual. She had spent a restless day, unable to rid herself of thoughts about what Jenli had said about being implanted with a violent seed. She wished that the day had been longer. She did not feel centered enough to lead these women in the ritual. Her thoughts of Jenli had been intermingled with her excited anticipation of seeing Braen again.

A moon's time without Braen had seemed like an eternity. She was also looking forward to seeing all the women gathered. Some of whom she had taught the basics of the healing mysteries. She put her purple cloak on over her white woolen robe. She wasn't sure how all these women, including herself, were going to get to the stone circle undetected.

She was happy to see Jenli standing with Dana, waiting for her. She nodded to the two women and smiled at Jenli. Jenli looked tentative as the three started toward the path that would lead them to the stone circle. Somehow, walking through the trees dressed in their robes, Henith felt very vulnerable. It certainly would be hard to disguise who they were, if they came upon any people along the way. Dana had reassured Henith yesterday that none of the townspeople knew about this path except her. This was the way she went to the circle, and except for one place where the path crossed a small road, they could travel undetected.

The three walked in silence, Dana first, followed by Jenli, and then Henith. They had planned to reach the circle at sunset. Henith and Braen would not have any time together before Braen cast the circle. Their reunion would have to wait until after the celebration. Henith found herself thinking more about Braen than about the ritual that she was about to lead. It had been a long time since she and Braen had been alone together. There were so many experiences that she had had that she wanted to discuss with Braen. She especially wanted to talk about Jenli's experience. She did not understand it, and it frightened her. She hoped that Braen would be able to help her make sense of what was happening.

They were very close to where Henith had first met Dana. She could sense that some women had already gathered. There was an energy in the air that made her almost want to run down the path. Her feelings of excitement began to win out over her feelings of foreboding. As they came into the clearing, Henith was thrilled seeing so many women—twenty-five or thirty.

Most of the women were already gathering in the circle. Some were waiting on the outside. She looked around for Braen and Shelagh. Dana went ahead into the circle, and Jenli followed, looking shyly at Henith. Henith smiled encouragement at her. As Henith was searching for Braen in the groups of women, she detected a movement behind her and noticed a hush come over the group. She turned to see Shelagh coming from the edge of the woods. The women who had been standing outside the circle moved to be inside the stones. Shelagh's ancient face glowed when she saw Henith. Henith looked past Shelagh as Zeena emerged from the edge of the forest. Zeena was radiant in her ruby red cape, her chestnut hair highlighted with gold falling gently on her shoulders. When Braen appeared, Henith almost lost her balance. Never had Braen looked so beautiful, so much a priestess as she walked, straight and tall, sure of every step. Henith had to remind herself to breathe. Braen waited as Henith followed Zeena toward the circle. The joy that encompassed Henith as she entered the circle was overwhelming. How could anything so beautiful be threatened?

The four priestesses reached their positions. Shelagh turned to the east. Just as Shelagh was about to invoke the powers of the east, a cold wind blew across Henith's back. She thought she felt something in the trees behind her. She tried to look at Braen. Did Braen detect it, too? Braen looked at Henith. She had sensed it. What were they going to do? Shelagh was halfway though the invocation. The cold wind blew again. Henith shivered. Some of the women in the circle noticed it, too. Henith was tempted to turn around to see what she could detect in the woods behind her. Then she noticed that Braen had started to cast the circle before Zeena and she had had time to invoke the other powers. What was she doing? She was going on the outside of the stones. Usually the circle was cast on the inside of the stones. And she was going very quickly. The women in the center started to move and whisper nervously. Shelagh detected the shift in energy and turned to face the women, a low hum coming from deep inside of her. The women close to her picked up the sound. Soon all the women were humming very softly. The nervous energy started to dissipate. Henith joined Braen on the outside of the stones. She reasoned that maybe two priestesses casting the circle quickly would be as powerful as one doing it slowly.

The low humming sound from inside the circle was eerie. Henith tried to imagine what they looked like. Two women almost running around the stone circle with their robes flying behind them. All of a sudden Braen stopped. A noise somewhere to their right was getting louder. It sounded like many footsteps, stepping on twigs, branches and leaves. In a voice Henith had never heard before, Braen shouted clearly above the low hum. "Scatter, now. Go in all the directions of the universe. Keep running until you can run no longer." Pandemonium broke loose. Some women screamed. Others started to run as directed. Some stood bewildered. Braen reached to pull Henith to her, "This way."

Henith looked for Shelagh and Jenli. Shelagh was too old to be running through the night even though her body was in fine physical health. "We have to get Jenli," Henith said to Braen.

"We can't." Braen was pulling Henith into the trees in the direction that they had come the first time they saw this circle.

"We can't leave her here," Henith struggled with herself, wanting to flee with Braen and wanting to find Jenli.

"We will just have to pray that she will be safe. There are only ten or so men and they are all coming from the same direction. If we all scatter, they will not be able to capture all of us."

"Why don't we stay and fight?" Henith asked, gasping for breath.

"With what? Those men may have weapons. How could we stand a chance against swords and knives?"

Henith could hear some of the women screaming. Henith could not detect anyone following her and Braen. "Could we slow down, Braen?"

"Not until we are a safe distance from here."

Henith and Braen continued to run into the night, thankful that the moon was lighting their way, but fearful that in so much moonlight they were not as well protected as they would have been in the dark of the new moon.

When the two reached the place where they had first camped, Braen started to slow down. The screams of the women became muffled.

"I think we will be safe here." Braen reached to pull Henith close to her. The touch of Braen caused Henith to cry. The tears just flowed and flowed. She could not stop them, and she did not want to. The two held each other for a long time.

The muffled cries of the women softened to a whisper. As the night progressed, even the whispers disappeared. Henith and Braen continued to hold onto each other.

❧❦

"Do you think the others escaped?" Henith tried not to think about what might have happened to Jenli.

"I know that most of the women will have gotten away, but I doubt if all of them did. I am sure some are still there, and may need your healing skills."

"My medicines are all packed in the wagon," Henith said, wondering if Dana had managed to get to safety and if their wagon was still at her place.

The two walked silently back toward the circle, listening for any sounds. As they came close to the edge of the trees, Braen indicated to Henith to go around to the south. She would go to the north and meet her on the other side. Braen stopped and held out her hand just as Henith was about to go through the trees to her right, but Henith had heard it, too. A soft moaning coming from the trees to the right. Braen followed Henith carefully through the underbrush. There hidden under a fallen branch, was a young woman. Henith recognized her as one that had come to learn about the healing mysteries. She was weeping. Henith bent down to her and gently removed the branch she was hiding under. Except for some cuts and scratches she appeared to be alright.

She looked at the two women and fear passed over her face. Braen put her fingers to her mouth to indicate that they should be quiet.

"Can you walk?" Henith whispered into the young woman's ear.

She nodded.

"Stay here until we come back. We are going to see who else is here. Do not move and be very quiet."

The young woman grabbed Henith's arm. "Do not leave me," the young woman pleaded.

"Can you move quietly to the edge of the trees?"

She nodded.

"Then wait for us there. We have to make sure there are no men left behind." Braen helped the young woman to stand.

As Henith continued to go south around the edge of the trees, Braen left and went north. Henith could hear moaning coming from the stone circle, and as she continued the moaning became louder and louder. She could not see into the circle from where she was in the trees, but the moaning had taken on a droning sound, getting louder and softer in an eerie pattern. When she reached the eastern edge of the woods, she had not found any other women. Panic started to rumble in her stomach. Braen should have been here by now. She decided to keep on around the circle. Maybe she miscalculated halfway, maybe Braen had found another woman, maybe Braen had been captured by a man. She dismissed that last thought. She continued walking quietly. To her left she heard a sound, and it sounded like her name.

She turned toward the sound and walked further into the forest. She remembered her experience years ago when she was an initiate, following someone calling her name in the forest and almost decided not to go any further when she saw Braen standing with three other women. They were looking down. As Henith approached she could see that it was Zeena laying on the ground. At first Henith thought she was dead.

"Is she alive?" Henith asked in a whisper as she approached the group.

"Barely," one of the women answered.

Another one spoke, "We want to move her to the circle, but we don't know if it is safe, she is barely conscious."

Henith knelt beside Zeena. Centering herself quickly, she began to run her hands lightly over Zeena's body. When she was finished she said, "We can't move her yet. You were wise to leave her. She has several broken bones. She has let go for some reason and does not want to return here. She may choose to leave us." Henith stood. "I need to have the medicines that are in the wagon at Dana's."

"Henith, first we must see to the others. Most have been carried or taken to the circle. Many have suffered injury not only to their bodies,

but also to their spirits. An evil thing has happened here tonight."
Braen looked at Zeena and the others.

"What about the men?"

"As far as we can determine, they have all gone, except the one
who is wounded on the north side of the circle. Jenli is guarding him."

"Jenli?" Henith exclaimed in relief. "And Shelagh?" She almost did
not want to hear the answer.

"Shelagh is fine. She is the one who suggested that the women be
gathered into the circle."

"One of you, stay here with Zeena. I will be back as soon as I can
get what I need." Henith and Braen walked out of the trees toward the
stones. From what Henith could see, the stones were still standing. She
had expected that the men might try to knock them down.

There were ten women lying on the ground, another three or
four were tending them. Shelagh came up to them. "I'm so glad you
escaped, now you can help heal these women."

"Are you alright, Shelagh?" Henith asked, hugging the old woman.

"My body has survived just fine, but my mind and my soul are in
agony. I hid just beyond the trees," she continued pointing to the east
side of the circle. "They came, as you know, from the west. When
Braen called for us to scatter, I ran, but I didn't go far. They caught
some of the women, but most of them escaped and hopefully are
far from here, safe at home. The ones that were caught were brutally
treated. Some may not recover, ever. What this has done to their spirits
is beyond all imaginings. Some of the women came back to help. I
think it is dangerous for them to stay here, but I couldn't move all of
the wounded by myself. They have been helpful."

"Where are the men? Why didn't they stay here?"

"I cannot explain it. At first they were everywhere, violating the
women they had caught. Sometimes two on one woman. I wanted to
scream and I wanted to kill them. I could not watch. I did not know
what to do. I could not just stay here, but what was one old woman
going to do against all of those men? I started praying to the Goddess
for help. I felt as if someone, one of the men, heard me. It was the
strangest feeling. I have never felt anything like it before. The closest

I can remember was when Henith's thoughts seemed to have been captured by one of the men that passed us that day when we were leaving my circle. All of sudden, one of the men started yelling for the others to stop. At first no one listened to him. But then gradually, each one let go of the woman he was holding. They just let them fall. Some did fall, because they had been so badly treated and some ran off. Most of the men started to leave. One of the men, however, started a fight with the one that had told the others to stop. They fought and fought. The one that had stopped the others was wounded. Most of the men had gone by then. The big one just left the other one lying there bleeding. Jenli is watching him right now. He's over there." Shelagh pointed to the north.

Braen and Henith stood amazed at Shelagh's story. Henith moved first. "I need my medicines. These women need to be tended to immediately, especially Zeena. Where's Dana? Have you seen her?"

"No, I think she may have escaped," Shelagh said.

"Oh!" Henith exclaimed.

"What is it?" Braen turned to see what had startled Henith.

"The young woman we left over there. She must be terrified."

"I thought we had found all the women that were still here. I wonder how many more may be lost or hurt somewhere," Shelagh looked concerned.

Henith motioned to one of the women, to go to the place where they had left the young woman and bring her back. Then she called another and asked to go to Dana's for her medicines.

Henith began to attend to the women who were badly hurt. With each one, she centered herself and felt the body of the woman with her hands.

As Henith approached the last woman, she noticed another woman coming into the stone circle. It was Dana. Henith was so relieved to see her that she left the woman and ran over to Dana.

"Thank Goddess, you are alive," Henith greeted her friend, "I was afraid I'd never see you again."

"I brought your wagon. It is in the grove where you were camped the first night."

"How did you know I needed the wagon?"

"I knew that some of the women were going to need what you had in the wagon. I wasn't sure that you would be here, but I knew that we may need the wagon to carry these women home. We cannot stay here much longer. I am sure that the men will be back soon. I am surprised that they have not already been back."

Panic started to take over Henith. "But some of these women cannot be moved yet."

"We will have to risk it. I am sure they will come back to destroy these stones as soon as it is light."

"Then we must hurry. Do you think we can get some hot water?"

"Unlikely—we do not have time for that. You will have to settle for cold."

Learning the healing mysteries on Mona had not prepared Henith for this. How was she expected to tend to all these women at once without any proper preparation? She looked around. There was still one woman that she had not been able to tend yet. Zeena! And what about the man? Was she expected to heal him also?

As she was approaching one of the women on the ground, Shelagh came up to her and said, "Dana said she brought the wagon and the medicines. I will take care of the six that are not in immediate danger and see that they get away from here as soon as possible. That leaves four plus Zeena. You and Braen can tend to them. Maybe we can get them to the wagon in the grove. At least they will be away from here."

Henith looked down at the woman at her feet. A gasp escaped her lips. "It's Celie." Henith quickly knelt beside the woman and started to determine what was wrong with her body. Celie was barely alive, but Henith could not determine any physical reason for her condition. Henith tried again. The woman was barely breathing. Her heart was beating tentatively, but Henith could not detect any injured parts of her body. Puzzled, Henith continued to try to locate the source of Celie's distress.

Henith could see the others busy at work. Braen was tending to the three women who needed extra attention. Shelagh and Dana were helping the others. The women who had come back to help had been paired with one of the wounded. Gradually most of the women had left.

Shelagh was helping Braen. They had decided to put the three into the wagon and take them to Dana's. It seemed safer to move them now than to wait here. They were waiting for Henith to decide about Celie and Zeena.

"I think we should move Zeena here to the circle."

"But, Henith, we are trying to move these women out of here as fast as possible." Dana was adamant.

"I know, but there is nothing wrong with Celie physically, at least nothing that I can determine. Zeena has some broken bones and some other internal injuries, nothing that will not mend in time. Her response is what is troubling. I think she and Celie have decided to pass from this life."

"What?"

"I think Zeena and Celie have decided to pass from this life, and I think we should help them do it. Dana, we will make a carrier for Zeena like the one we made for Jenli. We will bring Zeena here to be with Celie. We will do the parting ritual for them while Dana's gone. By the time she returns, we will be ready."

"What about the man?

"Oh, I had forgotten about him. Poor Jenli, she must be beside herself having to be so close to him." Henith wondered how Jenli was managing. "Maybe I should see him."

Henith was reluctant to leave the women to tend to a man.

"We can manage, Henith. Jenli will be happy to see you. Go ahead."

Henith picked up some of the medicines.

"Jenli," Henith called as she approached where Jenli and the man were supposed to be.

"Over here, Henith. Am I glad to see you," Jenli rose to greet Henith.

Henith looked around, "Where is the man?"

"Over there, he's not going far. He has lost much blood."

Henith went to where Jenli pointed.

There lying in the leaves totally saturated with blood was the man. He looked familiar to Henith, but that was unlikely as she had not known any men around here. The only one she really knew was Talendar, and this was not him.

She knelt beside him. He was not dead, but he was very weak from this excessive loss of blood. His eyes flickered open. He tried to speak.

"It is you," he said.

"What?" Henith said in surprise.

"It is you."

"Shh, do not try to talk, you have lost much blood. You must save your strength."

"It is you."

Henith managed to bind the wound that had caused all the bleeding. Something very sharp had pierced his body. It must have been a sword or something, Henith thought. Why would these men want to do this to each other? She still could not comprehend the violent ways these men treated other people. It was so far from her understanding that she could not make any sense of it.

"It is you."

"What?" The word escaped before she could control it.

"I have seen you several times."

Henith thought he must be delirious from his wounds.

"I have seen you in my mind."

A flash of recognition crossed Henith's face. Oh no, the man who could read her thoughts. Her hands started to tremble. It was dangerous to be so near him. He could read her mind. She rose to leave.

"Are you going to leave me here?"

Henith looked at him. Could she leave him here? Certainly no one would find him.

"What are we going to do with him?" Jenli asked keeping her distance from him.

"I am not sure, but he will be alright for the time being. We have work to do back at the circle."

"Should I stay here so he does not try to escape?"

A question puzzled Henith. Why would they want to keep him? It might be good if he just went away, but then he also might try to attack them again.

"We were not intending to attack. We were just going to watch. It just got out of control too quickly."

Henith was jolted by the ease with which he read her mind.

"I do not know what we will do with you, but for now you will have to stay here. I doubt if you could move far anyway. Come on, Jenli, let us get back to the others. We will have to deal with him later." Henith was shaking, thinking about this man who so easily had mastered one of the sacred mysteries.

When they had reached the circle, Braen and Shelagh had already moved Celie to the center of the circle.

"Let us get Zeena," Braen said as the four gathered again. A feeling of coming home washed over Henith. The four were again in a stone circle. "The dawn is about to break. We do not have much time."

The four took the carrier to where Zeena lay in the brush. Gently they moved her onto it. She was barely breathing. Henith thought she detected a calmness come over Zeena's body as she was being carried by the four priestesses to the stone circle. When they reached the circle, they placed her next to Celie, close enough so that their shoulders were touching. Henith prepared the oil for anointing. Shelagh lit the yellow and white candles that Henith always carried in her medicine bag. Braen started the invocation of the powers of the Goddess. The four priestesses took up the chant. When all was prepared, Henith, Braen, Shelagh, and Jenli stood facing each other, two on each side of the women on the ground.

"Here, O Mother, are Your daughters, take them safely home. Here, O Mother, are Your daughters, take them safely home." The chanting continued. Gradually the four priestesses, with arms held out at waist height, moved as if carrying the Celie and Zeena whose bodies remained on the ground at their feet. Slowly they moved to the northern stone, gradually lifting their arms.

The spirits of Celie and Zeena had gone back to the Mother.

They decided to bury their bodies in the center of the stone circle.

Henith smiled when she saw the intertwined fingers of Celie and Zeena, together at last.

Chapter 16

"Jenli, how long have you been feeling this way?" Shelagh asked.

"How did you know?"

Shelagh asked, "Are you pregnant?"

"Yes!"

"Have you told Braen and Henith?"

"Not yet, I wanted to be sure!"

"If all goes well, we should be arriving on Mona in time for the birth."

"What happens if it's a boy?" Jenli asked as a cloud passed over her face. Very softly, she continued, "I was thinking of ridding myself of the baby."

Shelagh reached out to Jenli. "That is a difficult decision for any woman to make. Let us talk about it with the others when they return."

Braen and Henith had gone to a house they had passed to inquire about the next town. Shelagh and Jenli had been left to make camp for the night. It had been about three weeks since they had left Dana and the others. No one had followed them that they had seen. They kept off the main roads for the first two weeks. Travel had been difficult because of the wagon and trying to avoid roads and villages. They had seen no one for those two weeks. For the past few days they had been travelling on a road. It was easier, but the potential danger was greater.

They had begun to see more people so they knew they must be getting closer to a major village or a town, although they had been told that there were no large towns in this part of Trenig.

The evening meal was being prepared when Braen and Henith returned.

"We are nearing a village. The good news is that there is a stone circle there, and a priestess from Mona. Can you believe it?"

"We have traveled further north than we had guessed. The woman at the house said we would reach there the day after tomorrow."

"That means we may be there in time for the moon ritual." Excitement filled the group.

"I wonder who is there. Do you think we are near Rento's circle?" Henith asked Braen.

"The woman said that it is a small circle. Not many women have continued the old ways. Some of the men from the new religion have been in the village for some time. She says it is easier not to have the rituals. She does not go to the village often, once or twice a year for the festivals. Her sister lives in the village and once in a while comes here for a visit."

"Has she heard anything about the last town we were in?"

"No! I guess news does not travel this way very often. We are in a very remote part of Trenig."

"I cannot wait to get to the next village to see the priestess from home. I wish we could leave right now." Henith sat down next to Braen.

"I like it here," Jenli said, "it is peaceful and quiet. I am not anxious to see many people."

"I am not either, but being with a priestess from home will be a special gift. It has been so long."

"Will we reach Mona then, before the Spring Rite? We must be nearer than we thought."

"Trenig is much more narrow from east to west in the north than the south. We might even be home by the solstice."

"I am pregnant," Jenli said when there was a pause in the conversation, "and I am not sure how I feel about it. In the first place, the child was conceived in violence, and I am not sure that I can ever forget that fact. In the second place, I am not sure I want this child. This is not a child of my choosing." Jenli started to cry.

Henith knew that there were some herbs she could give Jenli to help her rid herself of the child. The women on Mona chose when they wanted a child. Giving life was a sacred act. None of the women she had ever known would have chosen to rid themselves of a potential new life, because they were never in a situation where they would get pregnant without choosing to be so. Again she was struck by how different life in Trenig was for women than on Mona.

Shelagh spoke for the first time since Henith and Braen had returned.

"I have been thinking about Jenli's situation. There have been many times I have given women what they needed to remove an unwanted baby. It is always a decision that is difficult. In some ways it goes against everything we believe about the goodness of life and the joy of bringing a baby into this world. It is one of the most beautiful and powerful gifts women have been given. But in Trenig, women do not always have a choice about when. Jenli, whatever you decide, I will support you. I also would like to suggest that we stay here for a few days of silence and meditation. I know, Henith, you are anxious to go the next village, but we have been running away from the last town for too long. We jump at every noise we hear. We keep looking behind us to see if we are being followed. We are in no condition spiritually to approach another village, however welcome we may be there.

"Jenli has suffered severe trauma. Her body and her soul need time and space to heal. And now she is faced with the heaviest of decisions. If we stay here for three days in silence and meditation we will still have time to reach the village by the moon ritual."

Shelagh was quiet.

"Shelagh is right as usual," Braen said, "we have been running away from our fears. We do need some time to prepare ourselves for the next part of our journey. Jenli, I want you to take whatever time you need. It is impossible for me to understand how you are feeling. What happened to you is so far from my own experience that I have no way to identify with you. Henith, dear, how are you doing with the idea of waiting before we go to the village?"

"I know what you say is right. I am always overwhelmed by my desire to go home to Mona, to escape from the ways of Trenig, and to go back to where life is calm and orderly. I am tired of having to make life and death decisions as women here have to every day. I, too, need to re-center my energies. I am totally scattered. I had not realized it until you, Shelagh, began talking. Jenli, I cannot honestly say what I would do if I were in your circumstances. I always assumed that if I chose to bear a child, I would be participating in one of the Goddess's most sacred rites. It never occurred to me until now that there might be circumstances when that might not be true."

"Let us be in silence then until the evening meal the day after tomorrow."

Henith was surprised when she tried to remember how long it had been since she had so much silent time. She remembered her first three-day vigil many years ago, before she was initiated. The visions she had at the time had been so vivid she thought they had been real. She thought about Carog and wondered what she was doing. It had been a long time since she had thought about Carog. Was she on Mona living the peaceful life of a priestess? Henith thought about how long it had been since she had any news from Mona. In most of Trenig it was as if Mona didn't exist. She felt an impatience overtake her and a mild resentment of the others. Three more days to wait. She wondered if the priestess in the next village knew her mother. She thought about her mother and Morgan coming back from Trenig that time her mother had been wounded. She shivered when she thought about her mother being attacked like Jenli was. Henith had not even known what a man was then. She wished she did not know now.

❧❧

Henith was deep into meditation when she opened her eyes and saw the woman from the house down the road standing in front of her. She did not know where the others were. The woman looked embarrassed standing there in the trees watching her.

Henith was reluctant to break her silence, but the woman staring at her did not know that she was in silence.

257

"Hello!" Henith said surprised at the sound of her own voice in the stillness of this place. "I was meditating."

"I probably should not have bothered you, but I thought you would like to know."

"Like to know what?" Henith was curious why this woman had troubled herself to come here.

"I was not sure you were still camped here. I thought maybe you had gone, but I did not see you leave. I can see the road from my window. My house is up on a hill, you see. I can watch the people traveling on the road in both directions for some way. I was sure I had not missed your leaving."

"We decided to rest for a few days before we went into the next village and this is such a pleasant place." Henith thought maybe the woman was here under false pretenses, trying to find out what they were doing.

"You said you thought we should know something," Henith continued, trying to keep the impatience from her voice.

"You are far enough off the road here so you cannot see the travellers. There are not many, you know. You were the first in many days. That is why I thought you would like to know."

Henith could feel her impatience overtaking her body. She willed herself to remain calm and let the woman tell her what she wanted to at her own pace.

"When you came the other day asking if there was a stone circle here, I was surprised. Even though some people still follow the old ways, not many people pay any attention anymore. I have not heard anyone talk about it since the new priestess came last year. I cannot even remember her name."

Henith was surprised by this new information. The other day when Braen and she had visited this woman, she had been reluctant with information. It had not occurred to Henith to ask the name of the priestess. The woman had been so vague. She and Braen had silently agreed not to pursue the conversation by trying not to appear too interested, just in case this area had been taken over by the new ways.

They had been content to learn that there was a circle near here and that a priestess was serving there.

"It has been so long since I had strangers visit and ask about the circle, I was really shocked when another stranger stopped by yesterday asking the same question."

Henith's mouth fell open. "Another person?" Henith doubted if Jenli or Shelagh would break the silence to go and talk to this woman. "You said another traveller?" Henith's voice was trembling.

"Yes, a man, and a fine looking one at that."

"A man?" Now Henith's whole body was shaking.

"He came by yesterday, late in the day. He asked if there were any circles around here. I told him only an old abandoned one over that way." She pointed north.

"Did you tell him about the one to the west?"

"No, I began to wonder about all this interest in circles, and I did not want to lie to him. I told him about the one three days' ride from here."

"Did he ask anything else?" she asked, internally preparing herself for the answer.

"Yes, he asked if anyone, a woman, by any chance had come this way in the last few weeks."

"What did you tell him?"

"I told you I do not like to lie. Lying always gets you in trouble later on down the path. I was just about to tell him I had seen you, when it occurred to me that I had seen four women not one. If I said I had not seen one woman, then I was not really lying because I had seen four."

Henith chuckled at the cleverness of the woman.

"Thank you."

"Did I say right?"

"Yes, thank you. Can you describe him?"

"He was tall. His beard was a reddish blonde. He had nice eyes. Oh, he seemed to be favoring his left shoulder as if it hurt him somehow."

Henith remembered the man in the pool of blood with the red-blonde beard. She could still hear his voice saying, "It is you. It is you." She remembered the gentleness mingled with pain that she had detected in his eyes. Could it be the same man? How had he lived? It was true that they had placed him near the circle just before they left, in case his friends returned for him. The women had made him as comfortable as possible. They even prepared his body in case he might die before he was found, but then they had left him. They had traveled by an obscure route as best as they could to this point. Could it be him? Who else could it be?

"It was so good of you not to tell him about us. Did he by any chance tell you his name?'

"Let me see, I think he said his name was Colywn. Do you know him?"

"Not really. I saved the life of someone who fits his description. I did not know his name though."

The woman looked at Henith, hoping for more information, but she did not ask any questions. Henith remained silent.

"I guess I will be going then. How long had you planned to stay, in case you get more visitors?"

"We had planned to leave tomorrow, early."

"Well, it is goodbye then."

Henith rose and walked to the woman who stood before her. "Thank you again. You do not know how much help you have been. How far did you say it was to the stone circle?"

"Which one?"

"Oh, both I guess."

"Well, the one I sent him to find is three days' north. The one you want is a day and a half west."

After the woman had gone, Henith decided to wait until their evening meal before she told the others about the woman's visit.

Chapter 17

Henith could feel her body begin to tingle with excitement. In a few more hours at most they would reach the village. Henith wondered who the priestess was. Henith did not know all the women of her island, so she did not expect to know the woman serving here. But that did not stop the excitement she felt. Somehow just seeing another priestess again would feel like home. The old woman that she had talked to the other day had said that the priestess had only arrived here a year ago. That would mean that she would have news of Mona. Henith longed to hear about her mother and Morgan.

"Henith, we will be there soon. Do you think we should find a place to camp and prepare ourselves for the visit?" Henith heard Braen's voice in her reverie.

"What?"

"Do you think we should camp around here somewhere?" Braen laughed at her friend. "Where were you?"

"Oh, I was thinking of Mona and the priestess here, and wondering if she knew my mother, and what might be happening on Mona."

"What about finding a place to set up camp?"

"Oh, I guess I just assumed that we would stay with the priestess there. Do you think that is not wise?"

"I do not know. Maybe we should set up camp outside of the town, and you and I go to see the priestess. If this is really a safe place and if she feels that it is alright, we will come back for Shelagh and Jenli."

For some reason, Henith had refused to think of the possibility that they might not be safe. A town with a priestess from Mona had to be a safe place, but maybe Braen was right. Some caution might be in order. After all, there was that man who obviously was following them. But he could not be here yet if he went to the other circle first. He may never get here, if he keeps going north. Henith allowed a slight smile to cross her lips when she thought of him going further and further north looking for stone circles, but then a shiver crossed her body when she realized that he was also looking for her.

"You're right. Let us begin to look for a place to camp. I was just in such a hurry to find the woman from Mona, I forgot that it might not be safe for us."

"We will be back tonight, tomorrow noon at the latest," Braen said to Shelagh and Jenli, "if anything happens, we will send you a message. I doubt that we are in any particular danger. At least there is a priestess here, so things cannot be as bad as they were in the last town."

⁂

"Are you excited, Braen? I am. She must be in that cottage over there. The woman said it was the one on the edge of the village. I expect that she will be surprised to see two priestesses from Mona. I wonder if she will know who we are. Certainly if she has been here a year, she will know that we are wandering around Trenig." Henith chuckled thinking of the image of herself and Braen wandering around Trenig. "Just think, we are even here in time for the moon ritual which should be tomorrow night."

Braen took Henith's hand and gave it a squeeze as they approached the door. Just as they were about to knock, the door opened and a young woman their age stood staring at them. Braen felt Henith's hand tighten in hers, and felt Henith's body go very rigid. She looked from the woman who was standing in the doorway, with her mouth open as if unable to speak, to Henith who stood frozen next to her. Braen could not detect what had passed between the woman and Henith, but whatever it was, it had a long history.

Henith recovered first. "Hello, Carog, I guess I never expected to find you here. It has been so long since we have seen anyone from home that it was a shock to find someone I knew."

Carog also recovered. "I am sorry for staring, but I never thought I would see you again, especially here in this remote village. Come in, come in."

"This is Braen, from the east village. Maybe you remember, she was also initiated with us."

Carog nodded to Braen.

"How long have you been here, Carog? How are the women on Mona? What news do you have?"

Carog laughed, "How long has it been, Henith? I have been here almost a year, and you left several years before that!"

"How is Morgan? Did you ever see my mother?"

"I cannot possibly answer all the questions at once. Maybe I should start from the beginning, but first, would you like some tea?"

"Yes, that would be good," Braen said. "But before you start the storytelling, is this a safe place? We have been in some villages where it is not at all safe for women to be practicing our religion, and it certainly was dangerous to be a priestess."

Braen thought she detected a color shift in Carog and wondered if Henith had noticed.

"It is safe enough if you are careful and know how to deal with the men of the new religion."

"Are they here?" Henith sounded astounded. "How can it possibly be safe for you, if they are here?"

"You just have to know how to play their little games," Carog had turned away from the women, and Henith could not see her face. Henith began to detect that something was not quite right.

"What do you mean, play their little games?" Braen had also detected some uneasiness in Carog.

"Here is the tea. Oh, I will tell you about that later, but first let us catch up on all the stories. You also must have many stories to tell." Carog sat across from Henith. "Life on Mona was as boring as ever. Not like here. It is very exciting being here. I've met all kinds of people. It is so different than just seeing priestesses all the time, telling the same stories over and over."

"I think I would like that. Life here has been too dangerous. There is too much violence. The ways of the Goddess are slipping away. No one seems to care anymore."

"Oh, Henith, you always were so old-fashioned. Trenig is changing. You cannot keep holding on to the old ways forever."

Henith looked at Carog. "What do you mean you cannot hold on to the old ways? The old ways are important. They give meaning to life. Life was peaceful and calm before these invaders came. Do not tell me that you have given up the old ways." Henith's voice was getting louder and higher.

Braen reached over to touch Henith's hand. Henith felt the touch, but it was not enough. She could feel herself getting angrier and angrier.

Braen interceded. "Tell us some stories about Mona. We are hungry for the stories of home. We have been on a long and difficult journey, and we long to be home. Even the dullest detail to you will be music to us. Please begin the storytelling anywhere."

"Just after you left, three men landed near the south village." A groan escaped from Henith's throat. "The women overwhelmed the men. A fight ensued, and the men were all killed. Some of the women were badly hurt. The experience of killing those men was so terrible that some of the women became very ill. The deaths affected the whole island for many moons. Morgan went to stay in the southern village along with the keepers of the healing mysteries. Several moons passed before the energy on the island returned to normal, although some of the women believed that it never could return to the way it had been before the invasion. The holy space had been violated and the women were fearful. The fact that some women had actually killed other human beings, even in saving their own lives and the lives of their sisters, was such a violation of the ways of Mona that some felt that even though the men were dead, their ways had won out, and that the ways of the Goddess were gone forever. For days and weeks women went through the rituals as if they were not real. It was a difficult time for us. The great Spring Rite that year was very somber.

No one felt like celebrating. Something had been lost. Even though we did the same rituals, as women on Mona had been doing for centuries, something was missing. Everyone felt the shift in energy, but no one could offer a way to shift it back to the way it was before the killings."

Henith and Braen sat stunned listening to Carog. Maybe they did not want to hear the stories after all.

"All of the women recovered physically. Eventually Morgan went back to live at the center, and the healers went back to their villages. Over the year that followed, many different solutions were tried to regain the energy that we knew existed before the invasion. We met with different groups of women from the different villages, that was the best part. We were amazed how much we needed to meet with each other. We realized that we had led a rather solitary life, only knowing the women in our own village. That meant there was more activity on the island, women moving from village to village. Then someone thought that all the moving was working against our ability to re-center. So we spent more time in silence. Weeks on end spent in silence. I did not like that time very much. I am not disciplined enough to stay silent for weeks at a time. Nothing seemed to work. The energy shift resulting from the killing remained. After about a year, life returned to our old routines, except that it was easier to go and visit in the other villages. Friendships had been established that had not existed before. I think that was the good that came from the experience."

Henith thought about the one fear she had had about returning to Mona, that she would never see Braen again except for the Spring Rite. She found herself secretly relieved that something had changed on Mona.

"Have there been any invasions since?" Braen asked.

"None before I left. I have not heard about any since I came here, although I have heard that the invaders plan to take over all of Trenig eventually, and that includes destroying Mona."

"When did you hear that? Did you send a message back home?"

"I only heard it a few moons ago. I was not sure it was true, so I have not told anyone, except now, you two." Carog looked embarrassed.

The old familiar childhood feeling of mistrust came over Henith. Henith could not decide whether the feelings of mistrust she was experiencing were memories from years ago or whether she was discovering new feelings.

"Is there any other news? Do you know how my mother, Canth, is?"

"When I left, Canth was fine. She and Morgan had come to Trenig again, just to visit the villages closest to Mona. They were only gone for a moon's time. I told you that after the invasion there was a period of time when women met in groups all over the island. As a result of that, friendships were established and the women were reluctant to go back to their village and not see their friends anymore. Several women left their village and went to live in another village."

"That must have caused a great deal of confusion on the island," Braen suggested, trying to imagine not living in her own village.

"For a while it did cause a great deal of unrest, and for the first time that the storytellers could remember, conflict and jealousies between villages emerged. We spent many moons discussing whether our loyalty was to our own village or to Mona, or even to Trenig. After many days of very tedious discussion, we decided that it did not matter where we lived, as long as we were faithful to the ways of the Goddess. So, many women moved. It turned out that the villages stayed about the same size. One of the fears was that everyone would move to one village and the others would be left unbalanced. That is not what happened. One of the most unusual shifts was that your mother, Canth, moved to the center of the island to live with Morgan. As far as the storytellers could remember, there had never been more than the five High Priestesses living at the center. Some of the older women were concerned that that would upset the balance of energy even more. The debate had not been settled before I left. I expect that it caused many more days of tedious discussion."

Henith was stunned. Her mother and Morgan. Why not? She was with Braen. She still could not imagine it somehow. Morgan was the High Priestess. So what? From the little that Carog was telling them, Henith was having trouble imagining all of the changes that had taken place on Mona since she left. She had hoped nothing had changed there, that somehow she could go back again to the peaceful life she had known before she and Braen started this journey. A joyful thought did pass through her mind, however. The changes meant that she and Braen could live together in the same village. She looked at Braen, hoping Braen was thinking the same thoughts.

"How is your life here, Carog?" Braen interrupted Henith's thoughts again.

"Life is different here. It was lonely at first, then I began to know some of the people here," Carog looked down at her hands in her lap. Feelings of mistrust leaped at Henith again.

"You do conduct the rituals, don't you?" Henith asked almost in an accusing way.

"Yes, but not many women come anymore."

"We would love to join you tomorrow night."

Carog looked uncomfortable. "Yes, tomorrow night. I would be happy to have you join me, but do not be surprised if only a few of the town's women appear. Since the new religion has come to this area, the women do not want to bother with the old ways. There have been some months when I have been the only one there."

"Is it dangerous? Do they fear for their lives?"

"No, it just does not seem important to them any more. They do not want to leave their husbands. It is true that many of the men have forbidden their wives to continue in the old ways. One or two who are unmarried have continued to come occasionally. Most of the women have had to choose between their husbands and the rituals, and most have chosen their husbands. It has been a relatively quiet take over. Not many people have been hurt physically. Most of the women have just made different choices."

"But what about you? How do you manage to stay here? I would think that the foreigners would have destroyed the circle by now and would have harmed you in some way. That is what has happened in other parts of Trenig."

"I know the leader of the foreigners who came to this village just after I did. He and I worked out an agreement. He would not destroy the stones, if I would not try to keep the women coming to the rituals."

"What?" Henith shrieked at Carog. "How could you agree to such an arrangement? What about the ways of the Goddess we promised to protect? What about the women in this area?"

"Listen, Henith, I did what I thought was best. I have at least saved the stones for a little while longer. Did you want a blood bath? What happened on Mona, the killing of those three men, changed our ways forever. And here there are many more men. Women would have been killed. Is that what you want? At least the women are alive and the stones are safe," Carog was shouting back at Henith.

"But what about the mysteries? Who is going to keep them safe? What about the rituals, who is going to even know about them when you leave? What about the spiritual lives of the women here? Aren't those things important, too?" Henith was furious and near tears, thinking about what was being lost here.

"I do not have the answers to those questions. When you and I were on Mona, we never had to make decisions like that. We studied the mysteries, days came and days went, everything had been the same for centuries. And now it is changing. To save and protect the old ways we would have to be violent ourselves. We might even have had to kill another human being. Is that how you want this to be? You were not on Mona when the men were killed. You do not know what it did to the women there."

Henith sat silently staring at her tea. She remembered what happened to Jenli and the women at the last town. She remembered Celie and Zeena. She remembered the other women lying wounded around the stones.

Braen put her arm around her and held her tightly. Braen said, "We have not seen what has happened on Mona, but we have seen what has happened in other villages and towns in Trenig. We also have experienced much violence. It is hard for us to accept, but maybe your way is the best. At least the women are safe. We would still like to join you tomorrow night for the ritual, if you think that is alright. In your agreement with the leader of the men, did you also promise not to do the moon rituals?" Braen was looking straight into Carog's eyes. She noticed a flicker in them when she asked the question.

"Not exactly, it is just that no women come to the circle."

"Well, we will be there. We also have some friends that we would like to have there. That at least makes five of us."

Carog was visibly uncomfortable under Braen's stare.

"Yes, we will do the ritual," she said in a tone that was not at all reassuring.

Braen questioned herself as to whether it had been wise to push her.

"We should be returning to our friends. We will bring them to visit tomorrow if that is alright with you." As Braen started to rise, they all heard a horse ride up outside.

Carog jumped up from where she was sitting and ran to the door. Curious, Braen and Henith followed. A very familiar tall young man was dismounting from his horse. Before he noticed the two women standing in the doorway, he ran up to Carog and embraced her enthusiastically, kissing her and lifting her off her feet. Henith's knees turned to water when she recognized him. Carog was struggling to get free. Henith backed up into the room not wanting to be part of the next events, which were inevitable. Braen stood quietly watching the scene and felt Henith withdraw behind her.

Carog recovered her composure and, leading the young man to the house, started to introduce him to the women.

Upon seeing Braen, Talendar stopped, staring in disbelief.

Carog, not understanding what was happening, tried to pull him toward the women.

Braen and Talendar were staring at each other. Wishing for any type of escape, Henith had hidden behind the door.

Before Carog could speak, Talendar moved toward Braen. "Good afternoon, Braen, this is a pleasant surprise. I thought I would never see you again after that time in Boscawen. Whatever happened to you? I thought we were going to meet for instruction, and you never appeared. I waited many hours. You just disappeared into thin air. Is Henith with you?" Braen could tell he was trying hard to keep his voice even.

"You two know each other?" Carog exclaimed. "How extraordinary!"

"Yes, we met some time ago. Is Henith with you?" he asked again.

"Yes."

Henith came from behind the door. Looking at the ground, Henith said, barely above a whisper, "Good afternoon, Talendar."

"You know him, too?" Carog asked accusingly of Henith.

"Yes, we have met."

"Then I guess there is no need for introductions."

An uncomfortable silence fell on the group, no one quite knowing what to do next.

Henith broke the silence, "It has been nice seeing you again, but we had better be going."

"Can you stay for dinner?" Talendar asked. Carog shifted onto the other leg. "Carog and I would love to have you stay to dinner, wouldn't we?" Talendar put his arm around Carog.

Henith began to tremble again. She looked at Braen for help.

"We have other plans for this evening, but we would like to visit with you some other time. We do need to be getting back to our camp."

Carog looked relieved.

"Will we be seeing you again tomorrow, Carog?" Braen asked as if the previous plan did not exist.

"Come by for tea in the morning. There are some things we still need to talk about."

"Yes, it would seem so." Braen and Henith said goodbye and left the two of them standing there, Talenda's arm still around Carog.

Chapter 18

Henith and Braen walked in silence. Seeing Carog again was a shock to Henith, but to see her with Talendar, that was almost more than she could comprehend. She was disgusted and angry with Carog. How could she so blithely abandon the Goddess for Talendar? Henith could not understand what she had witnessed. How had Talendar found Carog anyway? She thought he was going north to marry a woman in a village. Henith stopped walking. Braen looked at her.

"Are you alright? What were you thinking about?"

"Oh Braen, do you think Talendar has married Carog?" Henith asked, not liking the words that were coming from her mouth.

"She is a priestess of the Goddess. She would not forsake her vows."

"But Talendar told us that he was going to marry a woman in a northern village. And he did say 'we' when he invited us to dine with them. Do you think that is why Carog was so fidgety when we were asking her about tomorrow's ritual?"

"I doubt if Carog would marry one of the foreigners."

"I do not trust her, I never have. My mother always told me to watch her and I would learn some valuable lessons about myself. She always made me so uncomfortable. What are we going to do about tomorrow?"

"I do not know. Talendar probably never knew that we were also priestesses of the Goddess. I wonder if knowing will change his attitude toward us. And I wonder if we are safe."

"Shelagh and Jenli are going to find this turn of events difficult to believe. I know I do."

"It cannot be more than five or six days walk to the village near Mona if Carog is here. Maybe we should just go home, and forget about Carog," Henith said after a long silence.

"But we do not know for sure she has married, and we do not know that she has given up the ways of the Goddess. You are only speculating because you are angry."

"You are right, Braen, I am being unfair and I am angry."

⊱•⊰

After supper, Henith suggested to her friends that she needed to spend some time alone to try to clarify some of her feelings. The others agreed to spend the evening in silence. They were unclear about what they should do next. Going directly to Mona was appealing to all of them. Jenli had been concerned about whether she would be allowed on Mona, because she was not a priestess and because she was pregnant. She had decided not to rid herself of the baby, even though it had not been her choice to be pregnant now, and even though it had been conceived under violent conditions. Henith and Braen both agreed that she would be allowed to go to Mona, because she really was a priestess in the full sense of what it meant to be one. They assured her that the women on the island would welcome her and the birth of her baby. No one mentioned the problem of what would happen to it if it were a boy. The time to make decisions about that possibility seemed so far away. No one could imagine what would happen on Mona after the women heard all the stories that Henith and Braen had to tell.

Henith walked toward the brook that was near the camp and started to follow it upstream. Water always calmed her, even if it were only a tiny flowing trickle of a brook. She had gone some distance from camp when she came to a clearing. From this vantage point she could see the smoke rising through the trees from their campfire below. In the distance she could see the houses at the edge of town where Carog lived. It was much larger than Henith had realized. She had been so upset at seeing Carog and Talendar that she and Braen had not explored the town further after leaving Carog's. The sun was setting in the west, somewhere over Mona. Henith looked with longing at the western sky, as shades of red and gold played on the clouds. Mona was there. Morgan and her mother, all the priestess of the Goddess were under that pink and purple sky. She knew the women would be preparing for evening renewal. She wished she were there, in the peace and tranquility of the evening prayers. She found a comfortable rock to lean against that was facing west. Maybe she could connect with them if she settled herself. Maybe their energy would reach all this distance across the hills and mountains and water that lay between them.

Just as Henith was closing her eyes and trying to focus on the island that she knew lay far away in the distance, she heard footsteps coming from the north. The footsteps were heavier that Braen's or the others. Besides, if they had taken a walk they would probably have approached from the other direction. Fear gripped Henith. She did not want to be found alone by a strange man.

Henith had started to get up from where she was sitting, planning to run down the path near the brook back toward her camp, when a man appeared heading directly toward her.

"Well, Henith, I see you have found one of the prettiest spots in northern Trenig."

Henith looked at Talendar standing before her.

"And I see you have found it by yourself, how convenient. At last we can be alone."

Henith started toward the path.

"Don't leave, I want to talk to you. It has been months since we have seen each other, and you have to admit, you owe me an explanation for your sudden departure. You know I looked everywhere for you and your friend. I thought maybe you had been kidnapped or something. I could not believe that you would just go off that way without even saying good-bye."

Henith did not know whether to run or to stay. She kept staring at the young man, who was different than she remembered. He seemed less shy, or stronger or something.

"Aren't you at least going to say 'Hello'?"

"Good evening, Talendar, I was not expecting to see anyone here. I was just sitting watching the sunset when I heard footsteps. I guess I was a little frightened."

"You do insist upon wandering around Trenig alone. I told you that was not safe when I met you in Boscawen. But you are safe here with me."

Henith did not feel comforted by his words.

"Do you mind if I watch the sunset with you? I often come here to watch it."

Henith sat down with her back to the rock again, looking out toward where Mona should be. The pinks in the sky were becoming more rosy in color. The almost full moon had already risen. The few clouds that remained in the sky were in the west. The rest of the sky was clear. One or two stars were making themselves visible in spite of the brightness of the moon's light.

Talendar sat next to Henith. Because the rock that she was leaning against was not large, his body was closer to hers than she would have liked. Strange feelings started stirring in her stomach. They were similar to the ones she had had when she had met him before. Breathing was becoming more difficult. Feelings of flight began to overtake her.

"Tell me, how do you know Carog?"

Henith did not know how to answer the question because she did not know what Carog had already told him, and she did not want to put herself in any more danger that she already was in.

"We have known each other for a long time."

"That is what she said, but how could you have known her? She said that she came from an island off the coast. Did you come from that island also?"

Henith looked at Talendar, who was looking out into the sky. Did he know Carog was a priestess or just someone who came from an island?

"Yes. Have you known Carog long?" Henith tried to shift to asking the questions.

"After I lost you, I came directly north. Remember I told you that we had been sent out to marry the women in the north. Well, I arrived here some months ago. Many of the men found women right away, but I was still thinking about you." Talendar paused and looked at Henith.

Henith shifted her body away from him, trying not to appear too obvious. She did not like what she was hearing. It made her body do strange things.

"You do not even know me," Henith said weakly.

"I knew what I felt back in Boscawen. I had never felt that before, and I have had many opportunities to feel it with many women. But there was something about you that I could not get out of my mind. You haunted me."

"But we barely spoke to each other."

"It did not matter. I knew that if there was any chance at all after the instruction in our religion, I would ignore the orders to go north and marry, and I would ask you to marry me."

Henith's face flushed. She tried to pinch herself to see if she were having another one of her visions or not. In spite of the words that she was hearing that were unbelievable in any case, her body seemed real and what was worse, so did the body of this man. She wished she could just fly away from here. She did not like what he was saying and she certainly did not like what her own body was doing.

"Talendar, I really must be going. The others will be worried about me." She tried to move. But he put his hand on her arm.

"Don't go!" She could not tell if it were a command or a request.

"I really must."

"Not yet, you have not even heard the rest of my story." His hand remained on her arm. "I could not believe it when you disappeared. I looked everywhere for you. No one had seen you leave. Even Tana did not know where you were. Where did you go? It was as if you had vanished off the earth."

"We went to Merchlyn." There was no need going into details, Henith thought, and it was true that they went to Merchlyn.

"You did not go there right away. I had men looking for you in all of the major towns. I even went to Lintern, looking for you. No one had ever seen you."

"We went by all the back roads and it took us a long time to get there." Henith was not used to telling half-truths, but she could not tell him about Shelagh's circle.

"It amazes me that you ended up here in Balquhain. It is a miracle. I do remember you saying that you were from the north of Trenig, so I hoped that I would find you here, but when I arrived no one had ever heard of you here either."

"What about Carog?"

"By the time I found Carog, I had given up ever finding you again. Trenig is a very big place to lose one woman." He smiled at her, his hand squeezing her arm ever so slightly.

"What about Carog?"

"What do you mean?" Talendar looked out into the darkening sky.

"You were very friendly with her this afternoon."

"We are friends."

"Friends?" Henith wondered why she was pursuing this conversation. She really did not want to know about Talendar and Carog. All she wanted to do was to go back to the others, pack the wagon and go home to Mona. These new sensations in her body were scaring her.

"Well, actually, Carog and I are married," he said.

Henith could not respond. A heaviness fell between them. To Henith the silence was worse than the discussion. She fell into a time shift. The silence went on into eternity. She could not move, she was suspended in the world between reality and illusion. She tried to bring herself back, but she was not sure she wanted to be back.

Finally, she heard a deep voice outside of her self.

"But it does not matter. I married her because that was what we were supposed to do. I could not disobey the orders much longer, so I married Carog. The strategists were right. It is far more effective than trying to take people by force. Almost all of the village has been converted, even Carog. She did resist at first, hanging on to all that Goddess nonsense. I even caught her sneaking off to the stone circle last month." Talendar looked at the moon and laughed. "She will probably try to sneak away tomorrow night. I should have had the stones destroyed, then she would not have any place to go, but it seemed like such a waste of energy."

The queasy feelings in Henith's stomach started to turn to nausea. "Do all of the women give in so easily?"

"No, but eventually they come round, especially when they start to have our children. Carog has not conceived yet, but I know it will not be long."

Henith felt as if she had been talking to two totally different people. One had been kind and gentle and the other had been one of the foreigners with their condescending view of women. How could Carog have been taken in by him? She even began to feel sorry for Carog.

"I really must be getting back."

"Can I see you tomorrow?"

"We will probably see Carog tomorrow. We have not finished catching up on all the stories."

"I mean can I see you tomorrow alone?"

"I do not think that would be wise. I am not sure what the others have planned," Henith tried to avoid the direct answer. She did not want to put herself or the others in danger.

"What time will you be coming to see Carog? I would like to be there and hear some of your stories, too. Why don't you come mid-morning? You could leave your chaperone behind." Henith thought she detected a sneer in his voice. As Henith rose to leave, he caught both of her hands.

"Henith, do come alone. I really would like to see you again. I have missed you very much," the tone in his voice had totally shifted from the sneer. Henith could feel her knees weaken as he held her hands in the moonlight. She was in danger and she knew it. She managed to pull her hands free.

"I will see you tomorrow, Talendar." Henith managed to sound polite and non-committal and started down the path toward her camp.

"Until tomorrow, then." He smiled at her and watched as she disappeared into the darkness.

Chapter 19

“Good morning, Henith, Braen.” Talendar nodded in the direction of the two women who were approaching the gate. Henith smiled slightly, but avoided his eyes. She knew he was displeased with her for bringing Braen. Shelagh and Jenli had decided to stay at camp. Under the circumstances, it seemed wise for the four of them not to be together too often. If anything happened to Braen or Henith, the other two might be able to help them.

“Good morning, Talendar, is Carog at home?”

“Yes, go on in, she’s expecting you.” Talendar had moved to stand very close to Henith. “Henith, may I speak with you? Braen, why don’t you go in and see Carog? I would like to speak to Henith for a moment.”

Braen looked at Henith, who was looking at the ground and shifting her weight back and forth on her feet. Henith had not told the others about Talendar’s visit last night. She was embarrassed by the feelings she was having and wanted to have time alone to try to understand what was happening to her. Braen’s look was one of both concern and curiosity.

Trying to make light of the situation Braen said, “Don’t be too long. We have many stories to catch up on.”

“Come, walk with me, Henith. There is something I would like to show you.”

She followed him down a well-worn path that led downhill from the north side of their house. They walked in silence, Talendar leading,

Henith following. The further and further they went into the woods, the more and more uncomfortable Henith became.

"We should be getting back." She turned to start up the hill.

"Wait, I have not shown you what we have come this far to see."

"How much further is it? I really need to be getting back." Fear was starting to creep into her voice.

"We are very close."

Henith looked ahead. She thought she detected water through the opening between some of the trees. "Is there a lake here?"

"Yes," was Talendar's only response.

They walked on until they came to the edge of the lake. It was beautiful. The water was a color Henith had never seen before, a warm greenish blue. She thought it would be a splendid color for a robe. She tried to think of all the dyes that she had used, and could not think of one that would produce that shade. She mixed colors in her mind, trying to imagine what colors could be put together to match the intenseness of this particular shade of green, or was it blue? Henith looked out across the lake. The trees on the other side were birches with white trunks and leaves that seemed to dance in the breeze. They were casting a reflection onto the still surface of the lake.

"Now, isn't this worth the walk?" Talendar was standing very close to Henith. She could feel the warmth of his body through her tunic. She moved away.

"It is breathtaking. You were right, Talendar. I wish we had brought Braen here, too, she also would have liked to have seen it." Henith moved toward a path that was leading off around the lake. She did not want to go any farther, but if she turned back she would be facing Talendar directly.

"Henith." He reached out to touch her arm. He was pulling her toward him. "Henith, you are even more beautiful than the lake. Come here, stop running off."

Henith wanted to run away from here, but she knew she could not run faster than he could. "Talendar, you are forgetting Carog."

"Stop worrying about her. I told you, I had to marry someone. Those were our orders, but I want you. Last night I could not sleep thinking about you. I could not believe that you just walked right back into my life. My only regret is that you did not come back a few months ago. Then I would have married you instead of Carog."

"Talendar, you are forgetting one thing. Suppose I do not want to marry you?"

He laughed. "You forget where you are. Women have no choice in whom they marry. Did you not know that?" He looked at her with a question on his face.

It had never occurred to Henith that women had no choice. She was always surprised to find one more thing that she had not known before and had just taken for granted. "But you are already married. Certainly you cannot have two wives."

"Our religion does forbid having more than one wife at a time, but it is alright for me to have more than one woman at a time." That awful sneer came back into his voice. He was still holding Henith's arm.

Angrily, Henith began, "Well, my religion—" But she stopped. She could not tell him about her religion.

He let go of her, "Do not tell me you still practice that Goddess religion. You and Carog." He was disgusted. "You will have to stop doing that, it is evil. Your souls are in danger. Do you not realize that our religion will save you from burning in the great fire after you die?"

"Our religion is not evil. How can you say such a thing? You do not even know anything about it." She was so angry that she said more than she ought to have.

"I suppose you also belong to one of those circles that meet by the stones." He was looking directly at her. She did not answer. "Henith, listen to me." His voice softened. "Your old ways are archaic. Once you understand about the new religion, you will see that it is the only way to salvation." He took both her arms. She was trying to resist gently, not wanting to raise his anger again. This aspect of Talendar was gentle and even comforting, but the one that was angry frightened her. She felt him pulling her against him. She started to shake.

Somewhere in her mind she could see this same scene, a man and a woman by a lake. The image was so real, but she could not remember where she had seen it before. It seemed to come from a long time ago. They heard twigs crackling coming from the path. Talendar let go of Henith, just as Carog, followed closely by Braen, came out of the woods.

"Well, Talendar, showing Henith our beauty? But you kept her too long. We have many stories to share. Come Henith, let us go back to our story telling." Carog reached for Henith's hand. Henith looked at Braen who was watching the events. Henith could not tell what she was thinking by the strange expression on her face. She could not risk mind-speaking to Braen, because Carog would also be able to listen. She tried to keep her mind blank and she buried the feelings deep inside of her to take out at some future time, when she could explore them without interruption. Carog was practically pulling Henith up the path. Henith struggled free and followed. Braen fell in behind her and Talendar came last.

"I'm going into town," Talendar said when they reached the house.

Both Carog and Henith looked at him in surprise.

"Oh?" Carog responded first, "I thought you wanted to hear the stories too."

Henith felt relief flood through her body.

"I have changed my mind." Henith noted a slight irritation in his voice. "I will be back in time for the noon meal."

Talendar went off toward town, leaving the three women staring after him.

"How could you marry, Carog, and marry one of the foreigners? What about your sacred vows, what about protecting our mysteries?" The words tumbled out. Braen looked at Henith with some alarm.

Carog turned to Henith, fire dancing in her eyes. "How dare you tell me what to do? You do not know what it is like here. To be all alone. To have your life threatened every minute."

"But marrying one of them? There must have been other choices."

"Henith, have you ever been with a man?"

Henith flushed. "What are you asking me, Carog? You know that we have vowed to hold the ways of the Goddess sacred in our bodies and minds. How can you even let a man touch you at all?" Henith could feel the heat rising in her cheeks.

"What we were taught about being with men isn't true. I like Talendar. I like the way his body feels next to mine. I like sleeping with him."

Both Braen and Henith gasped.

"What are the two of you so shocked for? You already know he and I are married. Of course we sleep together." Carog turned to go into the house. "Come, do you still want some tea?"

Braen and Henith looked at each other. Henith was visibly upset. Her body was shaking. Braen put her arm around her.

"Come, Henith, we might as well be polite," she said softly to Henith. Henith barely nodded agreement as they followed Carog into the house.

"Look, the times are changing. We cannot hold on to our ways. It is impossible. These men are determined to destroy the old religion, the old value system. I do not see anything that we can do to stop it. I am not sure there is anything that we can do to stop it." Carog sat at the table, joining the others.

"Don't you think marrying one of them is going too far, though?" Henith tried to keep the edge of irritation out of her voice.

"No. As a matter of fact it is using their own strategy against them."

"What? I do not understand."

"They think that the best way to conquer Trenig is to marry the women and have children. Eventually all of Trenig will be following their ways. Usually they destroy the stone circles. In the first wave of invaders, they killed many women and others who were trying to defend the stones and the old ways. So far Talendar has not touched the stones. He does not even go near them. And no one in this town has been killed. He thinks that I have totally capitulated to his will and need. And, in some ways, I have, but the stone circle is still intact. And if I have girl children, I will teach them everything I know."

Braen intervened, "That's what the women in Merchlyn are doing. Although after what happened there last month, I'm not sure how many will be able to continue with that plan."

"In Merchlyn? Are they still keeping the ways of the Goddess? Talendar had said that the old ways had been entirely wiped out there."

"There was one stone circle left. Somehow the foreigners had missed it in their first pass of destruction. Some of the women there were meeting in secret. They would drug their husbands at the time of the full moon and meet together at the circle to do the full moon ritual. One of the women was the High Priestess of the circle." Braen's eyes closed as she remembered Zeena.

"What happened last month?" Carog asked appearing to be genuinely interested.

Henith did not want Braen to continue. She still did not trust Carog and did not want to tell her any more details. She was not sure whether Carog would tell Talendar or not. She also was not sure whether or not he would go and kill the women who were still faithful to the Goddess.

Braen sensed Henith's discomfort. "A woman was killed. I expect that it will be a long time before any of those women gather again."

"That is too bad. How were they able to meet at all?"

"They gave their husbands potions of a sleeping herb. And when their husbands were asleep, they slipped out."

"That is very clever. I wonder if I should give Talendar a sleeping drink tomorrow, so we can celebrate the full moon together."

"Do you think that is wise? What if he finds out? He will surely have the circle destroyed," Henith said with an uneven voice.

"How will he ever know? And besides, if he finds out and threatens the circle, I will rid myself of his child."

Henith looked at Carog. "Does Talendar know about the child?"

"No, I have not told him yet. I have been trying to decide whether to keep it or not. Now I have a reason to keep it a while longer." The glint in Carog's eyes made Henith uncomfortable. "So shall we have our ritual?"

Braen and Henith looked at each other. "It does not feel very safe here for us," Braen said after a while, "but if you can guarantee that Talendar will be asleep and not find out, maybe it would be good for us to worship together." Braen had sensed the incredible tension in Henith's body.

"Didn't you say you had some others with you? Why didn't you bring them this morning for a meal?"

"They decided to spend their time alone." Henith did not want to tell Carog the real reason why they stayed in camp.

"Well, they will come to the ritual then?"

"I do not know, probably."

"Tell us some more stories from Mona. We are a bit homesick you know."

"When will you be going home?" Henith looked directly into Carog's eyes when she asked her the question.

"Henith, please, you know I will not be going back to Mona. I would never be accepted back as a priestess. And besides, this is home now. I am home. I live with Talendar, we will have children, and we will live here in Balquhain. I will never see Mona again." Henith thought she detected a slight sadness in Carog's voice, but maybe it was only her hope that Carog felt some remorse for the choices she had made.

"Talendar will be returning shortly. I had better prepare lunch." Avoiding Henith's eyes, she rose from the table.

Chapter 20

"It sounds as if Talendar brought home some of his friends," Henith could hear several men's voices coming from the yard. Henith and Braen looked at each other.

"Maybe we had better leave," Henith quickly responded, rising from the table. Just then two men followed Talendar into the house. The two men were staring at the priestesses from Mona as if they had seen a vision. The two women looked away from their stares.

"See, wasn't I right, two of the most lovely women in all of Trenig." Talendar walked up to Henith, and took her hand. She tried to pull away. "Come, Henith, let me introduce you to my friends. This is Henith, the other is Braen. They are visiting my wife for a while." Talendar practically pushed Henith at one of the men. Braen remained rigid in her chair.

The men started to laugh. "You were right, Talendar, I did not believe you, but you did not lie this time. They are beauties. I thought all the good ones had been taken by now. Where have you been hiding, my dear?" The taller one, with the dark brown beard walked up to Braen and started touching her hair.

She stood very suddenly, knocking over the chair. "Please do not touch me."

"Ho, this one is full of vinegar." He tried to put his arm around Braen. She moved to the other side of the table. "I like this one."

The other man was looking at Henith. She was staring at Talendar. "Talendar, what is going on here?" she said very softly, trying to keep the volatile situation as calm as possible until they could find a way to leave this place.

"What do you mean? You know that all the unwed women in Trenig have to marry one of our men. I thought my two friends here who have disobeyed the laws long enough should be made aware that there are two women here just waiting to be wed." Henith detected the sneer again. She felt her body go cold, as if she had fallen into an icy pond with no bottom.

"Thank you, that was very kind of you," Braen said, regaining her calmness, "but we prefer not to be wed."

"As I was trying to explain to Henith earlier, that is not possible. You must obey the laws of Trenig."

"What if I choose not to obey the laws of Trenig?" Henith could feel the rage rising inside of her.

"Then you will be have to be executed."

"Executed? For not marrying? What kind of a law is that? Do I not have any say in whether I marry or not? And whom I marry?" Henith was getting more and more agitated. Her face was very warm from the blood that was burning her cheeks.

"Of course not. Women have no choice. They marry whom they are told to marry."

Carog carried a tureen of soup to the table. "Why don't we sit down and have something to eat? Let us discuss this in a civilized way." She looked pleadingly at Henith.

Henith looked at Braen, hoping for some sign to indicate a plan for escape. It seemed unlikely that they would be allowed to leave even if they wanted to. Talendar pushed Henith into a chair. He sat on one side of Henith. The tall man with the beard sat on the other. She felt smothered being surrounded so closely by these men. Braen became very quiet. Henith knew she had gone to a different level. Henith tried to join Braen. Talendar's leg was pushing against hers. She could not move over because she would be too close to the man on her other side. Henith heard the loud voices of the men surrounding her. Henith and Braen had resorted to one syllable answers. The men kept joking with each other, sometimes asking questions of the women, but mostly ignoring their responses.

Braen spoke very quietly, "Henith and I need to be leaving now." She rose very slowly from the table. The calmness in her voice and the slowness with which she moved stopped the conversation. Everyone was watching her. Henith copied her behavior and rose very slowly from the table.

"Thank you, Carog. We will be seeing you again, I am sure," Braen continued to speak very softly. The others remained silent, just watching as the two women slowly left the house. No one said a word or made a move to stop them.

Braen and Henith continued in silence until they were very near their camp.

When they reached the camp, Braen said to Shelagh, who was sitting watching a brightly colored bird in the tree, "We have to leave immediately. We are in intense danger."

Jenli came into the clearing. "What about the ritual tomorrow? I thought there was a priestess from Mona here."

"I do not think we can risk staying here for the ritual. And, yes, there is a priestess here, but she has married one of the foreigners and can not be trusted any more." Braen's voice remained very calm as if it were coming from deep in the earth.

"I agree with Braen, I think we should leave immediately. I am sure that when they waken from the trance Braen cast upon them they will try to find us."

"Who are they?"

"Talendar, and two men."

"But will we be any safer moving?

"Carog thinks that we will be here at least until tomorrow. She thinks that we will be worshipping with her tonight. If we leave now, at least we will have a day's head start. But we cannot go directly to Mona, that would be the first place they would look, and besides that means going too close to Carog's."

"What makes you think that they would come after us?" Jenli asked.

"Talendar found two men to marry us," Henith answered.

"What?" Jenli started to laugh.

"Jenli, it's not funny." Then Braen also started to laugh. Soon all four women were laughing. Somehow the vision of Henith and Braen married to two foreigners caused them to roar with laughter.

Finally Shelagh said, wiping her eyes, "At one level it is very amusing to imagine Henith and Braen wed to two men, but if that really is Talenda's intent, we are in danger."

"Why would Talendar care whether you were married or not? It does not make any sense." Jenli moved to sit next to Shelagh.

Henith looked down at the leaves on the ground. She did not know whether to say any more. Finally she said very softly, "I think he wants to keep me near him."

Braen looked at her friend. Old feelings stirred from deep within her.

"But I do not want to be near him," she looked softly into Braen's eyes, "I want to go back to Mona." She left unsaid what she was really wanted, hoping that Braen was reading her mind.

"Where are we going to go then?" Jenli said, always asking the practical questions.

"The old woman that we met said there was a stone circle north of here. Maybe we could go there for a while."

"But isn't that where the old woman sent the other man?"

"Yes, but he will be ahead of us. He may have left by the time we get there. We could go there and just wait for several moons. Then we could slowly move down the coast to Brithdir. By then maybe they will have given up looking for us. We will still be able to be in Mona by the Spring Rite."

"Maybe we should go south. There must be somewhere to hide south of here," Jenli offered.

"But north is better. There are fewer foreigners to the north. It would be difficult to find any place south where four unwed women would be safe," Braen replied.

"I wish we could go directly toward Mona," Henith said wistfully.

"I do not think that is the safest plan, Henith." Braen wanted to take Henith home, too, but she also wanted to keep them all safe. "We had better start breaking camp. There is no way to tell how long they will be asleep."

Henith chuckled. "Braen, when they became quiet I wondered why they had become so passive all of a sudden, and then I realized what you had done. I wished I had thought of that. I am glad you were there with me."

After a few hours, the four women were in their wagon going to the east on the road that they had traveled not too many days before. The longing in them to continue west was strong. Soon they would find the road that went away from Mona. Henith hoped that Braen was right and they would be back to Mona by the Spring Rite. She thought about Morgan and her mother, and the women on Mona. She feared for them. What were they going to do? The wagon moved down the road, away from Carog and Talendar, and away from Mona.

Chapter 21

"It has been two moons since we left Carog's. Do you think it is safe to try to go to Mona yet?" Henith asked the women sitting around the fire in the late afternoon light.

"Talendar probably has given up looking for us, if he ever tried at all. He certainly did not send anyone in this direction. I think we would have heard about it if he had," Jenli joined the conversation.

"It has been a very peaceful two moons. The people in this part of Trenig have been kind. The foreigners have not come this far north yet, except for a few small raiding parties."

"It is remote," Jenli said, looking out over the rugged mountains to the north. "I wonder that anyone survives in this terrain at all."

"And what is more of a miracle is that these people are still faithful to the Goddess. The way of life here is so much calmer than in southern Trenig."

"In some ways it is sad to leave here." Braen looked at the others, knowing that the last two moons were only a rest on their journey.

"Let us leave after the next moon ritual," Henith suggested, anxious to be heading home.

A faraway look came over her face as if seeing something painful in the past. "I think Carog told him who we were. What if Talendar stationed some men in that village, knowing that we had to go there to find a boat to take us back to Mona?"

Shelagh looked at Henith, "Something about Carog has a hold on you. You have to let it go. She will destroy you if you continue to hold on to the fear."

"I know, Shelagh, but ever since we were children, I have not trusted her. It is difficult to let go now when the possibility exists that she told Talendar where we were going. He knows about Mona. She told him that she was from the island off the northwest coast of Trenig. She may have told him that we were, too."

"When we get near Brithdir, Jenli and I can go ahead and find out if Talendar is still there. He does not know me, and might not remember Jenli from the inn. We may be able to find out what has happened, and if he is waiting for you there."

"That is a good idea, Shelagh. But what about Colywn? We do not know where he is either."

"We know that he was here, from what the villagers told us, but that was moons ago. He left as soon as he discovered that we had not come here. He probably went towards Carog's circle," Jenli offered.

"I cannot help wondering why he also is trying to find us. It is strange to think that there are men who are following us around. It makes me feel very unsafe." Henith still could see him lying wounded on the ground, saying, "It is you." She had no idea what he meant, but it stilled raised her curiosity.

"When Shelagh and I go to Brithdir, we will also find out if Colywn has been there. Somehow I have the feeling that Colywn is not as dangerous to us as Talendar appears to be."

"But, Jenli, Colywn was one of the men who attacked Zeena's circle. He cannot be trusted."

"Do you think he will recognize you, Jenli?" Henith asked. "You were the one guarding him that night."

"I doubt it. It was dark, and I stayed some distance away." Jenli continued after some thought, "I think we should go west from here to the coast. That will keep us north for as long as possible. When we reach the coast, we will travel south. Shelagh and I will go ahead. We could make better progress if we had another horse."

"Where would we get another horse?" Braen asked in surprise.

"Are you thinking of putting me on a horse?" Shelagh looked at Jenli, her old face reflecting the light of the fire.

"Well, if we had another horse the two of us could travel faster down the coast. If it seemed safe then I could ride back to Henith, Braen, and the wagon, and they could begin to move. In the meantime you could be traveling on, gathering information. I would meet you, and depending on the situation, I would come back and tell them."

"That sounds like a very complicated plan. Don't you think it would be dangerous? Why don't we go west as you suggested, and travel down the coast slowly together. You could go on ahead each day and find out what how dangerous it will be for us."

"How are we going to do that with one horse?"

"Maybe we should abandon the wagon when we get to the coast and just keep the horse for Jenli to travel on."

"I had not thought about that, you are right. We will go as far south on the coast as is safe with the wagon and the horse, then we will travel the rest of the way on foot. Shelagh, do you think that you will be able to walk that far?" Henith asked the old woman with some concern.

"Henith, I have come this close to Mona, I will not give up now." A teasing wrinkle played at the corners of her eyes.

"Good, we will leave here in four days, after the moon is full. We will go west to the coast, and then south." A thrill went through the group. The thought of reaching Mona in the next month was intoxicating.

இ~~இ

"Jenli, what is happening? You look like you have been chased across Trenig. Look at this poor horse."

Jenli slid from the horse, "They are here. I came as fast as I could. They did not see me," she tried to catch her breath.

"Here, sit awhile, then tell us the story. We can wait a few more minutes. Calm yourself." Braen moved Jenli to a place to sit. Henith took the horse.

The three women gathered around Jenli.

"I reached the outskirts of Brithdir two mornings ago. I did not realize how close we were. There was a great deal of activity happening there. I could tell something was going on. I left the horse and walked

292

to the village center. As I was approaching, I met a woman; a knowing crossed my mind that she was from Mona. She said that some men had come a few months ago, looking for two women and questioning everyone in town. She had been sent to Brithdir to determine if they were planning another invasion of Mona. As far as she was able to determine, they were just looking for these two women. I did not tell her about the two of you." Jenli nodded at Henith and Braen. "I was not sure who I could trust after your stories of Carog. There were several men in town that obviously were foreigners. Then I thought I saw Colywn. I do not think that he saw me, but I had the strangest sensation that somehow he knew I was there. I do not know if Talendar was there or not, but obviously they were looking for you. When I saw Colywn, my heart sank. How are we going to get through that town unnoticed? It is a very small town. How are we going to get a boat without anyone finding out?"

"Did you get any more information from anyone?" Henith asked. "Did you find out the name of the woman from Mona?"

"She said her name was Oalii. Do you know her?"

"Yes, she is from my village." Henith remembered the night she helped Zendar deliver Oalii's baby. It seemed so very long ago.

"Can we trust her? We could ask her to come here. Maybe she can help us get to Mona."

"She must have a plan for getting back to Mona herself."

"You are right. How close do you think we can get to the village? Are there any places where you think we can camp without being detected?"

"I think we should leave the wagon here and put everything that needs to be carried on the horse. I think about a day's walk is as close as we can go. There are many people on the roads. There just seems to be a great deal of excitement in the area. We should not go too much closer than that."

"Then we can ask Oalii to meet with us."

"We will rest and pack tonight and leave in the morning. I think we should stay off the roads. It will be difficult walking through the underbrush, but I think we will be safer."

"Do you think we are close enough for you to contact Morgan, or the mind-speaker in your village, Braen?" Henith looked at Braen. The last few months had been a calm time in their lives. She was not looking forward to the next few days. She did not like the agitated energy she could already detect in the air. She did not like the fear that it generated in them.

"Tomorrow, when we get to the place where we will camp, I could try to reach Sinthea and Morgan, if Sinthea is still the mind-speaker in my village. We do not even know who is still on Mona."

"Carog said that Morgan and my mother were still there," Henith reminded Braen.

❧❦

"Oalii, is it really you?" Henith went up to the woman she remembered from her village.

"Henith? I was not sure whether to believe Jenli or not. It is difficult to know who to trust anymore. No one is above suspicion." The older woman greeted Henith with a hug. "What are you doing here? Your mother was very worried about you. We haven't heard from you for years. Morgan kept telling her that you and Braen would be alright. She knew that you would return."

Henith smiled, thinking about the time Morgan had asked her and Braen to go on this mission.

Oalii was looking at Shelagh.

"This is Shelagh. We are taking her to Mona, along with Jenli," Henith said.

"Oh!"

"There are so many stories to tell, but first we need to decide on a plan to reach Mona."

"Why didn't you just come to Brithdir? Why are you being so cautious?"

"Jenli said that there were men in town looking for two women. I am afraid Braen and I are the ones that they are searching for."

"Oh!" Oalii said with some recognition. "But there are four of you."

"Yes, but these men have not seen Shelagh and Jenli. Do you know the names of the men who are in town looking for us?"

"Talendar and Colywn. But it is strange. They do not seem to be together. Talendar is looking for two women, and Colywn is searching for one. It never occurred to me that they both were looking for the same women. Who are they?"

"Talendar is Carog's husband."

"What?" Oalii cried out not believing what she was hearing. "Carog's husband? But she was sent to a village last year as a priestess. How could she be married to one of the foreigners?"

"We met Talendar in southern Trenig, quite near Shelagh's circle and then again in northern Trenig. By the time we had reached Balquhain he and Carog were married. Carog is also pregnant with his child."

"I find all of this difficult to understand. Why would she do that?"

"She thought it was a way to keep peace in Trenig, to keep women from being tortured and killed, and to keep the stones safe."

"Things must be much worse than we ever imagined, if Carog went to such extreme measures to break her sacred vows."

Silence fell on the group. After a while, Oalii asked, "And who is Colywn?"

"He is a man that was with a group of men who attacked a stone circle while we were having a moon ritual. He was wounded and I tended his wounds, and apparently saved his life. He has been trying to find me since then. We do not know what he wants with us," Henith replied.

"I was to return to Mona in seven days," Oalii continued. "I do not know how we can get all of you to the boat without being seen. The coast along here is very dangerous as you may remember. Crossing the channel to Mona has always been treacherous. That is what has kept us safe for so many years. I am sure that if there were other places along the coast around here where it was safe to launch a boat, someone would have discovered them long before now. The only way to Mona is by boat and through Brithdir, and then it can only be risked at the slack of the tide."

295

"Do you know who the mind-speaker is in the eastern village?" Braen asked Oalii.

"Sinthea is still there. Many things have changed since you left. There is much more movement. The women live in the village they want to rather than the one where they were born. Your mother, Henith, lives with Morgan at the center. Many women were upset about that for a long time, but gradually things settled down. However, it has never been quite the same since the men were killed."

"Yes, Carog told us about that. I cannot imagine what a terrible time that must have been on Mona, but we also have seen some terrible things here in Trenig."

"Do you think we could try to contact Sinthea tonight to at least tell her to let Morgan know that we are returning?"

"We can try. I was not expected to contact them for several days. They will not be expecting a message and may be focused elsewhere. Also it is some distance still to Mona from here. I was never very good at mind-speaking." Oalii looked at the four women around her.

"Braen has the skill. I think we should try tonight around the time of evening renewal. Maybe we could even reach Morgan." Henith smiled when she remembered spirit flying so many years ago with Morgan and Braen.

❧

"Are you ready? Let us all calm ourselves. Braen will lead us. Let us focus our energy on Sinthea and Morgan, maybe one of them will hear us." The women sat in a circle, with eyes closed and hands held loosely in their laps. Braen led them into a deep silence. Henith could feel the strength of Braen's energy. She allowed herself to go with Braen, deeper and deeper into the silence. She let herself relax into the blueness that she experienced in these times of intense deepening. She found herself floating above Mona.

It had been so long since she had been here. She could sense Braen and Shelagh up ahead of her, flying to the center of Mona. As she tried to reach them she felt herself being pulled back. The more she struggled to reach the center of Mona, the more difficult it became. She felt as if someone or something was pulling her in the opposite direction.

She felt as if she were trying to swim upstream against a very strong current that was determined to wash her downstream. She was becoming exhausted. It wouldn't let go of her. She was afraid that she could not get free of it. She called out to Braen and Morgan. Something crashed into her. It was if she had flown into a wall of considerable strength. She was so stunned by the shock of impact that she let go of trying to reach Braen.

When she looked around she recognized parts of Brithdir. She and Braen had passed through here when they had started on their journey. She could see Colywn sitting in the woods staring into the fire. She knew she had to leave here at once, but she was afraid it might be too late.

She felt the pull of the river again, this time pulling her away from Colywn. Somewhere far away she could hear Braen calling her. She tried to focus on the sound of Braen's voice. She was being split in two. Her voice became louder and louder. She could hear the voice saying, "Open your eyes, Henith, open your eyes." She tried to obey the instructions, but her eyelids were heavy. "Open your eyes, Henith, open your eyes." The voice became more emphatic. The light from their fire startled her. She looked around at Braen, Jenli, Shelagh, and Oalii, trying to remember what she was doing here with them, trying to remember where she was.

"Henith, are you here?" Braen asked with some concern in her voice.

"Yes, I think so. What happened?"

"We were trying to contact Morgan, when I felt you being pulled away with great force. I tried to get you back, but I lost you for a while. Finally I found you in Brithdir with Colywn. He has improved his skill since he was in Merchlyn. I finally was able to release you from him with the help of Shelagh. Are you alright?" Braen was looking directly at Henith and noticed the cloud that passed over Henith's face as she was told what happened.

"Why do you think he is able to capture me when I mind-speak or whenever I try to spirit fly?" Henith was feeling very vulnerable. It was not safe for her to have someone who could so indiscriminatly invade her psychic space.

"I do not know, except that he is looking for you with an intensity that is even stronger than Talendar's. And now he knows you are near. If he has any intuition at all, he will begin to look for you more in earnest. We need to develop a plan quickly. I am not sure we can even wait for the next seven days before we return to Mona." Braen looked around to each woman in the group.

"Did you contact Morgan?" Henith asked.

"No, we started to lose you, so we gave up on trying to reach Morgan and started to try to hold on to you. I do not know if Morgan was aware of our trying to reach her at all."

"I am sorry, Braen, but I never expected to be drawn away so easily, I was not prepared for it. I did not know what was happening."

"We know now that we have to be more cautious than ever. I am not sure I know how you are going to protect yourself from Colywn finding you." Looking around the circle at the others, Braen asked, "Do any of you have any ideas about how we are going to get to Mona, knowing that Colywn probably knows we are here and that Talendar is waiting for us to arrive in town? Carog must have told him that we would have to pass through Brithdir on our way home, and that it was just a matter of being patient and waiting for us."

"Well, we need a boat large enough to carry four or five of us. We need to cross at the slack of the tide, and we need to be able to travel through Brithdir without being seen," Jenli listed.

"We could go one at a time in a smaller boat. The tide will be slack in the middle of the day and the middle of the night for the next few days," Oalii offered.

"But where are we going to get a boat? And crossing in the middle of the night can be extremely dangerous. And how are we going to get the boat back for the others?"

"I have never maneuvered a boat by myself," Shelagh said, "and I do not know these waters at all."

"None of us know the waters very well. A few women in the eastern village are the ones that ferry the others back and forth, and even then it is not very often. The cliffs are steep for miles in both directions. It is impossible to reach the water safely in most places. Launching a boat from anywhere except from Brithdir would be extremely perilous. Besides, it is unlikely that the four of you can get through Brithdir without being detected, except possibly in the middle of the night, and then it still will be dangerous even if we can find a boat to take us home."

"Besides Colywn and Talendar, how many other men are posted waiting for our return?"

"I would say about twelve or so," Oalii answered.

"We are not getting anywhere and time is running out." Jenli was getting impatient. "Why don't we drug them, find a woman who is still sympathetic to the Goddess and have her find us a boat?"

"How are we going to drug so many men?" Henith asked in astonishment.

"That is a good idea, Jenli, maybe we can drug them."

Shelagh laughed at the thought of all those men lying around drugged and said, "It is a good idea, but I am not sure how we can drug so many people all at once."

"That is a problem, but first we have to see if there is a boat that we can borrow."

"Maybe we could trade our horse for a boat." The group looked at Shelagh, and laughed. The idea was so simple and wonderful.

"Oalii, do you think that you could find someone to trade a boat for a horse? You are the only one that can safely travel about in Brithdir."

"I am not sure, but I can try. It might raise some suspicion, though, because I have been there for a few days now and I do not have a horse. Someone may wonder where I found a horse to trade."

"Well, you will have to find someone who is still faithful to the Goddess, someone who will not question a priestess of Mona, someone who will be pleased to help in any way."

"Are there still some women left in Brithdir who might fit into that category?"

"Yes, I have met a few while I have been here, but I do not know if any of them have a boat or not. This is not going to be easy."

"We will have to move much closer to town if we want to be able to get through it quickly. Are there any places that you have seen where we might stay?" Jenli asked Oalii.

"Why don't you and I go back tonight, Jenli? We can find a safe place for the others, then you can come back and get them. In the meantime I will try to locate some type of boat. We cannot wait too much longer. The slack of the tide will be in the early morning and early evening by next week, then we will have to wait another week."

"That is a good plan, are we all agreed? Jenli and Oalii will leave now for Brithdir, and Jenli will return when they locate a safe place for us to be for a short time. In the meantime, maybe Oalii will find a boat for us."

Oalii and Jenli rose to leave. "Be careful, we hope to see you both very soon," Braen said as she embraced each woman in turn.

"With any luck, by tomorrow night." Jenli and Oalii left the safety of the campfire and went out into the night.

PART 4:
The Homecoming

They were about half way across the dangerous channel when Henith thought she saw something glisten just above the horizon in the direction of Brithdir.

"Braen, did you just see something? Look over there," She pointed in the direction that she had seen the light.

"I did not see anything. I was looking toward Mona."

"There it is again. Look!"

"I think we are being followed," Henith said.

"That is impossible. Nobody knows we are here except Colywn and Jenli, and they would not tell anyone."

"What about Kare?" Henith asked.

"I am sure she will keep our secret."

"There could not be anyone there. Your fear is playing tricks on you," Braen tried to comfort Henith.

Henith was quiet for a long time, watching carefully to see if she could detect another boat behind them. They were approaching the most difficult part of the crossing. Even at slack tide, the waters seemed to be warring with each other. High standing waves appeared all around them. Hugh rocks came and went under the waves. In took all Oalii could do to steer through these rough waters. She could not take the chance of even looking back for an instant. Braen turned to Oalii and asked, "Can we help?"

"Do you know how the women from the eastern village navigate these waters? There must be something they know that I do not know." She sounded worried.

"I remember some of the women talking about the crossing. They asked the rocks to guide them across."

"Can you do that?" Oalii asked as the tiller lurched from her hand.

"We can try. I think it will be easier if I held the tiller though." Braen and Oalii quickly changed places.

Braen said to Henith and Shelagh, "Help me. I am going to let the stones guide us home."

Henith focused her attention on the rocks and on Mona asking for clear passage. She let go of the fear that she had that they were being followed. Shelagh joined them. Calm seemed to settle on the waters. Braen barely held onto the tiller. Some unseen force took the little boat in its hand. The waves became smaller and smaller, the rocks one after another became like beacons, marking a safe passage.

৵৽৽

In just a few hours the all-gathering would begin. Henith was amazed at how familiar everything felt even after all these years and all the changes. She was surprised that Morgan and her mother had met them at the shore when they arrived home several days ago. Morgan had said that many of the women had sensed that she and Braen would be arriving soon. So Morgan and Canth had temporarily moved to the eastern village to await their return.

Morgan had greeted Shelagh with warmth, recognizing the Goddess in her ancient body. Henith was worried about Shelagh. She was failing quickly. Zendar had been called to tend to the old woman. Zendar had told Henith that it was only a matter of a few days. Now that Shelagh had reached Mona, she was ready to leave this earth. Henith wondered if the all-gathering would be too strenuous for Shelagh.

Women had been arriving all day for the meeting, and Henith noticed that there was much more camaraderie among the women than she remembered. Women freely intermingled with women from the other villages. It was not like her first all-gathering, when she had to stay with the women in her village. They had waited for Oalii's return from Trenig before they had called the meeting. All the women were to be present, including the young women and children. Today would be an important day in the history of Mona. Henith thought about the changes that might take place as a result of her and Braen's report.

꙰

The storytelling had been going on for several hours. Henith and Braen described in detail what they had learned in Trenig, what they had learned about the foreigners, and what they had discovered about the women in Trenig.

Henith told them about Jenli, how she was raped, discovered she was pregnant, and chose to give birth to the child. She told them that Jenli decided to stay in Trenig for the birth of her child, which could happen some time soon. She had not wanted to make the difficult crossing in the middle of the night. She had also believed that she could keep them informed about the comings and goings in Trenig.

Taking a deep breath Henith said softly, "And then there is Colwyn." She paused and then continued, "Colwyn has incredible powers of mind reading. He apparently inherited this skill and a few others from his grandmother. He is native to Trenig and does not follow the new religion, even though he had been forced to join with the foreign men in their campaign to take over Trenig with their religion and value system. He easily read my thoughts when I was mind-speaking. He claims he wasn't doing it intentionally, but somehow my thoughts just randomly came into his mind."

Henith looked around the group, took another deep breath and said, "In spite of my and our initial mistrust of him, he turned out to be an ally. He helped us find a boat. He told us that he would help Jenli if she agreed."

The women started to ask questions all at the same time. The discussion flowed back and forth. Just as the red of the setting sun filled the western sky, Shelagh stood and addressed the gathering.

"Women of Mona, I only have a few more hours left before I leave you."

Henith felt a pain pass through her body.

"But before I depart, I would like to tell you what I have seen, and what I see." A hush fell over the gathering, even the birds stopped singing, and the breeze quieted.

Shelagh's voice was strong and clear as she continued, "The times you have known are passing. I have lived in Trenig and I have witnessed the changes. Most are not good for the women of Trenig, and certainly not good for the ways of the Goddess. The sadness I carry is in knowing that there is nothing that we can do to stop it. Many women have lost their lives in trying to resist the changes that this new religion and these foreigners are bringing. There will be a time, I do not know in how many suns, or in how many years or hundreds of years, but there will be a time when the ways of the Goddess are gone from the earth. There will be a long time when women in Trenig and all the lands that stretch far to the south will be treated as animals."

A gasp was heard, the only sound on the island.

"But there is also hope. You will have to keep the mysteries alive. Not here. But everywhere. You will have to leave Mona, establish yourself in Trenig and on other parts of the earth. Some of you may even have to marry. And most of you will have to have children. Girl children. You will have to tell the stories to your daughters. You will have to teach them the mysteries, and you will have to do this in secret. Eventually the people of the new religion will forget about us, will forget about the stone circles, will forget about the Goddess. And in those times, the lessons that you have taught your children, and in turn their children's children, will be made visible again. And then the mysteries of the Goddess will save the planet earth. None of us will be alive to see the rebirth of the mysteries, but all of us will see the destruction of our ways. It is a time when we have to be stronger than we have ever been. It is a time when we will be tested.

"If you are among those choosing to marry, be very careful to chose someone that will enable you to keep the mysteries. There are some men who can be trusted. We have met one, Colywn. Henith has already told you about him. But there are others, like Talendar, who has married Carog, who cannot be trusted. Be very careful in your choices."

"For those among you that choose to live your lives with another woman, your way will be very difficult. You will not be accepted into the communities of Trenig. You may have to live isolated and away from the cities and towns. I pray the Goddess will protect you, but I know that your way will be especially difficult for many generations to come."

"You must never let the hope die. In spite of what you see, in spite of what atrocities happen to you, as priestesses of the Goddess you must keep the mysteries alive. You must keep the hope of the future alive. It will not be easy for any of you. And you only have my knowing to assure you that your efforts will not be in vain."

Shelagh waited. The silence on the island pressed on the women as if the giant stones had fallen and were covering the women like heavy blankets. No one moved. After many minutes, Shelagh spoke again.

"It is time for my leaving. I would be honored if Henith and Braen would prepare my body for the passage." Shelagh walked to where Braen and Henith were sitting. The others continued the silence. Henith looked up into Shelagh's eyes and knew that she had spoken a great truth.

As Braen and Henith rose to greet Shelagh, the other women gradually formed a circle around them. Zendar gave Henith the oils that she would need. Shelagh slipped off her robe and her ancient woman's body glistened in the starlight as Henith and Braen anointed Shelagh's body with oil. After she had been anointed, Shelagh laid down on the blanket that Morgan and Zendar had prepared for her. Tears were flowing from Henith's eyes as she watched Braen kiss Shelagh.

As Henith bent to kiss her, Shelagh whispered in a voice lighter than air itself, "Thank you, for bringing me to Mona. Now I go to my home with our great Mother." Shelagh closed her eyes. Henith could tell that she had gone. Facing each other, Henith, Braen, Morgan, and Canth, with their hands outstretched, carried the spirit of Shelagh to the tall standing stones that marked the entrance to the circle of the moon.